OTHER TIT

War of Hearts (A True Immortality Novel)

Kiss of Vengeance (A True Immortality Novel)

Kiss of Eternity (A True Immortality Short Story)

Bound by Forever (A True Immortality Novel)

Other Adult Contemporary Novels by Samantha Young

Play On

As Dust Dances

Black Tangled Heart

Hold On: A Play On Novella

Into the Deep

Out of the Shallows

Hero

Villain: A Hero Novella

One Day: A Valentine Novella

Fight or Flight

Outmatched (co-write with Kristen Callihan)

On Dublin Street Series:

On Dublin Street

Down London Road

Before Jamaica Lane

Fall From India Place

Echoes of Scotland Street

Moonlight on Nightingale Way

Until Fountain Bridge (a novella)

Castle Hill (a novella)

Valentine (a novella)

One King's Way (a novella)

On Hart's Boardwalk (a novella)

On Dublin Street: The Bonus Material (a novella)

Hart's Boardwalk Series:

The One Real Thing

Every Little Thing

Things We Never Said

The Truest Thing

Young Adult contemporary titles by Samantha Young

The Impossible Vastness of Us

The Fragile Ordinary

Young Adult Urban Fantasy titles by Samantha Young

The Tale of Lunarmorte Trilogy:

Moon Spell

River Cast

Blood Solstice

Warriors of Ankh Trilogy:

Blood Will Tell

Blood Past

Shades of Blood

Fire Spirits Series:

Smokeless Fire

Scorched Skies

FEAR OF FIRE AND SHADOW

S. YOUNG

FEAR OF FIRE AND SHADOW

By S. Young

Edited by Jennifer Sommersby Young
Cover Design By Hang Le

Borrowed Ember

Darkness, Kindled

Drip Drop Teardrop (a novella)

PREFACE

Dear Readers,

Fear of Fire and Shadow was previously published under the title 'Slumber'. While this is an updated, re-edited edition of the novel, there are no major changes to plot.

This is an adult fantasy romance. FOFAS contains sexual content, violence, and a scene of attempted rape that some readers may find triggering.

MAP OF PHAEDRA

INDEX OF TERMS

The Rada — The Council
The Dravilec — Healers
The Glava — Psychics
The Azyl — Seekers
The Dyzvati — Evokers

Terms of Royalty and Nobility
Kral — King
Kralovna — Queen
Prince — Prince
Princezna — Princess
Vojvoda — Duke
Vojvodkyna — Duchess
Markiz — Marquess
Markiza — Marchioness
Grof — Earl
Grofka — Countess
Vikomt — Viscount
Vikomtesa — Viscountess
Baron — Baron

Might there come a time
When we stand over a grave
And mourn ourselves?
Mourn the past, a previous life?
Shall we weep for the passing of time?
Shall we grieve for unfulfilled dreams?
In my naivety; in my belief
In immortal youth,
I sleepwalk through life.
Someone ... wake me up.
Please.
Wake me up.
—*Slumber*

PROLOGUE

When I was a child, the world smelled of summer.

The heady perfume of dancing wildflowers hugged my senses as the breeze took them on a journey to soothe my cheeks from the heat of the afternoon sun. The scent of damp soil when the sun had pushed the sky too far and it wept rain for days before wearily turning the world back over to its golden companion. The refreshing aroma of lemons in the thick air of the house mingled with my mother's baking as she prepared our afternoon repast of bitter lemonade and thick warm bread, slathered with creamy butter made cold from the sheltering shade of the larder.

And my father's pipe.

The sweet odor of tobacco tickling my nose as Father held me close and whispered the stories of our Salvation and the mighty kral who lived in the grandest palace in all the land with his beautiful daughter, the princezna, how kind and gentle they were—and the reason my private world was one of innocence and endless summer.

My memories of that life never leave me. I can still hear my brother's laughter carrying back to my young, happy ears as we chased through the fields of purple and gold, racing over the farm to the brook that ran behind our land. I remember the gentle trickle of that stream and how it drew us each day, my brother sprinting for the rope swing he had looped around the strongest tree, the one with the trunk that seemed to bend toward the water as if thirsty for a taste of its pure relief. I was drawn to its coolness on my skin, its moisture in my dry mouth, its familiar smell ... like damp metal and wet grass.

Sometimes I hear my mother calling our names in my dreams.

There was no warning to summer's end. It began like any other day. I stretched alongside my brother beneath the shadow of an oak by the brook's edge, my young voice barely heard above the babbling water as I recounted the story my father had told me over and over. I could hear Father's rich voice in my head, had memorized every word, and as I recited it, I remembered to speak in the hushed, awed tones he used to make a story sound as magical as this one really was.

"Eons and eons ago, our people were the most blessed of mankind. Powerful and beautiful, we could tap into Mother Nature and draw from her powers. Magical beings, spiritual and wondrous to behold. But mankind grew envious of us, and wise as we were, we knew mankind, with so many wars already brewing among its people, could not withstand a war with us. Our wisest leaders persuaded us it was time to fade from mankind's Earth, to fade as one into a world of our own.

"We withdrew and imagined a paradise. Mankind melted around us as we fell deep, deep into the fade. When our people awakened, we found ourselves here, in a newborn land—a sky, a moon, a sun, trees, plants, water, and familiar animals awaiting them, waiting to begin the new world in peace.

"Fearful of our emotions betraying us as they had mankind, it was decided that the Dyzvati, a clan of magical evokers with the ability to lull the people and the land with peace, would reign as the royal family. The Dyzvati named our land Phaedra, splitting it into six provinces, giving a province to the clans with the most powerful magic. Sabithia, in the south, was taken by the Dyzvati, and they built a beautiful palace in the capital city of Silvera where the shores of the Silver Sea edge its coast with its vibrant silver surf.

"Clan Glava, the largest and most powerful of the mage with their many psychic abilities, whether it be reading the past, present, or future, or moving objects and summoning elements with their minds, was given Javinia to the east of Sabithia and also Daeronia in the northeast." I turned my head to smile at my brother who stared at me, enraptured. "And our own slice of haven, Vasterya, was given to the Clan Azyl, mage with the ability to seek whatever their hearts desired. Eventually, the Azyl became servants of the Dyzvati, using their abilities to seek whatever the royal family wished, helping the upkeep of the peace in Phaedra.

"Many centuries onward and the Azyl's magic evolved with their position, no longer able to seek that which they wished for themselves, only what others wanted."

My brother frowned. "That's a little unfair."

I nodded in agreement before continuing, "The province of Daeronia, beyond the northern borders of Sabithia, was given to Clan Dravilec, the healers, to keep them close to the Dyzvati." I thought on how much of a fairy tale this sounded now, a millennium on from the beginning of Phaedra. "Now there are so few mages left. Papa says there are none left in Vasterya at all. And now only the kral and Princezna Haydyn remain of the Dyzvati."

"What about Alvernia?" my brother asked in a hushed voice.

I shuddered at the thought of Alvernia; the stories I'd heard of the rough, uncivilized northern mountain people, terrifying tales of their macabre misdeeds and ignoble existence, all because the power of the Dyzvati waned toward the middle of their province.

"Alvernia was given to those of middling magical abilities. Several of the Glava went with them, as there were so many, and set themselves up in the southernmost point in the city of Arrana."

"Where the vojvoda lives?"

"Yes, where the vojvoda lives."

"I wish I was a vojvoda. Or a markiza. Or a vikomt!" he cried excitedly, pushing himself into a sitting position. "I'd have horses. Lots of horses. And gold! We could play treasure hunt!"

I laughed and nudged him playfully. "All those titles and you didn't choose the best."

"What?" He pouted.

I stood, bracing my small hands against my youthful hips, legs astride, chin defiant. "Why ... kral, of course!"

"Yeah!" He jumped to his feet now, mimicking my stance. "I am Kral of Vasterya!"

"And me?"

"My servant."

I growled in outrage. "Servant indeed."

I still remember the sounds of his beautiful laughter as I chased him for his teasing.

At the grumbling of our bellies, my brother and I reluctantly ceased playing and walked home. I held his hand as we wove through the fields. I remember the gust of wind that shook the gold and purple and blew my hair back from my face, sending shivers of warning down my spine. My feet moved faster then, and I tugged on my brother's hand each time my heart beat a little quicker.

I can still see the expression on my father's face when we appeared out of the fields, his countenance pale and slack, his eyes bleak. My mother clung to his arm, her eyes as glassy as my favorite doll's. At the sound of a horse's nicker, I turned to see strangers outside our home. Four men, all dressed in livery that matched those of their horses. My eyes were drawn to the emerald-and-silver heraldic badges with the silver dove crest in the middle. Our symbol of peace.

They were from the palace.

Fear gripped me and I had no understanding of why. I trembled so hard, I thought I must be shaking the very ground beneath my feet. Instinctively, I pushed my brother behind me, out of the view of the men looming ominously over our parents.

One of them descended from his beast. I realized he did not wear the livery. He alone came toward me like a serpent slithering on the ground, his purple cloak hissing in the breeze. His eyes were the deepest black and probing, so fixated on me I quivered in violation as if he had actually touched me.

"This is the one."

"You're sure?" asked the soldier who towered over my parents.

The serpent smiled, ready to strike his killing blow. "She is the one."

"No!" my father bellowed as my mother whimpered at his side. "Run, Rogan! Run!"

But I was frozen in place by their panic, an ice sculpture who watched two soldiers hold my father as he struggled in their arms, and a third pull a dagger from his belt and plunge it into his heart. My father twitched and stiffened in their hold, a horrifying gurgling noise making its way up from his chest to spurt a thick, bloody fluid out of his mouth and down his chin.

My mother's screams played the soundtrack to this memory before the dagger-wielding soldier strolled toward her crumpled figure, his black-gloved fingers stroking over her hair. They slid like leeches down to her throat and back up to her cheeks. And then he twisted her head between his hands with a jerk that sent an echoing crack around my world.

That's when I felt the tug on my hand and remembered my brother. With a thousand screams stuck in my throat, I whirled with him and began to run, dragging him with me into the cover of the fields, my father's last shouts reverberating in my ears. I drowned out the sounds of my shallow, panicked breaths, the hiccupping cries of my brother as I hauled him with me. The hollering and thundering behind us made me race faster.

When the thundering eased, I knew I had lost them in the fields. We were small and knew the land as well as we knew each tiny scar and line upon our palms. I headed east, picking up my brother when he tripped, shushing him when I was no longer sure we were alone. At last we reached the cave my father had punished us for hiding in only a year before. Bears, he had warned. But now I feared the soldiers from the palace more than the bears, the soldiers who wanted me and why, I did not know. They had slaughtered my parents to have me. Would they murder me too? My brother? At the thought, I burrowed him against me in the dank cave and his tears soaked my dress.

"I'm sorry," he whispered.

I wanted to tell him he need not apologize for crying, for grieving, but I feared if I spoke, all my screams would burst forth with terrifying consequences.

"I didn't mean to."

At that, I pressed him back until a shaft of light filtered over his face. He looked so lost, my heart broke again. He clutched his trousers, turning from me, and it was then the smell hit my nostrils.

I began to cry.

I did not want him to be ashamed of his fear. He was so little.

"It's okay," I whispered and made to reach for him, but his shirt slipped through my hands as he was whipped out of sight. I must have yelled, I think, as I stumbled blindly after him into a day that had suddenly turned gray, a day that had once blazed in a beautiful fire of heat and life. Now it was gone.

And as my eyes found my brother, I realized even the last sparks of the embers had been snuffed out, leaving only the fire's funeral shroud of smoke.

His small body laid at the mouth of the cave. The dagger

edged in blood from his throat slipped back into its place on a soldier's belt.

The serpent stepped over my brother's body and knelt before me.

"Say goodbye to your family, Rogan. A new one awaits you."

CHAPTER 1

I ached. I had never experienced such pain before. But I had never been on a horse for so long. It did not help I was stiff from trying to keep my body as far from the man who held me on that horse in his embrace. It was impossible not to touch him—his long arms encircled me in order to hold the reins.

I didn't know where we were. It was impossibly dark. The sun had been on our left for much of the day before moving to the right and setting. It had also taken longer to set than it did back home. If my father had taught me correctly, this meant we were moving south. I twisted my neck to look at Kir, who rode trapped between the captain of the Guard and the reins of his horse, Destroyer. Such a fitting name. He had helped the despicable mage behind me, Vikomt Syracen Stovia—one of the Glava—destroy my life, as well as Kir's.

The kral was dead.

Only Haydyn Dyzvati, Princezna of Phaedra, remained of the evokers. Kir told me Stovia was collecting those left with rare magic to help protect and reinforce the sovereign until Haydyn came of age and produced more children of the Dyzvati.

Kir was one of the Glava, a telekinetic.

"The Dyzvati power has waned," Kir had whispered to me, his eyes flickering to our guard. That had been only two nights after the murder

of my family. Kir had been with the Guard for a week. The other soldiers ate and talked quietly around the campfire. "Stovia has taken advantage of it. The way he talks ... as if the violence of his crimes is justified. He's protecting the sovereign and the peace of Phaedra with blood and cruelty. With a selfish pursuit for the last of the mage."

"But I'm not a mage," I whispered in shock. We were sitting together to the side of the fire. Strangers. But the wiry boy, a few years my senior, shared the haunted look in my eyes. They had destroyed his family too.

Kir had shrugged. "You must be."

But I wasn't. Was I?

I caught Kir's gaze as we rode swiftly and quietly into the small village. His face was taut, his eyes narrowed. Something was happening.

The horses drew to a stop with not even a snort, so obedient to their masters' will. An unpleasant shock moved through me at the feel of Stovia's hand in my hair.

"Now, little one," he whispered, "time to see how well that magic of yours works."

I shifted away from him. "I have no magic."

He chuckled. "You're one of the Azyl, child."

One of the Azyl? No. He was mistaken.

"I'm not."

With a growl, Stovia dismounted and none too gently ripped me from the saddle. My feet hadn't even hit the ground before he shook me, my eyes rolling back in my head with the force of it. "Stop pretending!" he hissed, careful not to raise his voice. He released me and I stumbled as he lowered his body so his austere face was level with my own. Those wicked black eyes bore through me. "In this village is one of the Dravilec. I want you to seek out my healer. Now."

At the command, a wave of energy crashed over me and my whole body hummed with tingling vibrancy. I turned to face the village. And I sensed her. The Dravilec. Six years old. Valena of Daeronia. We were in Daeronia. Thought so. We were growing closer to Sabithia. To Silvera. To the princezna.

Wait.

I am *an Azyl.*

I swayed at the thought. Every time my father had told me the stories, I'd wished desperately for a little piece of magic in our lives.

I had been a mage all along.

I wanted to cry. I wanted to be with my family.

What would Stovia do to Valena's family? Would he murder them in cold blood if they refused to hand her over? I knew, even without my help, that he would find Valena. He was a powerful Glava. Could sense magic. But that didn't mean I had to aid in the destruction of another family.

"No," I whispered.

"What?" Stovia growled.

I spun around, defiant, hatred blazing out of my eyes. I wished I were Glava with the ability to summon the elements. I'd set him on fire and watch him burn for what he had done to me. To Kir. For what he would do to Valena.

"I said ... no."

His fist connected with my face with such force, I flew to the ground. The breath whooshed out of me at the agonizing blow to my ribs as I hit the hard dirt. My eyes watered at the painful heat across the left side of my face. Blood trickled out of the corner of my mouth and I tasted copper on my tongue.

Kir cried out my name.

But Stovia wasn't done. He grabbed me by the clasp on my cloak and held me so he could slap me across the right side of my face. The world rang in my ears.

I refused to cry.

"Find me the healer, girl, or you'll wish you were dead."

"No!" Kir yelled.

"Shut him up," Stovia hissed.

I heard the sound of flesh hitting flesh, of Kir grunting.

No.

"No," I groaned, lolling limply in Stovia's grasp. "Stop."

"Will you find the Dravilec?"

I couldn't. "No."

"Lash the boy to the nearest tree. He's going to pay for Rogan's disobedience."

My heart lurched, and I shrugged around Stovia to watch through blurred vision as they dragged a bleeding, crying Kir to the nearest tree trunk. They tore at his shirt. One of them produced a horsewhip, and Kir whimpered in terror. Vomit rushed up my throat, but I willed the acidic show of weakness down.

"Stop," I murmured weakly. "Stop. Don't hurt him. I'll do it."

Stovia studied me, seemingly fascinated. Then he nodded at his men and they drew Kir's cloak over him before dragging him back to the horses. His right eye was already swelling shut, matching my left one.

"Tut-tut, Rogan," Stovia whispered. "You've just shown me your weakness. I imagine I could have battered you into oblivion and you would not have given in. But you won't let someone else be hurt because of you. Interesting. And useful. Now find me the Dravilec."

I was gripped with nauseating shame as I took the guards through the winding, quaint, peaceful village. By now we had made enough noise to rouse people from their homes, and they gathered on doorsteps nervously as their eyes took in the Royal Guard and the two beaten children with them. I came to a stop at the door of a shop. An apothecary.

"Here."

Stovia smiled at me, his eyes brimming with pride. I hated him. "Yes, it is. Thank you, Rogan."

He pulled the rope by the door and a brass bell rang. We heard hurried footsteps and then the door was thrust open by an older man. He was tall and imposing.

"Can I help?" he queried warily.

"I am Vikomt Syracen Stovia of the Rada. May I come in, Mr. Rosonia?"

Rosonia's eyes widened but he nodded, his oil lamp casting his profile against the shadows of the wall. Stovia turned and nodded at two guards who strode forward to follow at his back. He pushed me past the threshold and into the shop. Sadist. He wanted me to witness this.

Once inside, Rosonia stood with a stout, middle-aged woman who appeared frightened, clutching her robes tightly around her. Two girls stood behind them, one a tall, attractive girl, possibly around thirteen or fourteen years of age. Clutching her hand was Valena, small and frightened, her large, dark eyes too big for her face.

"I come bearing sad news." Stovia emanated power and intimidation. "The kral is dead."

The Rosonias gasped at the news.

"Yes. I am afraid it is true. Princezna Haydyn is now alone in the world, the weight of carrying the load of Dyzvati too great for her young shoulders. As the only mage upon the Rada, I felt it was my duty to seek whatever Her Highness needs to aid her in her mighty responsibilities."

"What can we do to help, my lord?" Valena's father asked eagerly, his eyes full of genuine sadness for the kral.

"Very little magic remains in our world. However, I've been collecting the strongest of that which does. Here." He put his deadly hand upon my shoulder and I fought not to shiver. "This is one of the Azyl, thought to be extinct. But she found you well enough."

Mrs. Rosonia gasped at my bloodied appearance. "What happened to the child?"

"One of my soldiers. He has been dealt with," Stovia lied smoothly. "But you have in your keeping someone who could help my little Rogan."

"Mama." The elder girl drew Valena closer. "Don't."

"Valena." Mr. Rosonia exhaled heavily. "She is one of the Dravilec, then?"

"You had your suspicions?" Stovia asked.

Valena's father nodded.

"She is needed. Your daughter is needed by her people."

"You want to take her?" Mrs. Rosonia's voice trembled.

Stovia smiled. "She will be well cared for at the palace. And you may visit. She will be taught by the Royal Dravilec how to use her power. She is strong. I could taste *her energy from Sabithia, it was so strong."*

The Rosonias stood in silence for a moment, mother and father silently communicating with one another. Finally, Valena's father turned to Stovia and nodded. "You may take her, my lord."

I gasped in outrage. My parents had died rather than see me in the hands of this snake of a man. And I wasn't the only one outraged. The elder girl shrieked and grabbed Valena to her, refusing to release her. Valena screamed and cried, terrified and confused.

Mr. Rosonia wrenched Valena free, and his wife took her upstairs to ready her for departure. She returned quickly with the little girl dressed for traveling. All the while, she cried. Her mother hugged her, quiet tears rolling down her cheeks as her daughter clung tightly. Mr. Rosonia came over and pulled Valena away, ignoring his elder daughter who sobbed from the corner of the room. Mr. Rosonia kissed Valena's cheeks and promised he would see her soon. Then he handed her into the arms of Syracen Stovia.

Sensing what only children could, she shrieked and writhed to escape. Careful to hide his disgust, Stovia thrust the squalling six-year-old into my arms. I pressed her close, ashamed for my part in this. Valena stopped struggling and instead looped her little arms around my neck, her legs around my waist, and bawled into my shoulder. A memory of my little brother doing the same not too many weeks ago when he had fallen from a tree and cut his leg flashed through my mind, and I squeezed the girl closer, as if I alone could protect her.

Stovia hurried us out of the house, and we walked a distance away to the bridge that would take us out of the village.

"Lieutenant Sandstone," Stovia called, and the soldier trotted forward on his horse. "Take Valena. I can't carry the two on my horse."

Sandstone dismounted and tried to pry Valena from me. The girl screamed, her tiny hands gripped to my cloak, my hair, refusing to budge. And even though I winced at her tight hold, I declined to hand her over.

"That's enough," Stovia grunted. He pushed Sandstone out of the way and gripped a hold of Valena, bruising her small arms as he ripped her from me. I cried out as he drew back his arm and slapped her into silence. I rushed at him in a rage, beating and pushing at him. I was pulled off by the soldier. Stovia, to spite me, hit Valena one more time. Sobbing, furious, I fought against the soldier, only to be beaten by the pummeling fists of the captain of the Guard. The next thing I knew, Kir joined the fray, hitting and punching those who tried to hurt us. I no longer felt pain. I was too angry, too immersed in my fury to feel anything else.

Eventually I was pinned to the ground by the captain and as he stared down at me, I noticed his eyes for the first time. They were blank. Empty.

"Captain ... after we leave the village, I want you to take two of your men and burn the apothecary to the ground. With the Rosonias inside," Stovia demanded from somewhere to my left.

The captain nodded robotically, and it was then I knew. With the evocation of the Dyzvati weakened by Princezna Haydyn's grief and age, Stovia's magic was able to penetrate it. He was compelling the soldiers to do his awful deeds.

As the captain hauled me to my feet, I was weighed down by my despairing heart.

Stovia appeared before me, holding Valena close, her little cheeks red from his slaps. "You attempt to disobey me, Rogan, and I will make you pay. For this disobedience, the Rosonias will pay. You now must live with the fact you killed Valena's family."

Stovia laughed gleefully at my horrified expression.

"Don't listen to him, Rogan." Kir struggled against a soldier, his face mottled with anger. "He was going to kill them anyway. Don't let him make you think you did it."

Stovia curled his lip in disgust. "I've had enough of you. Sandstone!"

The whip appeared in the soldier's hand and Kir was thrust into the dirt.

"NO!" I screamed, my heart lodged somewhere in my throat.

"NO!"

"NO!" I bolted upright in bed. The sheets twisted around my body, my skin clammy, my hair stuck to my neck. Almost immediately, I sensed I wasn't alone. Glancing left, I saw her sitting in an armchair by my bed.

"You were having a nightmare again." Her soft, gentle eyes were sad. "More memories?"

I nodded, my throat constricted with the nightmare that still held me in its talons. "More memories."

Haydyn sighed and slowly drew to her feet. I watched her float across my large bedroom suite and pull the heavy brocade curtains back from my windows. I winced as the sunlight streamed in, too bright, too adamant, willing my bad memories away whilst I steadfastly anchored myself to them.

"I told you I'd speak to Raj to see if he had a tonic to help you sleep without the dreams."

Raj was the Royal Healer; Valena was his apprentice. I shook my head. "I told you no."

"You're the only one who ever says no to me." Haydyn sauntered back to sit on my bed. Her pale hair gleamed almost silver in the sunlight, her countenance serene except for the teasing in her lovely eyes. "I wonder why I let you."

"Because you love me," I stated matter-of-factly as I pushed back the covers. I needed to ready myself for the day.

"Yes, I do."

The statement was so melancholy, I spun to face her. It was then I saw it. The gloom in the back of her eyes, in the dark purpling beneath them. Those exhaustion bruises had been appearing more and more over the last few weeks, and I didn't like it. "Something's the matter."

Haydyn shook her head. "Just tired is all."

"Perhaps we should speak to Raj about a tonic for *you*."

She wasn't amenable but as always, to appease me, she nodded. "Perhaps."

I grimaced when I realized she was fully dressed. Most times when Haydyn came into my suite, it was still so early she was in her nightclothes. "I overslept?"

Haydyn grinned. "Haven forbid, but you did."

I rolled my eyes at her teasing. "You know I hate oversleeping. It muddles up my entire day."

"I know. That's why I let you sleep." She grinned unrepentantly. Sometimes she really was like an annoying younger sister. "You need to loosen the reins on your life now and then, Rogan."

Making a face at her suggestion, I pulled on the servants' bell to let them know I was ready for my morning bath. They would come to me as quickly as they would to Haydyn. After all, I was her best friend, her family. I had been ever since I had been brought to the palace nine years ago by Syracen Stovia. I was only twelve years old at the time. Haydyn was ten. Upon our arrival, Valena was taken from me and given to Raj. Kir lived with Syracen and his family. And I lived at the palace with Haydyn.

Both grieving for the families we'd lost, it hadn't taken long for us to find solace in one another.

Haydyn's mother had died in childbirth, leaving Haydyn alone with her father. The Rada had pushed and pushed him to take another wife, to have more children, but he had loved Haydyn's mother too dearly. He couldn't bear the thought of making someone else his kralovna. That left only the kral and his baby daughter.

Two peas in a pod they were, Haydyn told me. Inseparable. She had depended on her father for everything. Love, comfort, affection, friendship, advice, security. With him gone, she was adrift. And I happened to be the float she grasped on to in his passing. She demanded I be given the suite next to hers where I had roomed ever since. I was also granted the run of the palace as if I were royalty. In return, she looked to me for love, comfort, affection, friendship, advice, and security.

I feared my presence was hindering Haydyn to become the truly independent leader Phaedra needed, but I gave her my strength because she was the only family I had left. And because, after a number of years of begging me to tell her why I screamed in my sleep, I told her what Syracen Stovia had done to my family, to Kir's and Valena's families as well. There was only my word against his. By then I had been at the palace for four years.

Kir had escaped only a year after our arrival, and Haydyn had grown strong enough that Stovia didn't chase him for fear of disrupting the peace. And Valena couldn't remember anything before being brought here.

But Haydyn believed me. And she demanded the Rada listen. She ordered that all twelve members of the Rada Council travel to Silvera to judge Vikomt Syracen Stovia for his crimes. Even if the captain of the Guard had not come forward and confessed what he remembered doing under the compulsion of Stovia, I knew Haydyn would not have stopped until the vikomt was punished.

She was only fourteen years old then. But I was her family. And he had wronged me.

I pledged my everlasting loyalty to Haydyn that day.

The Rada *were* disgusted by Stovia's methods and ordered him imprisoned in Silvera Jail—the lone prisoner. He didn't take the news well. I remember the sweat beading on his forehead and the nosebleed he sustained as he fought to break through Haydyn's evocation. Powerful as he was, he was strong enough to reach for Haydyn to use her as a shield in order to escape. The captain of the Guard did his duty, however, and killed the threat to the princezna's life.

Syracen Stovia's death didn't ease my grief. But I felt freer than I had since the death of my family.

❧

THE SERVANTS ARRIVED AND HAYDYN TOOK HER LEAVE WHILE I helped the girls fill the bath with the hot water. Like every morning, they swatted at me to stop.

"The Handmaiden of Phaedra shouldn't be doing servants' work."

I grunted at the nickname I had been given many years ago. It made me sound like something I wasn't.

After they were gone, I soaked in the tub and grew irritated at having lost productive hours in the day by oversleeping. I hurried out of the bath, toweling my long hair dry before braiding it. It hung heavy and damp down my back, the ends brushing the bottom of my spine. Quickly, I stepped into a dark rose dress of the finest velvet. All my clothing was chosen by Haydyn, and she loved clothes and jewelry. None of these things interested me but for Haydyn's sake, I wore everything she bestowed upon me.

"Ah good, you're dressed." Haydyn barged into my room without knocking. Lord Matai, second lieutenant of the Guard and a young vikomt of a good family, was Haydyn's newest bodyguard. He hovered protectively, even when she was alone with me.

I smiled indulgently at her before noting the slight strain in her features. "What's happened?"

"Nothing. I think." She shrugged elegantly. "Jarvis and Ava have requested me in the Chambers of the Rada."

I hid my concern. His Grace, Vojvoda Jarvis Rada, was the highest-ranking member of the nobility of Sabithia and the Chairman of the Rada, as well as the Keeper of the Archives. Grofka Ava Rada was a widow and the only other member of the Rada who lived in Sabithia. They were both good people, and they loved Haydyn dearly. But Haydyn relied too heavily upon their opinions, and oftentimes they forgot that Haydyn even had a voice. Particularly Jarvis, whose responsibilities and position—especially that of Keeper of the Archives, the very exclusive control over mage history (meaning no one but he was allowed entrance into the archives until his demise, and then only his appointed successor would have the privilege)—had given him an inflated sense of self.

It nettled me. But it wasn't my place to speak for her. Like a frustrated parent, I wanted her to find her voice and independence by herself.

"Well then." I threw both Haydyn and Matai a blasé smile. "We best go and see what they want."

CHAPTER 2

"Ah, Princezna." Vojvoda Jarvis rose to his feet, Lady Ava at his side. He bowed deeply whilst Ava dipped as low as she could into a curtsy. "Looking beautiful as always." Jarvis smiled at Haydyn like a doting grandfather. His eyes flicked to me and he gave me an expressionless nod. Jarvis and Ava were uncomfortable around me. They were ashamed of what Stovia did to my family.

"Your Grace." Haydyn gave a shallow curtsy. "My lady. I trust you are both well."

"As well as can be, Princezna. We do not bring good tidings."

Haydyn and I shared a worried look, and I followed her as she took her seat at the head of the long chambers table. I sat on her left, facing Ava. Jarvis took the seat next to the grofka.

"What's wrong?" Haydyn asked. That gloom crept into her eyes again, and I could have sworn she swayed in her chair. I was just about to reach for her when she seemed to shake herself awake. I withdrew my hand.

Jarvis cleared his throat, his expression grave. "I must ask, first of all, Princezna, whether you are feeling well? Are you in good health?"

I was surprised by his question. Unnerved, even.

"Of course," she answered, but it sounded hesitant to my ears.

"Why?" I asked, even though it wasn't my place to.

Ava's eyes were wide with anxiety. "Because it seems as if the evocation is weakened somehow."

Haydyn gasped. "Weakened? It can't be. I'm projecting the evocation at full, as always."

"We've received reports these last few weeks from the rest of the Rada, the most anxious of them being Vojvoda Andrei Rada, Keeper of Alvernia. The province is worsening; the uncivilized, loutish behavior of the mountain people grows steadily closer to his city in the south. He fears the people of Arrana may become contaminated by the aggression of the northerners and grows agitated by Silvera's 'negligence,' as he calls it."

Haydyn threw me a concerned look. "I had no idea things were so bad."

"There is more," Ava added.

"Yes," Jarvis continued. "I've had word from the city of Pharya. A rookery has sprung up on the border of Vasterya in the towns near the glass works. Gangs of thieves and smugglers are disrupting import and exportation."

Dear havens, I had never heard the like. "Thieves? Gangs? A rookery? In Phaedra?" I was aghast. We all were. My questioning gaze swung to Haydyn.

She squirmed as her emerald eyes filled with fear. "Don't look at me like that, Rogan. I don't know what to tell you. I don't feel a change in my magic."

Jarvis coughed. "Lastly—"

"There's more?"

He threw me an admonishing look for the interruption. "Yes. There's more. Markiza Raven Rada's guard is dealing with nomads—"

"The Caels?" Haydyn frowned as she referred to one of the

nomadic clans. "But the Caels have lived in Northern Javinia for decades. They finally made a place their home."

"Not the Caels, Princezna. The Iavii. These Alvernian nomads are not looking for peace. They've already stolen land from the Caels, and now they try to do the same with the Javinians. Tensions are high between the Javinians and the Caels, who are being held as accountable as the Iavii."

"That's not fair!" Haydyn cried. "The Caels are a peaceful clan."

"They are. *Were.* Nothing in Javinia remains peaceful. The Javinian guards are busy dealing with disputes and protecting Markiza Raven in Novia. She calls for aid."

The magnitude of the news silenced us both. How quickly our beautiful world seemed to have imploded.

"You're sure you're well, Princezna?" Ava queried again.

"Positive," Haydyn snapped, jolting out of her seat. I watched on, as wide-eyed as Jarvis and Ava. Haydyn never spoke harshly to anyone. "I will not be questioned again."

"Of course, Princezna. We meant no disrespect." Jarvis's brow furrowed deeply.

"Now, what is to be done?"

You *tell* them, *Haydyn*, I wanted to say. But I didn't. She already appeared so lost and afraid.

Jarvis sighed wearily. "Well, I think before we panic, we should discover the realities of the situation for ourselves. I say we send some of the Guard to Alvernia, Vasterya, and Javinia to report back their findings before we decide upon action."

Haydyn seemed relieved by his suggestion. She turned to Matai who stood on guard at the door. "Lord Matai, please have one of the footmen fetch Captain Stovia."

I flinched at her command and bit my lip, my heart picking up speed at the thought of Wolfe. Captain Wolfe Stovia. *Vikomt* Wolfe Stovia, now that his father Syracen was dead. A few years my senior, Wolfe had proven himself steadfast, loyal, hardworking, and a strong soldier. He was one of the youngest captains in the history of the Guard. And I didn't trust him one iota.

He wasn't long in arriving. Wolfe strode into the room as his namesake would have done. Sleek and watchful, wily and dangerous. As handsome as any man in Phaedra, the servant girls went into twittering spasms whenever he was near. It made me feel rather queasy, to be honest.

His light blue eyes drank in the room before they came to rest upon me. His expression was inscrutable. Wolfe favored his mother's side of the family in looks, for which I was grateful. It would have been awful to witness a young version of Syracen stalking the palace halls.

Wolfe bowed deeply and smiled at Haydyn, almost flirtatiously. "Princezna."

I rolled my eyes as Haydyn smiled prettily back at him. She may as well have batted her eyelashes. A person couldn't entirely blame her. If forced to, I could admit he was something to look at. Wolfe was strikingly tall, broad-shouldered, had a thick head of silky chestnut hair, olive skin, and beautiful almond-shaped eyes. His was a strong face, masculine and powerful. I, however, disliked it greatly.

"Captain," Haydyn said. "I need you to send the Guard on an errand for me."

I watched as Wolfe listened carefully to the news, his expression tightening as he learned of our situation. "I will send nine of my best men, Your Highness, three to each province."

"Thank you, Captain." Jarvis drew to his feet and helped Ava out of hers. "We appreciate it."

As they were about to depart, I stood and cleared my throat. "May I suggest we keep this among us? And stress the importance of keeping this information confidential to your men ... *Captain.*"

Haydyn's eyes widened. "Of course, Rogan is right. We don't want to cause panic until we have all the facts."

Wolfe nodded, but he never took his eyes from me as he smiled sardonically. "Of course, Princezna."

I glowered at him until he took his leave. Jarvis and Ava followed in his wake.

A solemn air hung between Haydyn and me as we strolled to her suite, Matai close on our heels. I was afraid to mention what had just been discussed.

"I keep waiting for you to cease your unpleasant attitude toward Captain Wolfe." Haydyn threw me a reproving look.

"You'll be waiting a millennium then."

"Rogan, really." She tsked. "He's not his father, you know."

I shrugged. I knew Haydyn thought it was unfair of me to dislike Wolfe, but I couldn't help it. He was a Stovia. No matter how much he ingratiated himself to Haydyn or into the Rada's trust, he would always be my enemy. His father had taken my family, and I had destroyed his in return. I was suspicious of his loyalty to Haydyn, when any normal man would have wanted vengeance for his father's death.

Haydyn did not share the suspicion. She sighed dreamily. "I don't understand how you can be so disagreeable with him. He's so handsome and strong."

I laughed softly at Matai's choked grunt behind us, and Haydyn threw him a teasing look over her shoulder. He would take his revenge for that.

We stopped at her suite and I checked the halls in both directions. It was clear. I nodded at them and Haydyn grabbed Matai's hand, disappearing into her suite with him. I stood guard.

Protecting Haydyn as always.

Protecting her secrets.

Protecting her love for Lord Matai.

I experienced a twinge of unfamiliar longing at the sound of her and Matai's intimate laughter beyond the door. Haydyn was akin to my younger sister, and yet she knew more of that mysterious intimacy between man and woman than I did. All I ever wanted was to be a source of wisdom and support for Haydyn. How could I be when she was more worldly than I? I was twenty-one years of age and remained unkissed.

I ducked my head, feeling silly and adolescent. I did not seek love. I'd never wanted it. However, a little romance perhaps might be nice.

I shook the thought from my mind. No. I had no time for romance. I was far too busy facilitating Haydyn's.

CHAPTER 3

"Mmm," I moaned, the sweet chocolate and fresh cream cake making my eyes flutter shut in rapture. "Cook, you've surpassed yourself."

Cook grinned broadly, rolling out pastry as servants bustled around us in the enormous kitchen. Valena giggled from her seat across from me, cream caught on the corner of her mouth. "I swear, Rogan, the sweetest expression you ever have on your face is when you're eating Cook's desserts."

I raised an eyebrow at her cheekiness and reached across to swipe the last of the cakes from her plate.

"Hey!" She leapt forward to grab for it but I held it out of her reach. If we had been standing face-to-face rather than sitting across a long table, she would have taken it easily. Valena was only fourteen, but she was also extremely tall, a good three inches taller than me. "Oh, don't, Rogan." Valena's eyes widened as I pretended to pop the cake into my mouth. "Cook only made a few today."

Cook shook her head at my teasing. "I swear it could be nine years ago with the way you act, Miss Rogan."

"Well, I wouldn't have to behave this way if you made more

than just a few cakes." I handed the desserts over to Valena, greedily watching as she scoffed one down in seconds. "Oh, you didn't even take time to enjoy that. Sacrilege. I should have eaten it."

"But it was mine." Valena grinned through a mouthful. "You're too honorable to have taken what was mine."

"Where did she adopt such an attitude?" I asked Cook, pretending beleaguerment.

Cook snorted. "You!"

Valena burst out laughing while I faked a scowl.

"Valena!"

We spun around at the sound of Raj's frantic voice, the kitchen coming to a standstill as he stumbled into the room. We all stared at him wide-eyed. My heart thumped as Raj smoothed back his white-blond hair and straightened his waistcoat. "Valena," he said, quieter this time. "I need you."

Valena didn't ask questions. She jumped from the table and made her way toward him. Raj gestured for her to walk before him and then turned his pale eyes on me. "You, too, Rogan."

I shared a brief worried look with Cook and hurried after the healers.

"What's going on?" I asked.

"I've been called to the princezna's suite."

I forgot all ladylike manners and lifted my dress, running as fast as I could through the palace halls to Haydyn's apartments. Servants gaped at me as I blurred by them, and I wanted desperately to shout back at Raj to hurry up. But if he did that, if he ran with me, then everyone would know something was wrong with Haydyn.

I knew *something was wrong!*

I cursed myself for not pressing her further, but ever since Jarvis and Ava had imparted the news of the hostility in Phaedra a few weeks ago, I was afraid to burden Haydyn.

Inside her suite, I found Matai. No other servant. Only

Matai, his expression frantic as he hovered over Haydyn, collapsed on the floor.

"What happened?" I rushed to them, throwing myself down beside my friend. Her skin was deathly pale and when I reached for her hand, I found it limp.

Matai met my gaze with a grim one of his own. "I don't know," he whispered to me. "We were only talking and then she ... she just fainted. I was afraid to move her. I've called for Raj. I didn't want anyone else to know ..." He trailed off as Raj and Valena came into the room. Valena shut the door behind her.

Raj shoved me out of the way.

"What's wrong with her?" I demanded.

"Give me a minute, Rogan, for haven's sake," Raj replied through gritted teeth.

Haydyn groaned, her eyelids fluttering open. As her eyes focused, they widened in panic. "What happened?" her voice was hoarse.

"You fainted," I snapped, as if it was somehow her fault.

She looked to Raj. "Why?"

Raj shook his head. "Lord Matai, help me move the princezna to the bed."

I stood back, and Valena gripped my hand to reassure me. The gesture was sweet but ineffective.

"Lord Matai, Rogan, please leave Valena and me alone with the princezna."

I objected, "No. I'm staying right here."

"Rogan." Matai grabbed my arm. "For once, do as you're told." I wasn't even given a chance to struggle. Not that I could. Matai was as big as Wolfe. He pushed me outside the suite and shut the door behind us, his large body blocking my entrance.

"I need to be in there with her."

"No. You want to be, there's a difference."

"Matai."

"Stop it, Rogan," he hissed. A flash of sharpness in his eyes revealed his deep concern. "For once ... just stop."

I slumped at his tone, my heart pounding so hard I was sick with it. "What's wrong with her, Matai? She won't tell me."

"I know." He grimaced. "She's been overtired lately. I've tried to talk to her about it but ..."

"She keeps saying nothing is the matter," I finished.

"Yes."

Our eyes locked. We both knew something was *definitely* wrong.

It seemed forever before Raj beckoned us back into the suite. It had probably only been fifteen minutes.

"What's the matter?" I rushed to Haydyn's side and grasped her hand in mine.

She was sitting up in bed now, color returning to her cheeks, and she smiled a bright smile that relieved me.

Matai stood hovering at the end of the bed. He threw Raj a belligerent look. "Well, man, what the hell is going on?"

I shot the soldier a chiding look. He and Haydyn were supposed to hide their feelings for one another, not make it obvious to even the most unobservant person.

Raj smiled indulgently, glancing from Haydyn to Valena. "Both Valena and I have examined the princezna. We sensed only the darkness of exhaustion and so we removed it from her. The princezna is feeling much better." He strode to her other side. "As for this not sleeping, I will have one of the servants bring a tonic from my stores that should help you find rest, Princezna."

"Thank you, Raj." Haydyn bestowed a grateful smile upon the healer. "I appreciate your help."

Suddenly I was exhausted by the fright she had given me. "Next time maybe you'll do as I ask and see Raj before you collapse on the floor."

The others looked a little shocked. Not Haydyn. She appeared remorseful. Because she knew me well. "I'm sorry, Rogan. I promise not to frighten you again."

"Pfft."

"Rogan?"

"If you're all better, I have things to do."

Matai and the healers glared at me, but I did not care for their opinions.

Haydyn narrowed her eyes on me. "Yes, you do have things to do." She threw back the covers and got out of bed with a surprising breeze of energy. "Tell Jarek to ready my horse and yours. We're going to the marketplace."

I clenched my jaw but strode toward the door to do her bidding. The marketplace! She knew I hated the marketplace. She was punishing me for my inability to admit I was frightened.

"Oh, and Rogan ..."

I stiffened. I did not like that singsong tone of hers. It meant she was up to something. "Yes, Your Highness?"

"After you speak with Jarek, please find Captain Stovia. We'll need an escort."

I grimaced and marched out of the room, her sweet laughter following me. Despite the distasteful thought of being in Wolfe's presence, I smiled at the sound of her laughter and shook my head at her mischief.

"There you are," I called as I came upon Jarek in the Silver Stable. We had stables almost as large as the palace because half of the Royal Guard was cavalry. There were a number of stable boys, and Jarek, a young man my age with a quick wit and warm smile, had been a stable boy up until recently. The old stable master had passed away, and I had suggested Jarek for the job. Yes, he was young, but we had been friends ever since my arrival at the palace and I had never met anyone with such an affinity for horses. There had been some upset at first when Haydyn appointed him as stable master. People assumed he was too young and not responsible enough. But he had the stables in tip-top shape in no time and now everyone could plainly see he was the best man for the job.

Jarek looked up from checking a chestnut bay's hooves. He grinned at me. "Where else would I be?"

"I don't know." I shrugged, sauntering leisurely toward him. "Any one of the other stables. Or the kitchen. Cook made cakes today."

He sucked in a breath of mock disappointment. "And I missed them?"

"Jarek, you would have missed them even if you'd been there. Valena and I devastated the plate within five seconds."

"Valena ..." He threw me a teasing smirk. "She's getting to be too much like you."

"Everyone keeps saying that." I frowned. "And what's wrong with being like me?"

Jarek studied me, his smile widening to a wicked grin. "Nothing. Absolutely nothing."

Despite myself, I warmed at Jarek's attention. We had been friends for a long time, but more and more lately, our conversations had taken a decidedly flirtatious turn. And he *was* extremely good-looking. However, that was the problem. I knew too many maids, and even a few noblewomen, who had shared Jarek's bed. Despite that reckless little voice inside that was eager to uncover the mysteries of intimacy between lovers, I didn't want to be just another girl he'd tumbled.

I cleared my throat. "Haydyn wishes to go to the marketplace right away. Will you ready Midnight and Sundown?"

Jarek nodded. "Is the Guard going with you?"

I winced. "Yes."

"You don't sound too excited about it. Here's a thought." He bent his head to mine, his breath hot on my ear. Goosebumps skated down my spine. "Why don't I be your guard for the day? I'd take very good care of you, Rogan."

"And Haydyn?" I murmured, my body vibrating with awareness of him.

Jarek laughed softly. "She has Lord Matai." He drew back only a little, our noses almost touching. "You can have me."

"Well, isn't this cozy."

I closed my eyes at the voice of interruption.

Wolfe.

Ugh, how I hated him.

Jarek sighed and retreated as I turned to face Wolfe. He leaned against the stable wall, glaring at us. "Apparently, I'm escorting you to the marketplace. When were you planning on delivering that message? A week, maybe two ...?"

I glowered. "Clearly it makes no matter since the message has been delivered."

Wolfe pushed away from the wall and strode toward me. Dear haven, he was tall. He towered over me and Jarek. "You," he bit out at Jarek, "the horses. Now. Hers"—he flicked a distasteful look at me—"the princezna's, Lord Matai's, my own, and three of my guard."

Jarek crossed his arms over his chest, not in the least intimidated. "Which three?"

"Worth, Vincent, and Chaeron," Wolfe replied through clenched teeth.

Jarek nodded tightly. His expression softened when his eyes fell upon me again, and he winked. "I'll speak with you later, Rogan."

"Jarek." I watched him leave, biting my lip against indecent thoughts as he swaggered out of the stable and into the next. Feeling Wolfe's eyes on me, I turned and met his sharp look with one of my own. "What?"

"What?" He guffawed incredulously. "The princezna has been unwell and everyone is agreeing to her outing to the market, and you're in here flirting with the stable boy."

"Stable master," I corrected, poking him in the chest with the words. "And don't take that self-righteous tone with me, as if I don't care about Haydyn."

Wolfe snorted. "Do you care? You were supposed to come

and inform me so I can protect you at market, and you're in here with your legs practically wrapped around Jarek."

How dare he? I sucked in a breath at the accusation. "You're lucky I don't slap you for that insinuation. Jarek is my friend. I came here to ask him to prepare the horses, and I was just about to come and find your sorry ass to let you know Haydyn required your company. *Not* that I should have to explain myself to you."

"*Sorry ass.*" Wolfe threw me a disdainful look. "Really? That's the language of the Handmaiden of Phaedra? Very refined."

Refined? I'd give him refined. I'd been around enough stable boys to know my share of curse words. "Oh, sod off, Captain," I threw over my shoulder as I departed the stables.

❧

THE CITY OF SILVERA GREW QUIET AND THE CROWDS PARTED as we moved through them on the cobbled streets. Their chatter hushed and then rose again as the people gathered together at the rear of our entourage, like a wave crashing to shore behind us.

I rode beside Haydyn on Midnight, she on Sundown. Matai was on Haydyn's other side and three of the Royal Guard were at our backs. Wolfe rode in front, his eagle eyes watching the crowds as we traveled past taverns, apothecaries, inns, butchers, bakers, and candlestick makers. The marketplace was in the large Silvera Square where people from the neighboring provinces came to sell their wares. Haydyn always had a particular interest in the artists and craftsmen of Raphizya and the beautiful glasswork of Vasterya.

"I've decided to hold a ball." Haydyn waved to Silverans who bowed and curtsied as we cantered past.

I raised an eyebrow. "A ball?"

"Hmm." Haydyn grinned excitedly. She seemed so young in that moment, despite her nineteen years. "A ball. I'll invite all the

Rada and all the noblemen and women of every province. A way of showing our solidarity in an unsettling time."

"A ball?" I still wasn't convinced.

"I think it's a fine idea, Princezna." Matai smiled at her.

I sighed. "No one asked you, Lord Matai."

"Rogan, be nice," Haydyn tutted. "Anyway, Lord Matai is correct. It *is* a fine idea."

My heart jumped a little at the determination in her voice and hope bloomed. Perhaps Haydyn was finally taking charge. And I might not like fancy balls, but ... it *was* a good idea. If only because it was *her* idea.

Her face fell when I didn't respond. Abruptly, she looked anxious. "Don't you think it's a good idea, Rogan?"

I cursed inwardly. Why did everyone's opinion matter so much to her? She was as smart and capable as any of us fools whose advice she solicited. I wished she'd remember she was fair and just and royal—she should not concern herself with my opinion, or anyone else's, for that matter.

Instead I gave her a soft smile. "Lord Matai's correct. It's a fine idea."

Moment of worry over, Haydyn's expression turned cheerful as we entered the marketplace. Again, all went quiet at the sight of us, but gradually, as we trotted over to the stables, the noise level rose again.

"Please, I want you to seek out the finest fabric for me, for my new ballgown, as well as the finest for yourself," Haydyn commanded politely as Matai helped her dismount. I was so shocked by the request, I dismounted without help, forgetting I wasn't supposed to do that in public. But Haydyn very rarely used my magic and never for something as frivolous as fabric shopping.

My body crackled from the inside out, drawing me toward a fabric stall deep in the crowds of the square. "Fabric?"

"Hmm." Haydyn nodded. "We want to look our best for such an important event."

"Not the key to world peace? Not the answer to shutting down a rookery or controlling nomads? *Fabric?*"

Haydyn exhaled wearily. "Must I repeat it, Rogan, when we both know you're being facetious?"

I shrugged. "Well, I just had no idea that the form of our fashion was so incredibly important to settling Phaedrian disputes."

"More facetiousness. Lovely."

"Fine. Away I go to seek and order the fabric." I glanced between her and Matai. "What are you going to do?"

Haydyn stared a little too adoringly at her bodyguard. "Lord Matai's going to escort me around the market while I choose some gifts to present to our guests at the ball."

I threw him a mock horrified look. "Lord Matai, may I say now how much I've enjoyed knowing you, for I fear it will be the last time I look upon you." I winced. "Death by boredom is such a tragic way to go."

He grinned. "I'm sure I'll survive."

"You don't have to sound so put upon." Haydyn sniffed.

I laughed, thinking about her well-known generosity. "And just where are all these gifts going? We didn't bring a cart?"

"I'll borrow one. Or buy one. I am the princezna."

I almost rolled my eyes. She asserts her authority when shopping. Wonderful.

"Don't let me keep you. Off I go. Shan't be long." I disappeared into the crowds before Haydyn demanded I take an escort.

I breathed deeply of the thick smells. It was a strange mixture of pungent sheep's wool, beets, chocolate, oil, sweet meats, bread, perfume, paint ... oh, it was a fragrance of all the variety of the market. Usually, I disliked the crowds, preferring to escape to the cliffs some miles from the palace. I loved the peace and quiet of watching the surf of the Silver Sea crash against the cliff walls. The sea's fierceness reminded me what it was to be alive.

But I was never alone. There was always a guard with me some way in the distance.

Today, as I swept past people, some who recognized me, some who didn't—merchants calling out to me to buy their wares, desperate for what they assumed was a noblewoman to purchase some expensive bauble from them—I loved the market in that moment. Because I was alone. All alone. Free.

I was quick on my feet, dodging persistent sellers and hopefully any of the Guard who may have followed me. In no time at all, I found the stall with the fabric that called to my magic. I recognized it immediately. Velvet, the color of lapis lazuli, made from the finest silk in the textile factories in Ryl. Haydyn would look wonderful in it. I reached out to stroke the beautiful fabric when a hand clamped around my wrist.

"No, no, miss." I looked up into the ruddy face of the market seller. "Not the right color for you, miss. Come see some of my silks." He tried to pull me toward the more expensive material. I tugged on his grip, but he was determined.

I grew irritated by his persistence. "Sir—"

"With a face and figure like yours, you shouldn't hide behind heavy textures. Fine silks, miss, fine silks for you."

I tugged again. Oh yes. *This* was why I hated the marketplace.

A large hand came down on top of the seller's, ripping it from my own and holding it tight. Both the seller and I looked up into the angry face of Wolfe Stovia.

"You dare to lay your hand on the princezna's handmaiden?" Wolfe growled at the man.

The seller blanched as he looked at me, recognition finally dawning. "Oh, my lady, I meant no disrespect."

Wolfe grunted and shoved the man away a little. "Lady or servant, I see you trying to coerce a woman again, and you and I will have words."

I'd never seen anyone look so green with fear. "Apologies, my lord. I was overexcited. It won't happen again. Apologies, my lady."

Oh, for haven's sake. "I'm not a lady," I snapped, furious at Wolfe for drawing attention to the situation and blowing it out of proportion. The overbearing lout. I glared at him. "You, sir, are a bully."

Wolfe frowned at me. "And you are the Handmaiden of Phaedra and as such, a *lady*. You are not to allow strange men to touch you."

"I'll allow a mountain man of Alvernia to touch me before I take advice from you, *Stovia*." Dismissing him, agitated by his presence, his ruination of my pretense at freedom, I turned to the seller. "I want one bolt of the lapis lazuli velvet and one of the emerald silk chiffon."

I relaxed a little at having completed my task for Haydyn, but then my body hummed with energy again. I turned without thinking toward a stall some quarter of the way back into the middle of the market. The fabric that would suit me most was in there somewhere. Damn Haydyn. Damn being an Azyl.

I spun back to the seller. "Have the fabric delivered to the palace and ask for Seamstress Rowan. You'll be paid well for your troubles."

He nodded, doing this obscene half-bow/curtsy thing that made me throw a growl in Wolfe's direction. Turning sharply from them both, I followed my magic across the marketplace and drew in a breath at the pleasant sandalwood scent that signaled Wolfe had fallen into step beside me.

I stopped abruptly. "What are you doing?"

Wolfe shrugged, refusing to look at me, refusing to leave. "Just one of the more unpleasant jobs of being captain of the Guard. Protecting *you*."

"We are droll, aren't we?"

"Some people think I'm charming." He grinned flirtatiously at a passing tavern girl who continued to eye him over her bare shoulder as we walked away.

"Some people don't know any better."

"Ooh, is that judgment I hear in the voice of the lady who was flirting with a mere stable boy this morning?"

I gritted my teeth. "Stable *master*."

Wolfe raised one annoying eyebrow. "As if that makes it any more palatable. You know he's bedded every woman in the palace. You're not special."

My blood boiled beneath my skin, as it did whenever I was forced to be in proximity to this man. I tried to take deep, calming breaths. I did. I really, really did. It didn't work. "Who I choose to converse with is of no consequence to you, Captain Stovia. And may I remind you to whom you are speaking?"

He threw me a mocking look. "So, there is a snob buried under all that 'I'm not a lady, I'm not a lady, I'm just like everyone else' piffle?"

"I *am* just like everyone else. *Except*," I snapped, "when it comes to you. *You* will talk to me like I'm royalty, Captain. As in ... don't speak to me at all."

Wolfe stiffened at my insults, his face taut with anger. Our dislike was definitely, *definitely* mutual. "If you want to make this about rank, Rogan—"

I flinched at his use of my given name. He'd never called me Rogan before. Not to my face, anyway. It had always been *my lady*, despite my lack of nobility.

"May I remind *you* that I'm the one with lord before *my* name? Don't speak to me like I'm dirt beneath your shoe."

Arrogant beast. I shook my head. Just like his demon father. I laughed humorlessly, a cold, brittle laugh that caused him to wince. "You don't need to remind me who *you* are, *Vikomt Stovia.*" With that, I veered from him, pushing through the crowds to escape him. I glanced back to make sure he did not follow. He didn't, but he lifted his chin in someone else's direction. It was an order.

Within seconds, Lieutenant Chaeron had pushed through the crowds to be at my side, his hand on the hilt of his sword.

My first impulse was to be aggravated and suffocated by his presence, but then I recalled Jarvis's words of warning. There was a reason behind Haydyn's idea for a ball. Quite suddenly, I was glad for our trained Guard. We had never needed them before.

But then there had never been crime in civilized Phaedra before.

CHAPTER 4

"What about Matai, Haydyn?" I hissed, knowing he stood outside her bedroom suite.

She glanced worriedly at the door. "Please, keep your voice down, Rogan."

I bit my lip against a tirade. I was so mad at her. I wanted her to wake up! My head swam with all Ava and Jarvis had informed us.

That morning, Haydyn had been called to the Chambers to speak with Jarvis and Ava: Last night, Wolfe's men had returned ... and they hadn't returned bearing good news.

"So ... it's all true?" Haydyn had asked as she sat clutching my hand tight in hers. I ignored the stinging pain of her long nails digging into my skin and tried to squeeze her hand in reassurance.

Jarvis nodded. He seemed to have aged a decade since we saw him but a few weeks before. "All three complaints proved true. Javinia is in unrest, and it seems rumor of the unrest is spreading through Sabithia. Alvernia is worsening. Even the Valley grows more uncivilized. Apparently, Arrana is the only civilized city left in the province. And as for the rookery in Vasterya ... well, it does exist."

Haydyn grew tense beside me, her young eyes round and fearful. "What do we do?"

Ava and Jarvis shared a look.

It was I who questioned it.

"Well." Jarvis cleared his throat. "Of course, we should send reinforcements into Javinia, and someone should speak with Markiz Solom Rada in Pharya—he needs to send his guard out to police the rookery. It's unfathomable that he hasn't already."

"Is it?" Ava murmured. It appeared Ava and I shared the same opinion of Markiz Solom.

He was my least favorite of the Rada. Spoiled, entitled, weak.

"What about Alvernia?" I queried.

Again, they exchanged a nervous glance.

Ava attempted to smile brightly. "We have a wonderful suggestion."

My intuition told me it wasn't that wonderful. "Suggest it, then."

"Rogan," Haydyn admonished.

Seeming unconcerned with my attitude, Jarvis leaned forward across the table, his eyes all grandfatherly and wise as he focused his attention on Haydyn. "You are of an age now, Princezna, and it's time to discuss the possibility of you marrying and carrying on the Dyzvati line."

I sucked in a breath, feeling Haydyn stiffen under my touch. "She's not a broodmare."

Jarvis flinched at my tone and narrowed his eyes on me. "I suggest no such thing, Rogan. Please dispense with the attitude."

"Rogan, please." Haydyn patted my hand. "His Grace is right. I am of age."

As I watched Ava and Jarvis share pleased looks, I just knew deep in the pit of my stomach what they wanted of her. "You want a match with Alvernia."

They seemed shocked at my deduction and Jarvis shifted nervously for a moment. Vaguely, I noted Matai stiffen at the door.

Jarvis held Haydyn's gaze. "We think you might want to consider a betrothal between Your Highness and Markiz Andrei of Alvernia—son of Vojvoda Andrei Rada. It would greatly improve relations between the two provinces and would be an excellent start toward civilizing the north."

Haydyn turned pale at the suggestion. She looked at me and winced at what she saw in my expression. Then she threw back her shoulders, her chin rising. In defiance of my opinion, it would seem. "I think it's a very good idea. And one we must consider. Vojvoda Andrei and his son are invited to the ball next month, are they not?"

"Yes," Ava replied, relief sparking in her eyes. "They are, Princezna. They're staying at the palace with the rest of the Rada and their families. It will be a wonderful opportunity for you both to get to know one another."

"Splendid." Jarvis clapped his hands and Haydyn smiled, glad to have pleased them.

THE WALK BACK TO HER SUITE HAD BEEN ICE COLD AS MATAI refused to look at either of us. He opened the door to her suite and shut it softly in our wake. Not one word had passed between the lovers.

"I just can't believe you're even considering marrying some stranger."

Haydyn's cheeks colored with a deep blush, and I knew she was growing impatient with me. "It may be what's best for Phaedra. I'm finally doing something worthy of a leader and you're angry at me?"

"You're not doing something worthy of a leader. You're doing what someone else wants you to do. As always!"

She flinched, hurt stark in her eyes.

I instantly felt awful but words of apology stuck in my throat.

"There was never a future for me and Matai," she whispered sorrowfully, pleading with me to understand. "He's not of a high enough rank."

"You can have any future you want, Haydyn." I gestured out the window. "You can do what *you* like, love who *you* love, *be* who *you* want to be. And there is nothing they can do about it because *they* need *you*."

Haydyn trembled, clasping onto a bed post. "No." She shook her head, growing wanner by the second. "Something's wrong with Phaedra and I have to fix it. Jarvis knows how. The betrothal is a good idea," she gasped, seeming out of breath.

I was too angry to pay attention. How dare she play the sacrificial lamb when we owed her everything. We couldn't just take and take from her, ensuring our safety and happiness at the expense of her own. "Haydyn, it's a good idea. But not the best idea. Not the only idea. Surely, we can come up with something else. You don't—"

"Rogan ..."

"—know if Andrei of Alvernia is a despicable lout like the rest of the mountain people are supposed to—"

"Rogan ..."

"—be. He could—"

"Rogan!" Haydyn gasped and fell toward me. My heart flared in panic as I rushed to catch her. Thankfully I caught her before she hit the ground, but her eyes rolled back in her head and she grew limp and lifeless in my arms.

"Haydyn." I shook her. "Haydyn." I shook her harder but her eyes wouldn't open. She was so pale. So deathly pale. I choked on a sob. "Haydyn! Wake up!" A sob broke out from the pit of my stomach. "MATAI!" I screamed. "MATAI!"

CHAPTER 5

The room was silent. Like death had crept into the palace and snuffed out all the candles, all the cheer, all the life. I looked around at my companions and swallowed past the constriction in my throat.

"I've called you all here for a reason." I forced out the words.

After Haydyn had collapsed in my arms, Matai burst into the room and he wasn't alone. For some reason, Wolfe was with him.

Unable to rouse Haydyn, I silently walked through the palace, terrified of spreading panic. I quietly ushered Valena and Raj to the suite. When Raj gravely informed us that he and Valena needed more time to discover Haydyn's illness, deep suspicion and fear coalesced inside me. I sent a messenger out for Vojvoda Jarvis and Grofka Ava and met them in the grand entranceway before I brought them to my suite where Wolfe and Matai waited.

They paled at the news of Haydyn's collapse and were outraged to learn it wasn't the first time. I bore the brunt of their anger.

Finally, Valena called us into Haydyn's suite. A passing maid's eyes widened at the sight of our illustrious group, and I shooed her away with a warning that she was not to speak of this to anyone. She nodded before hurrying away.

Inside we were greeted by a very grave Raj. And then he confirmed our worst fears. Haydyn had fallen ill to the Somna. The rarest of illnesses in Phaedra, the Somna, more colloquially known as the sleeping disease, was a mystery to us. No one knew where, why, or what caused it. There had been fewer and fewer records of the Somna over the last centuries, but now and again it took hold of someone without warning. It caused a growing lethargy that soon led to the victim falling into a coma-like state. If the victim was lucky enough to have a Dravilec nearby, the healer could hold off death by healing the sleeping person from starvation and dehydration. If not, death was inevitable ... unless one could find the rare leaves of the Somna plant, the only cure to the sleeping disease—a plant that was now said to be extinct.

I stared around the Chambers of the Rada at Jarvis, Ava, Matai, Wolfe, Valena, and Raj. Only we knew Haydyn was dying. It was the reason Phaedra was falling apart. Unbeknownst to her, her magic was waning with her illness.

I thought of my harsh words to Haydyn, the words that had been my last. I flinched and then gritted my teeth. They wouldn't be my last. Haydyn was *not* dying. Not while I had breath in my body.

"Someone command me to seek the Somna plant," I urged.

Wolfe's eyes widened as everyone shifted, as if waking out of a coma themselves. "Of course," he whispered, and they all seemed to admonish themselves for not having thought of it before. "Rogan—"

"Not you," I interrupted. I wouldn't be ordered to seek anything from another Stovia again. He threw me a wounded look I refused to believe wasn't a manipulation. Ignoring him, I turned to Jarvis. "Vojvoda."

He nodded militantly. "Rogan, I command you to seek the Somna plant."

Waves crashed within and I shuddered at the immense

current of energy coursing through me. I'd never experienced the magic like this before, my nerves buzzing and twanging, my muscles twitching. Even my gums ached with it.

As the knowledge of the plant's existence formed in my mind, I realized why the impact was so great this time. The Somna plant was buried in the northernmost point of Phaedra.

I had never had to seek anything so far from me before.

"It exists." I exhaled in relief, my heart in my throat, tears pricking my eyes.

"Where?" Matai croaked.

I braced myself. What a journey lay ahead of me. "The Pool of Phaedra."

Ava gasped. "In the mountains of Alvernia?"

"Is there any other?" I answered.

Jarvis eyed me worriedly. "You are willing to retrieve it, aren't you? Our kingdom is at stake."

Curling my lip in scorn, I replied coldly, "Of course, I will retrieve it. Not for our kingdom but for my princezna." Nothing else mattered but saving Haydyn. Saving the kingdom was just a consequence of succeeding in my mission.

"We'll send word ahead to Vojvoda Andrei Rada that I and members of the Royal Guard are coming to visit his province. Let him and everyone else think Haydyn has sent me to divine whether a possible betrothal between her and the markiz will suit her and the kingdom. Everyone knows Haydyn defers to my opinion, so no one will question it. In reality, I will spend only a day or so at Arrana and head into the mountains to retrieve the plant."

I barely took a moment to breathe before continuing, "At home, you will spread the tale that Haydyn has decided she would like some peace from palace life. She's staying in her cottage at Land's End." I took a moment to think who would be most trustworthy to accompany her. "She'll need a chaperone, for appearance's sake, so we'll send Seamstress Rowan with Matai, Raj, and Valena. Rowan can be trusted." I stared them all down. "No one must know the truth but us and Rowan."

They stared as if they'd never seen me before. Jarvis gave me what might pass for a proud look as he nodded. "It's an excellent plan, Rogan."

"How long will it take you to retrieve the plant?" Valena asked, her fingers worrying the handkerchief in her hand. She hadn't stopped crying since she'd helped Raj uncover Haydyn's illness.

I looked to Wolfe. He was the only one who knew the provinces well. He cocked his head to the side, considering it. "Without interruption? With the Royal Guard—"

I shook my head. "Not all of them."

"My lady, more and more criminal acts are being recorded. I will not take the Handmaiden of Phaedra across our land without an army."

"Stop calling me the Handmaiden of Phaedra."

"Just being respectful."

"I'd believe that if not for the mocking tone in your voice." I huffed as I realized how childish I was being in light of the circumstances. "Fine. Twenty men."

"A hundred."

A hundred men! Talk about conspicuous. I glowered, incredulous.

Wolfe sighed. "Fine, fifty."

I opened my mouth to argue and Jarvis held up a hand. "You will take fifty men with you, Rogan. That's an order from the Rada."

I grimaced but deferred to his wishes. "All right, so how long will it take us?"

Wolfe shook his head. "Difficult to say. Depending on weather and any other unforeseen circumstances, I would say between three to six weeks. What will I tell my men?"

Jarvis answered, "I assume you can trust Lieutenant Chaeron with the truth. Otherwise, exactly what Rogan suggested. This is merely a diplomatic trip on behalf of the princezna. If trouble brews and you must tell your men, then you must, but otherwise, keep it among you, Rogan, and Chaeron. May I suggest you leave Second Lieutenant Worth at the palace, just in case you and Rogan don't make it back in time before trouble arrives here?" Jarvis blanched at the thought of crime in Sabithia, as did we all.

"Of course." Wolfe stood. He projected calm and an air of capability that I knew reassured the Rada. They all looked to him as if he would take care of everything. "I'll see to my men."

"I'll see to Haydyn's quiet removal from the palace," Ava said, standing unsteadily. "Lord Matai, will you find Seamstress Rowan and explain everything? She will need to pack a few things. Raj, Valena, Lord Jarvis, we need to get the princezna out of the palace." She took me entirely by surprise by drawing me into her embrace. I stiffened. No one but Haydyn and Valena ever touched me. "Good luck, Rogan. I know you can do this. We shall see you in a few weeks' time."

I nodded, feeling emotion clog my throat. I cleared it and retreated from her. "I better gather my things." Before leaving, I pulled Valena into a tight hug and her tears wet my skin. "You take care of her. And yourself."

"Be careful, Rogan," Valena begged. "Please."

I promised I would and marched from the room, only now feeling what Haydyn must feel every day.

The weight of an entire world on my shoulders.

And now, like her, I would have given anything to ask someone else to help me carry the burden.

CHAPTER 6

Haydyn lay before me on her bed, peaceful and pale, her eyelids not even twitching to assure me she was dreaming somewhere inside herself. My throat was so tight, so sore with constrained emotion, and I gripped the bedpost lest I reach forward to shake her as I wanted to, to shake her awake and scold her for terrifying me. Her chest rose and fell in slow, gentle breaths.

"You're going to be all right," I whispered, bending down to brush a kiss across her forehead. I knew her as well as I knew myself, and I could not bear to live in a world where she did not exist. I choked back a frightened sob. "I promise."

I STRODE OUT INTO THE COURTYARD WHERE THE GUARD WERE busying themselves with their horses and the supply cart that would travel with us. I tugged on my leather riding gloves, my cloak billowing at my back as wind rushed in from the east. Jarek watched me carefully as I approached him and Midnight. My heart thudded rapidly as I willed my expression to relax into a soft smile.

"Thank you, Jarek," I acknowledged, taking Midnight's reins. As I stroked my mare's glossy, blue-black coat in greeting, Midnight nickered and bounced her head toward me in response.

"So." Jarek eyed me skeptically. "A diplomatic trip on behalf of the princezna?"

Avoiding his stare, I nodded and continued to stroke Midnight. "Yes. Haydyn's interested in improving relations with the Alvernians."

"It's such a hastily put-together outing." Jarek shook his head. "My boys nearly broke their backs getting the horses ready under Wolfe's command. Usually a trip such as this would take a week of preparation, at least."

I hated to lie to an old friend. Instead I opted to trust him with a little of the truth. I looked into his eyes and he tensed at what he saw in mine. "Alvernia is worsening," I informed him quietly, glancing around to make sure no one else was listening. "I'm going with Captain Stovia to discern the situation for myself and see what can be done. Speak of this to no one, Jarek, but Haydyn may consider a betrothal to Vojvoda Andrei's son."

Jarek's eyes widened. "Are things really that bad?"

I nodded.

"I swear, I'll tell no one, Rogan. It would cause unnecessary panic."

Smiling at his understanding, I took his hand. "Thank you, Jarek. Haydyn will be staying at her cottage at Land's End while I'm gone. The news has troubled her, and I think it would do her good to take some time away from palace life."

Jarek squeezed my hand. "And what of you, Rogan? You're to bear the burden of traveling and worrying and making the decisions? It hardly seems fair."

I was warmed by his concern. "I make no decisions. I merely offer an opinion. Which we all know I do often and well on many subjects."

"I will miss you while you're gone." He raised my hand and

brushed a soft kiss across my knuckles, his eyes twinkling. Such a charmer. I was no fool. I knew as soon as I departed, Jarek would return to flirting with the next prettiest maid who came along. But there was comfort and ease in being with Jarek, in being in Silvera, and to leave him was to leave the city and all the security I had known since I was blown adrift from my family so many years ago. I experienced a sudden panic at having to leave and abruptly pulled my hand from his.

"I won't be long, Jarek," I said, and let him help me into the saddle. "Take care of everyone."

He nodded, patting the rump of my horse, and stepped back as Wolfe cantered into the courtyard from the stables.

Wolfe eyed me solemnly. "Ready?"

"As I'll ever be."

I was surprised and annoyed as Wolfe sent Lieutenant Chaeron ahead of us to lead the cavalcade. It meant Wolfe could ride beside me while the Guard rode at our backs. Before I could suggest an alternative traveling formation that involved him being *gone* from my side, Wolfe spoke. "Vojvoda Jarvis has instructed that we will stop in Peza for the night to visit with Grof Krill Rada, and in Caera to visit with Vojvodkyna Winter Rada."

Visiting nobility on social calls on a journey to save Haydyn's life? Were they insane? Remembering rumors of an affair between Wolfe and Vojvodkyna Winter a few seasons ago, I wondered if Jarvis had been the one to come up with those instructions at all. I threw Wolfe a disbelieving look. "That's ridiculous."

Wolfe shook his head. "No, it's not. We can't expect to travel through the land with fifty of the Royal Guard and not have word reach the Rada that the Handmaiden of Phaedra is on a diplomatic trip to Alvernia. The Rada would be insulted if we didn't stop to visit with them. Just be thankful we're only traveling through Raphizya and Daeronia."

"Thankful," I scoffed. "Thankful? It's your fault for making me bring fifty bloody men with me. We could have gotten through the provinces undetected otherwise."

"Oh, really?" His tone was mocking. "So if you took off through Phaedra with a couple of men, you would retrieve the plant faster, is that right?"

"Exactly."

"And how would we explain your disappearance at the palace?"

"I'm at the cottage with Haydyn."

Wolfe grunted at my quick response. "Fine. What about the fact that even if you were disguised as a lumberjack, people would know you were raised a lady? You're a target, Rogan. Everything about you is. I doubt even a few men would be able to help you out of the trouble you would inevitably find if I weren't here to supervise you."

I was stunned into silence by his arrogance. He chuckled at having irked me into speechlessness.

"Perhaps I better swap places with Lieutenant Chaeron?"

I wanted to push him off his horse. "I think that would be wise."

Not too long later, Lieutenant Chaeron cantered at my side, happy to oblige me with pleasant, easy conversation. Our procession through the city was slow as folks dodged out of the way of the large entourage, not to mention some of the streets narrowed greatly here and there, hindering us even more.

I was surprised when Wolfe led us toward the Flower District, the wealthy neighborhood where Matai and Wolfe resided, where all nobility and wealthy business owners had beautiful townhouses. This route lengthened our journey out of the city. We drew to a complete halt outside a townhouse.

"What's going on?" I asked Lieutenant Chaeron.

He nodded to Wolfe as the captain dismounted from his horse. "Captain Stovia wanted to inform his mother personally of his departure. She worries." He smiled as if I would be moved by Wolfe's devotion to familial duty. Instead I had gone cold inside at the thought of Wolfe and his mother and the man missing from their lives. I looked away from the house as Wolfe entered it, fighting to keep my composure as images of Syracen flashed through my mind. Images that were always followed by my parents' horrified faces as they died, of my little brother lifeless at my feet.

"Miss Rogan, are you all right?" Lieutenant Chaeron asked.

I threw him a brittle smile. I liked Chaeron. A few years ago, I had asked him to stop calling me *my lady* like everyone else did. He began addressing me as Miss Rogan instead and for that, he held my affection.

I was about to reassure him when the door to Wolfe's home opened and he appeared there with a short woman at his side. He turned and kissed her cheek. She smiled warmly up at him before she waved to the Guard.

"Safe trip, good men!" she called softly.

"Thank you, my lady!" some of the men returned. She smiled prettily, still very attractive, not even a hint of gray in her chestnut tresses. Her eyes traveled over our entourage and finally found me. Vikomtesa Stovia stiffened and paled at the sight of me. She turned to Wolfe to whisper at him and he shook his head, muttering a reply. She nodded, but when she looked at me again, I could have sworn there was fear in her eyes.

Seeming to shake herself, she dragged her gaze from me to Chaeron. "Lieutenant Chaeron, take care of my Wolfe, won't you?"

Lieutenant Chaeron grinned. "Of course, my lady!"

Wolfe grimaced before he patted his mother's hand in reassurance and bounced down the stone steps to mount his horse with an ease and agility that made me envious.

I looked away sharply, shaken by Vikomtesa Stovia, even more so by her reaction to me ... as if I were the one to be feared, not them.

As soon as we were out of the city, Wolfe pushed us at a fast pace. When we could, we skirted villages; when we couldn't, we slowed so as not to cause suspicion. I hated those moments, having to wave to the villagers like I was royalty, when in truth I was a farm girl just like many of the Sabithians. Once we were out of the village and onto the main trade roads, Wolfe hurried on and we followed suit. My body ached three hours in, my bottom numb in the saddle. I tried not to show my discomfort. We wouldn't stop today as we had a late start. We would be riding on until nightfall.

Lieutenant Chaeron seemed to sense my ever-growing discomfort and talked to me about his family. We shared stories of farm life and I realized how similar the people in Vasterya seemed to those in Sabithia. But not once did I ever mention my family by name, and Chaeron didn't pry. Everyone knew my sad tale. Everyone knew I didn't *talk* about my sad tale. Instead, the lieutenant made me laugh as he spoke of his younger sister and her comical attempts to catch the man of her dreams.

"Donal is from coal mining country in the northeast of Sabithia," the lieutenant said. "Quiet, reserved people. He moved to Laerth to live with cousins, start a new life in farming. He wasn't prepared for the overwhelming attention of my sister."

I laughed as he described her outrageous tactics to win Donal.

"She succeeded, though?" I asked.

Lieutenant Chaeron snorted. "Kirsta had him wed in under two months. They've been married three years now and have two children, more to come, I suspect."

From his stories I gathered his entire family was close. It was what I'd always imagined my own would have been like had we been given the chance to grow with one another. I swallowed my grief and encouraged him to tell me more about his own wife and children.

As night fell, we crossed the River Silvera, and a while later, the River Sabith, and as we passed through a small patch of woodland, we saw lights twinkling in the distance between the trees. Coming out of the woods, I swatted at another insect that had decided my skin was a tasty treat. Not even twenty-four hours in and already I was irritated by the realities of travel.

"Sabith Town." Wolfe halted his horse, turning to us as he pointed at the large town in the distance. "We'll rest here for the night."

I swear I almost swooned in relief. And I was *not* a swooner. I grinned at the lieutenant, and with renewed energy, the Guard loped into a gallop, the men and the cart trailing behind us.

Seemingly familiar with the town, Wolfe took us straight to a large inn on the outskirts. I was thankful we wouldn't be trotting through the quiet cobbled streets at this time, waking everyone from their beds.

The innkeeper, a tall, stout woman with arms like rolling pins, came swaggering out to us, undaunted by our appearance. I smiled. Her robust confidence reminded me of Cook.

"Well, what a fine sight!" she called heartily as Wolfe dismounted. They shook hands, and it became clear that she and Wolfe were already acquainted.

"You bring me much business, Captain Wolfe." She nodded to us all, her eyes landing on me. She dipped me a graceful curtsy at complete odds with her ambling gait. "My lady!" she called up to me. I was beginning to realize that this woman never spoke—she barked. "Well." She turned to Wolfe. "You'll be needing a room for that fine lass. As for you and your men, I have five rooms free that I'm sure a good few can share. The rest will need to bunk in the stables."

"That's fine," Wolfe assured her. He spun around to address Lieutenant Chaeron who dismounted. "Lieutenant, you'll take the room in the inn nearest to Lady Rogan's. Assess the size of the other rooms and calculate how many of our men can comfortably share them. I'll bunk in the stables with the rest."

Taken aback by Wolfe's decision to sleep in the stables, I

forgot myself and began to dismount. I was almost to the ground when I felt a hand on my lower back. I knew his scent before I even turned. "I can manage."

"I know," Wolfe replied flatly. "But appearances, my lady, appearances."

I huffed in indignation.

"Child," he muttered and then took my arm like a gentleman. I tried to escape but he held me fast. "Can you behave for one night, Lady Rogan?" he hissed. "I have to show you to your room."

"You're such a fusspot." Yet I allowed him to escort me. I gaped in wonder at the openness of the inn. To our left was an arched doorway that led into a spacious eating area and bar. A fire crackled in a large hearth at one end and I shivered at the thought of its delicious heat. To our right was a narrow hallway I surmised led to guest rooms, and before us an open stairway led to the rooms upstairs.

"Room 11, Captain." The innkeeper approached, grinning broadly. She thrust the key toward us and Wolfe took it before I could.

"Thank you, Mags, you're the best."

She blushed at his smile and I groaned inwardly. Dear haven, if a woman like Mags fell for Wolfe's charm, no woman alive, except me, was safe.

"I'm sure I can find the room all by myself. I'm a big girl, you know."

He grunted and led me upstairs.

The room was surprisingly nice. A four-poster bed with clean cotton sheets and woven quilts sat at one end, and lo and behold, a lovely fire flickered brilliantly at the other. Very nice.

"I'll have Mags bring you up a meal." Wolfe strode around the room, peering here and there. What in haven was he looking for? "Everything seems in order." He marched stiffly to the doorway.

"What? No rookery thieves hiding behind the changing screen?" I asked sarcastically.

I was rewarded with a disdainful look. "Just lock the door behind me."

I shrugged in answer just to annoy him. As the door was closing in his wake, he said, "And stop flirting with my men, my lady. Some of them are married."

My cheeks flamed in outrage and the door took the brunt of my thrown traveling bag.

CHAPTER 7

Although Wolfe had promised to take it a little easier after having hurried us through the first day, he kept up what I considered a grueling pace. He only gave us a fifteen-minute respite, and although I understood (more than anyone) the importance of retrieving the plant in good time, I didn't think we'd get there any faster if we all died from exhaustion. Moreover, the men were befuddled by how quickly we journeyed on, considering this was supposed to be a casual diplomatic trip.

I managed to antagonize Wolfe into giving us a half-hour respite instead.

By the third day of our journey, we were close to reaching the northern border of Sabithia. The previous night we were provided shelter by one of the wealthiest farmers I had ever met. Chaeron told me the breeding of their sheep and the working of their wool were kept a strict secret and their staff were paid well to keep it for them. Whatever their method, Farmer Soel and his family produced the finest wool in all of Phaedra, wool only the wealthy could afford. And as Farmer Soel had welcomed me into his home, his face seemed familiar. Clearly, I had seen him at the marketplace in Silvera.

Lieutenant Chaeron led me into the house while the rest of the men camped outside or in the stables. Wolfe had insisted I needed a chaperone, and I insisted that chaperone be Lieutenant Chaeron.

After a wonderful sleep, it was jarring to get back on the horse, but as the hours wore on, I realized my aching muscles were growing used to the saddle.

Thank haven for small mercies.

The light faded as we cantered into what Chaeron called Lumberland. Most of northern Sabithia was covered in forestation, and the province purchased much of its wood for housing and furniture from the numerous forestry establishments.

Wolfe followed signs posted along a route that allowed travelers to pass safely. By the time we drew clear of the forest, the day had grown dark as it gave way to night. We trotted toward the small village on the forest's edge. A lumber factory on its outskirts marred its quaint beauty.

Despite the lateness of the hour, people milled about and noise levels rose at our appearance. Wolfe raised his hand and the lieutenant halted. I pulled on Midnight's reins to draw her to a stop. We watched as Wolfe approached a tall man who wore his shirt sleeves rolled up to his elbows. The stranger's face glistened with sweat and was dirty with grime. Wolfe spoke, and the man nodded before he strode toward the factory and disappeared inside.

Only minutes later, he returned outside accompanied by another tall, strapping man, perhaps in his late fifties. He spoke to Wolfe and then the captain led him over to us.

"My lady. Lieutenant," Wolfe addressed us. I saw weariness in the back of his eyes. We were all a little tired today. It *had* been especially hot. "This is Jac Dena. And this is the village of Woodmill. Jac owns the largest lumber establishment in northern Sabithia."

Jac grinned proudly and nodded his head at me. "Nice to make your acquaintance, my lady."

I nodded, too tired to find an appropriate response.

"Jac has graciously invited Lady Rogan and Lieutenant Chaeron to stay with him and his family. He will prevail upon the rest of the village to give the Guard shelter for the night."

"Thank you, Mr. Dena," I said gratefully. I was desperate for food and sleep. "That's extremely kind of you."

"Oh, not at all, not at all, my lady." He gave me a slight bow. "We are honored to offer hospitality to the Royal Guard and the Handmaiden of Phaedra."

I glared at Wolfe. Damn him repeating that stupid nickname. He smirked unrepentantly back at me.

I FOUND MYSELF SEATED AT A STURDY TABLE, IN A COZY kitchen, with wonderful aromas that made my stomach clench in anticipation. Lieutenant Chaeron sat beside me, looking as weary as I felt.

Jac's home wasn't overly large, but it was comfortably furnished, and it appeared as though his family had everything they needed. His wife, a pretty, petite woman, stammered in my presence (bloody Wolfe) and flittered around us like a wee butterfly. Jac sat at the head of the table, and after arguing quite profusely, I settled across from his two sons instead of at the other end of the table where Mrs. Dena normally sat and where they'd insisted I sit in her stead. However, I would never dream of entering someone else's home only to act like an overbearing, superior kralovna.

Mrs. Dena finally took a seat and we served ourselves. I became uncomfortably aware of the Denas' two sons staring at me. My cheeks flushed under their scrutiny. The eldest, Jac Junior, was around my age, the youngest, Leon, perhaps Haydyn's. I had never before been the target of such open attention, and I squirmed in my seat. From the corner of my eye, I saw Chaeron grip his knife a little too tightly.

Thankfully, Jac cut through the tension by asking questions about Silvera. I tried my best to answer them graciously. After all, they had opened their home to strangers, and I was more than thankful to be off my horse for a while. I'm sure Midnight was equally thankful.

I told them of the palace and when Mrs. Dena grew excited at the mention of the royal marketplace, I described the different items that could be found there.

Mrs. Dena opened her mouth to respond to my descriptions, but her son spoke first.

"By gee ..." Leon's dark eyes fixated on me.

My fork hovered halfway to my mouth, my eyes wide with surprise at the insolent expression of desire on his face. The boy looked as if he was picturing me naked. I flushed harder.

"You are the prettiest thing I've ever seen. And that's including Shera. Shera's the fairest girl in Woodmill, but she isn't as pretty as you."

Jac Senior began to reprimand, "Leon, don't—"

Jac Junior's slap across Leon's head cut him off. "Don't be speaking to royalty like that, Leon. And don't be speaking about Shera at all. I told you to stay away from my girl."

"She's not your girl," Leon hissed, purpling with anger.

I unconsciously slid toward the lieutenant as the boys' argument grew more heated. Neither listened to their parents' demands to cease embarrassing them. I flinched as the discussion became aggressive in light of some personal revelations.

"What do you mean you kissed her?" Jac Junior dove at his brother, and the two crashed to the floor, chairs and all.

As fists met flesh, images of Kir on the muddy ground, a giant soldier towering over him in the dark, pierced my mind. I stumbled from the table and the fight, my skin prickling unpleasantly. Lieutenant Chaeron strode across the room, pushed Jac Senior out of his way, and hauled Leon off Jac Junior. He shoved the boy aside and stood between them as the eldest son jumped to his feet. He moved to lunge at his brother and Chaeron pushed him back.

"Enough!" The lieutenant bellowed before he turned to glare at Jac Dena. "What manner of behavior is this in front of Lady Rogan? If these boys ever hope to become men, I suggest you teach them some discipline."

Jac's face was bloodred with humiliation. "I apologize, Lieutenant. I've never been so ashamed in my life." He grabbed his sons, growling as he pushed them out of the room and into the back of the home. I looked at Mrs. Dena who looked so confused and alarmed by her sons' behavior that realization hit me with sudden dread.

Silent communication passed between me and Chaeron.

This was it.

The Dyzvati magic was failing in Sabithia.

People who were inclined toward temper would no longer be affected and soothed by Haydyn's evocation. They would react as they would do naturally, the heat of anger no longer tamed by my friend and her magic. It never even crossed my mind that it might be natural for brothers, close in age, to fight so. To Phaedrians under the Dyzvati spell for so long, *natural* was to curb any instincts that may disrupt the peace, despite any inward feelings of anger, passion, or violence.

That night, Chaeron insisted upon sleeping on a pallet in the room the Denas offered me.

I didn't question it.

His presence was reassuring.

CHAPTER 8

Wolfe was visibly concerned when Chaeron told him what happened as we readied to leave the next morning. He glanced around to make sure none of the men were listening and then looked at me. "Are you all right?" he asked, brows furrowed with anger.

I retreated from his penetrating stare, perturbed by what I sensed was worry.

For me.

Yet that couldn't be.

Wolfe stared at me a moment too long, and I realized his concern was not for me but for the kingdom. For a brief second, I wanted to reassure him.

But then I remembered who he was and turned from him to mount Midnight.

It rained in Raphizya.

Not light, showery rain to ease our hot skin but hard, pelting rain that pummeled in large drops as if punishing us with its fury at having been dominated by the sun for too long. My cloak stuck to my dress like a second skin, making movement on the horse difficult. Not to mention I had to keep pulling my cloak closed because my muslin dress left little to the imagination, plastered as it was to my body.

We stopped at an inn that night and I stood naked by the fire for so long, the backs of my legs turned blotchy and red. I didn't care. I was blissfully warm.

The next day the sun returned, not so hot as before, and we gathered together for a milder, more comfortable journey. I winced as a chorus of sneezing sounded from the men behind me and prayed that none of them were very ill.

When Wolfe stopped for lunch, it was in a massive, open field. In the distance we saw cows and sheep in neighboring farmlands. The grass was as green as green could be, as green as a master painter's imagination, and a single, beautiful willow tree attracted the men as they dismounted. Some gathered around it, talking and laughing as they sipped thirstily from their canteens and munched on bread we had bought from the people of Woodmill.

I fed Midnight an apple and then left her to graze with the men. I required a moment of peace. Alone. I didn't wander far. They were still in sight, but now their voices were mere murmurs on the wind.

I noted Wolfe sitting with Chaeron and a few others as they ate oatcakes and laughed together. I shrugged off the uncomfortable feeling that perhaps I'd misjudged Wolfe and had unjustifiably blamed him for his father's deeds. So far he had proven himself to be strong and fair. His men loved him, obeyed and trusted him, despite his young age.

Surely that said much of his character.

Thoughts of my parents, however, caused guilt to roil in my gut. I could never trust a Stovia. If I felt this strongly—this hateful—toward Syracen for what he had done, surely Wolfe felt the same way toward me for exposing Syracen's evil.

Frowning, I wrenched my attention from the captain and

grew interested in two soldiers who appeared to be training. They parried and thrust with their swords—easy, fluid, strong. I'd always wanted to learn how to sword fight, but it was considered inappropriate for a lady to do so.

I realized that I'd probably never have a better excuse to thumb my nose at convention than I did now.

I lifted my skirts and strode toward the two soldiers.

"Officer Stark, isn't it?" I enquired as I came upon them. "And Officer Reith?"

They seemed surprised that I knew them by name, but I had an excellent memory.

"My lady." They both offered polite bows.

"Please." I held up my hands. "It's Rogan. Or"—I noted their appalled looks—"Miss Rogan, if you must. But I'm not *lady* anything."

"Miss Rogan," Officer Stark said, clearing his throat, "how can we assist you?"

I wasn't a terribly good flirt, but I had learned from Haydyn that a soft smile went a long way. And she was right. They seemed to puff their chests under my feminine attention. "I was watching you train; you're both very good."

They flushed and murmured their thanks. I calculated their heights with the happy realization they were the perfect men for the task in mind. Not too tall nor too broad.

"I wonder if you might teach me how to use a sword."

Reith's jaw dropped before he remembered himself and smoothed his expression. "A sword, Miss Rogan?"

I offered him an even sweeter smile in gratitude for calling me Miss Rogan. "Yes. Nothing too difficult, of course, but I do think with us traveling into Alvernia that it might be of use for me to know how to defend myself."

The men shared a look, and I was relieved to see they weren't too shocked by the idea. In fact, Officer Stark nodded determinedly. "If you wish it, Miss Rogan, then we shall teach you."

I grinned, excited, unable to believe they had acquiesced so easily. I was so used to being treated like Haydyn, like I was a piece of precious glass that would shatter at the slightest touch.

Reith, the shorter of the two, approached. He drew close as Stark spoke of eight basic angles of attack while Reith demonstrated where they were on my body. Then he walked behind and leaned into me as he held out the sword. "You must learn to hold it just so," he said as he wrapped his hand over mine around the hilt.

So engrossed in their teachings, laughing with them as I thrust the sword like a limp noodle, I didn't hear his approach.

"What the bloody hell is going on?"

Reith jumped away from me as if I were poisonous, his face flushing guiltily.

I turned to face Wolfe. "We were—"

"I wasn't asking you," Wolfe snapped. "Officer Stark?"

Officer Stark shifted uncomfortably. "Miss Rogan asked us to show her some basic sword training, Captain. We didn't see any harm in it."

"Any harm? Any *harm*?" Wolfe seethed. "She could have walked into the damn thing, for haven's sake."

Blood flooded my cheeks and I bit my tongue from screaming at him like a banshee. "Captain Stovia," I fumed. "I am not a fool. I am perfectly capable of avoiding the sharp end of a sword!"

"And"—he ignored me entirely, knowing how much it would further enrage me—"*Lady* Rogan is to be addressed as such."

"I asked them to call me *Miss* Rogan," I retorted.

He growled, "Well, I'm un-asking them." His eyes sparked like blue fire. "From now on, if *she* requests anything, you ask me first before you acquiesce."

"Yes, sir." They obeyed.

Wolfe marched away, his spine stiff with irritation.

"I have a name!" I called out to him lamely. *She* indeed.

As soon as he was out of earshot, Officer Reith whistled. "I don't know what it is about you, Lady Rogan, but you're the only one who ever makes Captain lose his composure."

I frowned and Officer Stark nudged his partner, silently telling him to shut up.

Understanding dawned on Reith's face and he flushed with embarrassment. He'd remembered then that it was I who had forced Wolfe's father's demise.

"Yes," I replied wryly, "a man tends to react that way around his archenemy."

I began to walk away, deflated that Wolfe had ruined my lesson. Then I stiffened when I heard Reith mutter to Stark, "I'm not sure that's what gets Captain so hot."

I grimaced and kept walking, finding Wolfe among his soldiers as he ordered the men back onto their horses. Of course he saw me as his enemy. Why else was he always baiting me? I wasn't an idiot—Wolfe hated me as much as I hated him.

And I'd be waiting when he finally came to take his vengeance.

Knowing how to use a sword in the event of such a situation would be useful.

I grumbled under my breath. The man was an antagonistic prig.

❧

I REFUSED TO SPEAK WITH WOLFE AFTER HE HUMILIATED ME in front of his men; he, in turn, refused to speak to me for enlisting his men's help behind his back.

He rode ahead the entire way to Peza, and I glared at his back without distraction. Lieutenant Chaeron kept making amused little sounds from the back of his throat but I ignored him, somehow thinking if I stared long and hard enough, the power of my mind might knock Wolfe off his horse and onto his ass.

Having sent one of the men ahead to let Grof Krill Rada

know we were arriving, we were met at the gates by Grof Krill's guards and escorted through Peza to the grof's home. I stared in wonder at Peza, almost oblivious to the people and their waving and exuberant calls of welcome. I was amazed by the similarities to Silvera. It was as if Silvera had been copied by a master artisan and plunked down in Peza. The architecture was the same, the street plan was the same—even the market square seemed the same, if only a little smaller.

The difference, however, was in the splashes of vibrant color everywhere. Tapestries hung on the outsides of buildings and murals were painted on brick work. I winced at the thought of having to clean and replace those tapestries, and at having to refresh the murals every few years. But this was the city of art—it made sense that the people wished to display their work wherever they could.

The lieutenant caught my astonished expression and grinned. "Remarkable, isn't it?"

"Extremely." I was truly charmed by the colorful city.

The grof's guard quickly led us out of the hubbub of the city to a gated district where large mansions surrounded a beautiful park. When they pulled to a stop outside the largest mansion, I gaped in wonder. I did not know that such buildings existed outside of Haydyn's palace. With its pillared columns and gothic arches, the mansion was a jumble of architectural ideas ... and yet somehow it worked. It was intimidating and palatial.

"Captain Stovia," the captain of the grof's guard announced loudly, "Vikomtesa Laurel Sans"—he pointed to the smaller mansion next to this one—"has graciously offered her house and stables for some of your guard. The rest of your men will find rooms and shelter with his lordship. Some will have to sleep in his stables, but I assure you they are spacious and comfortable."

Wolfe nodded. "Thank you, Captain." He turned to Chaeron. "Take a group of the men to the vikomtesa's and introduce yourself. Get some rest. We leave tomorrow at sunrise."

"So soon, Captain?"

We all turned toward the voice. It belonged to an elegant man who strolled toward us from the house, a huge wolfhound following at his heels.

A footman opened the enormous gates for Grof Krill Rada. His eyes found me. "Rogan," he called up to me familiarly, and I noted both Wolfe and the lieutenant share a disapproving look. "It's been awhile."

The last I had seen Grof Krill was three years ago. I had taken him for a quiet man, watchful and intelligent. We had barely spoken, at least not enough for him to address me so informally. Remembering why I was there, however, I offered a polite smile. "My lord." I bobbed my head. "It is good to see you. I trust you are well."

He smiled, his eyes traveling down the length of me. "I am now."

I narrowed my eyes at his open flirtation.

"Well, Captain, help the Lady Rogan down from her horse," Grof Krill snapped, and Wolfe dismounted quickly. I noted a muscle ticking in his jaw.

A flash of anger rippled through me at Krill's attitude. Wolfe was not Krill's captain to command. I reached for Wolfe without complaint as he lowered me from my horse. His eyes widened marginally, as if shocked I'd allowed him to touch me without resistance. Our gazes, still heavy with suspicion, locked, and the captain held me a moment too long. His hands seemed to burn through my dress where they gripped tight to my waist. My skin prickled with awareness.

I drew in a sharp breath at the sudden heat that coated my skin, and Wolfe relinquished his hold with such speed, one might think he'd pricked his fingers upon thorns.

"Rogan." Grof Krill breezed past Wolfe to loop my arm through his. His stare was low-lidded and smoldered, much to my alarm. "I have such grand plans for us this evening. How does dinner and the opera sound?"

Exhausting, I thought.

"Wonderful," I mumbled.

"I'll accompany you," Wolfe announced.

Grof Krill arched an eyebrow at him. "Oh, you will, will you?"

Wolfe strode to us, his face implacably hard. He matched Grof Krill in height and outweighed him in strength. "Lady Rogan goes nowhere without a royal escort, my lord."

The grof sniffed haughtily. "We'll be accompanied by *my* guard."

"I said *royal* escort, my lord," Wolfe reiterated arrogantly and then dismissed the grof by turning to the lieutenant. "Take the men to the vikomtesa's, Lieutenant Chaeron. Ready them to leave by sunrise tomorrow."

❧

Dinner was a strange affair.

I was bemused by Grof Krill's outrageous advances as he had never treated me with such overt flattery before. Surely the women at court would have mentioned Grof Krill if he was such a lothario. I definitely remembered him to be a somber, refined, and reserved man. I hadn't known him very well, but I had thought him one of the more intelligent members of the Rada. What on haven had happened to him?

I patted the head of Krill's wolfhound, Strider, as he lolled it in my lap, his eyes staring up at me adoringly. I really shouldn't have slipped him that bite of chicken at the dinner table. We shared a frustrated look with one another as Grof Krill told me how beautiful the ladies of the opera were this season, although nowhere near as beautiful as me, he added. I nearly snorted. Just what did this character want from me?

Somehow, I managed to get through dinner, despite the grof's appallingly bad flirting and Wolfe's monosyllabic responses to questions posed by the Krill. I was so tense I was sure one pull of the laces on my dress and I would snap like a piano wire.

Things only grew worse. I had no dress to wear to the opera, so Grof Krill provided me with one. I flushed as his maids helped me into the red dress. *Red.* I had never worn red—it was a deep scarlet in plush velvet—not to mention I had never worn a gown with such a low-cut neckline. Oh, it was very fashionable, and all of Haydyn's dresses were cut just so, but I had never really been comfortable displaying my somewhat voluptuous bosom. I blanched as they pulled my hair up off my neck, fastening pins here and there with expertise.

I looked like a fashionable lady of Peza. If you were clever like Haydyn, fashionable was elegance and refinement.

Fashionable on me was a little too bold and dangerous.

"I can't wear this. Isn't there another dress I could wear? Something a little less daring."

The maids gasped. "No, my lady, you must wear this, you look wonderful."

My reflection offended me. I didn't look like myself. Exhaustion prodded my eyelids and pinched at my muscles. I just had to get through the next few hours and then I could find sleep.

As I descended the grand staircase in Grof Krill's home, I watched as Wolfe walked into the entrance hall. The grof had obviously lent him evening wear; the crisp darkness of the tailored suit made his hair burn gold under the chandelier. I stopped to watch him as he stared up at a tall painting of the Silver Sea crashing against the cliffs. One could see the palace depicted in the distance. Wolfe examined the painting as I studied his handsome profile. What was he thinking? He looked so stark, so alone.

And I suddenly felt as if I knew him.

A strange flutter in my lower belly made me stumble and as I righted myself, I caught Wolfe's attention. I flushed beneath his unwavering stare and met him in the middle of the hall. His jaw clenched tightly as he took in my attire.

"What?" I snapped, already feeling stupid and in no mood for his quips.

Wolfe cleared his throat. "You look beautiful."

I narrowed my eyes. Obviously, he was mocking me. "Will you cease with the sarcasm for one evening, Captain?"

His mouth fell open at my rebuke but his riposte was interrupted by Grof Krill.

"Rogan!" We turned as he greeted me. For a moment he looked astonished at my appearance and then he smiled—a real, genuine smile—as he took my hand and placed a gentlemanly kiss upon the back of it. "Why, you look beautiful, Lady Rogan."

Sensing he was being sincere, I smiled politely. "Thank you, my lord."

Wolfe grunted at my side but I ignored the good captain as the grof escorted me from the mansion.

THE OPERA WAS WONDERFUL, THE SINGERS BREATHTAKING, THE sets incandescent. My senses were overwhelmed by the vibrancy and decadence of the opera hall, the wealthy, glittering audience and vivacious singers who took to the stage. The scent of jasmine hung in the air, mingling with tobacco. I had been to the opera in Silvera with Haydyn, but there was something different about being at the opera in the homeland of opera. Even the ogling nobility who recognized me from royal events and balls in Silvera did not sway my attention from the stage.

It would have been an unspoiled evening if Grof Krill hadn't begun his insincere pursuit of me again. His fingers kept brushing my arms, my skirts, even my breast as he squeezed past me. I scowled, ready to eviscerate him if he tried it again. Thankfully, Wolfe hadn't noticed the grof's forwardness on that occasion.

Unfortunately, my enjoyment of the effervescent opera crowd and its stars was ruined by Grof Krill flirting. I attempted to lean away from him, trying to keep as much distance between us as possible.

Grof Krill placed my hand on his arm and with Wolfe at our

backs, the grof led me out of his opera box and through the crowds outside it. He descended the stairs ahead of me and I understood his plot as he "accidentally" tripped on a stair, pulling me down so I was captured in his arms.

I grew flush with anger at his games and apologies as he kept hold of me, pretending he was trying to right my footing, even though I already had. I struggled little in his arms, desperate not to cause a scene. A warm, strong hand wrapped around my biceps and I looked up to find Wolfe glaring daggers at Grof Krill.

"Release her," he demanded under his breath.

The grof smiled blandly and let me go.

I allowed Wolfe to hook my arm through his and the three of us descended the stairs, no one else having noticed our little tussle. My mind whirled with confusion. I knew now why Grof Krill didn't flirt. He was awful at it! Which begged the question ... why was he trying so hard to flirt with me?

I was grateful as Wolfe helped me into the carriage and sat beside me before Grof Krill could.

And then I tensed as I realized I'd been thankful to Wolfe.

Thankful for his presence.

Guilt filled me and I sidled a little away from him as the carriage departed.

HAVING SHOOED AWAY THE MAIDS WHO WERE WAITING FOR ME in the guest suite, I undressed and practically threw the offending gown into the garderobe. I dug through my traveling bag in agitation and drew out my nightgown. I was so angry. Furious and confused and I didn't know why. I took a deep breath, pouring cold water from the ewer into the basin to splash my face. Afterward, I pulled on the nightgown and flopped down onto the stool by the dressing table. My face reflected in the oval mirror situated atop it, eyes dark with worries and fears and frustration. Gradually they blurred, and I grew numb as my face became more and more unfamiliar. Tears trembled on my eyelashes and I didn't know why.

"You're just tired, Rogan," I whispered to myself.

I stilled at the sound of a key turning in the lock in my door. My pulse jumped wildly in my neck. Shooting to my feet, I delved quickly through my traveling bag and removed the dagger Matai had given me before I left. Sweat dampened my skin as I tiptoed barefoot across the room and stood behind the door.

Slowly, sinisterly, it opened inward. A black-booted foot appeared first. I waited as the familiar figure stepped inside and shut the door behind him. Disgruntled at my height, or more so his, I lunged up onto my toes and looped an arm around his neck, drawing him down so I could press the dagger in my other hand to his throat. He let out a startled yelp and halted, immobilized at the feel of cold metal against his skin.

"Grof Krill," I growled, shocked and terrified that he had come into my room. Pride willed my body not to tremble.

"Now, Lady Rogan." The grof held his hands away from his body, the key to my room glittering between his fingers. "I mean you no harm."

I pressed the dagger until it pinched, and he hissed in pain. "No harm, indeed. What do you want with me?"

"Your magic."

I was so taken aback by his answer, I inadvertently loosened my hold and he ducked out of it, spinning to face me. I thrust the dagger at him and he took a wary step back. "What do you mean?"

"I need your help," he replied, his eyes sad, desperate.

"Is this the reason I was subjected to your abysmal attempts at seduction this evening, my lord?"

He flushed, groaning, running a hand down his face in mortification. "I'm not a very good flirt, my lady. Please accept the apology of a foolish man."

"Why the flirting?"

He shrugged. "I thought if you liked me, you might be more inclined to help me."

"With what?"

"I want you to find the woman I love."

I shuddered as the wave of my magic crashed through me. I sensed her. Beautiful and gentle, Ariana, who worked in Javinia … as a governess. I threw Grof Krill a speculative look, glad he had no idea that my magic had already obeyed his command.

"The woman you love?" I queried, curious despite my exhaustion. A spark of indignation lit within me. "You intended to seduce me to help you so I could reunite you with the woman you love?"

Grof Krill winced. "Not the most honorable plan, I know."

"I should say not."

His shoulders slumped, his throat working as if trying to hold back emotion. "I wouldn't have, my lady, but … Ariana. My lovely Ariana. Ward of our family friend the Baron Roe. She was the daughter of his cousin who died when Ariana was twelve. I hadn't seen the baron for years—we were school chums. He returned to Raphizya from Daeronia three years ago. Ariana and his daughter, Dru, were of an age, both seventeen. I fell in love with Ariana almost instantly." He sighed. "She isn't like those twittering idiots at court. She's intelligent. Quiet. Gentle. I miss her every day."

"What happened?" I whispered, finding myself lost in his heartbreak despite his terrible behavior.

He smiled humorlessly. "We were like two peas in a pod. We loved one another very much. But my aunt discovered my love for Ariana and was furious I wanted to marry someone of low birth. She blackmailed Ariana. She'd gotten wind of Dru's affair with one of the stable boys and threatened to expose her." He snorted. "So cliché, I know, but a word from my aunt and Dru would have been ruined. And Ariana loves Dru, so she took up the situation my aunt offered and disappeared. My aunt wouldn't tell me where she'd sent her and then my aunt died a year ago, leaving me no clues. I've hired people to find Ariana, but nothing. My aunt was a conniving old witch, but a clever one."

"So you want me to seek her?"

He nodded, coming toward me in his excitement. I held the dagger back up. "I won't hurt you, Lady Rogan."

"No, you won't," I bit out.

Part of me ached for him, and the other distrusted him as I did most men. What if he'd hurt Ariana somehow and she had wanted to disappear, wanted to stay gone? A plan formed in my mind. "You better leave, Grof Krill, before I scream for Captain Stovia and you are charged with trying to force the princezna's Azyl to work for you."

"No." Krill shook his head. "I would never force you. I just want your help."

"I can't help you, my lord. My duty is not to you. I work only for Her Highness. Now please leave."

I watched the light dim in his eyes, his expression haggard. "Of course, my lady. I shall leave you in peace. I apologize for my untoward behavior. I overstepped."

He left quietly, the door closing behind him. Futile though it was, I turned the lock.

I sighed wearily. I would never sleep now. Instead I hurried to the dressing table and rummaged through the drawers until I found stationery. I dipped my pen in ink and began my letter.

Dear Ariana,

You do not know me. I am Rogan of Vasterya, Princezna Haydyn's Handmaiden and one of the Azyl. I have been fortunate enough to enjoy the hospitality of Grof Krill Rada of Raphizya whom I am told you are acquainted. I write to you on behalf of a desperate man who tells me he loves you. I have not informed him where you are, although the grof did command me to seek you, so if he lies and yours was not a relationship of mutual love, then fear not, he will not find you.

Did you know the grof had no inkling of his aunt's blackmail until after your disappearance? Did you know his aunt is dead, thus freeing your dear friend from any consequences of her blackmail? Grof Krill desperately seeks you, Ariana. He has been looking for three years. He loves you.

If you love him, you are free to return to him.

Yours sincerely,

Rogan

I SIGHED AND FOLDED THE LETTER INTO AN ENVELOPE, addressing it to Ariana. I snorted at my own foolishness. The girl would probably think the letter a hoax. I shrugged and pulled on a dressing gown. Still, it was the only thing I could think to do for Grof Krill without putting all my trust in him.

I hurried from the room, my candle battling the shadows as I marched through the mansion and out into the cold stable yard. I shivered and rushed to the stables, coming across a man on guard whose hand immediately leapt to the hilt of his sword before he jolted in recognition.

"My lady," the officer whispered. "What are you doing out here? Are you well?"

I nodded, my teeth chattering. "Here." I thrust the envelope at him. "You must find a messenger immediately and have this delivered in Javinia." I handed over the coins to pay the messenger.

Like a good soldier, he nodded unquestioningly. "Of course, my lady. But please, I insist you return inside."

"Thank you. I have every intention of doing so." And without another word, I hurried into the mansion. That deep, buried, romantic part of my soul hoped my letter reached Ariana.

CHAPTER 9

Had I ever been so tired?

Mistrustful, I couldn't sleep. I'd sat up rigidly in bed until sunlight spilled through the cracks in the curtains of the guest suite. By the time the maids arrived to help me dress, I was ready for the day, having washed and then adorned a riding gown. I'd fashioned my hair into a simple braid.

I knew the maids were shocked by my "unladylike" behavior—haven forbid a lady actually dress herself—and I imagined I'd be a prime bit of gossip amongst the servants of Grof Krill's home when I departed. But by that point I was so numb with exhaustion, I couldn't give a damn.

The grof was not at breakfast, and the butler informed me Wolfe had already eaten and was in the stables with the men, preparing to continue our journey. I scoffed down some toast and black coffee, hoping it might energize me. All the coffee did was make me jittery.

Surmising Grof Krill would not wish to see me off after the previous evening's embarrassing encounter, I ventured outside to find the Guard waiting for me. I was annoyed that no one had come for me sooner. I hated being the one to keep everyone waiting, like I was *that* woman. Tiredness made me grumpier, and I huffed in annoyance as Lieutenant Chaeron helped me mount Midnight with a cheery, "Good morning."

"Lady Rogan." Wolfe urged his horse toward me from the front of our cavalcade. He nodded a dismissal at the lieutenant who left my side to mount his own horse, Snowstorm. Together they sidled away from Wolfe and I, giving us privacy.

I frowned against the morning sun, wishing I was more inclined to wearing bonnets. But they annoyed me—I liked to be aware of my surroundings, and bonnets cut off too much of my peripheral vision.

"Captain Stovia," I mumbled, hoping I wasn't in for some kind of lecture. This could end in a screaming match. A weary one, but I'd give it my best effort.

The sunlight brightened his eyes to a golden aquamarine as they washed over me. "Are you all right, Lady Rogan? After last evening, I mean?" His mouth twisted in consternation as we both remembered Krill's appalling behavior.

I nodded, suppressing a yawn. "Yes, Captain, I'm quite well. Grof Krill explained his unseemly behavior last night and apologized."

Wolfe stiffened at the news. "Oh, he did, did he? And what exactly did he tell you?"

I shrugged. "He was trying to ingratiate himself to me. He wanted to use my magic to find someone."

"That piece of ..." Wolfe pressed his lips together in fury as he glared bloody murder at Krill's mansion. For a moment, he appeared ready to dismount and head inside. The man really took his duties too seriously. My amused smirk turned into a yawn as Wolfe growled at the building, "How dare he abuse a lady's feelings in such a manner."

"I assure you I knew from the start that he was up to something, Captain. I'm not the sort of woman men make fools of themselves over."

Wolfe's head whipped toward me, his expression slack with disbelief. We stared at one another a moment before he seemed to shake himself. With a snort of derision, the captain gathered his reins and turned his horse forward. "And yet so many of them do."

Too tired to argue with his nonsensical comment, I stayed silent as Wolfe trotted to lead our procession. I acknowledged Lieutenant Chaeron with a tremulous smile as he returned to my side; I fought against the rhythmic sway of Midnight's movements as we followed the captain.

I barely remember leaving Peza. Everything was a blur as I battled to keep my eyes open, my body tense so it didn't fall asleep. The city disappeared behind us and the land grew quiet, our small army passing farms off the beaten track. I was lulled by the peace and began to give in to my body's need for respite. Feeling nauseated with the exhaustion, I struggled to keep my head up. We couldn't waste any more time after stopping at Peza. Every time my eyes slid shut for brief moments, Haydyn's smiling, beautiful, serene face danced across the blackness of my lids, and sparks of aching pain shot out of my heart and across my chest. I snapped my eyes open and gripped the reins harder, determined to go as fast as Wolfe was leading.

My body was in total disagreement. Perhaps three, maybe four hours into our journey, all I was aware of was the heat of the sun burning through my dress, the distant sounds of the clip-clopping of horses' hooves, and the soldiers' murmured chatter that resembled insects buzzing around my head.

And suddenly I was lying outside in the grass by the cliffs of Sabithia. It was a hot summer's day and my mind lazily drifted into slumber.

"Miss Rogan," I heard a voice call in the distance. My eyes popped open at the happy sound and I stood up. I gazed behind me to see Haydyn approach and was shocked to find her all alone. She was barefoot like me as she walked through the cool grass.

"Your Highness," I teased. "I missed you."

Haydyn took my hand. "I missed you too."

We grinned at one another and then turned to stare out at the calm sea stretching away from the cliff edge.

"That water looks wonderful," I whispered.

"You know today it looks calm enough to swim in."

"We're too high up."

"Be adventurous, Rogan."

Frowning, I took a step closer to the edge, the drop at least a hundred feet. "It would kill us."

"Not today." Haydyn shook her head. "Trust me."

Heart pounding at the thought, I gripped her hand tighter. "Together? On three?"

She laughed, exhilarated. "One. Two. Three!"

"Miss Rogan!"

And then I was falling.

Blissfully falling.

EVERYTHING ACHED.

I did not want to open my eyes but a strange feeling of disorientation forced me to.

And I found myself staring up at an unfamiliar ceiling. It was dark, nighttime. There were a few lit candles in the room.

Where the hell was I?

"Ah, Miss Rogan, you're awake."

Calming instantly at Lieutenant Chaeron's voice, I turned my head on a soft pillow and saw him sitting in a chair by my bedside. His brow creased with worry as he leaned into me, offering a glass of water. He helped me sip it and then settled back in the chair.

"What happened?" I asked hoarsely. "Where are we?"

He made a clucking sound with his tongue, disapproval marring his usually friendly expression. "You should have told us how exhausted you were. You could have been killed."

Now I was very confused. All I could remember was talking to Wolfe outside Grof Krill's mansion. "What happened?"

"You fell asleep on your horse." He sighed like a wearied parent. "If I hadn't been at your side to catch you, you would have landed on the ground and possibly been trampled."

I swore softly at the thought, chastising myself for my stupid pride and hell-bent determination to get to Alvernia in record time. "Thank you, Lieutenant."

He nodded and patted the hand I reached out to him. "No need to thank me. For now, we've stopped at a farm. We've all been resting. We're going to stay here through the night. Captain is not at all pleased with you."

I groaned. "I've slowed us down."

Chaeron patted my hand again. "That's not why he's angry. He wishes you had told him you were exhausted. He takes your safety very seriously. We all do."

I nodded vaguely, annoyed somewhere inside but too tired to cling to the emotion. Feeling my lids grow heavy again, I mumbled, "He needs to find himself a pastime."

Distantly I heard the lieutenant chuckle, and then he whispered, "Sleep well, Miss Rogan."

CHAPTER 10

Guilt was an emotion I disliked greatly. So I smothered the feeling with anger and directed it at Wolfe. The next morning he barely acknowledged me. He was cold, distant, and it irritated me more than it should have because generally, I preferred his indifference. But his annoyance only compounded how stupidly I had behaved, making me feel like the simpering handmaiden I was so adamant I wasn't.

Lieutenant Chaeron threw a few bolstering looks my way and as usual tried to keep up a pleasant conversation as we rode through Raphizya. Wolfe controlled our pace, and it was deliberately slow. It smacked of condescension. I huffed in the saddle, wanting to speed up, and poor Midnight faltered a little at my mixed signals. I leaned over to stroke her face, apologizing quietly in her ear. I forced myself to relax in my seat and ignored Chaeron's knowing grin.

With my renewed energy, time seemed to pass a little more quickly. Before I knew it, we were crossing the stone bridge across the River Kral, called so because it was the longest in Phaedra, passing through not only Raphizya but Vasterya too. We were closing in on Ryl, the second-largest city in Raphizya, famous for being the only city in Phaedra that wasn't a capital, and also for its factories.

Almost as large as Peza, it was home to factories that mass-produced textiles, paintings, pottery, and lots of other knick-knacks, designed by the artisans of Peza. They sustained much of Raphizya, supplying employment and a large exportation income.

Knowing the plan was to stay with Matai's cousins, Mr. Zanst and his wife and their two small children, I wasn't surprised when Wolfe led us through the outskirts of the city toward the Factory District. Ironically, the Factory District wasn't in fact where the manufacturing took place. The Factory District was home to the mansions and large townhouses of the *owners* of the mills and plants. Mr. Zanst owned a large textile mill and was said to be wealthier than his vikomt cousin, Matai. I had met Mr. Zanst and his wife at court. They were a nice couple, friendly and open, and a refreshing diversion from the titled nobility and all their manners and dos and don'ts.

When we arrived, Mrs. Zanst was there to greet us, her husband not yet returned from his office at the factory. She was young and attractive. I hid a smile as some of the Guard tried not to stare at her. They had been deprived of female companionship for longer than some of them were used to, and she was a lovely sight. Sighing, I dismounted with Chaeron's aid and was enveloped in a friendly hug by Mrs. Zanst.

"It's such a pleasure to see you again, Lady Rogan." She smiled widely as she pulled away to take in my appearance. "I must say, you're looking very well for a young lady who's been traveling. And without a carriage, no less." She frowned, looking over the Guard.

I shrugged inelegantly, happy to be around someone who didn't care if I shrugged inelegantly. "I thought a carriage would be more of a hindrance than a help."

Mrs. Zanst didn't seem to agree but she said no more,

clasping my hand in hers as we walked inside and left the Guard to organize themselves. It would seem there wasn't enough room in the stables or the mansion for all of them, so some would have to venture into the city for accommodation. I rolled my eyes as many eagerly volunteered, knowing from conversation I'd overheard that the excitement was due more to finding a bed partner than an actual bed.

"Oh," I gasped as we stepped into the entrance hall. "Your home is lovely, Mrs. Zanst." And I meant it. Her expression brightened, a little flush of pride cresting her cheeks.

"Thank you, Lady Rogan. I do try."

In all the homes of the wealthy I had ventured into, the floors of the entrance hall, hallways in general, were always white and black marble, or, as at the palace, pure white marble flecked with sparkling crystal. But Mr. and Mrs. Zanst had forgone the cold marble aesthetic of the wealthy and instead had beautiful, wide-slatted, wooden polished floors that reflected the glow from the stunning but simplistic chandelier spiraling from the ceiling. I stared at the corkscrew of crystals, surprised by its originality. It was like a piece of modern art in itself.

Careful not to encumber the light, airy quality they had created, there were no drab oil paintings or heavy tapestries, only pale, buttercream walls. Adorning one of the walls was a mural depicting a blurry forest with gorgeous wood nymphs and other rustic creatures. A few silver mirrors were dotted here and there and flowers in soft pastel shades rested in ornate vases.

"It's like a fairy tale," I whispered. "Haydyn would love this."

Mrs. Zanst blushed even harder. "Do you really think so?"

I nodded, giving her arm a friendly squeeze. "You, Mrs. Zanst, have a gift for interior design."

"Oh, I'm pleased you think so. Many of the women here"—her voice dropped to a murmur—"think my taste unfashionable."

"On the contrary, I think you might set a new fashion for interiors. Wait until we get you back to the palace to decorate

Haydyn's private parlor, Mrs. Zanst. Then all the ladies will wish you to decorate their homes."

Wide-eyed, she pulled me into her equally quaint and beautiful parlor. "Do you really think so?"

❧

HAVING APPARENTLY MADE A FRIEND FOR LIFE IN THE charming Mrs. Zanst, I felt awful when I tricked her. Desperate for some time alone, to be away from the Guard and the Factory District, which was buzzing with the news of our arrival, I knew I had to make my escape before the neighbors started calling on Mrs. Zanst to meet me.

I faked a headache and fatigue from the journey and was shown to a spectacular guest suite with wonderful views of Ryl. There I hastily wrote a note to Mrs. Zanst informing her where I'd gone so she wouldn't worry, and then threw on a dark cloak, creeping out of the room. I was forced to hide twice—once in another bedroom and then in the music room on the second floor. I halted at the sound of children squealing and realized the nursery must be near. Afraid of being found by an impish child, I scurried down the next flight of stairs and then cursed under my breath when I came face-to-face with the butler.

"May I help you, my lady?" he bowed, gracefully, the tallest butler I had ever encountered.

I gulped, thinking fast. "I'm going for a walk. Mrs. Zanst suggested I follow the main road out of the Factory District to arrive at the center of the city ..."

He frowned, shaking his head. "That cannot be correct, my lady. Mrs. Zanst must have meant for you to take a right and then a left once you reach the entrance to the Factory District."

I smiled inwardly. "And that takes me straight into the city?"

"You cannot miss it, my lady."

"Thank you."

And as easily as that, I was out the door. I held my breath, almost skipping as I shot down the driveway and through the gates. As I hurried along, I glanced back at the house and saw some of the Guard still organizing themselves at the stables. Afraid to be spotted, I took off at a run, no longer caring which of the neighbors saw.

As the wind rushed into my face, tearing my eyes, my skirts billowing a hindrance around my legs, I grinned and pushed harder. It was wonderful, so freeing.

Skidding to a stop at the end of the Factory District, I peered over my shoulder to make sure I wasn't being followed. I couldn't see anyone. I smoothed my skirts and straightened my cloak and walked sedately toward the city. There were still a few hours until nightfall, plenty of time to have a look around.

Quite suddenly, I found myself in the hubbub of the city, lots of people rushing around as if they had somewhere important to be. In fact, as I stared around at the rather drab appearance of the city, with its towering industrial factories in the distance and the squat little shops, I realized how different it was to Peza.

Or so I thought.

Like stepping into an oil painting, I walked through an arched alleyway and was lambasted by color as I entered the market square. Everywhere were people and stalls in a multitude of hues where quiet sellers stood patiently offering help and information. Never before had I seen such serious, hushed sellers. I walked around the stalls, my eyes widening now and then. Their products were beautiful, no matter if they were mass-produced.

I stopped, drawn to a stall with beaded jewelry. The jewelry I owned was of the finest precious metals and stones. But I trailed my fingers over a bracelet made with pleated leather; three beautifully painted beads in emerald, aquamarine, and rose decorated the end near the clasp. A little silver bird hung between the beads.

I saw my mother taking a bracelet from my hands as a child, pressing a soft kiss to my head and telling me it wasn't to be played with, but when I was older, it would be mine. It had been a leather rope bracelet, no beads, but a little bird had hung from its center.

"How much?" I asked, a little dazed, holding up the bracelet.

The seller smiled. "Five coppers, miss."

Five coppers? That was all? Haydyn would like one, too, I was sure. "I'll take two."

She smiled pleasantly as I handed over the money. She then wrapped the bracelets separately in tissue paper before popping them into a little paper bag for me. I thanked her and walked away, bemused by my impulse buy. I wasn't really much of a shopper.

I wandered for a while among the glitter and awe of the splendid market and then eyed a confectionary store in indecision. Finally, at the little growl in my stomach, I shrugged and went inside to buy a cream cake. Once outside, I stood away from the crowds by the corner of the shop where it met a narrow alley between buildings. There I ate my cake in peace.

Although the cake was good, I couldn't help feeling a little unsatisfied. It was nowhere near as good as Cook's, I grimaced. I wondered if Valena was eating all my cakes as well as hers. Smiling wryly at the thought, I wiped at a smudge of cream on my lip and readied myself to return to the Zansts'. I was lucky to have gotten away for this long. And I just knew I was in for a severe lecture from Wolfe.

Just as I made to take a step forward, I heard a scuffle behind me. My pulse skittered.

A grimy, sweaty hand clamped down on my mouth and my feet left the ground as I was dragged back into the darkness of the alley. I tried to scream against the hand but all that came out was a muffled whine. I beat at the head behind me, trying to wriggle free from the strong arm around my waist.

"Stop it, or I'll break your neck," a gruff voice spoke in my ear, and I trembled as decaying breath hit my nostrils. I stilled, feeling the strength in his hold.

"Do it," someone else said.

How many were there? I turned to look just as a musty hood came down over my face, drowning me in darkness. Panicked, I thrashed and beat out at my attackers. More hands clamped down on me and muffled grunts and curses lit the air as they tried to lift me off the ground. I was terrified, furious to be so helpless and vulnerable, with one of my senses disabled.

The familiar sound of a sword hissing from its scabbard halted us all, and one of my captors growled, "Deal with him."

One of the Guard!

I'd never been so thankful to be followed!

So busy attempting to hear the exchange, I wasn't paying attention to my captors and stupidly allowed one of them to throw me onto a hard shoulder. Grunts and a shout of pain hit my ears. I hoped the officer's sword had just found one of my captor's bellies. The clatter of steel hitting stone made me tense. Then all I could hear was flesh smashing into flesh—grunts, groans, hisses of pain.

"Stop, or we kill the girl."

I heard heavy breathing and then silence.

Fearful, I squirmed, beating down on whatever body part I could find.

"Stop it, or we will kill your bodyguard," the man holding me said as an insolent hand swatted me hard on the bottom. Tears of humiliation sprung in my eyes but I stopped fighting, realizing they had both me and the officer in an untenable position. If one of the Guard had been disarmed, then there must be too many of them to fight.

"What will we do with 'im?" a rough female voice asked from somewhere to my left.

"Bring 'im. 'E'll only send people after us otherwise."

I began to fight again in earnest, taking pleasure in the yelp of pain I produced when I bit what I assumed was an ear through the hood over my head.

"Blood 'ell! Prick her!"

A sharp, short pain flared in my arm and I cried out. Heat rushed up the appendage at a dizzying speed and flooded my brain in a gush of warmth and bright colors. The colors burst like fireworks in the night sky until they faded, leaving only a numbing darkness.

CHAPTER 11

A shaft of light pried at my eyelids causing a sharp pain to ricochet through my head. I moaned through lips that were dry and cracked.

"Rogan?" a familiar voice asked.

I jolted and my eyes flew open. Blinking against the light, I turned my head and winced at the feel of cold stone beneath it. A tiny window was the source of the annoying illumination in the dank cellar. I scrambled quickly to a sitting position, grit and dirt pinching my palms. At the sight of Wolfe sitting near me, looking tired and pale, I experienced more than a flicker of panic.

"Are you all right?" he asked.

I shook my head, trying to get my bearings as I looked around the large room with the low ceiling that had nothing in it but us and a changing screen in the corner. A door made of thick metal bars stood at one end. It was as if I were in a dream. I couldn't remember how I had gotten there. Flashes of images, of unfamiliar faces, swept through me.

Then I remembered being jostled. Someone tried to feed me.

"Where are we?" I croaked. My throat was dry.

Wolfe sighed and pushed a cup of water to me.

I gulped it thirstily.

"Do you remember being taken in the market at Ryl?"

Fear shot through my body and I trembled, dropping the cup. I could still feel that clammy, dirty hand over my mouth, hands on my body as they tried to restrain me. "You were the one who followed me?"

He nodded gravely. "We've been kidnapped by the Iavii."

That was the last thing I had been expecting. Although, to be honest, I didn't know what I'd been expecting. The last time I'd been kidnapped, it was for my power; I assumed this was the reason behind our current situation. "The clan from Alvernia that have been causing havoc in Javinia?"

"The very ones." He grimaced. "They drugged us. We're in Javinia, but we've only been out for a few days, I think, which means we must be near the border."

My heart thudded. I felt sick. "A few days. At the mercy of those people?"

Wolfe's jaw clenched and he turned away in frustration. "Well, you would have to defy orders and take off on your own."

Furious heat shot through me. "Oh, it didn't take long for the lecture to start, did it, Stovia?"

"I'm not the one who got us into this mess," he hissed, gesturing around at the cell. "They have a Dravilec, Rogan. And they're well armed and can fight. God knows what else they have up their sleeve."

"A Dravilec?" I was momentarily thrown by the fact that the clan would have a mage among them, considering there were so few left.

"Yes. The healer took the effects of the drugs away so we would wake up. I was then informed of who they are and what they want with us."

Feeling guilty, I exhaled. "What *do* they want with us?"

He snorted humorlessly. "They find themselves fortunate enough to have in their hands the Handmaiden of Phaedra and the captain of the Royal Guard. We're bargaining chips, my lady.

They're going to hold us for ransom—they want land from Markiza Raven."

I scoffed. "Are they idiots? Even if they managed some temporary agreement with Novia, once we're free we'll just send in the entire Guard to arrest them for what they've done."

Wolfe shook his head. "Not if they refuse to free us but merely guarantee our safety while we're imprisoned. They know how much the princezna cares about you."

An awful understanding dawned. "They mean to keep us here indefinitely?"

"That would be my guess." He nodded. "They'll promise to look after us, keep us alive. But they won't hand us over until they're certain of their position. If ever."

Acid curdled in my stomach and I dragged myself along the floor so I could lean my head against the wall. The tight, fearful knot that had begun to grow within me since we learned of the increasing crime in Phaedra was suddenly nauseating. "This is because of Haydyn ... isn't it? Because her power is waning?"

Wolfe sighed and followed my lead, leaning back against the wall, his light eyes hard as flint. I looked away, unnerved by the focused, ruthless expression. "Yes. It is," he replied finally.

"We have to get out of here." I jumped up to rush at the cellar door. My legs were wobbly with disuse but I pushed through the sensation.

"Rogan ..."

I pulled at the door but it was useless. Ignoring the prick of tears, I peered through the bars. There was nothing there to see. Just a narrow, dark staircase leading upward into the house. I whirled around, my focus on the window. I ran at it but couldn't reach it. I twisted around to glare at Wolfe. "Can you get your ass up for a minute to see if these bars will shift?"

He pinned me to the wall with a disgusted look. "I'm the captain of the Royal Guard, Rogan, not an idiot. I tried the window and the door as soon as they left us in this damn cellar."

I deflated but refused to show my fear. "Well, we have to do something."

"The only chance we have of escape is if they let us out of the room."

Reluctantly hearing the wisdom in his statement, I nodded and returned to my spot against the wall. I slumped to the ground. It was then I became aware of how much I needed a bath. I wrinkled my nose in disgust.

Wolfe grunted and muttered a curse under his breath.

"If you've got something to say, say it," I huffed.

"Oh, it's nothing." His words were laced with heavy sarcasm. "Just relaxing, you know, thanking my fortunate stars for being the one who was put in charge of protecting you."

"No one asked you to protect me. To follow me!"

"I'm the princezna's captain, Lady Rogan, and you are the most important person in her life. Not to mention the last of the Azyl and the only bloody person who knows where the Somna plant is. It's my job to protect you. And you make it *very* difficult."

"I went for a walk!"

"And got us kidnapped by the Iavii!"

"Oh, dear haven," I groaned, closing my eyes. "Please get over it so we can move on."

He spluttered, "Get over it? Get over it? Do you have any idea what this could do to me? What if I can't get us out of here, Rogan? What if something happens to you?"

"Relax. It's not like they'll blame you and you'll lose your job." I sighed. "I can't believe I got kidnapped with Captain Wolfe Stovia. Talk about fun."

"You are such a brat."

I smiled, enjoying the thought of irritating him. "And you are such a pompous, untrustworthy snake."

I heard his indrawn breath and determinedly squished my remorse.

Before he could reply, a key turned in the lock. A huge, burly man with long, dark hair pulled back into a messy queue strolled into the cellar. He seemed to take up the entire space as he watched us, like a predator studying its prey.

"We've brought ye food." He had a slight accent, his words rolling and unrefined. He nodded at someone and a young man came into the room carrying a tray. "One move and I run ye through," the big man warned, his hand going to the hilt of a sword strapped to a belt around his hip.

I looked at Wolfe for guidance. His attention was trained on the larger of the men. The young man came forward, keeping his distance, and set the tray on the ground. He looked at me as he picked up one bowl and slid it toward me. He did the same for Wolfe's bowl, his eyes never leaving me, and I squirmed under his strange regard. He watched me with a clinical interest that was extremely disturbing. I waited for Wolfe to do something. But he just sat there.

"I need to use the ... I have need of ... I need to relieve myself."

"Relieve yerself?" The big man grinned. "Ye mean ye need to use the piss pot?"

I flushed at his crassness but nodded, hoping he would let me out of the cellar so I could note our surroundings for Wolfe.

"There's one in the corner." He grinned harder. "Behind the changing screen."

I was horrified. "You are jesting?"

He shook his head. "If ye're that desperate, ye'll use it."

Disgusted, I could do nothing but wait with bated breath for them to leave and then I turned on Wolfe. "Why didn't you do something?"

He shrugged and grabbed the bowl and bread that had been left for him. "He had the upper hand. Plus ... I'm hungry."

How could he be so blasé? Infuriated with not only him but myself for not having the skills to save myself, I snatched my bowl. "Wonderful. Just wonderful. Let me know when you decide to start working on that whole protecting-me thing you keep spouting on about."

He threw me a look but didn't retort, which annoyed me more than I would have liked.

When we finished eating, he looked at me with a mischievous twinkle in his eyes. "You know, if you need to ... *relieve* yourself ... I could hum or sing so you're not embarrassed ... you know, by the noise—"

"I understand your meaning, thank you." I blushed so hard my face could have warmed the Guard around a campsite.

"I'm just saying I—"

"You could sing, yes, yes, very funny."

He nearly choked himself to death laughing when three hours later, I made him do just that as I darted behind the changing screen to use the chamber pot.

Worse still, he actually had a very nice singing voice.

CHAPTER 12

"I really am tiring of people manhandling me," I muttered, covering my fear with bravado at the bite of the dagger at my neck. I tried not to think how ironic it was that only a few days ago, I had someone else in the position I was now in.

"Rogan," Wolfe warned.

I shrugged, and the clan member at my back pressed the blade harder against my skin. I winced as it nicked my skin.

"Hey!" Wolfe growled in outrage, making a move toward me. The two huge Iavii holding him reeled him in.

"I told ye, the girl gets it if ye make a move to attack." The man holding me was the one from yesterday with the messy queue and hand-me-down gentleman's clothing. The arm he wrapped around my waist tightened so I was flush with his body. "And ye," he whispered softly in my ear, "keep quiet. Or I'll find a far more pleasurable way to occupy yer mouth."

Aghast and repulsed, humiliated at being treated this way in front of Wolfe, who eyed the man as if he'd just signed his own death warrant, I decided it would be best if I shut up.

"Now," the Iavii continued, "we're going for a little walk outside. And ye're both going to behave." I noticed how measured his words were, as if he had to concentrate on his enunciation.

I tried to catch Wolfe's eye to see if he had a plan, but our captor pushed me ahead and I stumbled, my throat nearly catching the blade edge again.

"If you want me to behave, you better stop putting her life in danger," Wolfe warned in a tone that would have intimidated a lesser man.

The man grunted but was more careful with me as he took us upstairs. I really only caught a glimpse of a cozy parlor while we were taken out the front door of the modestly sized farmhouse. He dragged me down porch steps, and I gaped at the fields spread out before us. Dozens of tents sat on the farm—dogs, cats running around, horses grazing leisurely, some sheep and cattle off in the distance. In the center was a huge stone campfire, unlit, but still surrounded by the comings and goings of the Iavii.

"Come on," the man demanded and pushed me ahead. We strode past a few tents, and people stopped to stare. Eventually he brought us to a halt outside a small tent made from blue, purple, and red patchwork.

The dagger fell away from my throat.

"Vrik," a soft, husky voice called, and we all turned as a dark-haired beauty sauntered over to us. Her hips swished her drab skirts back and forth. Her worn blouse and gray skirt did nothing to detract from her loveliness. My spine stiffened in insult as she instantly dismissed me. She turned to Wolfe, and her eyes narrowed in appreciation as she dragged her gaze down his body and back up again. "These are the two?" she asked without taking her eyes off Wolfe.

The man behind me answered so I assumed he was Vrik. "Yes. Selena wants to see them."

She nodded, eyeing Wolfe like he was a meal. "Can I have this one, Vrik, when ye're done with him?"

My heart picked up pace as Wolfe stared back at her, expressionless.

Vrik snorted. "Scarla, we haven't even sent the message off to Javinia that we have them. A little patience, please."

She flashed her black, cat-shaped eyes at him. "But I want him."

"I'm sure the lad will be more than happy to see to ye when we reach an agreement with Markiza Raven. But until then, he's a prisoner and off limits."

Scarla pouted and reached out to trail a hand down Wolfe's chest. "I'm not happy about this, Vrik. Perhaps I should speak with Papa?"

"Papa will tell ye the same thing. Now leave, Scarla."

So these two ill-mannered beings were siblings?

Scarla huffed and then went up onto her tiptoes to whisper in Wolfe's ear. Whatever she said caused a manly blush across the crest of Wolfe's cheeks. My heart thumped and I glanced away, gritting my teeth.

When Scarla left, Vrik grabbed my arm and thrust me into the tent. The men holding Wolfe did the same with my companion.

My eyes adjusted to the dimness of the tiny tent and I started at the sight of the older woman before us. The interior was bare; grass beneath my feet, the only piece of furniture a stunning library desk that would have looked more at home in a study at the palace. The old woman sat behind it.

"Here ye are, Selena. Our prisoners." Vrik pushed me to her, and I caught myself on the desk. "Let us know if ye see anything that'll tell us about any future land agreements we may come to with that damn Rada."

Selena looked at him with a bland expression, as if he were below her interest. "Take the girl outside. I wish to speak with the boy first."

As I was dragged past Wolfe, I threw him a questioning look.

But he was focused solely on Selena. Who an earth was this woman? What was going on?

Outside, I found myself discomfited by the Iavii and their curious stares. I turned so my back was facing camp. Vrik watched me, his arms crossed over his chest.

"What's going on?" I asked, more than a little impatient now.

"Be quiet."

"Who is Selena?"

"I said, be quiet."

"You know you're really rather impertinent."

The beast bared his teeth. "And ye are getting on my last nerve, Princezna."

Trying to pretend that his animal behavior didn't bother me, I sniffed. "I'm not a princezna."

He made a face. "Ye look and act it."

I do not, I huffed. I think all in all, I had been taking my kidnapping extremely well. Especially considering the terrible memories it brought back of being carted off by Wolfe's father. I hardened in remembrance. "You haven't seen anything yet."

Vrik raised an eyebrow and then he had the audacity to grin. "Ye might be fun after all, Princezna."

Before I could offer a disgusted retort, Wolfe was shoved out of the tent by the two Iavii at his back.

"What happened?" I asked, moving to him. Vrik gripped my arm and wrenched me away.

Wolfe snarled at him and then turned to me. "Nothing. The old woman is useless."

One man walloped Wolfe across the head.

"Hey!" I yelled in outrage at the offending clansman and was rewarded with a bewildered look from Wolfe as I was pushed back into the tent.

"Anything?" Vrik asked Selena without preamble.

She shook her head. "He blocked me somehow."

"Blocked ye?" Vrik appeared stunned. My head swiveled between them. I was completely at a loss.

"Hmm," she answered. "Keep a careful eye on him."

"What is going on?" I demanded.

Selena arched an eyebrow at me and then smirked at Vrik. "We've got a live one here."

Vrik chuckled, a dark, sinister kind of chuckle that sent shivers slithering down my spine. "Seems so."

The old woman smiled at me. "Give me your hands."

I tucked my hands behind my back. "Why?"

She winked. "I'm not going to hurt you. Just give me your hands ... or I'll make Vrik hold you while we do this."

I snapped my hands out so fast, she cackled. "Don't think she likes you too much, Vrik, so I wouldn't be getting any ideas."

Vrik grunted behind me.

Selena snatched my hands in her extremely cold ones, and I felt every wrinkle and crevice of that sandpapery touch electrify through me.

She was a mage.

Seeing the question in my eye, Selena nodded. "I'm one of the Glava, little Azyl."

Dear haven, they had one of the Glava and a Dravilec among them. I wondered if they had been collected as Syracen had done with me, Valena, and Kir. "Your specialty?" I asked.

"I'm a reader."

"You read people's minds?"

"No. Just their futures."

I gulped and shook my head, trying to withdraw my hands. "I don't want to know my future."

She cocked her head, her eyes studying me curiously. "What happened to you, girl, to make you so afraid of the future?"

"Well, for a start, I was kidnapped by the Iavii."

Vrik smothered a chuckle behind me as Selena glared.

"*We* won't hurt you, girl. No. You fear something else."

"You said you can't read minds."

She laughed softly, condescendingly, like I was a small child before a teacher. "I don't need to read minds to know that a young, intelligent, pretty woman with her whole life ahead of her should be excited at the prospect of the future. You clearly aren't. So why are you frightened?"

"I'm not frightened. I'd rather live each day as they come than know what lies ahead. Knowledge can cause a person to alter their own path."

Her whole face lit up with pleasure. "What a wise thing to say."

"So ... may I go now?"

"No." She tugged harder on my hands and I lurched forward. A sick feeling swirled in my stomach as Selena closed her eyes. She was still for so long, my heart raced harder and louder. I was sure they must hear it in this tiny, sparse tent. Finally, Selena grinned. Her eyes popped open. "Nothing to fear," she assured me. "You'll marry one of the Glava and be very happy about it."

I scoffed and pulled my hands free. "Doubtful, madam, as I have no intention of marrying anyone. Ever," I emphasized. I began to feel better. Perhaps she wasn't really one of the Glava after all.

Selena shrugged. "I'm never wrong."

Wolfe was right. This was nonsense. I rolled my eyes and pulled from her. "May I go now?"

Seeming amused, Selena nodded and Vrik strode forward, frowning. He grabbed my arm and I winced. He would leave bruises with his rough handling.

"That's it?" he hissed at Selena. "Nothing about an agreement? About land?"

She shook her head, holding up her hands. "You know I only receive visions of what's most important to their fate."

"And you determined marriage was mine?" I snorted and turned to Vrik. "You might want to purchase a new Glava because this one is definitely broken."

Vrik forced me forward and out of the tent. Wolfe was nowhere to be seen. Panic flickered inside me. "Where's Wolfe?" I asked and received no answer. Vrik tried to lead me toward the house but I wouldn't let him, digging my feet into the dirt. "Where's Wolfe?"

"He's fine," Vrik snarled and used both hands to pick me up and put me down in front of him. He pressed his hands into my back and pushed me forward. I struggled all the way.

"Damn it, tell me where he is!"

"He's fine," he reiterated. "Now get yer ass in this house before I do good on my earlier promise to shut ye up in a way that I'll definitely enjoy but ye won't."

Rage pervaded my good sense and I elbowed him, hard, as he pushed me forward. "Just tell me where he is?"

"Having a better time than me, probably."

There was a sickening lurch in my stomach. Was Wolfe off with the Iavii girl while I was being mauled? Irritated beyond rationality, I lifted a knee and kicked backward, catching Vrik in the thigh. He yelled and grasped a handful of my hair as he forced me—kicking and shoving—into the house and down the cellar stairs.

"Where's Wolfe?" I screamed for the millionth time as I was thrown into the cellar.

I landed with a wounded grunt, my ribs hollering in pain as they impacted with the stone floor.

I heard a curse and then Wolfe's face hovered over mine. "Rogan, are you all right?"

He was here? In the cellar? I groaned and relaxed, thumping my head against the hard ground. "Ouch."

"Rogan?" His fingers were on my face. My eyes flashed open and my heart lodged somewhere in my throat at his proximity. I could see the gold striations in his blue eyes, his dark lashes enviably long. Suddenly I felt a strange, my skin was too hot, and squirmed at his concerned expression.

Distrusting it, I flinched away and watched the concern disappear. He sighed and retreated from me. "I take it you're fine."

"Yes, I'm fine." I struggled to a sitting position, willing my heart to slow. I pushed my skirts back down into some semblance of modesty. Not that it mattered. I was torn, smelly, and unwashed. Feeling Wolfe's unwavering gaze, I stopped fussing and glared at him. "What?"

"Nothing." He shrugged. "I've just never heard you say my name before."

"What?"

"You were yelling 'Where's Wolfe?' over and over again."

I flushed, not wanting him to misunderstand. "I thought they were separating us, and we have a better chance of escape if we're together. And you've heard me say your name before."

Wolfe shook his head, smiling wryly. "No. It's always Captain or Stovia or Captain Stovia. Then there's *vikomt*—you usually spit that one at me."

Uncomfortable for reasons unknown and not wishing to have anything that could qualify as an actual conversation with him, I deflected. "Well, *Vikomt*, how do you suggest we get out of this?" I gestured around the cellar. "Now that we know they have a Glava and a Dravilec."

Something like disappointment darkened Wolfe's countenance before he seemed to shrug the sentiment away. "I wonder if they have more mages here. I hope they've not been ..." He threw me a wary look before he continued quietly, "Collecting them."

My throat worked against the memories, but I refused to drop my gaze. My expression hardened and Wolfe's eyes blazed with an emotion I couldn't interpret. Was it anger from the memories of me destroying his family?

"So what do we do?" I murmured, wearily wondering when this uneasy truce between us would end, when Wolfe would finally take his vengeance.

"The only thing we can. I heard our guards talking about festivities this evening. Apparently, you and I are attending. When we're there, I'll create a distraction. You have to keep your wits about you, Lady Rogan. Watch me all the time. When I make my move, you make it with me, and we run."

I blinked, hoping I'd heard wrong. "That's your big plan? A distraction?"

"Yes. It's good, right?"

"You're going to get us killed."

"Well, since you got us kidnapped in the first place, you're in no position to judge."

CHAPTER 13

I schooled my expression as I was inspected by an older version of Vrik. The man stood by the campfire, shadows of flames flickering across his dark skin, pinpricks of light reflecting in the blackness of his gaze.

Around us the hubbub of noise was now a hushed tide, rising and falling with little bursts of laughter and conversation, as the Iavii enjoyed ale and food around the fire. Wolfe stood beside me in the darkness. We were guarded by Vrik and three other men, but not tied up, not held tight. It was as if, for now, they wanted us to feel less like prisoners and more like guests.

At the sound of a whimper, my attention was drawn to a girl sitting on a log, squashed in the middle of two rough-looking women. One of them grasped her hair, forcing her head back. Tears streamed down her face as one of the women held the dagger she'd been using to cut her apple up to the girl's eyes. My face tightened in anger at their bullying and the man before me frowned, turning to follow my gaze.

He seemed amused by my reaction and offered me a lazy shrug. "She's one of the Caels. Her brother was resistant to handing over his land, so we took her as punishment."

My blood ran cold, crystallizing until I was frozen solid in my anger. "And what of her brother, her family?" I asked through clenched teeth.

He shrugged again. "Dead."

The man seemed to flicker before me, his features merging with the man who had destroyed my life. They even had those same black eyes. "You son of a bitch," I spat as I lunged, but Vrik wrenched me back.

Wolfe tensed beside me but I couldn't look at him. Not with the memories. Not now.

Not caring if my outburst would provoke a lash of anger, I waited sullenly for a reaction. To my surprise the man laughed. "Ye were right, Vrik. She's feisty. She'll do well here."

I lowered my eyes to regain my composure and then lifted them when I was able to project boredom. "What do you mean?"

The man waved the question away as if batting away an annoying pest. "First, introductions. My name is Tiger. I am leader of the Iavii."

"What do you want from us?" Wolfe demanded.

Tiger seared him with a look. "I only want ransom from *ye*. Ye"—he shook his head and chuckled humorlessly—"the famed captain of the Royal Guard. I was expecting ... more."

"Really?" Wolfe smirked. "Funny, you're just what I expected. You're just a fucking leech, sucking land that's not yours and growing fat on it. Like a bully"—he nodded at the girl who was being tormented, his eyes blazing with indignation—"in the schoolyard, taking what doesn't belong to him and having the audacity to call himself kral."

My heart thudded at Wolfe's impassioned speech. An unexpected feeling of warmth took me by surprise. He looked at me when he was finished, and I dropped my gaze, glad for the shadows of the night that would hide my flushed cheeks.

I frowned, confused.

"Yes," Tiger sneered. "That's what a pampered prince who's lived in luxury and peace his entire life *would* think. We've traveled for too long in Alvernia, across Daeronia. We like Javinia, it's warm. It's home. Nomads no more, we want land. But ye wouldn't understand that. Ye haven't had to suffer the harsh lands of the mountains and deal with uncivilized folks like us. The uncivilized breed uncivilized."

"No." Wolfe shook his head. "You choose to act this way, *be* this way. Dyzvati magic stifles emotions and actions that can lead to unrest and chaos. Not having that magic doesn't turn people into automatic animals. It just makes sure those who would act that way can't. Don't blame your actions on lack of the evocation."

"Shut him up," Tiger directed the man beside Wolfe, and he raised his fist.

I lunged between them before he could hit.

"No!" I cried, putting my hands up to stop the blow. The man looked to Tiger who shook his head. The clansman lowered his hand, and I turned to find Wolfe glaring at me. Ignoring him, I addressed Tiger, "What do you want?"

"Tomorrow morning I send a message to Markiza Raven. In it, she will be told I hold ye both ransom—yer lives for land. Then we'll have to wait while she informs the Rada and the princezna. When we get the land, we'll keep our promise not to kill ye. *He*"—he stabbed a finger at Wolfe—"will be kept a prisoner until such time as I see fit to release him."

"And Lady Rogan?" Wolfe bit out.

Tiger smiled, his eyes running the length of me in a way that caused the hair on my nape to rise. I almost gripped Wolfe's arm in comfort. "Lady Rogan is something ye're not, Captain." He strode toward me. I flinched as he reached up and gripped my chin. "She is one of the Azyl ... and I find that I am in need of an Azyl."

I glowered in disdain and unfurling rage. "You're a collector."

"Yes. But ye're different. I've heard good things about ye. When Selena is impressed, I'm impressed." Abruptly, he released me. "Bird!" he called beyond me. Almost instantly, the tall, skinny boy who had served us food earlier—the one who had stared at me in detachment—appeared before us. Tiger put his arm around the boy and grinned. "This is my adopted son, Bird. Say hello, son."

Bird smirked at me. "Hello, son."

I almost rolled my eyes at his rehearsed insolence.

"Bird," Tiger continued, "is one of the Glava."

"Another mage?"

"Ye said it yerself, I'm a collector. I found Bird when he was five years old."

I moved as if to lunge at him again and was surprised to find Wolfe's hand on my wrist, squeezing it in restraint. I bared my teeth at Tiger. "You mean you took him."

"Semantics." Tiger waved my fury away. "Bird, show 'em what ye can do."

His eyes laughing, Bird turned and looked at the Cael gypsy girl. She emitted a frightened yelp as we watched her hair float up into the air, strand by strand. She whimpered, and the two women beside her chortled and scooted away as first one arm popped up into the air and then the other. Finally, her entire body rose from the log as if held up by unseen hands. Panic suffused her, and she thrashed and screamed as she rose steadily higher.

"Stop!" she shrieked in terror. "Make it stop!"

None of the nomads seemed too distressed by the sight, although I noticed a few on the other side of the campfire glaring at Bird in disgust. I, too, was disgusted and was just about to reprimand Bird when Wolfe snarled, "You've had your fun. Let her go."

Bird arched an eyebrow at Wolfe's demand and then looked to his father. Tiger smirked at Wolfe. "The boy thinks he's a hero."

"Please," I added, pleading with my eyes. Tiger frowned and then nodded at his son. He dropped the girl, and she fell with a hard thump onto the log and let go a howl of pain. "You bastard!" I yelled, forgetting myself.

"Now, now," Tiger admonished and seemed to share a look with Vrik. "Ye're right, son, perhaps she would do better for ye. I'm not sure Bird can handle her spirit."

"Then give her to me." Vrik reached and wrenched me to him.

"No!" Wolfe tried to come for me but was dragged back by the two Iavii. They held him fast and tight as he violently resisted.

Bird shrugged. "She's not much to look at, Papa. I don't care if ye give her to Vrik."

I trembled in disbelief as these men casually decided among them which one would rape me.

Vrik trailed his fingers across my cheek. "I didn't see the appeal at first either, but the more she snaps and snarls at ye, the prettier she seems to get." He chuckled and then ran a hand down my waist and around my hip before he squeezed my bottom. "Plus, she's luscious enough to bear healthy children."

I winced at his manhandling, afraid to look at Wolfe who struggled and cursed at them all.

"I've changed my mind." Bird turned to his father like a petulant little boy who had just discovered the boring toy he had given away did something interesting. "I want her."

"Very well," Tiger agreed. "We'll do the handfasting on the morrow."

Marriage!

I struggled in Vrik's arms as he argued, "Papa, she clearly doesn't want him—give her to me."

"I don't want any of you!" I screamed, fighting against him, but he wouldn't yield. "You can't do this to me!"

Tiger strode forward and pulled his hand back. I braced myself. His palm cracked across my cheek with a slap hard enough to roll my eyes back in my head. Harsh heat shot up the left side of my face and my eyes watered at the needles of pain. "You'll be given to Bird. The Glava marries the Azyl."

So that was Selena's game, telling me I would marry one of the Glava.

Old, manipulative witch.

Suddenly, a shriek echoed around the campfire and I opened my eyes to see the fire in the center of camp roar high, high into the night as if it had been jerked awake from a deep slumber. The Iavii stumbled away from it, fleeing the site as the flames licked out at them like arms trying to snatch them back into the scorching death of its embrace.

Wide-eyed, I looked to Wolfe and found his eyes narrowed in concentration. Bird screamed and Vrik released me as a wall of fire encircled his father and adopted brother. Ignoring the blazing heat stroking my skin, I stared at Wolfe, feeling the crackling of his magic.

His magic?

His magic!

Wolfe was one of the Glava.

He reached for me, his arms encircling my waist as I was pulled into him, his chest to my back. Another fire shot up around Vrik and his men, another around the tents. Wolfe, still holding me, strode forward and grabbed the girl from the Caels who sat immobilized in shock. He dragged the child from the log and holding our hands, he began running, a wall of fire rearing up in our wake to block the Iavii from following us.

Wolfe headed to the house where two horses grazed. The girl seemed to come out of her frightened daze at the sight.

She ran toward the mare and jumped into the saddle like an acrobat. She grabbed the reins expertly, turning the horse to the west. Her eyes caught Wolfe's and they swam with gratitude. "Thank you!" she yelled and then kicked her heels against the mare's flanks and bolted away.

"Where is she going?" I yelled against the noise of the chaos behind us, still cold with shock despite the heat of the fire at my back.

"Back to her clan," Wolfe grunted. "Come on, Rogan, move."

He vaulted onto the stallion and then reached a hand down for me. I just stared at him, still not believing what he had done, how powerful he was.

"Rogan!" he yelled and pulled at my arm. Shaking myself of my stupor, I reached for him and let him pull me onto the horse. His arms came around me, squeezing me tight, as he took hold of the reins and pushed the horse into a gallop.

CHAPTER 14

We rode in silence, pushing the horse to his limits to get as far from the Iavii as we could.

Wolfe was correct—we were very close to the border and soon, just as the stallion's coat was beginning to sweat, we came to a stop on a hill. We stared down on a valley in the distance where the glass factories of Vasterya shaded the border. It had grown much bigger since I was a child, lots of dark, crooked buildings surrounding the factories. This was the rookery.

"We need to be extra careful here," Wolfe warned, his voice pinched with tension. He dropped the reins, and I turned awkwardly to see what he was doing. He was shrugging out of his emerald military jacket. He threw it on the ground behind us.

"Won't you be cold?" I asked, trembling a little myself.

He shrugged. "Doesn't matter. From now on, I don't want anyone to know who we are until we've returned to the Guard."

Seeing wisdom in that, I nodded and let him move the stallion forward. I still hadn't asked about the magic. For the first time, I felt real and true anger toward Wolfe—not angry at him because of who his father was but hurt and angry at him for his deception.

No one knew Wolfe was one of the Glava. Evidence suggested he was a powerful one too.

I stiffened as I began to understand why I was so mad at him.

"You all right?" Wolfe asked. I nodded, trying to ignore the heat of him at my back and the way my body wanted to relax into his.

I was angry because somewhere along the way, I had begun to trust this man. *Stupid, stupid, stupid!* How could I? Were the nightmares, the memories, that huge gaping hole in my heart not enough to remind me not to trust a Stovia?

I stewed in silence, sensing Wolfe's tension. He was probably on tenterhooks waiting for me to ask why he had hidden the fact he was a mage. Dear haven, what awful vengeance he must have been planning.

And yet, why would he save me from the Iavii? Vengeance seemed incongruous to the man I'd come to know.

Stop it! I yelled at myself. I didn't know him, I didn't know him at all, and it was that silly kind of *girlish* thinking that was going to get me killed.

Wolfe was keeping me alive because I was the only one who could save Haydyn.

NOT LONG LATER WE WERE INSIDE THE WALLS OF THE rookery.

The change in atmosphere was intense. Something ominous slithered over me and clung to my skin, causing chill bumps. There was a malevolence here. People hurried past, not even glancing at us, their heads down as they determinedly rushed to get inside out of the dark, dank, dirty streets. Urine and horse manure mixed with the smoke and smells from the glassworks. Houses and shops were shabbily constructed, soulless and frightened-looking buildings jammed together in crooked rows. There was little light here, streetlamps sparsely spaced between streets.

I could feel Wolfe's shock matched my own. This was unbelievable.

"How could Markiz Solom Rada let this happen?" I whispered and turned to see Wolfe warily eyeing a boy who was staring at us.

"I don't know," he bit back. "We should have been told. We would have stopped this."

"We will stop this," I murmured, determinedly. "For now, we need a plan to return to the Guard."

"I have a few coins I kept hidden. The Iavii didn't get them. We'll find somewhere with lodging so we can eat, rest, and send a message to the Guard in Ryl."

"Will they still be there?"

"Yes. They'll send some men out to search but they won't move perchance we return to them. I'll ask Lieutenant Chaeron to bring the men and meet us in Caera at Vojvodkyna Winter Rada's home, as planned."

I gave a brittle nod, thinking his plan sound, and sighed, deciding to trust him. For now. "We need to get a move on. We've already lost too much time."

"I know."

Wolfe had to stop and ask someone where the nearest inn was. We were pointed in the direction of a drinking tavern we were told had rooms above to rent. There were stables behind the tavern and we secured the horse, handing over coin to the stable boy who kept guard over the clientele's horses.

Chilled as the night grew later, we headed into the tavern. We garnered the attention of all its occupants and conversation hushed. I was surprised when Wolfe's hand slid into mine; I jolted at the fissures of pleasure that shot up my arm at the feel of his rough, warm fingers entwined with mine.

He gave a slight shake of his head, his blue eyes startling in the light of the barroom and warning me not to make a scene, to just go along with the hand-holding. I responded with a subtle nod and he relaxed a little, leading me past the chairs and tables, ignoring the other patrons. The noise rose again as we approached the bar, and the burly barkeep came over to us, a wide grin appearing in among his massive ginger beard.

"Well, good evening. What can I get you?"

I relaxed at this warm welcome, such a jarring contrast to the streets outside.

Wolfe nodded congenially. "Good evening. We would like a room, if you have one available."

The barkeep's eyes lit up, I gathered at the thought of earning the extra money from renting a room. He looked me over before turning back to Wolfe with a wink. "Aye, I'd be wanting a room, too, if I were you."

I flushed despite being used to overhearing such talk among the Guard and servants back at the palace.

Wolfe squeezed my hand and shrugged at the barkeep. "My wife and I are tired—we've been traveling a while," he lied, and I knew it was for my sake and my sense of propriety, a sense that seemed a little redundant considering everything we'd just experienced. "I'd like a room and some food sent up. Also, we had a little mishap on the road. You wouldn't have some clean clothes we could purchase from you?"

"Not a problem, lad." He reached under the bar and brought up a key. "Room 2 is available." He pointed to stairs hidden in the shadows of the room. "Just up there. I'll have my wife bring you a dinner plate and some clothes."

"And some hot water," I interjected, desperate to wash at least some of the grime off my body.

"Of course. That'll be three and twenty."

I tried not to gape at the outrageous charge, knowing we were deliberately being ripped off. Did we really look that desperate? I noted Wolfe's irritation in the slight tensing of his jaw. However, Wolfe handed over the money and took the key, and he almost dragged me out of the barroom and upstairs.

"Are you trying to pull my arm out of the socket?" I snapped as we stepped onto the landing. Wolfe didn't acknowledge my comment until he'd hauled me inside Room 2 and slammed the door shut with the heel of his boot. He locked it.

"I was trying to get you out of the bar before I had to fight those bloody men over you."

My eyes widened as he strode toward the fire in the room and set about lighting it. The room was small with only a double bed (I noticed with a strange thump of my heart), but it was clean. "What are you talking about?"

Wolfe snorted. "These people have been left to live in squalor for too long. We should have known about this. Instead we sit on our plush cushions in Silvera, thinking the world outside happy and adoring and at peace. This isn't peace." He pointed outside the window as he glared at me. "Where have we been, Rogan? We've let our people come to this and we dare to look down our noses at them. Those men haven't seen anything as fine as you in a long time, and I was making bloody sure we were out of there as fast as possible before they took it upon themselves to have you."

"I didn't notice." I shook my head wearily, falling onto the bed. "I look a mess."

Wolfe sighed and looked away, provoking the fire to life. "Wearing rags, you would still carry yourself like a lady."

Ignoring the silly flutter in the pit of my belly, I tried to force our old dynamic and retorted stupidly, "I'm not a lady, Captain. I'm a farm girl."

Wolfe stood and strode toward me, his eyebrow arched. "You *are* a lady, Rogan. Even if you'd remained on your farm, it's just who you are."

I desperately wanted to say something droll to quell the sudden tension between us but his compliment flustered me. His strange behavior struck me mute, and I was grateful when our supplies arrived to divert our attention.

The barkeep's wife and two barmaids brought us food, clothing, and hot water, and then quickly departed, but not without the girls throwing come-hither looks at Wolfe. Dear haven, it was ridiculous how much female attention he garnered wherever we went. Ridiculous and irritating.

He didn't seem to notice and as soon as the door closed behind the women, he locked it again. Without so much as a glance in my direction, he picked up the dress they had brought and threw it at me. "Get cleaned up and dressed. There's a screen behind you."

I tried not to blush at the thought of stripping naked in the same room as Wolfe. Pretending the same indifference he seemed to feel about the situation, I strode, head held high, across the room and disappeared behind the changing screen.

"There must be some stationery in here," Wolfe muttered, and I heard him pulling at drawers and rummaging. At his sound of triumph, I was relieved to realize we would get word to the Guard. It had been a number of days since we'd been taken in Ryl, and I missed the comforting presence of Lieutenant Chaeron and the rest of the men.

A crash sounded from downstairs and I jumped, my dress falling to the floor. "What on Phaedra ...?"

Wolfe grunted as yells followed more crashing. "Tavern brawl."

A tavern brawl? My goodness, we were far away from home, weren't we.

The noise below made me tense, and I tried to concentrate on the sound of Wolfe's quill scratching against paper. If he didn't seem too concerned, then I gathered I shouldn't either.

My undergarments were in need of a wash, and I peeled them off with a sigh of relief. I'd just have to leave them here and make do with the rough blue dress the barkeep's wife had brought me. It would scratch my skin but I'd rather that than have to put dirty undergarments back on. I draped them over the top of the screen, vaguely aware that the scratching of quill against paper in the background had paused.

With the cloth and hot water the barkeep's wife had provided, I gave myself a quick scrub, trying to be fast so the water wouldn't be too cold when Wolfe used it. After a moment or so, I thought I heard Wolfe make a strangled sound and then the scratching of quill against paper resumed.

"Nearly done," I told him, thinking perhaps he was getting impatient. I drew on the blue dress, a demure, work-worn thing, but it was clean and not too rough against my skin. Without my undergarments I'd feel the cold, but perhaps I could get Wolfe to procure a cloak for me.

When I stepped out, Wolfe was staring at the screen as if in a daydream.

"You better hurry," I said, taking my undergarments off the screen and rolling them into a ball. "The water's getting cold."

He nodded, his lips pinched tightly. He brushed past me, barely sparing me a glance. I arched an eyebrow at his behavior but said nothing, having now given up on trying to understand anything about the man.

Speaking of which ...

I tucked into the food that had been left, my trembling stomach glad for it, and waited as Wolfe, once clean and changed into a rough-looking pair of trousers, shirt, and waistcoat, ate his meal. Then I couldn't stand it anymore. We were both sitting by the fire, enjoying the tranquility of the moment, and I couldn't stop myself from ruining it.

"So, you're a Glava?" I asked, even though there really was no question of it.

Wolfe stiffened. When he made no reply, I grew irritated.

"Why didn't you tell anyone?"

"I don't want to talk about," he dismissed, standing to take some coverings from the bed to make another bed on the floor.

"Seriously?" I stood. "You just destroyed an entire nomadic camp and *you* don't want to talk about it?"

"No, I don't."

"How can you expect me to trust you when you've lied about this?"

Wolfe snorted and finally glanced over at me. "You don't trust me anyway, Lady Rogan."

I ignored that, especially because it might be true, and snapped, "I demand to know, Captain Stovia."

"I don't give a rat's ass what you demand to know. I'm tired and I'm going to get some sleep. You should too."

But I wasn't quite ready to give up, and I did excel at pressing people's buttons. "The princezna will be so eager to hear that a mage was living in Silvera all this time and he didn't see fit to tell us."

This time I flinched at the force of Wolfe's severe look. "I would advise you to keep it to yourself, Rogan."

My hands flew to my hips in outraged defiance. "Are you threatening me?" Then the words were out before I could stop them. "Dear haven, you are just like your father!"

I'd never seen Wolfe move so fast. One moment he was on the other side of the room, the next he was inches from me. His eyes were white, his face mottled red with a rage I thought *I'd* only ever felt. "I'm *nothing* like my father!" he bellowed. "*Nothing*!"

I paled in terror, remembering the awesome power at his fingertips.

Wolfe blanched and cursed as he stumbled away from me, giving me his back.

Not knowing what to do, my heart pounding, my cheeks burning, I just stood there as he bedded down on the floor. The silence was so thick, so uneasy, I was shocked either of us could breathe beneath the weight of it.

"You better get some sleep." Wolfe broke the silence. He sounded defeated.

Guilt consumed me for I knew what I'd said had inflicted damage upon him.

I hurried over to the bed and slid under the sheet he'd left me.

"Here."

I looked down at the floor to see Wolfe holding a paper bag up to me.

"Thought you might want those back."

Frowning, curious, I reached over and took it. It contained the bracelets I'd bought for Haydyn and me.

"How did you ...?" Some emotion I couldn't identify constricted my throat.

"You dropped them in the alley. I picked them up before they drugged me. I thought they might be important to you."

A sharp ache bloomed in my chest and I stifled a noise of distress. Wolfe had been with me the entire time at the market. Why had he taken the time to rescue the cheap little bracelets that only meant something to me? I rolled over, fighting back tears, wishing that the man didn't cause me so much turmoil.

He was the last man in Phaedra I should ever trust, should ever feel anything toward.

But there was no denying my perception of Wolfe was changing.

CHAPTER 15

It was an understatement to say I was sore, cranky, and sleep deprived the next morning. My worries, and the man shifting restlessly on the floor all night, had kept me awake. Suffice it to say that come daylight, we shared little more than grunted responses to one another. Wolfe ordered breakfast to be brought to the room, still convinced I had the potential to cause trouble, and we shoveled down some horrible porridge as quickly as possible.

We then solicited the help of the jolly barkeep to retrieve a messenger for us. We had to wait in a dark corner of the nearly empty tavern looking anywhere but at each other.

Eventually, a tidy, well-put-together young man came in and spoke to the barkeep who in turn pointed in our direction. The young man turned out to be the best horseman in the rookery and made a nice income as a messenger. The barkeep swore we could trust him. Wolfe handed over the sealed letter and paid the messenger to deliver it to the Zansts' home in the Factory District in Ryl.

"Can we leave now?" I asked, not quite able to hide my impatience. The messenger had departed and yet we remained, Wolfe gazing across the barroom as if in a daydream.

He flinched at the sound of my voice as if it bothered him. A pang of something like hurt flared within me but I refused to recognize Wolfe was capable of eliciting such an emotion from me.

"Yes," he replied in a low, scratchy voice, and I took some satisfaction in the fact that he hadn't slept either. "Let's go." He grabbed me by the elbow and pulled me to my feet.

"You don't need to manhandle me," I hissed as we waved goodbye to the barkeep.

"I need to keep you close in order to protect you." His grip loosened and moved down my arm until he slid his fingers through mine to hold my hand.

A shiver tingled down my nape. Trying not to focus too much on the heat from his touch—or the not-unpleasant sensation of it—I quipped, "I would have thought you'd be happy to see something happen to me."

"I'd be happy if you suddenly lost the will to speak."

I slid him a dark look, which he ignored as he led us across the backyard to the stables. There was nothing and no one in sight.

Including our horse.

"What the ..." Wolfe released me as he peered into the empty stables. I walked away from him, checking around the back of the building. It was empty too.

I drew in a breath. How on earth were we going to make it back to Ryl without a horse?

A muffled thud sounded from over my shoulder.

"Wolfe—" I spun around only to find him crumpled on the ground, unconscious, a trickle of blood sliding down his temple.

Wolfe!

Standing over him were three of the dirtiest thugs I had ever seen, each holding a weapon. The tallest leered at me and his yellow teeth flashed as he bounced a mallet off the heel of his palm. The second tallest was an older man, not quite as grubby, his hand-me-down, unwashed clothing that of a gentleman's. His large hand sat on the hilt of a sword. The third appeared to be the youngest and as he kept jabbing the air with a dagger, I thought perhaps he might be a little deranged. He had a wild look in his eyes that sent a shiver of foreboding down my spine.

I wanted to tend to Wolfe, amazed that these ignorant thugs had crept up on us. Wolfe would never live it down if his men found out how easily he had been felled ... again. The fact that I was the common denominator in his failures had not escaped me.

A sound from the thugs drew my attention back to them. "What do you want?" I was proud how brave I sounded, considering my fear.

The man with the mallet quirked an eyebrow. "My, my, we are a haughty wee thing, aren't we?"

Wolfe chose that moment to groan and my heart skipped a beat in relief.

"Aw shit, Jesper," the older man spat, "we need to get them back to Boss before this 'un wakes up."

"You two pick him up." Jesper gestured to Wolfe, his eyes on me. "I'll take care of her."

Oh, dear haven, what the hell had Wolfe and I gotten ourselves into now?

I wanted to collapse and shriek and weep with exhaustion and fury. Didn't these people know my friend was dying? That if I didn't save her, then we were all doomed? That I would be doomed? I couldn't possibly live in a world without Haydyn.

How dare they endanger her!

Just like that, something within me snapped.

As Jesper reached for me, I kicked up between his legs as hard as I could. He let out a bellow of pain and dropped to his knees. Before any of the others could make a move, I slammed my booted foot into the hand that held the mallet, and Jesper cried out as the weapon tumbled from his grip.

"Get her!" he snarled, clutching his hand to his chest.

I dove for the weapon and came up brandishing it as the two thugs crept toward me, the light of violence in their eyes.

"I'll cut you up you, little bitch, if you don't play nice," the young one hissed, swiping the air with the dagger.

"She's not to be injured!" Jesper shouted as he regained his footing.

"I won't harm her, Jes-Jes," the young thug singsonged. "No, she'll like what I do to her, won't you, pretty-pretty?"

Revulsion filled me at the idea of this insane miscreant touching me.

He didn't know who he was trifling with.

I had a job to do.

I had to get to Alvernia, and no other son of a bitch would get in my way!

Conjuring all my strength, I pulled my elbow back and launched the mallet with all my worth at the young thug's head. It made perfect aim, clocking him across his skull with a sickening thud. His eyes slammed shut and he fell back with a dull sound, sprawled spread-eagle across the cobbles.

The older of the thugs stared at his downed colleague in shock while Jesper cursed. "For goodness' sake, lass." He shook his head in disbelief and then glared at me. "Now you've downed Little Sin. We'll have to come back for him. You won't get me or Dandy here, all right. We ain't gonna hurt you, am under orders from Boss not to. So, Dandy here is going to take you, and I'm going to take the boy here, all right? Now, if you don't make a fuss, I won't slit the boy's throat."

"What do you want?" I whispered, wishing Wolfe would wake up.

"That's up to Boss to tell you, lass."

I had no choice but to walk with Dandy as Jesper carried Wolfe over his shoulder, an impressive feat considering how large the captain was. He grunted and groaned about Wolfe's weight the entire time we walked. My outrage grew as we strode through the dank streets of the rookery and people ignored my pleading looks as we passed. They flinched away from my silent pleas, their eyes washing over my companions in fear before they turned away as quickly as possible, pretending they hadn't seen a thing. I knew then that I was in the hands of one of the rookery gangs. Someone back at the tavern must have sold us out. Wolfe had been right all along. We spoke too well, held ourselves like a lady and a gentleman. I could only imagine we were being kidnapped for possible ransom.

Again.

Jesper and Dandy slowed as we approached a substantial, crumbling building, the glass panes of its windows broken and cracked, the wide double doors covered in splashed paint. Jesper banged on the door three times and it swung open. A young man with a knife in each hand stood back to let us in.

"Got 'em then, Jesper?"

Jesper laughed and swatted Wolfe's bottom. "Looks like it, don't it."

The boy eyed me as Dandy pushed me inside. I stared around the open space with its large ovens and broken glass, with the grains of sand littering the floor. I guessed we were in a disused glassworks. At the back of the space was a wall, the upper half blocked in with glass that was cracked and shattered in some areas. A doorway led into darker places beyond. There were pieces of old furniture here and there, perhaps a dismal attempt to make the place look cozy.

I froze, taking in the flickering candlelight and the gang of men and women who lounged around the room, their beady eyes watching me. They were like a plague of rats.

"Take 'em through the back to Boss's room, 'e said." The boy jerked his head toward the rear of the building.

"He in?"

"Nah. Won't be long, 'e said."

Jesper grunted and shifted Wolfe up on his shoulder. I stayed close as we walked through the space, Jesper calling greetings to gang members. I felt a tug on my skirts and turned to see a young, haggard-looking woman clutching at me. She sat sprawled over an old chair, and I yanked out of her hold as she licked her lips. "Jesper, ask Boss if I can have this one." She grinned up at the man before turning that wicked smile on me. I blushed in understanding, which made her laugh.

Jesper clamped his hand down on my arm.

"She's for Boss, Nalia. Don't get any ideas."

Nalia's lips twisted into a pout. "But I wants her. She's pretty, like silk. You knows how I likes silk, Jesper."

Jesper grunted and pushed me forward before I could dare the little witch to touch me at her peril. We were silent as we walked through steel-gray hallways, until Jesper came to a halt and thrust his foot against a door, shoving it open. The space beyond resembled what could pass for a normal room in this hovel. A brass-framed bed sat in the corner covered with colorful quilts and cushions. A fireplace had a tin bathtub in front of it, a cozy armchair sat off to the side, and knickknacks rested on the mantelpiece. Well-made furniture was placed just so around the room with men's clothing haphazardly draped here and there.

And the bedroom was clean. Surprisingly so.

"Boss's room," Jesper grunted, and then dropped Wolfe on the stone floor as if he were nothing more than a sack of potatoes. I cried out and rushed for the captain just as his eyes began to open. "Shit!" Jesper sighed and reached across the bed for something. In the next moments, I watched helplessly as he tied Wolfe's wrists to the bottom spindles of the heavy bed frame.

"You're next." Jesper strode toward me and I tried to kick out at him again. He dodged and clucked his tongue at me. "Not that again, you wee bitch."

He lunged, trying to wrench my arms behind my back, but I shrieked and punched and pummeled at him, vaguely aware of Wolfe shouting and struggling from his prison on the floor. Then Jesper's huge hand came toward me and he hit my face with an almighty blow. My head snapped back and my legs gave way. I was barely aware of Jesper tying my hands behind my back and throwing me onto the bed. Water streamed out of my right eye and I hesitantly lifted my throbbing cheek, wincing at the blazing heat that scored down my face.

"Stay here and behave!" Jesper cried. "Boss will be in soon."

I struggled into a sitting position as the man slammed the door and turned the key in the lock.

Feeling eyes on me, I looked down at Wolfe.

"Are you all right?" he asked hoarsely, his gaze on my cheek, his jaw clenched so tight, I thought it might shatter.

I huffed and shimmied toward him, trying to get a look at the cut on his head. "Am I all right? Wolfe, they knocked you unconscious." I hissed at the bloody sight of his wound. "We need to get that cleaned up. Are you feeling well?"

He winced, stretching his legs out before him as he pulled at the ropes. It was futile. He slumped wearily. "I feel a little dizzy."

"You were out awhile."

"Noted. Where are we?" He glanced around the room.

I sighed. "We're in an abandoned glassworks. We've been taken by what I assume is a rookery gang."

Something forbidding burned in his blue eyes. "Did any of them touch you?"

I grinned, thinking about Little Sin. "I knocked out the one who tried."

Wolfe quirked an eyebrow. "Knocked out?"

I quickly told him how I had incapacitated Jesper and then launched the mallet at Little Sin. Wolfe shook his head in amazement. "Perhaps I *should* let the men train you."

Surprised, I grinned. "I told you so."

He rolled his eyes. "So humble."

"Pot, meet kettle."

Wolfe tugged at the ropes again. "We need to get out of here, Rogan."

Ignoring the ripple of sensation that tickled down my spine every time he said my name, I stumbled onto the floor and tried to maneuver myself in front of him.

"What are you doing?" I could hear the amusement in his voice.

"I thought you could use your teeth to get the ropes off my wrists," I explained over my shoulder, thrusting my arms backward at him.

"Rogan, please tell me you're kidding. Have you seen how thick this rope is?"

"Well, how else are we—"

I hushed at the sound of a key turning in the lock. Wolfe brought a leg up, pulling me back into him so I was sitting between his legs. I realized it was an attempt to shield me from whatever was coming. I felt his indrawn breath on the back of my neck.

We waited, hearts racing, and the door swung open. At first, I couldn't make out anything except the silhouette of a tall man. And then he strode inside, slowly, leisurely ... and I let go a yelp of surprise.

I recognized those green eyes and that jet-black hair, that defiant smirk. He was taller, older, and his face was harder now, but it was no less handsome than it had been when we were young.

"Kir!" I gasped.

The smirk on his face fell as he came to an abrupt halt. "Rogan? Wolfe?"

"Kir!" I laughed a little hysterically, relief flooding through me.

"Holy mother of—" He dropped to his knees and grasped my shoulders, his eyes wide with shock. "I can't believe it's you."

"Well, it is," Wolfe grunted from behind me. "Fancy untying us?"

Stunned, he sank back onto his heels, taking a moment.

It was then realization struck.

"You're Boss?" I asked, trying to keep the condemnation out of my question.

Kir must have heard the accusation anyway, for he winced regretfully. "Yeah," he admitted. "I'm Boss."

Wolfe peered over my shoulder, and I tensed with awareness of his proximity. "So, any intention of letting us go, then?"

The men shared a long look. "I can't believe it's you. How are you?"

I was surprised by how congenial the two were, considering Wolfe's father was Syracen and the fact that Kir had had to live with the bastard for a year. There seemed to be a depth of meaning in his query that I didn't understand.

Wolfe nodded. "I'm all right, Kir. Except for being kidnapped, that is."

Seeming to shake himself, Kir gestured to me. "Turn, Rogan. Let me get those off you."

I shimmied out from Wolfe's embrace and managed to twist, holding my hands out behind me.

"I'm going to use a blade, so keep still."

As soon as I was loose, Kir freed Wolfe. He eyed the top of Wolfe's head and frowned. "I told them not to do any damage. Mind you"—his gaze flickered over Wolfe as he slapped him on the back—"considering how big you've gotten, they probably had no choice."

Wolfe grunted and stumbled to his feet, rubbing his wrists. "Not that it isn't good to see you, Kir ... why the hell did you have us kidnapped?"

I rose to my feet, watching the two men as they faced one another. There was no tension or animosity between them. In fact, they both appeared happy to see each other. I was growing steadily more confused by the second.

Kir sighed. "I didn't know it was you. I got word that a fancy gent and lady were here and I knew the markiz would be interested."

I gaped, feeling disoriented and lost. "The markiz?"

Kir nodded grimly. "Things have been changing in Vasterya for a while now, Rogan."

Wolfe frowned. "Changing how?"

Gesturing to the bed for us to sit, Kir slumped down into the armchair opposite. As I took a seat beside Wolfe on the bed, I noted how much older Kir appeared than Wolfe, despite them being the same age. It would seem life had treated my old friend with more unkindness, or at least difficulty, after his escape from Syracen.

"Who do you think set up the rookery, Wolfe?"

Wolfe sucked in a breath. "Markiz Solom."

"What?" I squeaked, any color in my cheeks surely having leached out now. What on haven were they talking about? Why would the markiz create the rookery?

"The markiz cottoned on to the fact that the princezna's powers were weakening in Vasterya. Suddenly, all these ideas and feelings he had buried inside himself were bursting forth, being allowed free rein. Markiz began making plans."

"What kind of plans?" Wolfe asked.

"I was working for him, he found a Glava useful, and he paid me well. When things began to change, he put his plan to take over the sovereignty into action."

My stomach plummeted. "Take over the sovereignty? Is he insane?"

"Yes." Kir nodded. "Quite possibly. He's training an army. He paid me to create the rookery, hoping a gangland at the border of the city would deter outsiders from visiting and then carrying tales of the markiz back to Silvera. So far, it's worked."

Wolfe was frowning. "I sent men in only a few weeks ago. There was no mention of an army."

"No, there wouldn't have been. The army is trained out in the west near the sand dunes. And the people of Pharya are almost religious in their belief in the markiz and would never betray him. Without the Dyzvati power, these people are easily brainwashed, especially with food and money." He snorted and gestured around him. "Even I've been brought low by it."

I narrowed my eyes, understanding his role in this. "You

would have let him do this? Bring an army into Silvera? Betray Haydyn?"

My old friend remained expressionless as he replied in a flat voice, "I suspected Haydyn was unwell and that it was being dealt with. I expected this madness to be over soon and that I would return to working for the markiz who would remain a markiz, not a kral."

Remembering the boy who had fought so savagely against Syracen when he hurt me, who had taken a lashing unlike anything I had ever seen, I wanted to believe him. But there was a hollow darkness in Kir's eyes that hadn't been there those many years ago.

Wolfe cleared his throat, breaking the strained look Kir and I shared. "So what were you planning on doing with us?"

"Making sure you weren't spies. I thought the markiz would pay good money for you. And he certainly would pay good money to get his hands on the captain of the Royal Guard and the Handmaiden of Phaedra." Kir shook his head, grinning wryly. "But he won't find out about you. I would never let any harm come to either of you."

I exhaled sharply, my relief palpable. "Thank you, Kir."

He threw me a boyish smile, one so genuine we could have been children again, planning new ways to harass Syracen, consequences be damned. He looked me over, and his gaze sharpened. "Rogan, sweetheart, look how well you turned out."

Wolfe stiffened beside me while I laughed off Kir's roguishness. He'd been a terrible flirt even as a boy. In fact, he'd once kissed me on the cheek when he'd accompanied Syracen on a visit to the palace. Kir had gotten away from him and come to find me. I think I'd been hiding out in the gardens, terrified to be in the same building as Stovia. Sensing my unease, Kir had teased me into playing a game of tag. A few games in and we heard Syracen bellowing for Kir from the bottom of the gardens. Kir's eyes had hardened but when he saw me watching, he'd turned his bright smile on me and swooped down, planting a kiss on my rosy cheek, promising he'd return for me.

"You haven't changed a bit."

His expression told me he disagreed before he turned to Wolfe. "What about you, Wolfe? How is life treating you these days? Got a wife yet?"

Wolfe grunted.

Kir chuckled at the captain's monosyllabic response. "Well, you look like you both could do with a bath and some food."

Haydyn's face swam across my vision. "Actually, Kir, we really need to leave."

"Where are you traveling to?"

I wasn't sure we should share that information with Kir, and apparently Wolfe agreed when he lied. "Ryl."

Wolfe didn't quite trust Kir either. I felt a pang of guilt that I shoved away. Nothing and no one could get in our way of saving Haydyn. Not even an old friend.

Kir nodded. "Well, you'll need horses, which I can supply, but I need time to acquire them. I have a lot of explaining to do to the gang, and well ... you both look like you could do with some freshening up. Let me have the bath filled, and Wolfe, you need to take care of that wound."

I opened my mouth to argue but Kir shook his head. "It'll take me time to get the horses, so you may as well bathe and rest here in the meantime."

Kir had men fill the bathtub with hot water, and I left the room with Kir while Wolfe bathed. He took me to another room down the hallway, away from the gang members. It, too, was kept quite clean—a couple of armchairs, painted theatre posters on the chipped walls. I sat down, confused by the strange mix of alien and familiar in being with Kir. I smiled in thanks as he handed me a glass of water, which I greedily drank.

My eyelashes fluttered when Kir touched my face, but he was just tipping my cheek to the side for a better look. His green eyes darkened to the color of the forest at night.

"Who did that?" he bit out.

Not really caring if I got Jesper in trouble, I told him. Kir cursed profusely yet his fingers were gentle on my skin as he stroked my cheek.

"I'll kill him for that."

I pulled away when his gaze dipped to my mouth. "Please don't."

He quirked an eyebrow, retreating. "You don't want me to punish him for beating you?"

"I think I punished him enough."

Kir laughed. "I forgot how bloodthirsty you can be. What did you do to him?"

I told him, and Kir laughed harder.

Wiping tears from his eyes, he sighed, his expression soft with nostalgia. "I have missed you, little Rogan."

Smiling sadly, I shrugged. "It's been a long time, Kir."

"It has," he agreed. "But we went through a lifetime together in only a year."

As we both remembered, a chilly silence fell over the room. I flinched, still hearing his screams as the captain of the Guard lashed him over and over again with the horsewhip.

"Do you dream about it?" he asked so quietly, I almost didn't hear him.

My teeth clenched tightly as I gave him an imperceptible nod.

His rough hand clasped mine. "No one understands, Rogan. How could they? No one understands but you."

I nodded, feeling as if the last eight years were melting away and I was huddled in Kir's arms as we cried together by a campfire. In Silvera we saw one another once or twice a month, but I remembered how empty I felt when I heard he had run away, like some of kind of bond between us had snapped. "You left me," I whispered.

His features hardened as if he were in pain, and he grasped my hand tighter. "I had to get away, Rogan, please understand."

"I do," I replied. "I do."

"You could stay. Here. With me."

Shocked, I could only stare at him.

His lips quirked up at the corner. "It's not such a strange request. We were close once. We loved one another as children."

Tears stung my eyes because what he said was true. We had clung to one another with a fierceness born of our grief, and we'd tried to protect each other. "I can't stay, Kir. Haydyn needs my help. I can't stay."

"She *is* ill, then?"

Biting my lip, I gripped his hand tighter, pleading with my eyes. "Please don't tell anyone."

His eyes widened and he cupped my cheek. "I would never do anything to hurt you."

I believed him.

But ...

"What about Wolfe?"

Kir frowned. "What about Wolfe?"

"You seem surprisingly friendly with him considering you had to live with his family for a year."

As I studied him, his eyes narrowed. "I have no problem with Wolfe. He was a good lad when we were young. As much a victim as any of us."

I struggled to breathe evenly. My heart thudded hard. How could Kir ... what did Kir know that I didn't? How could Kir forgive when I couldn't? "What do you mean?" I was desperate to know. I needed to know.

He leaned in close, his expression quizzical. "Why do you care?"

"I—" I had no answer for him. And even if I did, I would have been distracted by the heat that sparked to life in his eyes just as his mouth descended toward mine. Kir was going to kiss me!

Was I going to let him?

"Boss."

Kir pulled back, muttering curses under his breath. He whipped around.

Jesper stood in the doorway, grinning at us. "The Hawks want to talk to you, Boss."

"The Hawks?" I queried, confusion wrinkling my brow.

Kir smiled and pulled me to my feet. "My gang are called the Hawks."

I threw him a sardonic look. "Why? Because you always catch your prey?"

He grinned wickedly. "Always, beautiful Rogan. Always."

I rolled my eyes at him and he laughed, and by the way Jesper's mouth fell open in surprise, I was guessing it wasn't something Kir did often.

"I'm sure Wolfe will be finished with the tub. Why don't you go along and check and I'll be back soon with some food?"

We strolled down the hall together, and when he and Jesper disappeared around a corner, I was so in a stew about what had almost happened between us, I forgot to knock.

"Oh," I gasped as Wolfe stood before me shirtless, droplets of bath water falling from the strands of hair at the nape of his neck to his shoulders, running in tantalizing rivulets across his muscled abdomen.

He was beautiful.

My gaze followed the trickle like a magpie following a diamond ... and then I gasped again at the raised scar on his lower stomach. "What ..." I trailed off as Wolfe wrenched a shirt over his head, covering what I had just seen.

Wolfe had been branded.

A dark horseshoe burn scar branded his lower stomach.

Who would do such a thing?

"Wolfe—"

The door burst open, slamming into my back. I stumbled forward.

"Oh, Rogan, I'm sorry." Kir righted me as he came in, patting my shoulder in apology. "It's just—we have a problem."

"What kind of problem?" Wolfe refused to look at me.

"I'm about to have a bloody mutiny on my hands if I don't hand you over to Solom."

I paled, instinctively wanting to edge closer to Wolfe. Reminding myself I was an independent woman, I stiffened my spine in resolve. "So what do we do?"

Kir's stare pinned Wolfe to the wall. "I'm sorry, Brother, but I had to."

Panic made my heart race. "Had to what? What's going on?"

"Does she know? About your ...?"

Wolfe nodded stiffly.

Kir relaxed. "I know you tried to keep it hidden, but it was the only thing I could barter with."

"I understand."

My head swiveled between them. "Understand what?" I snapped in burning frustration.

Finally, Kir turned to me. "I told them about Wolfe being a mage."

I gasped. "You knew?" Suddenly, I felt hopelessly betrayed. What was it that these two men shared? Why was Kir so amiable to Wolfe? Why couldn't he have told me he and Wolfe were friendly? Why was I the only one who didn't really know Wolfe?

And why on earth did it bother me so much?

Kir nodded. "Yes, I know. I managed to convince the Hawks that we could sell Wolfe to Solom."

"No!" I yelled, outraged at the idea. "Over my dead body! No!"

The two of them raised their eyebrows at me and grinned.

What on haven were they grinning about?

Then it dawned on me.

I flushed in mortification. "You're not really going to sell him, are you?"

Kir huffed in indignation. "Of course not. I'm going to let them think I am. They're sending a messenger to Pharya to have someone come and collect Wolfe. That someone should be here in a few days. For now, I want you to rest up for the night, have some food. And then tomorrow when I come to get you, we're going to pretend Wolfe blasted me with his powers and you escaped, when really I'll be letting you out the back door where I'll have a couple of horses waiting."

I impulsively threw my arms around him, drawing him in for a hug. Kir laughed and held me tight against him. "Thank you," I whispered.

"Worth it just for the hug."

LATER, AFTER I'D BATHED AND BOTH WOLFE AND I WERE FED, Kir apologized before leaving and locking us in the bedroom. Wolfe had claimed the armchair, so I lay down on the bed, thinking about Kir, about Wolfe, and about the horseshoe brand marring Wolfe's body.

"I was surprised at your vehement refusal to let Kir sell me to the markiz," Wolfe remarked. "I thought you wanted me dead."

"I thought you wanted *me* dead," I replied honestly, turning to look at him. His handsome face was a mask of complete shock.

Shock that soon gave way to fury.

"What do you mean, you thought I wanted you dead?"

Was he really so surprised I'd think that?

I'd had his father killed.

I was so weary of a sudden. I didn't want to be locked in a room with a man I realized I didn't know at all. I wanted wildflowers and summers by the stream. I wanted tobacco in the air and lemonade on the tongue.

Why would Kir protect Wolfe? Why would Wolfe protect me?

Fighting tears, I turned my back to him. "Never mind," I

finally answered. “I’m just starting to realize I don’t know you at all.”

“Yes, you do,” came his hoarse response. “You just hate that I’m not what you need me to be.”

Trying desperately to ignore that enigmatic comment, I slammed my eyes shut ... and dreamed of my little brother’s laughter.

CHAPTER 16

The mattress on Kir's bed was lumpy and uncomfortable so I tried to blame my lack of sleep on it and not on my hyperawareness of Wolfe.

I kept seeing that brand on his stomach, the pain in his eyes when he caught me looking at it, the secrets and friendship I knew he shared with Kir. There was something I was missing.

I'd assumed that because *I'd* wanted revenge on the man who destroyed my family that Wolfe would want it too. But maybe Wolfe wasn't built like me. Maybe I was wrong and Haydyn had been right all along.

My guilt was compounded by Wolfe's tossing and turning. The need to offer him comfort came over me, and I curled my hands into fists to stop myself reaching for him. When at last his breathing evened out, the tension drained from my weary body and I relaxed into the mattress beneath me. With his fall into slumber, I finally found my own.

TOO QUICKLY, I WAS AWOKEN BY SOMEONE SHAKING MY shoulder. Forgetting where I was, I assumed in my semiconscious state that Haydyn had come into my bedroom with some delicious secret. Last time she'd awoken me this early, it was to tell me she'd lost her virginity to Matai.

"What now?" I mumbled. "You with child?"

"What? Rogan, wake up," an irritated voice snapped.

Wolfe.

I shot up on the bed and cracked my head off his. "Ow." I winced. Wolfe's face hovered inches before mine, his pale-blue eyes narrowed in pain. He rubbed his forehead, already swollen in the upper corner from the blow he'd taken yesterday.

"It's like waking the dead," he grouched as he retreated across the room.

I rubbed my cheek sleepily and then cried out at the pain that shot up my face. "Wow, that hurts," I whimpered and watched warily as Wolfe's face turned black as a thundercloud.

"If I see him again, I'm going to kill him."

No need to ask who he was talking about. "Does it look awful?"

Wolfe walked over to me and lowered to his haunches so we were at eye level. The air whooshed out of my body as he reached up to touch my bruised cheek, his features etched with concern and some other emotion I couldn't quite decipher. I had the urge to buss into his touch like Haydyn's cat, Z, when one of Cook's cakes was in the vicinity.

A hot rush of tingles exploded across the top of my skin as our eyes connected. My stomach flipped. I couldn't breathe.

Clearing my throat, I pushed his hand away and stood, brushing past him with such force I almost knocked him on his ass. There was a mirror above the fireplace, dirty and broken, but it had enough of a reflection to show the red-and-purple swelling on my right cheek. Beautiful.

I sighed and caught Wolfe's eyes in the reflection. "Is it almost time?"

He nodded, frowning. A strange tension sprung up between us. If I were honest with myself, it had been there since we'd been taken by the Iavii. For someone who had spent the last decade quarreling with Wolfe, I had never once been this ill at ease around him. I didn't like it. Not one bit. I was so afraid of what it meant, so afraid of disappointing my family's memory.

The key turned in the door lock and Kir was there, smiling and befuddling me even more.

"You ready?" he asked, shutting the door and striding in, every inch the confident rookery gang leader.

I didn't look at Wolfe. "Yes."

"Great—" Kir cursed under his breath as he reached me, his hand cupping my chin. "That looks bad this morning."

Feeling Wolfe's burning stare, I tipped my chin out of Kir's hold. "I've had worse."

"I remember."

Not in the mood to take a trip down nightmare lane with him, I put my hands on my hips, trying to exude the strength I wasn't feeling. "All right, so now what?"

"Now you make your escape. Remember"—his eyes moved between us—"to get out, you take a left, a right, and the back door is at the end of the hall. I left it unlocked." He stared at Wolfe. "When you attack me, you have to make it look real."

Wolfe's expression grew taut.

Kir sighed. "I mean it, Wolfe."

"Is it really necessary?" the captain asked.

Kir pulled back his shoulders. "Yes."

Wolfe frowned.

A dark mischief entered Kir's eyes. "Fine. Then I guess I'll just have to make you want to."

Abruptly he caught me around the waist and I squawked in undignified surprise. I pushed against his hard chest as he crushed me to him, his other hand winding into my hair to bring my lips against his in a hard kiss. The hand on my waist slid down my back and squeezed my bottom.

Fury flushed through me, and I was just about to knee him like I'd kneed Vrik when his body was wrenched from mine. I watched as Kir soared across the room and straight through the door. That's right. Straight *through* the door.

I gaped. Kir collapsed around the wooden splinters of the door in the hall and then groaned as he drew himself into a sitting position.

"Come on."

I blinked down at the large, familiar hand wrapped around my wrist and then up at its owner. An extremely angry Wolfe.

He led me out through the fragments of the doorway, into the hall, and then pushed me behind him as furious yelling filled the hallway. Jesper hurried toward us with Nalia at his back. Wolfe stared them down in concentration. I felt the heat of his energy blast into me as he threw the two thugs back up the hallway with the force of his thoughts. They crashed against the back wall and crumpled in an unconscious heap on the floor.

Hearing Kir groan, I turned and gasped as he clasped his hand over the wound on his arm.

"Are you all right?" I made to rush toward him but Wolfe tried to pull me in the opposite direction. "Hey!"

"I'm fine, Rogan," Kir assured me, wincing as he pushed a large chunk of door off him. "Go. Just go."

We shared a long look as Wolfe continued to haul me up the narrow corridor, and just as we turned left, I mouthed "thank you," unexpected tears threatening to spill over. He gave me a small smile and a nod just before I lost sight of him.

"You can move things with your mind," I hissed at Wolfe as we hurried along the next hall.

"Be quiet, Rogan."

I raised my eyebrow at his tone. I could either argue with him or get out of there. Mind made up, I yanked my arm free and picked up my skirts. As I ran, Wolfe ran with me, and we burst out through the back door.

Only to be confronted by two of Kir's thugs.

They stood in the courtyard, smoking tobacco and staring in

confusion at the two horses tethered to a drainpipe on the next building.

Shocked to see us, they dropped the paper tubes containing the tobaçco to the sodden wet ground. Without a word, Wolfe flicked his hand and sent the two men soaring. At the sounds of flesh hitting brick, I decided now was probably not the time to question Wolfe about his abilities.

Instead we moved in tandem, hurrying to untie the horses Kir had procured for us. We hurried into the streets of the rookery, the horses' hooves echoing loudly against the buildings. Amazingly, the horses worked against the slickness of the cobbles with more proficiency than I would have expected, and soon we were out of the rookery, past the glassworks, and into the green land of the Vasterya I remembered.

As we galloped down the muddy trade road, past farm country, Wolfe slowed a little until my horse was abreast his.

"Rogan." He licked rain from his upper lip, seeming afraid to meet my eye. "We need to get somewhere safe. I know you don't want me to use your magic ..."

Understanding he wanted permission to utilize my magic to find a safe place to stop, I decided it was the perfect opportunity to pry some answers out of him. "If I let you ... will you tell me everything?"

He scowled at me, his eyes a piercing blue against the dullness of the gray sky. "What do you mean?"

"You!" I gestured to him in anger. "Tell me why you hid whatever magic you have. I want to know about you and Kir. I want to know about the horseshoe brand."

"That's none of your business, Rogan!" Wolfe yelled to be heard over the pounding rain and the cantering horses. Uneasiness strained his features.

It *was* none of my business. But not knowing was driving me mad with curiosity, and I needed to remain focused on Haydyn. This distraction had to be dealt with. "I'm making it my business."

"If we don't find a safe place to stay, that's on you."

"No." I shook my head. "That's on you. What's so important you can't trade for this?"

"It's private, Rogan. My personal business. There is no reason for you to know it."

"Yes, there is."

"What reason could there be?"

I couldn't meet his eyes. Nervous butterflies agitated my stomach, all the while guilt pricked me. I saw my brother's face in my mind and clenched my teeth. Finally, I met Wolfe's curious, frustrated gaze. "I don't know why."

He searched my face ... and then. "Fine."

"You'll trade?" I was shocked by his sudden capitulation.

"I'll trade."

"Then ask away."

"Rogan, I need you to find us someplace safe to stay via a secure route."

My magic washed through me in a warm, tingling wave, and I was almost sorry when it was over and my skin turned cold again in the downpour.

I sensed the pull of the little farm over the border into Daeronia. I grinned wearily. "Follow me."

CHAPTER 17

It took us a few days but we crossed the border into Daeronia with little problem (except hunger and exhaustion), and soon our olfactory senses were bombarded by the sweet, yeasty smell of the large brewery to the west as we headed toward Caera.

Caera was another half-day ride onward, so I led us off the main trade road and into fields toward a tiny farm owned by an elderly widow I'd sensed through my magic.

The widow was lively and peppered us with questions about who we were and what our business was. Since my magic led me to her, Wolfe thought it safe to tell her he was one of the Guard and that we'd gotten into some trouble at the rookery in Vasterya.

"Oh, I heard about all that mischief at the border." She nodded, leading us past her little sitting room and into a spacious farm kitchen. The smell of home-cooked stew caused my stomach to rumble; I clutched it in embarrassment. The widow threw me a sympathetic smile and gestured to the table for us to sit. "Sounds like the two of you were lucky to get away."

"Yes, ma'am, we were," Wolfe agreed. "We really appreciate your hospitality."

"No thanks needed." She bustled about, ladling huge amounts of stew into bowls. I felt the saliva building up under my tongue. "I ain't got much room in the house, I'm afraid, but I got a barn outside with a nice, warm hayloft. I got some blankets you can take up there. That should keep you cozy for the night."

Even though I didn't fancy a night in a barn, I was grateful for her kindness. "That sounds perfect." I smiled gratefully as she put a bowl of stew and a cup of ale before me. I shared a happy look with Wolfe and we broke bread, scooping the stew as if we hadn't had a decent meal in ages. And to be honest, we hadn't. The old widow was almost as good a cook as Cook.

"This is delicious," I said between mouthfuls.

She smiled cheerily, watching us scoff it down, seeming happy to have someone to feed.

Once our bellies were full, we sat with her awhile, engaging her in conversation about herself. Finally, seeing her eyelids droop, I suggested we get some sleep. After handing over some blankets and an oil lamp, the widow drowsily wished us a good night and turned to ascend the stairs to her bed.

Wolfe and I strolled outside to the barn. It wasn't huge, and when we climbed up into the hayloft, we shared a wary look. It was certainly cozy. I flushed at the thought of being in such close quarters with him.

We spread the blankets and then tentatively sat down next to one another. I could feel the heat from his skin inches from mine, the scent of him tickling my senses.

After a while, I couldn't take the silence. "So, you're quite a powerful Glava?"

Wolfe tensed. I wondered if he was going to go back on his word and not tell me all I wanted to know.

"Well?"

He exhaled. I almost felt bad for pressing him about it.

But not badly enough to stop.

"Wolfe?" I placed a hand on his arm.

He looked down at it, his eyebrows raised in surprise. When

he lifted his eyes to meet mine, I flushed at the intensity I found there.

I jerked my hand away, breaking the connection.

"I hid it," he offered.

"But why?"

He shrugged, staring off into the dark rafters, his jaw taut with suppressed emotion. "Because ... because I was afraid the magic would mean I was like my father."

The vulnerable honesty in his answer hit me with an impact I had not expected. It was as though he'd reached out to take me by the shoulders to shake me from a dream.

A sick feeling swam in my gut.

Guilt.

How could I have been so wrong?

"Kir ... Kir said you were as much a victim as we were. What did he mean?"

Wolfe's eyes slanted toward me, dark pain and fury fencing in his gaze. I knew he didn't want to tell me, that I was using his sense of honor against him. If I were a better person, I would have allowed him to keep his secrets. However, my selfish need to discover the real Wolfe held my good conscience hostage.

"My father ..." His voice cracked. "He didn't treat me and my mother very well. As you know, he was a cruel man."

"What did he do to you?"

"Mostly manipulative mind games played to make us feel inferior, subordinate. But when Haydyn's father died ... well the situation worsened. Not just for everyone else, but for my mother and I as well."

Shock robbed me of my voice. In truth, I wasn't sure I wanted to know what Syracen had done to Wolfe. It was one thing for a man to abuse strangers, but to hurt his own flesh and blood ...

"He, uh ... he horsewhipped my mother. Many times over the years."

Bile rose in my throat as I remembered the agony Kir endured when I witnessed it happening to him.

To do that to your own wife. My goodness.

"And that scar ... the horseshoe?"

A bitter, twisted little chuckle escaped Wolfe, and he shook his head. "I made the mistake of attacking my father a time he took the whip to my mother. Kir helped me because my mother was kind to him. My father beat Kir ... but me ... he took a hot horseshoe and branded me with it. He told me I was his son, not hers. Like horseflesh, I belonged solely to him and as such, he expected me to obey him as my master."

I couldn't comprehend what he was confiding. My chest flared with sharp, needling pain. Hot tears stung my eyes and I couldn't speak. My throat closed with the enormity of emotions I felt for him. Including my remorse. All these years I had been horrible to him, painting him with the same brush as I'd painted his father. I had been so sure he would want to hurt me for what I did to Syracen.

"I got my revenge, though. I helped Kir escape," Wolfe continued.

So that explained their camaraderie.

Kir knew Wolfe better than I.

Why did that bother me so much? I wrapped my arms across my stomach.

Wolfe must loathe me for the way I've treated him. The thought made me so ill, I could barely breathe with it.

"I'm so sorry," I choked out as a tear escaped. I brushed at it impatiently and was surprised when Wolfe caught my hand.

He stared, seeming amazed, watching as I lost my fight with another tear and another. His thumb caught one and he smoothed it gently into my cheek.

My breath caught at his nearness.

"Are you crying for me, Rogan?"

I nodded. "I'm sorry."

"Why are you sorry?"

"Because he hurt you. Because I've treated you terribly because of him." I trembled as my feelings became almost too much contain. There was a part of me that never wanted to leave the hayloft but another that wanted to run as far from Wolfe as possible in the hope of shedding the weight of my emotions. "I thought you detested me, that you were planning to take some kind of vengeance for my part in Syracen's death."

He furrowed his brow. "*That* is why you're snotty with me?"

Snotty? How dare he—

I caught myself before I could castigate him. It was amazing how quickly my feelings turned to irritation around him. But to be fair, he was not wrong in this instance. I sniffed a little haughtily, but it was in acknowledgment that he spoke the truth.

Wolfe's lips curled at the corner. I could tell he was dying to laugh. He smothered it with his hand, rubbing it across his mouth. And then he nodded. "I think I understand. But you should know I felt nothing but relief when he was killed. My mother and I were free. Our lives changed that day, for the better."

I wanted to reach out and offer some kind of comfort, some kind of apology that would make up for the last ten years of disdain. Haydyn would be pleased to know she had been right about him all along.

When Wolfe tensed, I understood why when he asked, "What exactly did my father do to your family?"

The rage burst open across my chest like a tidal wave after a landshake, and I drew in deep breaths to calm myself. "Are you sure you want to hear about that?"

"Only if you're up to telling it."

So I told him. About a perfect summer's day ending in tears and bloodshed, of my subsequent grief and impotent anger. His golden skin grew pale as my story wound on. I even told him about Valena and how Syracen had ordered her family killed even after they willingly gave her up. I didn't even realize I was crying again until Wolfe, eyes bright with sorrow, handed me a handkerchief. I wiped at my tears as thick silence descended over us.

For a while, all I could hear was our soft breathing and the blood rushing in my ears.

"No wonder you hate me." Wolfe's voice was hoarse.

With his shoulders slumped in dejection, he looked younger than his years ... and so lost. I disliked seeing him so vulnerable. Wolfe was always so strong and sure of himself. It made my heart hurt to see him take his father's crimes upon his shoulders.

And that was not the way a person reacted to someone they hated.

"I don't hate you," I whispered. My pulse throbbed hard, racing harder as our eyes collided.

His eyes widened ever so slightly and the color returned to his cheeks. His gaze was searching and fierce. "You don't?"

My cheeks burned hot. "No, I don't. I've been willfully blind, Captain. I'm sorry I didn't treat you the way you deserved."

He smirked. "I wasn't exactly charming to you either."

I laughed. "You were just reacting in kind."

"Yes, I suppose I was. It was galling, you know. You're so sweet to everyone else."

I wrinkled my nose. "Sweet? I'm not sweet."

"You can be."

I waved off his compliment, uncharacteristically nervous and embarrassed.

"Rogan?

I lifted my gaze to his and admitted, "You're a good man, Wolfe."

Those beautiful aquamarine eyes rounded at my praise. Then he smiled, a boyishly wicked smile that caused a riot of butterflies to awaken in my belly. "You think so?" he murmured.

I flushed but nodded.

Then abruptly, his smile dropped, his expression growing dull with sadness.

"What?"

Wolfe shook his head. "I'm still the man whose father killed yours."

I didn't know how to respond. My emotions were overwhelmed.

Because I was attracted to him. Deeply so.

And yet I felt I owed my family better than that, even if Wolfe was not to blame for his father's crimes. Surely caring for the son of the man who killed them was still a betrayal of their memory?

Turning his body toward mine, Wolfe shifted a little closer. Unconsciously, in spite of the turmoil raging inside me, I moved into him. It was as though we were two magnets, inevitably drawn together.

"I wanted to kill him, you know."

I frowned. "Who?"

"Kir." Wolfe gave a rueful shake of his head. "I wanted to kill him ... and all he did was kiss you."

I recognized the intensity in Wolfe's gaze, the flicker of something I saw sometimes when he looked at me, that I'd never understood.

Until now.

He wanted me.

Wolfe, who caused women all over to swoon if he smiled at them. For goodness' sake, according to palace gossip, he'd had a love affair with Vojvodkyna Winter Rada, the woman whose court we were heading to. She was an incredibly beautiful, sophisticated, wealthy young widow.

And yet he wanted me?

"I—"

Wolfe suddenly clasped my nape in his large hand, cutting off whatever banal thing I might have said to fill the heavy silence.

I swallowed hard, feeling so hot I thought I might combust. The way he looked at me ...

No one had ever looked at me like that before. Like I was the most—

"You're so beautiful," Wolfe said hoarsely.

Maybe I was naive, but I believed he really thought so.

And then I wasn't really thinking about anything but the fact that his mouth hovered inches from mine. A gasp escaped from between my lips as Wolfe leaned in and brushed his across mine in soft, feathery, butterfly kisses. They were all at once excruciatingly wonderful and frustrating.

"Wolfe," I murmured in complaint, wishing for more. Then I smirked against his lips, teasing, "Is that the best you can do?"

He accepted my challenge, loosening his grip on my neck but only to wrap his arms around me. I was pressed flush to him, my breasts crushed against his chest.

His kiss was hard and persistent and I pushed into it, intoxicated by the feel and scent of him all around me. A strangled sound erupted from the back of my throat at the feel of his tongue against my lips, and he took the opportunity to sweep into my mouth. It drugged me with the unfamiliar dark pull of the kind of kiss Haydyn had told me about but I'd never experienced. I must have stilled, unsure of what to do, letting him kiss me and enjoying it, but afraid to participate in case I did it wrong.

Wolfe stopped, breaking the kiss. He pulled back to frown at me.

I blushed, feeling like an idiot. Wolfe was used to experienced women, not twenty-one-year-old virgins.

"You've never been kissed properly before?" he asked, stroking my flushed cheek. I was still wrapped against him and despite my embarrassment, I didn't want to pull away. I was addicted.

"No."

"But I thought you and Jarek—"

"Me and Jarek what?" I huffed. What in haven was he insinuating? Or had Jarek said something? Had Jarek spread lies about me? No, he wouldn't ... would he?

Wolfe arched his eyebrow. "What was I supposed to think? You're always flirting with him."

I pressed my hands against his chest and attempted to push him off me but he only held me tighter and grinned. Smug. Annoying. "You are the most—"

"I'm glad I was wrong." He cut me off, his eyes narrowing with lustful intent. "Now kiss me back."

With my usual aversion to appearing weak or vulnerable, I stuck out my chin in defiance and declared, "I don't know how, so we should stop."

Wolfe laughed. "Not a chance. Just follow my lead, mimic what I do." His breathing grew labored as he leaned in toward me.

My heart pounded, and I hated to admit it, but I didn't want to stop. I wanted him.

This time his kiss was gentle, teasing, coaxing me to open my mouth. When his tongue touched mine, I reciprocated. Wolfe groaned and I felt it reverberate through me in delicious waves. I gasped at the feeling. This must be what Haydyn was always talking about.

The kiss grew more frantic and I freed my arms so I could wrap them around him, my breasts flat to his chest, every inch of my body as close as I could get to the heat of his. We collapsed back against the blankets, Wolfe's body covering mine, his thigh pushing my legs apart. I shivered at the feel of him against me, my brain no longer able to work against the sparks and explosions shooting off around my body as his intoxicating kisses went on and on. His strong hands slid up and down my waist seeming desperate to touch me but afraid to move higher or lower.

When I arched into him, Wolfe shook against me. He reluctantly pulled away, both of us gasping for air as he rolled off me. I didn't know what to do with my body—my nerves were twanging, my hands shaking. I noticed Wolfe's were, too, as he exhaled heavily, running a hand through his mussed hair.

"We have to stop. You drive me crazy, Rogan," he whispered gruffly. "You always have."

My heart was struggling to calm down, and I laughed at the strange, awesome but awful turn of events. "Well, you took the perfect revenge."

He turned his head to look at me and grinned. Smug.

I swatted at him. "Very nice."

"What?" He laughed, rolling up onto his elbow and reaching out to brush my hair off my face. "After spending the last few years panting after you, it's nice to know you want me back."

My eyebrows rose in surprise. "The last few years?"

Laughing, Wolfe pulled me into his embrace and tucked my head under his chin. Despite how strange it felt, it was also lovely. I snuggled into his heat. "Let's stop the questions for now, Rogan. We need to sleep."

I was skeptical that after our passionate interlude, I would be able to fall asleep. But surprisingly, with Wolfe keeping me safe, I drifted off quickly into a dreamless slumber.

CHAPTER 18

I couldn't see her in the crowds. Where was she? This was her night. Smiling benignly at a Raphizyan baron and his insipidly vapid wife, I made my way out of the noisy ballroom and into the foyer. I had already asked Vikomt Matai, her newest bodyguard, if he had seen her. He had turned his back for one minute and she was gone. I knew the man felt terrible, losing the princezna in a crowded ballroom two weeks into his new post. I tried to reassure him. Haydyn could be a minx, and he'd have to get to know her to understand her better. Once he had, looking after her wouldn't be a problem.

Two footmen stood guard at the entrance. "Have you seen the princezna?" I asked, before reminding myself to stop anxiously twisting my hands in case they thought something was amiss.

One of the footmen stepped forward. "Her Majesty left the ballroom a few minutes ago, my lady. She was headed in the direction of the orangery."

I nodded my thanks and lifted my gown, my steps picking up pace as I followed the luxuriously gilded hallways of the palace to the large glasshouse in the east wing with views of the Silver Sea in the distance. Not that you could really see the views past the exotic plants and citruses Stena, the gardener, had populated it with.

Briefly, I closed my eyes, wondering what on Phaedra I'd find when I got there. This was supposed to be Haydyn's proper debut as Princezna; she was eighteen now, no longer a child. But something had been plaguing her all day.

I stepped inside the humid air of the orangery, the scents somewhat overwhelming. But Haydyn liked it here. She said it made her feel like she was somewhere else. I relaxed a little upon finding her on a bench at the back of the room. She glanced up at my appearance.

"Haydyn," I whispered, moving toward her, the rustling of my skirts sounding overly loud in the quiet space. With a deep exhalation, I sat beside her, our elbows bumping. "Why aren't you at the ball enjoying your debut?"

She huffed, "It's not as if they haven't seen me at a ball before."

"True," I muttered, desperately trying to keep the laughter out of my voice. "But this is a special evening, and you really should return to your guests."

Haydyn shrugged.

I frowned. "I know you aren't blind to the superficiality of some of your court, but you've never treated them with disdain. You've always been so friendly and polite to everyone. Tonight, I'd be surprised if you had stretched your lips once into a smile. I even thought I misheard you telling Lady Viskt that if the people of Alvernia were half as well-fed as her cat, Phaedra would have no tribulations. Now I think I didn't mishear it at all."

She laughed lightly. "No, you didn't. But, Rogan, she's awful. All she talks about is that bloody cat of hers. As if the princezna wants to discuss an overfed spoiled brat of a cat that scratched me last time she brought it to court, over her donating money to the charity I wanted to start for the mountain people of Alvernia."

A wave of fondness made me smile. "Dear, not everyone is as open-minded about the Alvernian mountain people as you."

She snorted. "Including you."

I shrugged, unabashed. "They're under the same evocation as the rest of us. If they wanted to be civilized, they could be."

"But—"

"You know I'd be more positively inclined toward this rapidly failing

philanthropic idea of yours if I thought for one second it had been your idea."

Blushing, Haydyn shrugged. "Darren is very passionate about these issues."

Now I did snort. "Darren is an arrogant troubadour with an inflated sense of importance. He's never even been to Alvernia! The farthest he's been is Ryl. Not exactly the best troubadour if you ask me ... traveling minstrel, my left butt cheek!"

Haydyn burst into raucous laughter, shaking her head. Once she'd controlled her giggles, she stared up me with love shining bright in her eyes. "Perhaps you're right. He did write me the most awful poetry the other morning. Something about hair the color of the moon and a sweet lady granting him a boon. I think he may have been trying to get me to kiss him."

I narrowed my eyes. "You didn't, did you?"

Pinching her lips together, she gave a sharp jerk of her head. "No. I did think about it, but he's not really what I expected. None of this is." She swept the room with a dainty hand.

"What do you mean?"

"I don't think I can do this," she confessed hollowly. "Decisions and choices and pandering to the court. It's all so much responsibility. The coronation ceremony is only five years away, and then I'll be crowned kralovna. Somehow that makes it sound all that much more frightening.

"Why don't we go away?" She clutched my arm, her emerald eyes pleading. "We'll jump on a boat and sail the coast to Alvernia. See for ourselves what the people are really like."

"Hay—"

"Or we could take off on Midnight and Sundown, head for your old family home in Vasterya. We could run through the fields and play by that stream you always talk about. It sounds like paradise."

I smiled sadly at her and drew her into a hug. "Haydyn, you know we can't."

"Why not? You're the only one I care about and the only one who cares about me. We'll have a grand adventure."

"You know you care about the people here, Haydyn. You're just over-

whelmed, and that is to be expected." I turned so I was facing her. "Phaedra needs your magic, Haydyn. And it needs your goodness. I know it's a lot to ask of a young woman, but we've all had to sacrifice something for our land."

Her eyes welled with tears. "Oh, Rogan, you must think me terribly selfish and childish."

"No. I think you're young. I think you're scared. But I know how smart and kind and good you are. And like you said, you have me. I'll help you through. I'll always be there for you. You're all that matters, and nothing will get in the way of that. Nothing ..."

A STRIP OF HEAT TINGLED ACROSS MY FACE, SLOWLY BRINGING me out of sleep. I peeled my eyes open, blinking against the stream of sunlight coming in from a crack in the rafters.

Where was I?

It took me a moment but then it all flooded back and I stiffened, my head whipping to my side. The place where Wolfe had slept was empty. He was gone. My heart raced. No, he was probably just in the house, I reassured myself. I groaned and sat up. Despite feeling less exhausted, I still ached all over. *All over*. Why, oh why, had I kissed Wolfe last night? I groaned, burying my face in my hands. It was such a silly, stupid thing to do!

You were exhausted.

Yes. I was exhausted. I wasn't thinking clearly ... *clearly*.

I was in the middle of rescuing my best friend, my sister, the one person in the entire land of Phaedra who meant anything to me. I couldn't be distracted by kisses from the most inappropriate man imaginable. His father killed my family. He was a vikomt and I was a farm girl. He would marry and I ... definitely *would not*!

But what to do now? When I went into the house, how should I act? My stomach churned. I dreaded an actual conversation with him about it. Oh, surely Wolfe would know it was a mistake. A bleary-eyed, adrenaline-rushed error in judgment. I should just act like nothing happened. I bet that was exactly what he would want.

Nodding, happy with my decision, I scrambled down out of the hayloft, nearly falling on my bottom I trembled with nerves so badly. The sun was bright and hot outside, and I winced at the thought of riding to Caera in this heat. Heaving a huge sigh, I braced my shoulders as if readying for battle, and headed into the widow's house. Wolfe was nowhere to be seen; the widow bustled around the kitchen, the smell of breakfast heady and thick in the air. My stomach grumbled a plea.

"There you are." The old widow smiled at me. "I hope you slept well."

I nodded, confused. Where was Wolfe?

"Your man is out back getting washed up at the trough."

I glowered. "He's not my man. He's my ..." I realized I didn't know how to finish that sentence.

Chuckling, the widow lay out the breakfast for us. "I'm just going out to feed my pig. Be back in a minute."

"Thank you." I gestured to the food and sat down, answering her cheery smile with a half-hearted one of my own. I never knew confusion could be so physically disorienting. Shrugging it off, I dug into the delicious food, salivating as it melted on my tongue. Perhaps we should take the old widow back with us, employ her in the palace kitchens. My lips twitched at the thought. Cook wouldn't be amused by that turn of events. Ah, Cook. I missed her. And Valena. And Haydyn ... but that went without saying.

At the sound of a creak behind me, my ears perked up, and then his familiar scent hit me. I sensed Wolfe behind me. The press of his lips against my neck was startling, and I flinched back from him, staring at him incredulously. Wolfe took a step back, a wary aspect flickering across his gaze. Whatever he saw in my expression made him sigh heavily as he took the seat beside me to tuck into the breakfast.

"Last night was a dream, then?" he asked with a definite edge to his voice.

I took a moment, shaking off the delicious tingling on my neck where he had kissed me, desperately trying to ignore the way my stomach flipped at the sight of his aquamarine eyes and wicked mouth. Finally, when I was sure my feelings wouldn't betray me, I replied, "Not a dream. Just a mistake."

Somehow Wolfe managed to glare at me out of the corner of his eye, and it wasn't hard to fall back into the way of things, bristling at the condescending expression he slid on and off his face as easy as a mask. "A mistake?" He shook his head. "I should have known you'd wake up as skittish as a mouse. I shouldn't have left."

"It's got nothing to do with that. And I am not skittish! I never skitter."

"You *are* being skittish. But I'm willing to forgive your less than pleasant reaction and give you some time to think about things."

Whatever else I had been feeling, whatever doubts, whatever confusion, rushed out of the window at his patronizing. "You arrogant, condescending, arrogant—"

"You said that already." He flicked his fork at me, amusement playing on his lips.

He thought I was kidding. He thought we were having a disagreement. I took in a deep breath, willing my nerves to calm. "I'm completely serious, Captain," I told him, hating how he flinched as I reverted to calling him Captain. "I'm sorry to have misled you in any way ... but what happened last night will not happen again."

Wolfe studied me, perhaps trying to discern how earnest I was. Then he shook his head, angry confusion in his beautiful eyes. "Rogan, don't. I know this is ... difficult ... but we can figure—"

"Don't." I stood quickly, my plate rattling on the table. "I'm going to wash up." Before he could argue any more, I hurried out of the kitchen, brushing past the bewildered old widow.

The trough was right out back, hidden in the shade of the house so the water was still chilled. It was delicious, shocking, and refreshing as I splashed my face, rubbing water droplets into my neck and behind my ears. It wasn't perfect, but it would do.

For a while, I just stood by the trough, staring at the open land around the old widow's home. The land here wasn't as lush and green as Vasterya. There was a brown-bronze tinge to everything that suggested the land existed in a state of near autumn all year round, contrary to the heat of the sun. There was more rainfall in Daeronia during the summer months than anywhere else bar Alvernia. It was colder, too, the farther north you crept.

However, I decided I liked the air in Daeronia. Not only were we still close enough to breweries to smell the sweetness in the air but it was joined by a crisp freshness that could not be found in the other provinces during the summer. It was always so humid everywhere else.

I had prolonged my visit to the trough as long as I could, so I headed back into the kitchen, dreading what was awaiting me. Wolfe stood watching for me, his expression carefully blank.

"There you are," he said gruffly. "I have the horses waiting."

The old widow bustled back into the kitchen, a pack clutched in her hands. "Here." She thrust it at me. "Here are some provisions just in case, but you should reach Caera before nightfall."

I thanked the widow, as did Wolfe before he gestured to the doorway. His eyes had hardened. "Ladies first."

My instinct (call it years of disliking him) was to be peeved, but I realized that *I* had been the one to wrong *him* when I allowed his kisses. So I pinched my mouth closed and headed past him.

"Be patient," I heard the old woman say, and Wolfe grunted. I glanced back with a little furrow between my brows as the two shared a look—hers amused, his exasperated. Curious, I threw him a questioning look and then quickly whipped back around at his ferocious glare.

It was going to be a long ride to Caera.

❧

WE RODE THE HORSES HARD. WITH THE TWO OF US ANGRY AT me, I was emotionally and physically exhausted when we reached the city. I almost wept with relief when we crossed the beautifully sculpted bridge over the River Cael and into the gates of Caera. I had never been to Caera before, but I'd heard about the bridge. It was wide enough for horses and carts to pass one another and was made of thick, sturdy stone, polished to brilliance. On either side were walls made of the same stone that reached Wolfe's shoulders.

Massive stone statues stood guard at either entrance—two ethereal female mages at the entrance and two powerful male mages at the exit. Some say it was Vojvodkyna Winter's sense of humor: Caera was a woman's world, and the rest of Phaedra belonged to men. Statues of winged creatures beckoned from the walls of the bridge, and I stared wide-eyed. How much money had Winter spent on this bridge? It was beautiful ... but wasn't it wasteful? I was sure Jarvis would think so.

As soon as we were inside the city walls, I sensed Wolfe's urgency to get to the Guard as much as my own. We made haste through the thronging masses as they hurried to and fro. The marketplace in Daeronia would be busy; they didn't have anything to export except beer and coal, so much of the business was in import. I had to admit as I followed Wolfe out of the main streets to quieter cobbled ones, I was impressed by the vojvodkyna's white-stone city. It really was spectacularly beautiful. Much like Her Grace. I winced, remembering we were heading to the home of Wolfe's ex-lover.

That wouldn't be awkward at all.

Unlike the other wealthy districts of Phaedra, the Radiant

District was walled and had a gatekeeper. When Wolfe explained who we were, one of the soldiers disappeared behind the carved wooden doors that kept us out. Wolfe glared his disapproval at the three other guards. They looked anywhere but at him. I almost sympathized with them. I knew how stinging that glare could be.

"Captain!"

We both turned at the sound of Lieutenant Chaeron's voice as he came through the gates, directing the guard to open them so we could trot through.

"It's good to see you, Lieutenant." Wolfe nodded down at him. Chaeron nodded back. Men were such funny things.

I smiled brightly at Chaeron. "Lieutenant. So good to see you."

"You too, Miss Rogan." He looked up at me with concern as he walked by my horse. "I do hope you are well."

Realizing he was genuinely distressed that I had been taken whilst under his protection, I sought to reassure him. "Of course, Lieutenant. Captain Wolfe and I looked out for one another."

We both ignored the grunt from said captain's direction.

"The vojvodkyna has a suite waiting for you. She realizes how exhausted you must be and has given you leave to retreat to your room."

Given me leave? I wanted to snort at that. I was going to my bloody room, leave or not. I didn't say that, though. That would make me sound jealous. And I wasn't. Not a bit. "How kind of her."

Several members of the guard were waiting outside of Vojvodkyna Winter's white-stone mansion. It was like a small replica of the Silveran palace. Hmm. I raised an eyebrow but kept quiet. I wouldn't have been able to comment, even if I'd wanted to. The soldiers circled me and Wolfe, peppering us with questions until Wolfe took pity on me and ordered his men aside so I could go inside.

"Lady Rogan," Wolfe called as I walked away. I stiffened at hearing him so formal. I turned slightly, face expressionless.

"Yes, Captain?"

"I would prefer if we stayed here for a few days instead of one. To regain our strength."

I returned his nod with a brittle one of my own. I could understand the wisdom in the suggestion, despite my desperate need to get to Alvernia ... except I wondered if it was just wisdom on Wolfe's part or if he wanted some extra time with the beautiful vojvodkyna.

Shaking off the strange pang of hurt I felt, I followed Lieutenant Chaeron who introduced me to the butler, a beautiful older woman. I'd never met a female butler before. It wasn't really the done thing. Yet it did not surprise me to find one in Winter's home. The butler's auburn hair was tied back in a fierce knot, streaks of silver darting through the sides. I was surprised that Winter had such an attractive butler, thinking perhaps her vain enough to want to be the prettiest woman in her home.

But when the butler called for two maidservants to help me to my room, I came to a better understanding. The two maids were stunning young creatures, their auburn hair and wide blue eyes a striking counterpart to their dark work clothes. Then again, even their work clothes were the finest I had seen.

It was then I realized something obvious: Vojvodkyna Winter Rada was obsessed with beauty. And so far the servants resembled her in coloring. It was strange to say the least, and I wasn't just being snotty because of her history with Wolfe. I found it all a little narcissistic. Not a little. A lot.

As I followed the stunning little creatures to a lovely bedroom suite where a bath already awaited me, as did a tray of food, I snorted at the maids' beauty. The Royal Guard must be in haven here.

It was a wonderful sleep. Comfortable. Warm. Luxurious even. I did dream of Haydyn again, but I had given in to the idea that until I saved her, she was going to be a regular visitor in my subconscious. The next morning, I awoke to a maid setting a tray over my lap. She informed me I had missed breakfast but that once I was refreshed, I was invited to join the vojvodkyna in her parlor for tea.

Not particularly looking forward to that, I made an agreeable noise from the back of my throat before tearing into my toast. The maid stared at me a little wide-eyed, probably unaccustomed to a lady taking out her anger on harmless toasted bread. She gave me a tremulous smile and then bustled around the room, laying out a dress from the luggage the Royal Guard had kept safe. It would be nice to wear clean clothes again.

I followed another pretty maid to a room with white double doors edged in gold. A handsome footman with burnished brown hair and pale-blue eyes pulled the door open for me, and I swept inside, my gaze returning to the footman who was strangely familiar.

"I see Arnaud has captured your attention," a husky voice curled around me, drawing my attention away from the footman.

My spirits depressed. I forgot the impact of Winter's beauty. Contrary to her name, Winter was more autumn in coloring. Striking auburn hair, wide cobalt eyes, and fine features. Her pale skin was the only thing about her that could be considered winterish. No wonder Wolfe had wanted this woman. Which really made me wonder what on earth he found appealing about me. She was all sunny autumn morning, and I was all ... thunderclouds and rain with my black hair and dark eyes. Wolfe—

Wolfe! I turned around again to stare at the footman but he was gone, the door closed behind him. The footman had Wolfe's coloring. My gut twisted and my jaw clenched.

"He's rather delicious, isn't he?" Winter laughed, a throaty laugh meant for seducing boys and men.

I replied with a half smile. "Very."

Winter drew to her feet, her white dress as stunning as a ball gown, the neckline cut low, the waist cinched so everyone could see how tiny it was. I smoothed the plain gown I wore, wondering why I was letting the obvious differences between us bother me. I had never cared before.

"Come, sit down, you look exhausted." Winter clasped my hand and led me to the armchair. I took a seat, surprised by the genuine concern on her face as she eyed the fading bruise on my cheek. "You've been through such an ordeal. The Vikomt Stovia told me all about your abduction by rookery gang members." She shook her head in disgust. "I had heard of this so-called rookery in Vasteryian Borders but to face the reality of it—you're very brave, Lady Rogan. You are to be commended for handling it so well."

I smiled in spite of myself. "Thank you, Your Grace." Wolfe hadn't told Winter about the gypsies. He'd only told her a half truth, a truth she was already aware of. Good. We were sticking to the plan, not panicking anyone with the growing unrest in Phaedra.

"Tea?" Winter asked.

I nodded, feeling tongue-tied. I really didn't know what to say to this vivacious creature. Haydyn was always so good at talking to the Rada. I winced. Then again, Haydyn was as beautiful as Winter, perhaps more so.

"Arabelle." Winter waved a dainty hand to the maid in the corner and the girl came forward at a graceful float. She had her servants as well trained as debutantes.

Once tea was sorted, Arabelle was dismissed and Winter relaxed into the settee. "I do hope you slept well last night, Lady Rogan. I gathered you might need the rest."

"I did." I actually smiled at the thought of the luxurious bed upstairs. "Thank you, Your Grace, for your hospitality. It feels like the sun after a very long bout of rain."

Pleased with my poetic thanks, Winter hurried on to pepper me with more questions about my well-being until I began to feel guilty for judging her so harshly. She didn't seem like a shallow socialite at all. In fact, if I remember correctly, Haydyn had told me she liked the vojvodkyna. She said Winter was smart and opinionated and cared not who knew it—the kind of woman I might have called friend ...

Just as we were discussing Haydyn's plans to hold a ball next season in the hopes of addressing some Phaedrian issues, a knock sounded at the door and Wolfe strode in. He looked like his old self again. At the sight of him, my pulse increased. I bitterly tried to ignore my reaction.

"Vikomt!" Winter rose to her feet, her eyes alight. The smile he bestowed upon her was wide and brilliant. He bowed over her hand and pressed an intimate kiss to the corner of her wrist.

I experienced a painful twist in my chest. Seeing them together, as they turned to me, I realized just how handsome they looked together. How right. Winter was a little older than Wolfe, but with his maturity and sense of responsibility, the age difference seemed inconsequential.

"My lady." Wolfe nodded at me, his expression carefully blank.

I wanted to scowl at him in outrage. Instead, I nodded back as if I were unaffected by the difference in temperature of his greeting compared to the one he'd given Winter.

"Oh, my lord, it is lovely to have you to tea," Winter said in that husky undertone, leading him to the settee to sit closely by her.

I did not think it was deliberate, but now that Wolfe was in the room, nothing else existed for Winter. She huddled into him, availing him of her recent deal with a factory owner in Raphizya that she swore would bring more income and work for the people of Caera. Wolfe listened aptly, his eyes never leaving her, drinking in the vivid, intelligent woman's every word. I was completely cut out, and the longer they sat talking, the angrier and more hurt I grew. I felt as if a small creature was gnawing on my ribs.

I was jealous.

Hatefully, painfully jealous, and there was nothing I could do about it.

If only there was some way to end my attraction to him. I mulled over this for a moment. There was Haydyn. Once Raj administered the cure and she was well and back to full strength, perhaps she could manipulate my feelings for Wolfe. Make me feel indifferent to him.

I chewed on the idea for a bit before dismissing it. No. Haydyn needed all her strength for the peace evocation.

Well, that was that, then. I just had to avoid Wolfe at all costs.

I stood, smiling brightly, falsely, down at them. "Thank you for tea, Your Grace, but I promised Lieutenant Chaeron I would meet with him."

"Oh, of course." Winter smiled at me.

"Good day, Your Grace. Captain." I managed to meet his eyes before hurrying past.

"Lady Rogan, wait," Wolfe clipped out.

I spun and raised an eyebrow at his demanding tone. "Yes?"

"Where are you going?"

"I just told you," I snapped.

Winter raised an eyebrow, and Wolfe glowered. And then as I looked at them pressed together on the settee, I realized I was not only jealous, I was angry. Just two nights before, Wolfe had been kissing *me*. Now he was romancing his old lover under my nose. I had been right to brush off his attentions as a mistake. It had been nothing but a weak moment during a trying time. Wolfe was nothing but another Jarek.

"I don't remember any such plans," Wolfe drawled.

"I want Lieutenant Chaeron to train me. With a sword.

Considering what happened. You yourself said it wasn't a bad idea."

He frowned. "It's not. But I'll train you."

The thought of him putting his arms around me frightened me. Not because I was afraid of him. Only of how he made me feel.

Weak.

"No, thank you." Without another word, I spun around and left them to stew in the wake of my rude departure.

CHAPTER 19

Training with Chaeron the day before had really taken my mind off the Wolfe situation. I was still not amused that Chaeron hadn't taken my word for it that Wolfe was allowing me to be trained to use a sword and had gone off to ask permission from the man himself. But when he returned, a little sheepish, I decided that learning to fight back was more important than being peevish.

Chaeron proved to be a patient and adept trainer, and I really felt as if I had learned something from him. I now knew how to hold the hilt of a sword properly, which was more important than I gave credence to. He taught me how to use an opponent's weight and height against them, considering most men were going to be taller and stronger than I was. He could still back me into a corner, but not so quickly as before.

"Lieutenant." I waved to him as I crossed the courtyard. He and a few other soldiers were already busy at practice. "May I join you today?"

"You've come back for more punishment, Miss Rogan?" Chaeron teased.

I raised my eyebrows in mock hauteur. "I'm nothing if not resilient, Lieutenant."

We smiled at one another before he set about procuring me a sword. We went over a few basics again and he had a few of the men, of different heights and weights, come at me, calling out instructions on how best to deal with their attack.

"See how Smythe keeps attacking low—despite my best efforts to break him of the habit—he's trying to sneak past your defenses. But now that you know the pattern of his thrust and parry, you can use it against him, sweep up, strike at him as his sword comes at you ..."

We had only been training for a half hour when Wolfe appeared in the courtyard. The men hurried to appear vigilant, even though there was nothing to be vigilant about.

"Lieutenant." Wolfe nodded at Chaeron. "Why don't you and the men take a break?"

I frowned as Chaeron nodded and gestured for the men to follow him out of the courtyard, dispersing them in seconds. "You just got rid of my sparring partners."

Wolfe remained expressionless. "Follow me."

What on haven did he want? Still furious at him, I considered telling him to stick his sword where the sun didn't shine.

But curiosity won out.

I followed quickly as he led me out of the courtyard and down the stone servants' steps that led into the walled gardens. I hurried along, trying to keep up with him, my heart thudding as I gripped the hilt of the sword in my sweating hand. What could be wrong to have put Wolfe in this strange state of tense calm?

When he disappeared into the high hedges that hid us from the view of the house, I'd had enough. "Wolfe!" I called sharply, drawing to a halt.

He spun around, and I bit my lip. Damn it, I'd used his given name again. Shrugging off my embarrassment, I glared at him. "Well? What is the matter? I'm not following you any longer until you tell me what is going on."

Wolfe shrugged and headed toward me, his movements slow,

almost predatory. "I merely wanted privacy to continue your training."

An angry flush colored my face. "I was in the middle of training. I don't need your help."

"I'm the best swordsman in the Royal Guard," he said without arrogance, and I knew it was true. "Don't you want to learn from the best?"

"I was learning from second best, which is quite all right with me." I thrust my chin in the air, running my eyes down the length of his body with a look of distaste. "Why don't you return to your mistress, Captain? I've heard she enjoys a bit of swordplay."

Wolfe laughed, a true happy laugh that sent a shiver through me. I stepped back, but he followed until I was pressed up against a hedge, the branches pricking into my skin through my dress. He loomed over me, inches from me, intimidating me. "Are we going to spar or not?"

Determined I could withstand his nearness, I gave him a stubborn nod and pushed him away. He immediately encircled me, his arms coming around and covering my hand on the sword.

"I've already been shown how to hold it," I said hoarsely, my skin tight and sensitive at his proximity. I could feel his breath in my ear, his hard thighs through my skirts.

"You've not been shown how to hold mine properly," he replied in a low voice, his lips brushing my ear. My cheeks must have bloomed bright red as understanding dawned. The lascivious son of a ...

"Why, you—" My indignation trailed off into silence at the surprisingly sweet kiss he pressed against my neck. He held me tight as if trying to offer comfort more than passion. I almost melted into him. But then ... I have an excellent memory.

I swear, I've never met a man who knows how to use his mouth quite so well.

Winter!

I stiffened. I remembered overhearing her one night at the

palace two summer seasons ago. She and her friends had been discussing her liaison with Wolfe with pride and relish.

I would pay all the gold in Phaedra to be showered in that man's kisses.

Feeling stupider than stupid, I shoved away from Wolfe, hard. He staggered a little. Turning to face him, I found his eyes bright and narrowed with frustration.

"I'm not one of your women," I hissed, hating the sting of tears in my eyes. "It's not like that between us. Go back to Winter."

His face hardened and he bristled. For a moment, I had forgotten how much larger he was than me, his height casting me into shadow. "I'm not having an affair with Winter," Wolfe growled. "It's been over between us for a long time."

I wanted to believe him. Wolfe wasn't the kind of man who lied. And I knew, deep down, as I sneered at him and composed myself, because it was easier that way, I was deliberately choosing to believe otherwise. I shook my head, the message in my eyes clear. I felt his glare burn through my back as I hurried out of the gardens and away from him.

DINNER WAS EXCRUCIATING. I WORE MY BEST DRESS, WHICH wasn't saying much considering all I had packed were traveling gowns. I sat next to Chaeron, hoping his soothing presence would get me through the ordeal of sharing dinner with Winter and Wolfe. Winter sat at the head of the table with Wolfe at her side. As per usual, she was dressed as perfectly as a doll, flawless and refined. A lady.

Wolfe and I refused to look at one another, and I knew Chaeron was confused by the tension at the table. A tension that grew worse when it became apparent that Winter had cooled in her regard for me.

The few times she deigned to speak to me, it was with a tight smile and hard eyes. My protective lieutenant bristled beside me at her rudeness, but as Winter was Vojvodkyna and Chaeron a mere Mister, I placed a quieting hand on his arm to reassure him and received a blistering look from Wolfe for my trouble.

I had never been so thankful to get away from a room in my life. I hurried to my suite and locked myself inside.

But I couldn't sleep. I kept thinking of our journey ahead in the morning. Soon we would be in Alvernia and I would have to brave the mountains for Haydyn's cure. But brave them I would, and then I would hurry home to bring her back to us. I needed her more than ever. I refused to think of what was happening back in Silvera. If I did, I'd panic and lose the little focus I had.

Finally, after having tossed and turned the sheets into a tight tangle around my legs, I shoved myself out of bed and into a dressing gown. Winter had a library on the ground floor. I would pick out a book and read for a while, hoping it would send me off to sleep.

I was surprised to discover the sconces still alight out in the hallway, and as I walked, it became apparent that the vojvodkyna kept her house lit even when the household was asleep. I clucked, shaking my head. The lady really was wasteful.

I hurried through the hallways and tiptoed down the stairs, my bare feet cold against the marble floor. I hopped quietly from rug to rug to save my poor feet from the chill. As I drew closer to Winter's parlor, the sound of low voices drew me to a halt. *Was that Wolfe?*

Heart thudding, blooding rushing in my ears, I sidled along the wall until I drew up to the door. Peering tentatively around the door frame, I sucked in a breath at the sight before me. I hated that I wanted to cry. I hated that he made me feel that way.

Wolfe was sprawled in an armchair, his long arm draped over the edge, a brandy snifter dangling from his fingers. Winter stood over him, between his legs. She gazed down at him in longing.

I wanted to scream.

"Darling, you're being impossible," Winter purred as she leaned down, bracing a hand on each arm of the chair. "I've missed you. Two nights in the same house and not even a peck." She finished by pressing her lips to his cheek.

To my horror, Wolfe groaned, that familiar groan that I thought was all mine. Stupid fool. Stupid, inexperienced child.

But then he shocked me by pressing a hand to Winter's shoulder to push her away. With a sigh, Wolfe rose to his feet, towering over the vojvodkyna who was even more diminutive than I. I couldn't look away. Even as he stared at her so intensely. I watched as he brushed his fingers gently down her cheek. Winter stared back at him, wary and bewildered.

"I told you no," Wolfe said in a low voice. "I'm sorry, Winter."

Holding in my breath, I waited for Winter's response. She didn't seem like the kind of woman who would take kindly to being rebuffed.

Indeed she turned from him, her spine ramrod straight. "You can't possibly love her," she whispered. "She's nothing special. She's not even beautiful."

My jaw dropped. I may have questioned who on Phaedra they were discussing but I knew how much Winter admired beauty ... and I was anything but beautiful.

"I think she is," Wolfe whispered back, and my heart pounded so hard, it was as if the organ itself was swelling. My legs trembled; my toes curled into the marble floor.

Winter shook her head and turned back to him. "I'm such a fool. Even back then, your eyes followed her everywhere. I told myself you were only doing your job, watching over her."

"I'm sorry," Wolfe repeated, looking remorseful.

"Stop saying you're sorry. So what? You're going to give up what we could have again for a girl who doesn't even care for you?"

Wolfe flinched, and that awful pang resonated again and

again like a vibration in my chest. I wanted to cry out to him. It wasn't that I didn't care for him. It wasn't that at all. I just couldn't *be* with him.

"Rogan is confused." He rubbed his forehead in that familiar way of his. "But I'm willing to wait."

Winter shook her head, as if she thought him a fool. Mayhap she saw something in me that he didn't. "You do love her, don't you?"

My breath caught.

Wolfe sighed and walked over to the table. Slowly he placed his brandy snifter on it and then straightened, reaching for Winter in a comforting gesture. "I do. I love her."

At his pronouncement, I thought I might be sick. The blood rushed out of my face and seemed to abandon my body. No. *No.*

I quietly backed away from the door and snuck down the hallway before I raced to my room. For a while, I just stared at nothing, balancing on the edge of my bed.

Wolfe loved me.

Wolfe.

Loved.

Me.

How had this happened?

I thought of the way I had hurt when he told me what Syracen had done to him, what the sight of the horseshoe brand did to my heart. Of the way I had come to enjoy arguing with him so long as it meant being in his company. Of the way my stomach flipped when he turned his wicked smile on me, and the way my body came alive when he kissed me. Of the ache, deep and gnawing, in my chest when I thought he and Winter had resumed their affair.

Oh, haven's no. I closed my eyes, frustrated tears clogging my burning throat. I couldn't love him back. I just couldn't.

There were too many obstacles between us. Too much history. Too much hurt. The blood of the man who had destroyed my family ran in his veins. I wouldn't. I wouldn't betray my family by marrying Wolfe. A Glava. I thought of Selene and her prediction. Well, I'd prove her wrong.

From now on, I would put a world of distance between me and Wolfe. Soon he'd stop loving me. He'd be fine. He was a catch. He could have any woman he wanted.

And me?

I only wanted one thing, and Wolfe kept getting between me and it.

Focus. Utter focus on retrieving the Somna plant.

Saving Haydyn. Just the thought of her name. Haydyn. I knew it would help me keep Wolfe at a distance and give me the strength to go it alone.

CHAPTER 20

He knew what I was doing. The frustration and anguish on Wolfe's face when I gave him formal, clipped responses to his queries almost undid me. But I chanted *Haydyn* over and over in my head to keep me strong. And after the third hour, Wolfe finally glowered like he really hated me and sped off in front.

Feeling Lieutenant Chaeron's curious study, I stared straight ahead, my eyes blank, features expressionless. The quicker Wolfe forgot about me, the better it would be for all of us.

Despite the horror of the significance behind our journey across Phaedra, despite the terrible close calls I'd already had with the world's less civilized creatures, and despite the turmoil I felt over Wolfe, I actually looked forward to venturing into the coal mining district of Daeronia. I'd heard it was a close-knit community of friendly people.

As we trotted into the first village on the main trade road, I was more than a little surprised by the chill in the eyes of the villagers we passed. It was dusk, and people strode quickly to their homes, covered in soot and grime. Others, clean but still dressed ruggedly, traveled in the opposite direction toward the mine. But all of them stared up at us with hard eyes and bristling bodies.

I gaped at them in confusion, drinking in their squalid little homes and their gray little world.

No one stopped to greet us, and Wolfe, who rode a few yards in front, made no attempt to stop to speak with them. The lines of his own body were stiff, and I noted his hand sat on the hilt of his sword. Swallowing nervously, I kept my eyes forward. We were in the southernmost village in Daeronia. It was more than possible that the evocation had waned here.

Sharing a glance with the lieutenant, we shifted the horses at a faster trot. Wolfe crossed a small wooden bridge on the other side of town and stopped in the clearing beyond it. He turned, and the lieutenant and I did the same. None of us said a word. We just waited for the entire Guard to make it through the village. When the last two men trotted over the bridge and joined us, I finally exhaled.

"That was chilly," I said to Chaeron.

He answered with a brittle nod and looked over at Wolfe in question.

Wolfe sighed. "It's nearly dark. We should camp here. I think we'll be fine as long as we don't ask them for a place to sleep." He flicked a glance at me before staring straight ahead again. "I'm afraid it'll have to be a campfire bed for you, my lady. I hope that doesn't distress you too much."

He had said it loudly to needle me in front of his men. I sensed the anticipation in him, waiting for me to retaliate. He *wanted* me to. He wanted something, anything from me. I turned away, ignoring the shaking in my hands. "I think I can manage well enough, Captain."

Feeling his eyes burning into me, I slid off my horse, letting my hair fall to cover my hot cheeks.

"Tyler, Szorst!" Wolfe called out. He dismounted his horse and approached the two men, holding out a bag of coins. "Go back into the village and procure us some coal. It should keep us warm at camp and perhaps soften the locals." He nodded in the direction of the bridge to some villagers who had come out of the village to peer at us making camp.

As the two men started off on foot, I worried my lip between my teeth, watching them. Remembering the looks on the coal miners faces, I decided that sending the men in alone was a bad idea. But I couldn't very well say that to Wolfe and I couldn't rush off alone—that had not worked out well for me in the past.

"Lieutenant." I approached Chaeron as he settled the horses with some water.

"Yes, Miss Rogan?"

Telling Chaeron I thought his men were in danger wouldn't work. The Royal Guard were somewhat arrogant about their prowess and didn't take lightly to having it called into question. I'd have to approach the subject sensitively. "We've been riding all day and I really would like to stretch my legs. Would you walk with me into the village?"

He frowned. "Miss Rogan, you saw how unfriendly the people were."

"Then perhaps a few of the other men would like to stretch their legs with us." I used my take-no-prisoners tone that Haydyn hated. She could never deny me when I used that tone. I usually brandished it when she was daydreaming during her tutorials or refusing to get out of bed.

I blanched inwardly at the thought of her. Shaking off the familiar growing panic that thrummed beneath my skin, I raised an eyebrow at Chaeron as he just stood there. I remained unwavering and he finally drew himself up. "Of course, Miss Rogan."

As we passed two men, Chaeron called to them to come with us, and then informed Wolfe that he was escorting me into the village. Discerning the coming argument by the look on Wolfe's face, I drew out my heaviest artillery and stilled him with a look so cold, it made him flinch.

I gulped down my guilt and hurried on, my skin prickling and muscles twitching at the feel of his eyes on my back.

As soon as we crossed the bridge, I felt the charge in the air, a sense of violence and anticipation. Chaeron and his men must have felt it too because suddenly, we were hurrying into the town and through the narrow streets to get to the main village courtyard. Sure enough, Tyler and Szorst stood with their hands on the hilt of their swords, surrounded by a group of angry coal miners, spitting and shouting at them. Just one spark, I thought. That's all it would take.

"Halt!" Lieutenant Chaeron bellowed, and I startled in surprise. He sounded terrifying and intimidating, and looked it, too, as he strode forward with the two guards at his back. The villagers stumbled a little but did not move away from Tyler and Szorst who looked relieved to see us. "An attack on the Royal Guard is a high offense and will result in imprisonment!"

Some of the villagers seemed to deflate, their faces drawn and wary. Others grumbled but slumped away. Others grew even more aggressive. A tall, stout man with a round face hardened with hatred stood forward from the group to face Chaeron.

"Who gives a damn about the Guard? We're left to stew in this forsaken place, working our fingers to the bone in eighteen-hour shifts in the mines under order from management! Three months ago, we worked good hours, decent hours, until management started adding an hour here and there until eventually we exist on no sleep, bad food, and broken bodies. Our children grow sick! Our wives grow weary! Where is the Royal Guard in that, I ask you?"

Chaeron was as shocked as I at the explosion, and the rabble-rousing yells of agreement. What on Phaedra was going on here? What this man said, it couldn't be true? But as I looked around at the desperate faces, I found the truth in their eyes.

Impulsively, I strode forward past Chaeron who tried to reach for me, but missed. "There must be some mistake," I implored the man. "We didn't know."

He looked at me with such revulsion, I tensed. And then he made a groggy noise in the back of his throat and spat in my face. Chaeron's blade was against his neck before I even could comprehend what had happened. Humiliated, I wiped at the phlegm dripping down my cheek and glowered at the man who now stood stiff against Chaeron's sword.

"Your name?" Chaeron growled in his face.

"Den. Den Hewitt."

"Den Hewitt, you just committed a crime. Do you know who this lady is before you?"

The rabble-rouser paled somewhat as he really looked at me, his eyes showing a little of his panic as he wondered who he had just offended. "No," he replied hoarsely.

"You just assaulted the Lady Rogan of Silvera. The princezna's handmaiden."

The gasps of the people around us made me want to curl inside myself. Den blanched, fear turning his mouth white. Still shocked at his treatment of me, a woman, a lady, I let him stew on it. They thought his punishment would be grave indeed. However, although stunned by his offense, I was more concerned by his accusations.

"I didn't know." He wilted a little.

"No. I imagine you did not." Chaeron shifted the sword from his throat. "Den Hewitt, I charge you with assault against the Lady Rogan of Silvera. You will be placed in my custody and taken back to Silvera for trial."

"Lieutenant." I shook my head, not wanting this man punished severely for an act of stupidity born of frustration.

"But Lady Rogan?" Chaeron frowned.

"All I want is an apology." I crossed my arms over my chest.

Hewitt looked between the two of us, his expression filling with hope as he waited for Chaeron's decision. The lieutenant finally nodded, although his eyes blazed, and Hewitt breathed a sigh of relief before turning to me. "I am so sorry, my lady. I am so sorry."

I nodded. "If you had merely told us your grievance, we would have dealt with it, Mr. Hewitt. I assure you that none of us were aware of these conditions you speak of. Let us return to our camp and I will speak with the captain of the Guard. He will investigate the matter." It was perhaps obnoxious and forward of me to assume Wolfe would take care of this situation, but I couldn't leave these people as they were. They were so volatile. Just one spark ...

Den Hewitt thanked me and apologized some more, relieved at escaping severe punishment. The men and I withdrew from him and turned back for camp. I could feel Chaeron's disapproval, but I was the one who had been spat on. I should be the one to mete out the punishment.

Before I could approach Wolfe, Chaeron charged ahead. He cornered the captain.

By the time Chaeron was done, Wolfe's face was hard as stone. With an efficiency and lethal determination that demonstrated just why he was captain, Wolfe rounded up a group of ten men and they mounted their horses. As they cantered toward me, I stood to the side and kept my eyes on the grass. I saw Wolfe's horses' hooves come into view and then stop.

"Next time, ask me before you offer my services." He snapped.

I scowled at him. "Are you saying you would leave them this way?"

He frowned back. "You know I wouldn't. But I don't appreciate taking orders from you, Lady Rogan."

My apologetic smile was brittle. "Apologies. It won't happen again."

Again, seeming startled and disappointed by my compliance, Wolfe nodded and began to pull away. Just as I was relaxing, sure Wolfe would take care of the issues the villagers had put forth, he threw over his shoulder. "I'm fining Den Hewitt for assaulting you."

"But I don't want that!" I cried, rushing to catch up with him. I could see the other men trying to look uninterested in our exchange. "You can't do that!"

Wolfe drew to an abrupt halt and glared down at me. "I can do anything I want, Lady Rogan. I am captain of the Guard." He seethed, his face mottled with anger. "He assaulted you, Rogan, and that I will not stand for." Abruptly, he turned and jerked his reins, galloping over the bridge and into the village, unmindful of his surprised Guard who took off after him.

Wolfe had just betrayed the intimacy between us by using my given name.

❧

It was with a mixture of relief and pain I realized Wolfe had had enough and was no longer speaking to me. He returned to camp some few hours later and told Chaeron what had happened. I tried to eavesdrop, but the collective snoring of the Guard drowned out their voices.

The next morning, Wolfe refused to look at me, let alone speak to me, and as we moved off away from the village, I had to ask Chaeron for the details of Wolfe's venture into the village.

Apparently, Den Hewitt had not exaggerated. After investigation, Wolfe discovered the manager of the mine, a wealthy baron no less, was working the villagers to the bone to keep up with the competition from the local mining communities surrounding them. Discovering sick children and ill workers, worn out and hopeless, Wolfe was furious. The village had had two deaths in the last month caused by exhaustion and dehydration.

He fined the manager (and Den Hewitt) and threatened him with criminal charges if he did not return to the normal working procedures. To ensure his obedience, Wolfe left two of his men to guard the workers and sent a messenger to Vojvodkyna Winter Rada explaining the situation. He asked her to send some of her men to relieve the Royal Guardsmen and to assign a replacement manager for the mine.

I rested easier knowing Wolfe had taken care of it. I had

known he would. I sighed wearily and stared straight ahead, worrying about what we would find in the next village we passed through. I had so much to tell Haydyn once she was awake and well. Our problem wasn't just the evocation. Our problem was that outside the cities governed by the Rada, the people were ignored and left to go about their business. Those with power took advantage of those with none. That had to change.

I straightened my spine with determination.

When this journey was over and my task complete, parts of Phaedra would need reform.

CHAPTER 21

To my utter relief, the next few days through Daeronia passed uneventfully. We stopped in two other mining communities, and neither was suffering under the conditions of the first. From their disposition to the state of their homes and their fervent hospitality, they were fire to the southern coal mining village's ice.

And I? I was confused. Perhaps I had merely wanted to put the prior manager's attitude partly down to Haydyn's evocation, but the northern coal miners were wonderful in manner, and surely if the waning of the evocation was part of the problem, then they would be the ones to feel the effects more so than the south.

My forehead was in a perpetual state of wrinkles.

The situation with Wolfe hadn't changed. In fact, it had worsened. He had Lieutenant Chaeron pass along anything he wished me to know, and the night we dined in the home of the manager of a large coal mining town called East Winds, Wolfe flirted with their twenty-year-old daughter and ignored my existence.

I ignored the fist of agony in my chest. His behavior was of my own making and I had no right to feel anything toward him.

❦

We had been following the River Cael and were closing in on the border between Daeronia and Alvernia. A constant knot of anxiety now lived in my stomach, the need to get to the Pool of Phaedra an obsession, sharp and unrelenting. I was impatient when Wolfe stopped us by the river for our midday break and was about to voice my disgruntlement when I remembered I hadn't spoken to him for three days. Plus, it was unseasonably hot, not even a wisp of that crisp Daeronian breeze I had come to love.

I told Chaeron I needed a moment alone and wandered along the bank of the river that flowed on the left side of the trade road as the men gathered near the woodland on the right. They stopped, sliding down to lean against tree trunks and eat the hard biscuits that had come to form their unsatisfying daily diet.

I was still in sight, but I used the horse to cover me as I took off my shoes and stockings to dangle my feet into the river. I sighed at the blissful cold water on my skin and thanked goodness I hadn't had to walk too much.

Reluctantly, I pulled my feet out of the water and reassembled my clothing before Wolfe sent someone to collect me. However, as I strolled back to the men, my eyes darting over them, there was no sign of Wolfe ... or Chaeron. Puzzled, I searched for them.

Just as I was about to draw near the first group, I caught a flash of color out of the corner of my eye. Turning toward the trees, I saw Wolfe's green military jacket. He'd had to borrow it from one of the Guard. Curious as to why Wolfe and Chaeron were huddled in the woods, I eyed the men to see if any were watching me. I was somewhat disappointed to see that none of them were, too busy eating and talking among themselves.

Excellent guarding, gentlemen.

Rolling my eyes, I snuck away and edged closer to Wolfe and

Chaeron. I left my horse and stopped a few trees back from them, hidden in the shade.

"I just don't know if it's a good idea." Lieutenant Chaeron exhaled.

"I have to," Wolfe insisted, his voice flat.

"I could do it."

"No, it has to be me." Wolfe shook his head. "If Rogan's going up into the mountains, then I'm going to be the one protecting her."

Chaeron sighed again. "Things are difficult between you as it is."

"I know. But I won't let my feelings get in the way of my duty. Which is to protect her."

"What will I tell the men?"

"Tell them I've taken Rogan on a tour of Alvernia, to let her see for herself what the area and the people are really like, so she can report back to the princezna."

"They'll think it's insane. They'll wonder why you've gone alone, perhaps even speculate ..."

"If any one of my men utters a derogatory word against Lady Rogan, I want you to deal with them."

Chaeron sucked in his breath as if insulted. "You know I would, Captain."

"Good. Tell them the Alvernians are paranoid, suspicious. A royal entourage traipsing around their land would be seen as an act of aggression. Tell them that Lady Rogan and I are going incognito."

"All right." There was a moment of silence between them before Chaeron peered at Wolfe with genuine concern. "Wolfe," he said softly, surprising me by using his given name, "you've never been into the mountains. A few of the men here have. They'd be better suited to escort Miss Rogan."

Wolfe shook his head determinedly, his jaw set. "I won't let her go into that without me." He shoved a hand through his hair in obvious frustration, appearing vulnerable and lost. "I would not be able to ... It would drive me mad thinking of her out there without me ..."

Chaeron placed a hand on Wolfe's shoulder. "All right."

I backed away as stealthily as I could, the blood rushing in my ears and flooding my cheeks. I walked numbly back to the men with my horse; I saw nothing and heard nothing as we mounted and set off.

Wolfe was furious with me but he still cared. Cared enough to follow me into the heart of the Alvernian Mountains where the chances of us both coming to harm was great.

No. I shook my head, ignoring Chaeron's concerned looks. I wouldn't go into the mountains with Wolfe. I had to keep my distance. I had to stay focused on finding the plant, and I couldn't do that if I was worrying about Wolfe.

I had to get away from him somehow.

When we reached Arrana, I had to leave and set off into the mountains alone. It didn't matter if I had an escort. Only I knew the way to the Pool of Phaedra, and my magic would get me there. I just had to be careful and remember the route up so I could get back down the mountain without fault.

THAT NIGHT, WE MADE IT TO ARRANA. SMALLER THAN THE other cities, Arrana was also more heavily fortified, with a fifteen-foot wall snaking around its border. Like one of the keeps used thousands of years ago when the mages first came to Phaedra, the city had a moat, drawbridge, and armored guards. We had to wait for permission to enter, and as we crossed the sturdy bridge into the city, I frowned in disapproval. There were no wars in Phaedra. No need for city walls and moats and drawbridges. I understood the vojvoda was nervous of the mountain people of Alvernia—I was nervous of them and I had to walk right into their midst—but his fortification sent the wrong message. It isolated

Arrana, made it a lone entity, separate from Haydyn's Phaedra.

What must the people of Alvernia think? Or any people who crossed the border into Alvernia? It was unwelcoming and superior. Worse, it was aggressive.

This, too, would have to change.

❧

THIS WOULD NEVER DO, I THOUGHT GLUMLY, WATCHING Markiz Andrei follow the servant girl's bosom with his eyes whilst his father, Vojvoda Andrei, tried to convince me that his son would be a brilliant match for Haydyn. I found it difficult swallowing my fish as I dined with them. I studied the junior Andrei as he smiled at me, and I bemoaned the vapidity behind his eyes. The poor boy wasn't lascivious or cruel. He was just ... silly, and ... well, not very intelligent. He was so wrong for my Haydyn. Haydyn needed someone as clever and passionate as she was, someone who stood up for her and to her.

Someone like Matai.

All of a sudden, I felt unbearably sad.

I let Wolfe and the vojvoda do all the talking. I smiled enough so as not to seem unpleasant and bored, but I was sure the vojvoda was puzzled as to why Haydyn would send an advisor on her behalf who had barely opened her mouth.

But I was buried by the troubles of Phaedra. Buried and useless. I needed Haydyn to wake up. I had needed her to wake up before she fell ill. I only hoped that she would once I provided the cure and told her all I'd learned. To begin with, marrying Andrei would be a terrible mistake.

So lost in my problems, I barely noticed that Wolfe had finagled it so that he was the one to walk me to my room. As we drew closer and his arm brushed mine, my awareness of him drew me out of my musings.

I glanced at him, experienced more than a twinge of desire,

and looked away. We hadn't talked or been this near to one another in some time. Not since Caera.

"In the morning, you and I will leave for the mountains." Wolfe stopped and I drew to a halt, turning to him. We looked one another in the eye for the first time in days. "We're going to pretend we're taking a tour of Alvernia and its people, but in reality we're going to retrieve that plant."

I knew if I didn't try to dissuade him after all we'd been through, he'd be suspicious. I had to give a little argument, even though I already had my plan at the ready. "Do you really think that's wise ... considering?"

"Considering?"

"Considering you hate me." I held my breath, waiting for him to dispute it. I knew he cared. I just needed him to admit it.

Haven, I wished my heart would make up its mind!

I felt a sharp pain somewhere near the said organ when he shrugged. "It's my duty."

I bit back a hurt retort. "Fine. I want it noted that I dispute the idea. For future reference."

"Noted."

I nodded and turned to go into my room, disbelieving this would be the last thing I said to him before heading into the wilderness. I might never return.

I stilled as his hand wrapped around my upper arm. I glanced up nervously as he sidled closer, his eyes challenging me to stop him. I didn't. I let him kiss me. I thought it would be a hard kiss meant to dominate, but instead he surprised me with a soft, seductive brushing of lips and tongue, meant to melt me. Even as he kissed me, giving me what I wanted, I ached with longing.

When he pulled back, Wolfe's cheeks were flushed and he gazed at me again with that soft curl of his lip, bright gold in his blue eyes. "I want it noted that I don't hate you. For future reference."

Before I could stop it, a small smile tilted the corners of my mouth. "Noted. Although I must protest that you keep forcing unwanted kisses on me."

"Unwanted indeed." He raised a knowing eyebrow.

Arrogant knave.

I shook my head, feeling sad and happy at the same time. "Why do you persist, Wolfe?"

His grin was slow and wicked as he retreated. "Strategy."

"Strategy?"

He cocked his eyebrow. "At first I thought imposed isolation would make you miss me—"

"Why, you arro—"

"But then I realized that it's being near me you can't resist. And there are only so many kisses you'll take before you give in to me completely, Rogan."

Ignoring the flush of excited heat that moved through me at his hoarse tone and serious expression, I gripped the handle of the bedroom door behind me and guffawed. "We'll see, Captain. We'll see."

I slammed the door in his face, huffing at the sound of his cocky chuckle.

For a moment, all I could do was stare at myself in the mirror, touching a mouth that now tingled with the taste of Wolfe. I closed my eyes, hating that thrum in my body that never used to be there before he first kissed me.

I wasn't even sorry for kissing him. I was thankful that our last moment together—before Wolfe truly did come to dislike me—was sweet, in that dysfunctional way of ours.

Completely discombobulated by him, or rather my muddled feelings for him, I scrambled about, ringing the bell for a servant and gathering some coins. Grateful when a young girl in rough servants' clothing appeared, I explained what I needed and showed her the money. She stared at the coins in wonder. There was more money there than she probably earned in two years of hard work.

"Well?" I asked, my heart stuck in my throat.

For an answer, she scooped up the coins and pocketed them, grinning broadly. "I'll help ye, my lady," she replied in the soft burr of the Alvernians.

Breathing a sigh of relief, I went over again what I needed, and then waited for her return. She wasn't long in reappearing, a few bundles in hand. In one was a pack with food supplies and a canteen of water. In the other was boy's clothing, stolen from one of the stable boys. Hurriedly, the girl helped me into the trousers; they hugged my figure in a way that would make me blush if Wolfe ever saw me in them. I then pulled on the over-large shirt, waistcoat, and warm overcoat to see me through the bitterly cold nights in the mountains. The boots she brought belonged to her—they were worn and soft, but still foreign to me, and I hoped my feet would cope in them.

Lastly, I pinned my long, thick locks in a bun and hid the hair under the woolen cap she brought. Hopefully, in the dim light, if I kept my head low, I could pass for a boy. If I removed the over-coat, no one would ever believe it. I just had to make sure I never removed it. Lastly, I stuffed the dagger Matai had given me into the pack.

I thanked the servant profusely, and then we hurried through the darkened house and out to the front gates where she had a horse ready and waiting.

Once mounted, I gave the house one last look. Wolfe was going to be furious. But I was counting on him not to be foolish enough to follow me into the mountains without the Guard. He knew my magic wouldn't get me lost, but he didn't know the way.

I sighed. I had to put all my trust in Lieutenant Chaeron. He wouldn't let Wolfe leave without him.

CHAPTER 22

Fear wasn't new to me.

I'd first encountered the feeling, with its jaw of sharp teeth and painful clawed grip, when Syracen killed my parents and I ran through the fields with my brother. For years, that fear never really went away. And it had shown up in little spurts these last few weeks, perhaps not as toothy as the first time, maybe not as adept at holding me down, but it had been there, taunting me.

Now it was back.

I was blind, galloping out of the city walls and down into the valley beyond Arrana. It took awhile for my eyes to adjust to the night, and with my heart already racing at the thought of getting caught, I wasn't sure I wouldn't upchuck all over my poor horse. But I held strong, my hands biting into the reins, as I widened my eyes, desperate for them to acclimate to the darkness. By the time I put Arrana at a fifteen-minute gallop behind me, I could see more than just shapes and shadows ahead.

I drew the horse to a stop, sorry that I didn't know his name so I could soothe him better. I could feel his muscles tighten beneath me as he attuned to my tension.

The land before us dropped into a steep valley that stretched for miles, the mountains peaking over it in the distance.

I was all alone.

I snorted at the irony of it.

All I'd ever wanted was a moment of peace, to be truly alone, and now that I was, I was terrified. This land before me was alien and unknown. I didn't know the towns and the people in them. My magic was the only thing keeping me together, that and the coat protecting me from the icy night air. I had never known it to be this cold at night during the summer months.

Stroking the horse's face, I leaned over and murmured soothing words to him. His ear flicked against my mouth, tickling me, and he scuffed his hoof back, giving a little snort. He was ready. I smiled. At least I'd have him with me for the journey through Silveran Valley—named so because it was the one area in Alvernia, other than Arrana, closest in temperament to the capital city. In Alvernia, that wasn't really saying much. I reckoned it was called so more out of hope than reality. I trembled a little, thinking of the reports from the vojvoda that the valley people had grown more uncivilized.

I'd have to move through it inconspicuously, in a hurry.

With a jerk of the reins, we took off, the horse steady on his feet as we followed the steep trade road down into the valley. Once on level ground, we took off at a faster gallop; I hoped to put as much distance between Wolfe and me as possible. The last thing I needed was him catching up.

In the dark, I couldn't see much. I wouldn't have even if I'd wanted to, I was so determinedly concentrating on getting to those mountains. The trade roads were rougher in Alvernia, less traveled, and we stumbled a few times along the way.

Until my consideration for the horse overrode my need to reach my destination at speed.

I'd wear him out if I didn't stop soon.

Every little noise I heard over our galloping made cold sweat slide down my back. I was thankful when the sun broke the horizon. It burst out over the mountains until the brownish-green rolling plains of the valley became visible. We grew closer to the mountains towering over the valley in the distance, mountains like monsters beckoning travelers into nightmare. Thick, brutish, looming trees the Alvernians called the Arans covered what appeared to be every inch of the mountains, the lushness of those deep, black-green trees a sharp contrast to the sickly pallor of the plains I was passing through. The mountain people of Alvernia lived among those trees, their homes shrouded by the darkness, their lives sheltered in ignorance and ungoverned isolation.

My stomach lurched and I pulled the horse to an abrupt halt. Thankfully I made it off the poor horse and to the side of the road before I vomited up last night's fish.

❧

AFTER A QUICK RESPITE, I WAS BACK ON THE HORSE, RACING him faster than ever as the mountains drew closer. I didn't see much from the trade roads, only a farm or two visible from the road, but I wasn't interested. My magic was beginning to hum and vibrate through me the closer I drew to the Somna plant.

The Silveran Valley wasn't huge; most of Alvernia was covered by those mountains. It could be crossed in under a day, and as midmorning crept past, the horse and I were finally enveloped within the shade cast by the mountains.

Up close, they were utterly mammoth.

I watched a bird circle up ahead and then fly in among the trees.

Disappearing forever.

"Stop being maudlin," I hissed at myself.

Soon we drew around a bend in the road and the Aran trees stood before me, an entrance into the wooded hills, dark and foreboding. I slowed the horse and trotted forward. The horse snorted again, feeling my thighs squeeze him in my fear. My stomach was so full of butterflies, they were brimming over and touching my heart, their stupid wings tickling against the organ and urging it to react in kind. When we drew closer, I could make out a crude wooden sign nailed to one of the trees:

ALVERNIN MOWNTINS
TRED WIF CAYR

I CLOSED MY EYES, TRYING TO DRAW IN BREATH AND CALM. Shakily I slid off the horse, leading him over to a humble lane cut into the surrounding field. Pitched into the ground was another sign in the same carving:

HEVERS FARM

I SOOTHED MY COMPANION AND THANKED HIM BEFORE hitting his rump, sending him into a canter up the lane where hopefully the Hevers would find and take care of him. I couldn't take him up into the steep mountains. It would slow me down and be unfair to him.

For a moment, I stood at the opening of the woods, looking up the hill into the gloomy forest. I could hear the creak and twitch of the woods themselves, branches snapping, woodpeckers pecking. Insects buzzed around me, small animals skittered over crushed leaves and twigs, and in the far, far distance, I even thought I heard the howl of a dog. I shivered.

I imagined the overwhelming aroma of the forest might calm

me with its musky floral, honey, laurel, and freshly cut grass all breathing beneath the heady scent of rich, dark soil. It *was* wonderful.

But I was still quaking.

With another deep breath, I straightened my shoulders and took my first step into the mountains.

"Only for you, Haydyn," I whispered, and continued on in resignation.

The climb was almost immediate. One, two, three steps and the ground began to tilt upward. There were no more signs posted to the trees giving me directions to towns or settlements or whatever it was these people had in here, but I was following my magic, managing to keep to the rough track that already wound its way up through the mountains.

The longer I climbed, the more I wondered where the people were. My ears were practically pinned back, my heart jumping at every little noise. I must have stopped and spun around a hundred times, my eyes probing the shadows between trees for signs of life. So on edge, I wasn't going to sleep tonight.

I climbed for hours, my feet blistering inside the maid's boots. I fought off the pain by refusing to think about it, thinking only of the growing darkness within the woods and how cold it was becoming. By dusk I was beginning to panic that there were no signs of life. My magic told me the Pool of Phaedra was still days off yet, and I had hoped to find some safe place to shelter for the night.

Safe, I snorted.

Was that even a word in the Mountains of Alvernia?

I stopped, my ears kicking back at a familiar noise.

Water!

The trickling in the distance set my heart racing again. Surely where there was water, there would be people! I followed the noise, tripping over a thick root and taking my first tumble of the day. I landed on soggy leaves and damp soil, dirty circles staining my trousers at the knees. I grunted and got back up, determined not to feel foolish considering no one had seen me. The sound of water drew me to a stream, and I followed it, making sure it didn't pull me too far from the direction of my magic.

Surprise rippled through me as the woods broke, the stream leading out of the trees and into a clearing.

Stretching before me, encircled on all sides by the Arans, was a town. Shacks I gathered were houses dotted here and there, some by the stream, some farther off until they looked like little black squares in the distance. Lights shimmered in the dark. An extremely well-lit larger shack, some way off, caught my eye.

"Can I be helpin' ye, son?"

I jerked and then froze, my mouth falling open, my eyes wide, my palms and underarms instantly giving in to cold sweat. Slowly, afraid of what I'd find, I turned to confront the gruff voice with its strange burr. A man, exactly what I had in my mind when I thought "mountain man," stood before me, burly, tall, and wearing a frown of suspicion. He was wrapped up warm in worn clothes, a furry hat covering his head. I gulped at the sight of the huge ax laid casually against his shoulder.

I was threatened by more than just his height. I was a woman alone, and I had been caught by a strange man. But then ... he'd called me "son."

Glancing down at my boy's clothing, feeling the boy's cap on my head, I exhaled in relief. He thought I was a boy. I deepened my voice and tried to emulate a rough accent.

"Just lookin' for a place to rest before I pass through."

He straightened a little, eyeing me closely. "Oh yeah? And where you be headin', boy?"

I'd never heard such an accent before. It was clipped and tight with trilling *r*'s and dropped *g*'s. I shook myself from my momentary distraction and thought about my answer. It was well known to everyone in Phaedra that the Pool of Phaedra was considered mystical and fascinating. There had been many an adventurer who'd dared the mountains to find it.

"The Pool of Phaedra."

The man smirked. "An' what would a sprite like ye want with the Pool?"

I shrugged. "I'm on a spiritual journey and that is all I wish to say on the matter."

He laughed, and I bit my lip. I'd sounded far too well-bred. But he didn't say anything, just chuckled. "Well, don't be gettin' all ornery, yer business is *yer* business." He laughed again, shaking his head. There was something jolly about him. I began to relax.

"My name is Brint," he told me, his booming voice carrying beyond us. "Brint Lokam. I'm about the closest thing Hill o' Hope has to a mayor."

"Hill o' Hope?" I asked in confusion.

Brint grinned and gestured to the open land before us. "Hill o' Hope." He winked. "We here at Hill o' Hope have what some folks call an ironic sense o' humor." He drawled out the *i* in *ironic*.

I couldn't help but return his smile. "My name is Ro—" I stopped, remembering I was supposed to be a boy. "Rolfe. My name is Rolfe."

"Nice to meet ye, Rolfe. Well, ye don't look like ye can cause much trouble. Why don't ye join us at Hope Tavern?" Brint pointed to the larger shack lit up in the distance. "They'll give ye some gristle and grub, maybe a splash o' ale." He winked again. "It's no' much but it's somethin'. Plus, folks are in a good mood lately, what with the Iavii people who used to crawl all over these parts havin' taken off for greener pastures.

"Once yer done fillin' up, ye can come back with me." He jerked a thumb over his shoulder, and I noticed the shack up the hill behind us. A single light flickered in the window. "The wife will be more than happy to put a pallet by the fire for ye so ye can get some rest before movin' on in yer spiritual journey."

I smiled at his teasing. I knew I probably wouldn't get a better offer, so I nodded in thanks and followed him down the hill toward Hope Tavern. My first encounter with an Alvernian mountain person was not unfolding as I'd always imagined. The preconceived notion that they were all awful, uncivilized, ill-mannered people was further challenged when we entered the tavern. Brint introduced me to the roughest-looking people I'd ever seen. Even rougher than gypsies and the rookery thugs. I couldn't decipher age among them; they were all so weather beaten and worn, laughter wrinkles tickling the corners of everyone's eyes.

Despite the obvious fact that their lives were hard, that they didn't have much of anything, they were so friendly and jolly and happy. I couldn't believe what I was seeing and hearing. No, they weren't well-mannered as a rule, but in spite of that, no one was ill-mannered to me. And, if I were to go by the stories they regaled me with, amidst this uncivilized, isolated community of theirs was a true civilization of camaraderie and teamwork.

More shocking for me still, I watched the barkeep—who had thrust a plate of strange food and the darkest ale I'd ever seen at me—kiss a man who slid over the bar and wrapped his arms around him. Wide-eyed, I glanced around to see if anyone was looking, but no one cared.

Brint caught my look and laughed, explaining the two men were old lovers. Back home in Silvera, I knew of rumors of men who preferred other men, but society pretended it didn't exist, happy to ignore it as long as the men in question kept it hidden. I'd always believed that people should be free to love whomever they chose, and it amazed me that up here, in the heart of savage country, people were freer and more loving than back in Silvera.

My worry eased. The situation in Alvernia wasn't nearly so bad as we'd been led to believe. Mayhap Haydyn need never marry Andrei, whose father perpetuated the telling of tales of the uncivilized Alvernian mountain people.

Once again, I had been ignorant and prejudiced.

I decided then and there, as I enjoyed the rambunctious company of the people of Hill o' Hope, that I would never again draw an opinion on a subject until I'd researched said subject thoroughly. I thought of Haydyn's long-forgotten failed philanthropy regarding these people. If we'd listened to her, we would have done a lot of good. Once again, I was ashamed.

After I'd eaten, I relaxed beside Brint, listening as his neighbor Dru regaled me with the story of Brint, who organized a search party for a little girl who'd been kidnapped by the Iavii.

"We were lucky that the group who'd taken wee Amelia were few, because no matter what, Brint would be ah takin' us into the woods to fight the buggers and bring her back."

I stared at Brint who looked marginally embarrassed by the story. "And did you?"

"Oh, indeed," Dru went on. "We snuck up on the buggers and dealt them out a booting they wouldn't forget. We got wee Amelia and brung her home to her folks. The Iavii departed the mountain no' too long after that."

"You were very brave." I lifted my cup to them.

"Are ye brave?" A girl appeared at my side, swishing her dirty skirts and smiling at me, her teeth yellowed. I squinted, feeling warm and fuzzy from the ale. She would have been pretty had she been given the comforts of Silveran living.

"No," I replied promptly.

"Ye've come into the mountains by yer lonesome. There's a certain amount of bravery to be said for that." She brushed her fingers down my face before dropping into my lap.

Bewildered by her sudden proximity, it took me a minute to realize she was reaching to kiss me. I squealed under my breath and jerked back, thankful when her weight was lifted from me.

Brint gave her a look and patted her bottom. "Be on with ye, lass. This one is shy."

The girl huffed in disappointment, striding off before throwing me one more longing look over her shoulder. My cheeks felt hot and Brint laughed again.

"Tera is a bit free with her favors." He shook his head. "Gotten worse since the Iavii have gone. Everyone be a bit more relaxed these days."

"I can't believe the gypsies were that awful to their own." I bit my lip. Up here, Haydyn's evocation did not reach, up here where life was hard enough as it was.

Brint glowered now, looking as fierce as I first imagined him to be. "We weren't their own. You never knew which hill they'd come barrelin' into next, takin' that which wasn't theirs to take."

"Then I'm glad they've left you alone."

"Me too, son. I pity the buggers who they be botherin' now, though."

I grunted. *I* would be one of those buggers.

I shook off my memories and smiled, looking around me. "The mountains aren't anything like I was told they'd be. Everyone is so friendly and nice."

Once again, Brint's lips thinned and he leaned in. "In Hill o' Hope, we are. We be good people. But don't ye be gettin' all mistaken, son. There are folks in these here mountains who've gone crazy with the isolation. Ye watch yerself in this journey o' yers. Stick to the trails. There's a place one hill from here called Shadow Hill. Ye be bypassin' around the outskirts o' Shadow, ye hear? No' nothing there for strangers but a world o' suspicion and sorrow. And the closer to the Pool ye reach, be warier. There be dogs in packs up that way, hungry and feral as any an animal starvin' and uncontrolled."

I gulped.

My fear returned.

I should have known it couldn't be as easy as I'd begun to hope.

Hah, I snorted inwardly. Hill o' Hope. It was really called so because it gave hope that the mountains were as kind and easy-going as the people here.

"Thank you," I replied softly, grateful for the warning.

Brint nodded grimly, as if seeing past my deception and into the truth of me. He seemed concerned.

"Come." He stood. "Let us get ye home and to some sleep."

It was even colder out now.

I thought about the nights ahead. I wouldn't have a home to sleep in, a roof to shelter me, to give at least the pretense of safety. I thought of Brint's caution. The thought of sleeping under the stars was nothing compared to the thought of facing the horror in his eyes when he issued his warning.

CHAPTER 23

Brint's wife, Anna, was just as friendly as her husband. She laid out blankets by the fire and stoked the flames to life to keep me warm. She insisted I stay for breakfast in the morning, but I explained I had to leave extremely early. I was afraid of Wolfe and the Guard catching up to me. Anna ignored my protests, insisting she and Brint were early risers. But I knew I couldn't stay. However, I told them I would, and made sure I thanked them so they'd know, when they found me gone in the morning, that I had been grateful to them.

I slept a little, but I was so nervous for the day ahead that I was up before the sun broke the horizon. I slipped through Hill o' Hope before the roosters woke everyone up. I held on to my magic like a child holding a parent's hand tightly in the marketplace, terrified of being lost to the wildness of the mountains.

The morning air was chilly, but as the sun rose and filtered through the trees, I grew warm in the humid environment of the forest. I had to take off my jacket. With no one around, the fact that the trousers were beyond indecent on me wouldn't matter.

Stopping at midday for a quick snack and some water, I mulled over Brint's words of warning. He'd told me the next town up from theirs was full of good people. However, I decided I wasn't taking any chances. I'd been lucky with Brint and his townsmen and women. Remembering how badly things had gone in the past, I wasn't going to press that luck. Instead, I stayed on the outskirts of the town, keeping to the trees and treading slowly and quietly so as not to draw any attention.

Through the trees, a town, smaller than Hill o' Hope, flashed in and out of view. Children helped their parents milk cows, sort out wool being clipped from sheep, and collect eggs from hens. They worked in tandem, a machine of teamwork, just like Hill o' Hope.

By late afternoon, I was exhausted. My shirt was soaked with sweat underneath my waistcoat and my feet were in searing pain from the blisters populating my soles, toes, and heels. If I kept walking, I didn't feel it so much. But then I'd make the mistake of stopping for water, and when I moved to walk again, the agony would start over tenfold.

I pushed on through the night until my eyes began to droop. At the sight of a tree with a large root curling around the soil like an arm, I took off my pack and slumped down behind it, hidden from view. Every muscle in my body screamed. The pain in my feet made me whimper. I shook my head in disgust. When had I become this soft, genteel creature who couldn't withstand a little exertion? I felt miserable and incompetent.

When I'd lived on the farm, I could run for miles without stopping. I could climb trees like a trapeze artist, walk and climb and walk some more and never want to stop. Living outdoors had been second nature. Now I was pampered and useless, and everything my parents had abhorred. I thought of Wolfe and had to hold back frustrated tears. I just kept betraying them over and over again.

Even angrier at myself for being pitiful and maudlin, I exhaled and looked at the little bed I'd made for the night. A large spider with spindly brown legs crawled slowly up from the soil onto my leg. It tickled through the fabric of my trousers. Gently, I leaned over and scooped up the spider, putting it down on the ground behind me so it could scuttle off and not get squashed beneath me as I slept.

Watching it, I was reminded of my little brother. He hated spiders, was terrified of them—said he didn't trust their fast little legs. It was the only thing he ever squealed at, and I knew to come running to rescue not only him but the poor spider from his fear. Despite the spider, he would have loved this, I thought, gazing up through the thick branches of the Arans above me, hardly able to see even a drop of sky. He would've thought this was quite the adventure.

I dug through my pack and pulled out my dagger, clutching it in comfort as I waited for exhaustion to give in to the inevitable. Somehow I did drop off to sleep, fatigue tugging me under despite my nervousness about being alone in the mountains.

My neck tingled, the feeling turning to something sharp enough to pull me out of semiconsciousness. I groaned and slapped my hand to the spot and pulled away a huge centipede, its legs clambering frantically as it dangled between my fingers. I yelped under my breath and threw it away, shuddering as I touched my neck to make sure there was nothing else there. I winced. The damn thing had bitten me!

I jumped to my feet, flinching at the forgotten blisters, and shook myself out. Not sure I was safe from the insects, who obviously liked the Aran root as much as I did, I curled into a ball in the open soil, glancing around to make sure there was nothing else near me.

Oh haven, I hated this.

THANKFULLY, I MUST HAVE DRIFTED BACK TO SLEEP FOR I woke up lying flat out on my back, the forest ceiling above me now giving way to the blue of the sky.

The blue of the sky!

What time was it?

I cried out and lunged sleepily for my things. It was definitely past sunrise. Probably midmorning. I'd missed a good few hours of light for walking. Grumbling at myself, I chewed on a biscuit and sipped from my canteen as I hurried upward, remembering to hold back the whimpers from the pain in my feet and body. Those first few steps were agonizing. I sucked in air and took a few more tentative steps, building momentum and chanting Haydyn's name as incentive to keep moving.

At the thought of Shadow Hill, I chanted inwardly, sure I was close to the town by now. I didn't want to be heard.

By afternoon, the sun was stronger than ever and wearing me down. But my feet. The pain was unbearable. At the constant sound of the stream to my right, I gave in. It didn't deviate from the direction of my magic, only from the worn track that kept me from the thick of the woods and all the plants and twigs that would trip me. The thought of cold water against my sore feet was too terrible a temptation to ignore.

I headed off, stepping carefully, until I found the wide stream rushing past. I could almost feel its soothing, cool liquid. I smiled wearily and sat down to remove my boots.

"Ahh ... hsss ..." I whimpered and hissed as the boots knocked against sores. I pouted like a little girl as I peeled off my stockings, a garbled shout of pain escaping before I could stop it, as the stocking, stuck with sweat, ripped open a blister.

I glared at the boots.

Perhaps taking them off hadn't been such a good idea. They might not go back on without a fight. Slumping at my losing battle with my feet, I slid them into the stream, wincing at the stings. And then the cold water did what I had hoped it would, numbing my swollen appendages until I didn't feel a thing.

When they'd had enough, I kneeled and ripped off the jacket and waistcoat and scooped water up to clean my neck and behind my ears as best I could. Feeling sweat along my hairline, I tugged off the cap and uncoiled my hair, sighing in satisfaction as my scalp drew breath.

The crack of a branch made me flinch and stiffen.

I was terrified to look behind me.

I heard the heavy breathing and my heart spluttered in absolute horror. A smell drifted upwind. Stale. Dirty. Human.

"What be here, then?" he growled in my ear.

CHAPTER 24

Huge arms encircled my waist, dragging me back from the stream as if I weighed nothing more than a sack of flour.

I shrieked and reached behind me, clawing at skin and pulling at hair. The stranger merely grunted until I was shunted up onto his shoulders, high off the ground.

He was huge.

I wriggled and screamed and fought and pummeled, and was merely slapped at for my troubles. My heart raced so fast it hurt, bile threatened to rise in my throat, and I was shaking so hard, my teeth chattered.

Frustrated tears welled in my eyes.

I was so stupid.

Brint had warned me about the Shadow Hill people. Had I listened? No. I'd wandered off the path because my feet hurt! Not only that, I'd unbound my hair.

I beat at the man's back once more with fury. "Put me down!" I cried, exhaustion making my voice weak.

How was I to escape these people? My feet hurt, I had no energy, I was useless. Once again kidnapped and taken. I could only hope the people showed me mercy.

The stranger's hand slid around to my buttocks and he squeezed, making me blanch in revulsion. "Good," he commented gruffly. "Very good."

What the haven did that mean?

The more we trekked, the more my magic wailed at me to turn back. He was deviating from my path!

Just as I was about to yell at him again, he slowed, walking up a few stone steps before I heard the creak of a door. I swung my head up, looking around us. We were still in the woods! As we entered the dimness of a tiny shack, an awful realization dawned on me. He wasn't one of the Shadow Hill people. And we were all alone.

As he set me on my battered feet, I ignored the pain and tried to dart away from him. His huge sweaty hands wrapped around my waist and he yanked me back against him. I trembled at the feel of his wet lips against my neck and fought the urge to be sick. I yelled in outrage and raked my fingernails along the skin of his hands. The stranger growled and whipped me around. I caught a glimpse of a rough face, drooping eyes and a toothless mouth surrounded by a beard, before his meaty hand walloped me across the cheek.

Ringing burst into song in my ear as I crumpled to the ground, dazed, my left cheek blazing with heat and throbbing with pain. Disoriented, darkness fell over my eyes.

A few minutes later, as I came to, I felt a tugging at my feet and looked to see the huge mountain man tying my ankles together with rope. Disbelief cleared my head and I thrust my legs, trying to get away from him. Horror flooded me when I saw he'd already tied my wrists so tight with rope that the slightest movement caused the scratchy material to chafe.

Distantly aware of his hands sliding along my legs, I searched the room, looking for anything—a weapon, some way out. I lay on a soggy pallet in the far corner. And there was nothing. Nothing else in the room but a large hunting knife, a pail, and a door. There was one window. Tiny. Not nearly big enough to climb out.

No. No!

My eyes widened as his hand crawled up the inside of my thigh. I snarled and shook him off me. Mountain man did nothing but smile and crawl alongside me, the stench of his body odor making me gag.

"Now, now," he admonished, and I shrunk back at the bright lust in his eyes. My stomach roiled and my lips quivered. Tears splashed down my cheeks.

I choked on a sob and he grinned wider. "No tears, wife." He shook his head as he touched me between the legs.

I roared like an animal in his face and he flinched back in surprise. Then he gave a huff of laughter. "Good wife."

"I'm not your wife!" I screamed through tears and snot. "Let me go! I'm not your wife!"

I was rewarded with another heavy slap, across my right cheek this time. My teeth pierced through my lip at the impact and I tasted blood on my tongue.

Glaring through my lashes at the mountain man, I noted his fascination with the blood staining my lip. My heart stopped at the brightness in his eyes. The lust had deepened. I swallowed back a rush of vomit.

Mountain man reached out and touched my cut lip. "Yer ma wife," he growled, pushing his face into mine. I closed my eyes, holding my breath so I didn't have to inhale his stink. "I find ye. Ye be ma wife."

Brint had warned me. Brint had told me there were people out here who had gone crazy with the isolation.

"I'm goin' huntin'. But I be back. I be gone awhile. But I be back, wife. I be back and feed ye, wife. And then ye be seeing to my husbandly needs." He stroked himself and I turned away, biting back screams of denial.

Whimpers escaped between my pinched lips.

I shuddered at the feel of his fingers on my face. He gripped my chin, jerking my head around. I didn't have to open my eyes to know his face was inches from mine. His lips came down wet and hard on my mouth, his beard scratching me as I struggled against him, my lips tightly closed. A large hand encircled my neck and squeezed. I gasped, giving him the opening he needed. His tongue forced its way into my mouth. I gagged on the foul taste of him, his rancid stench clogging my senses. No matter how much I jerked my head this way and that, he followed, his lips drinking me in like a fish gulping for air. The skin around my mouth was raw from his beard and wet from his fetid saliva. I was running out of air, close to hyperventilating, when I felt his hand squeeze my breast.

My anger turned into a blaze of fury.

Fury at myself and my stupidity. At this man, this mountain man who thought he could just take me like I was a deer in the woods. It coursed through me in an unthinking rush. Instinctively, I brought up my tied hands, suffusing as much strength and force into the upswing as I could, and abused him between his legs.

He broke away from me with a strangled shout and fell back, clutching where only minutes before he'd been stroking. I immediately vomited on the crude wooden floors beside the pallet. The room now reeked with the vilest of human stench, and I emptied what was left in my stomach.

I struggled to draw breath, the room spinning. I had to get out of here. I had to.

I thought of my kidnapping by the Iavii people. Of Kir's rookery gang. None of it had been so bad as this. Nothing this horrific had happened to me in a long time. I didn't think anything could match watching my parents and brother die. But if I stayed here, if this man used me and broke me ...

I sobbed, tears blinding as I drew my tied hands down onto the floor and used my upper body to drag myself along the wood. The door was just there. I had to get to it.

A bellow echoed around the shack and I was yanked like a

rag doll and thrown against the back of the hut. A sickening vibration shot through my body as my head hit the wall.

I slumped on the pallet and watched through blurry eyes as the mountain man approached me, his face mottled with hatred, lechery, and anger. I became a little more alert at the sight of the large hunting knife in his hand.

"Bad wife," he growled, brandishing the knife. "Teach ye a lesson, I will."

I beat at him uselessly with my tied hands as he grabbed me by my shirt. And then he tore open the shirt, revealing the curve of my breasts.

"No!" I cried out and swung my hands back up, catching his jaw. The mountain man barely blinked.

"Yer goin' to behave." He pointed the knife in my face, and I glared back at him, ignoring the hot tears rolling down my cheek. I took deep breaths as he smiled at me. I let a shaky calm envelop me. If this was to be my end, then I wouldn't give him the satisfaction of enjoying my fear.

I jutted my chin in defiance.

The mountain man tutted and gently placed the tip of the blade at the bottom of my throat. It was menacingly cold as he gently drew it down my skin, scratching me, until he came to the rising curve of my left breast. The blade pressed deeper, and I muffled a cry of shocked pain. He scored a shallow cut along the top of my breast, watching my expression. Blood trickled from the wound and clenched my jaw to keep from looking at the injury.

Mountain man pulled the blade back, grinning the entire time, his eyes alight with excitement. The knife disappeared into a pouch on his hip and he stood. He was huge. Massive. His entire shadow cast me into darkness in the shade of the shack.

He tugged at his trousers and licked his lips. "I like red on ye, wife. It's good. When I get back, I be bedding ye, ma wife. Bedding ye with a little more red."

At that, he abruptly turned and left, picking up some crude

hunting gear I hadn't seen. It lay near the door. The door opened, and I searched it greedily for a lock. It slammed shut behind him and I heard his footsteps disappear. I blinked, stupefied by what I'd seen.

There was no lock on the door.

At his sudden departure, the realization of what had just happened—and what was *going* to happen if I didn't get out of there—rushed in like a storm against the cliffs of Silvera. Terrified sobs broke out of me in rib-cracking force, and I shook and trembled, damning my stupid pride and fear that had made me come up the mountains without Wolfe.

"Stop it," I bit out, impatiently brushing the tears from my face with the tips of my fingers. I couldn't just sit here wallowing. I had to escape. The longer I stayed, the more likely he would return. If that happened, we were all doomed. Haydyn was doomed. I had to get to that plant. I had to get back to Haydyn. And when she awoke ... I'd tell her all that had happened. All that I had discovered. That there were good and bad people all over our world—that background, upbringing, and proximity to the Dyzvati evocation mattered little.

I'd lived my life with blinders on, convinced that my harsh jolt out of childhood innocence somehow made me wiser than others. But I wasn't. I was still a child who'd only been thrust into womanhood on this journey. This journey to save Phaedra from losing the evocation.

A journey that had taught me—I sucked in a painful breath—we didn't need the evocation. For centuries we'd feared the fire and shadow, the worst of human nature. But that fire and shadow was a part of us, whether we liked it or not. And it roared and crackled to life when people were treated unjustly.

What we needed was a stronger government. We needed to take care of our people, no matter the province they belonged to. The evocation wouldn't change the issues that made people act out as soon as its strength waned. But perhaps a better governing of them could get us closer to fixing the issues. Get us closer to ridding the world of men like the one who had come upon me and taken me as if I were a body without a soul ...

All this I'd tell Haydyn ... if I ever got out of here.

With renewed determination, I thumped my bound hands down onto the floor, ignoring the bite of splinters from the wood. I dragged myself along the ground. I didn't have great upper-body strength but I might have managed more easily if it weren't for the stinging pain of my feet and the throbbing cut on my breast needling my brain and slowing me down.

I made it to the door, but I was already soaked with sweat. It took another five minutes to wobble up onto my feet so I could pry open the door. As soon as it opened and the fresh forest air rushed against me, stealing me from the stink of the shack, I was submerged in dizziness. I leaned against the door frame to collect myself.

Finally, I opened my eyes. My magic reached out to me, beckoning me back onto the path. If I could manage to hobble far enough, perhaps I could find some way to untie the ropes. Carefully, concentrating, I balanced my body just right and hopped down onto the first step out of the shack. I wobbled a little, making my heart pitch in fear, but I was still standing. I took another breath and hopped again. This time I lost my balance and crashed with a painful "oof" onto the forest floor. A little winged bug stared up at me before flying off. I growled in frustration and tried to pull myself into a standing position. Five falls later and I was back up.

That was the pattern of how my day continued. I couldn't even remember how far I had fallen, hopped, and dragged myself. I kept freezing at every sound, trying to hear over the blood rushing in my ears. By nightfall, I was covered in sweat and mud and forest. But with no coat and a ripped shirt, I was thankful for the heat of the exertion. The shack seemed long gone now, but still I remained terrified. I had no idea how far I'd traveled.

Night had fallen a few hours past when I heard a loud snap of a tree branch. I stilled, my heart fluttering like a snared animal. I glanced around, trying to see in the dark. A large plant rustled and I whirled around. I could feel eyes on me. Boring into me. Trapping me.

Terror taunted me.

A rush of warm fluid slid down my leg.

The rustle sounded again, another crack of a tree.

Beady eyes appeared in the dark, low to the ground. I let go of my breath, my whole body sagging as some kind of opossum darted out of the bush and away from me. Realization dawned, and I looked down in the dark at my trousers. I could smell the stench of urine.

Silently, I began to cry.

I MADE ANOTHER MISTAKE.

Sometime during the late night, perhaps early morning, my mind blank with agony and exhaustion, I had fallen again. I had only intended to take a minute to collect myself. But when my eyes finally peeled back open, it was because a stream of sunlight was begging them to.

I blinked, confused. Where was I?

"Finally, ye be wakin'."

The nightmare that had unbelievably been real came rushing back at the sound of the mountain man's voice. I closed my eyes as I was roughly turned around; I tasted soil on my lips.

"Open yer eyes!" he bellowed in my face, the putrid breath bringing back memories of the day before.

Not wanting to, but somehow needing to, I did as he demanded, opening my eyes to see his ugly face inches above mine, his large hands gripping my upper arms.

His eyes blazed with rage. "Ye goin' to be gettin' it bad, wife, for runnin' off."

He dragged me into his arms. I struggled. I was in so much

pain already, his pinches and slaps didn't stop me from giving him hell as he strode in long lurches back to his shack.

The magic screamed at me again as he pulled me from its path.

When the shack appeared, I stopped struggling, slumping in his arms. We had walked perhaps thirty minutes using his long strides.

It had taken me hours to get thirty minutes away from this beast.

I gave a roar of rage and clobbered my bound hands against his head in impotent wrath. He snarled at me, giving me a wounded look as if he were the victim, not I. The fact that this man was deranged made my fear increase. There would be no reasoning with someone like him.

I was thrown down on the pallet as he slammed the shack door shut. The stench of dead meat filled the small room, and I gagged at the sight of an animal in the corner. But the carcass was the least of my worries.

My heart froze as the mountain man began undressing. I struggled away from him, my back pressed against the wall of the shack, frantically searching for a weapon as he loomed over me, naked.

Fuck the chafing! I pulled my wrists back and forth, desperate to be free. I could hear him laughing as he lowered himself to the ground, but still I rubbed my wrists together, growling and crying at the agony as I ripped my flesh raw. Saliva and tears dripped off my chin as I refused to look at the man.

I slammed back against the wall, wide-eyed as he crawled over me, straddling me. I looked into his face with so much hatred, I hoped it incinerated him. His stench overwhelmed me as it had the last time, and my stomach lurched in response. His stale sweat and bad breath would have been enough to make me sick, but the odor of blood and old meat lingered on him too.

He smelled like death.

I closed my eyes and pushed away from him as his hands

pawed at me, the muscles in my body twanging and twitching like the taut strings of a lute.

"Ye better start playin', wife, or I'm goin' to get mad."

Despite his threat, I couldn't stop flinching from his touch; I couldn't have even if my mind had told me it was the safest thing to do. Instead I incurred his anger over and over again, pushing and struggling and jerking to get him off me. One of his huge hands slid down over my face, and he pushed me, slamming my head off the wall. The minutes after that were distant and unclear. My head lolled on my shoulders, and I could only see and hear images. I swore I heard Wolfe's voice, saw Haydyn's face.

But they weren't here.

As the present came back to me, my situation had worsened. I was flat on my back on the pallet, the mountain man still straddling me. My shirt had been ripped fully open by the knife in his hands. I was covered in little shallow cuts.

I let out a garbled cry and swung at his head with my hands, a weak hit, but enough to give me a moment to summon my energy. I bucked under him, trying to throw him off. I swung at him again, causing him to jerk away, providing me the momentum I needed to shake him off. I screamed like a banshee the entire time, using it to call up furious adrenaline that might infuse me with temporary strength.

The mountain man roared and clambered over me, the knifeless fist swooping down and connecting with my face. Blood gushed out of my nose as my eyes watered. He used my disorientation to unbutton my trousers.

"No, no," I mumbled, tasting the bitter copper of my blood. I shook my head. No. I began to hyperventilate as his body drew flush with mine, his face hovering above me with lascivious eyes and a lusty grin.

I heard the clatter of the knife as he threw it away and gripped me by the throat to keep me in place.

My eyes rolled back in my head.

Then ... the mountain man flinched, a startled cry falling from his mouth. He stared straight ahead at the wall above me, his eyes wide.

Then he snarled and rolled off me, and my own eyes widened at the sight of an arrow sticking out of his back. I threw my tied hands out and dragged my body away from him, gasping at the vision of a man, cast in the shadow of the doorway, a huge machete clutched in his hand. Beside him stood a girl. Young. Perhaps Haydyn's age. She held a crossbow pointed at the mountain man.

I watched in a stupor of horror and hope as the mountain man lunged to his feet to attack the intruders. The girl let another arrow fly with calm expertise. Mountain man staggered as the girl armed the crossbow with another arrow. The man beside her laid a gentle hand on her shoulder, holding her off.

I wanted to complain. To tell her to shoot. Mountain man was still standing. But as I watched, his face slackened.

And then he collapsed with an almighty thud.

"This her?" the man at the doorway asked, nodding at me.

"Stupid question, Papa. 'Course it's her," the girl answered.

I slid away from them. I couldn't trust anyone here.

The man nodded and moved tentatively toward me. I shimmied back until I hit the wall again. I glowered at him.

He stopped, and as my eyes adjusted to the light, I saw his face. He appeared upset. Concerned. "I'm not goin' to hurt ye, little one. I'm goin' to untie those ropes for ye, so ye can be gettin' yerself together."

My heart beat unsteadily as I glanced between the two strangers. I so needed to believe them. "Who are you? What did you do to him? Don't come near me!" I screeched as he edged closer.

He sighed heavily and the girl huffed, "Well, that be a grateful response. We isn't goin' to hurt ye!" She shook her head. "Papa, she's as soft as goat's cheese. No wonder she be landin' in this mess and causin' a rumpus!"

I blinked in confusion, still dazed from my beating. Who was this girl? This man?

"L, be nice," the man admonished. "Help the poor girl, will ye? She's been through what ye like to call an *ordeeul*."

An ordeal? I wanted to scream. *An ordeal?* Being kidnapped by the Iavii, running from rookery thugs, that was an ordeal! This ... I shook my head. I looked back over at the mountain man and then to the two people who had attacked him. Had they really saved me? Why?

The girl—L, her father had called her—sighed. "Look here, Rogan, we isn't goin' to hurt ye. We're rescuing ye from Crazy here. My arrow was tipped in a poison he won't be comin' back from. Bugger won't be hurtin' no one again." She curled her lip in disgust at the mountain man.

I stiffened in suspicion. "How do you know my name?"

The man sighed. "My girl is one o' the blessed. A mage. She's got the Sight."

"A Glava?" I raised my eyebrows at her.

"That be me," L huffed. "I felt yer terror. So Papa and I set out to rescue ye. Now ... ye goin' to repay our kindness by no' takin' a fit o' the vapors as we untie ye?"

There was something genuine about the girl's gruffness and her father's gentleness. Relief crashed over me and I began to shake. Tears glittered in my eyes but I fought them, noticing L watching me carefully. "Of course."

The man reached for me and gently cut the ropes around my wrists.

He hissed at the mess. They were red and bleeding. I imagined, overall, I wasn't a pretty sight, covered in blood and bruises. Not to mention my trousers still stank of my fear. "Ma will have to be puttin' some o' her special medicine on to be sortin' that mess out."

I didn't argue. I couldn't continue my journey without getting cleaned up and hopefully fed. When Papa had cut the rope from my ankles, which were in much the same condition as my wrists,

I numbly refastened my trousers and tried to pull the shirt together.

L stilled my hands, briskly pulling off her jacket and tugging me into it. She buttoned it for me. Up close now, I could see her eyes. A multitude of emotion lived in them. She wasn't as unaffected by the state she'd found me in as she'd like me to believe. I stumbled forward on my blistered feet, and L exhaled again, throwing her father a look. "Ma will need to be sortin' her feet out, too, if this one is to be gettin' to the Pool."

L and her father reached to help me out of the shack, their arms around me as I hobbled along with them. L's comment meant she knew who I was and why I was here.

"Where are you taking me?" I asked wearily as we wandered into the woods. I numbed myself to the pain, only focusing on my relief.

L's father answered, "Back to our home so ye can get cleaned up. I'm Jonas, by the way."

"Hello, Jonas. Thank you for rescuing me."

L coughed.

"You too, L."

After a moment of silence, the numbness and overwhelming relief gave way to a need for answers, for more reassurance. "Where is your home? What else do you know, L? Is it—"

"Questions later, Lady Rogan." L sniffed. "Let's just be gettin' the blazes out o' here."

I obliged her, not once looking back.

CHAPTER 25

L and Jonas guided me onto the trail and my magic hummed with relief as we headed in the right direction. I hobbled between them, attempting to bite back whimpers of pain and not always succeeding.

"We be headin' near the outskirts of Shadow Hill," L whispered abruptly. "Ye need to be keepin' that pain quiet."

I didn't reply. I just heeded her warning.

Sometime later, when I heard voices way off in the distance, I guessed we were at Shadow Hill. Jonas and L had grown tense beside me and walked with a stealth I tried to mimic. I could tell they were worried I'd somehow give them away, but after what I'd just gone through, I had no intention of putting myself in a position to be abused again.

There was a horrible moment when we heard crashing of bracken in the woods to our right; the whips and rustles of trees and plants, the hard thud of a heavy foot in the soil. My rescuers looked at each other wide-eyed and then quickly pushed me behind a thick tree trunk, warning me with their eyes to stay still. They scurried off to find a tree each for cover. I didn't dare peer around the tree. My heart *thud-thud-thumped* as I heard a man whistling and humming under his breath. I then heard a hissing noise and saw L roll her eyes from her place behind the tree across from me. I think perhaps the man was relieving himself.

After a while, the whistling and noise of him crashing through the woods faded into the distance, and a grinning L came out into the open, Jonas following suit. I glowered, wondering what she had to be so carefree about when I was a nervous wreck. I'd never met a girl as cocky as this one. Without a word, they put their arms around me, helping me, and we set off again.

Half an hour later, quiet tears rolled down my face.

I was in agony.

The back of my head throbbed, my cheeks were stiff and bruised, and the cut on my lip stung. The knife injury on the rise of my breast pulsed painfully and my wrists were raw, the pain from the broken skin sharp and nipping. My ankles were the same. And my feet. They felt shredded and swollen.

I expected L to make a comment on my tears but she just looked at me and increased her pace. I tried to keep up, and as dark fell over us, L and Jonas led me off the trail path into the thick of the woods. Wariness clung to me, but I tried to shrug it off. L and Jonas were helping me. I really believed that but the fear and suspicion seemed like leftovers from the shock of my ordeal.

We walked perhaps another hour, this time deviating enough from my magic for it to tug at me, like a child pulling a friend's hair in frustration. I didn't care this time. I needed to rest. Just for a minute. Only a minute.

Finally, a well-built shack appeared in a tiny clearing in the woods. There was a vegetable garden and a goat tied to the wooden framing of the porch. It was the homeliest-looking place I'd seen since venturing into the mountains, like something from a fairy tale. As we hobbled up the rough-hewn path, the door to the house burst open, candlelight from inside streaming out to greet us. I almost wept in relief. A woman's silhouette framed the doorway, a child's face appearing from behind her skirts.

"Thank haven," the woman whispered into the night. "I was gettin' worried."

"Ma, we need some o' yer medicine," L called out as we drew toward the porch. Jonas and L helped me hobble up the steps until I faced the woman. Her expression changed as she took me in, her smile morphing into angry concern.

"Dear haven, what did he do to that child? Get her in here." She gestured us inside. It was easy to see who L had inherited her gruffness from.

As I stepped inside, I glanced down at the little boy who stared at me in horror.

I must look horrendous.

I looked away from him to take in my surroundings. We were in the main room of their home, it included a sitting area and kitchen. Two rocking chairs sat on either side of a large, glowing fire. There were two doors, one at the back and the other on the wall opposite the fire. I gathered it led to their bedrooms.

L guided me over to the table that took up most of the room. There were empty plates and cups on it. From the kitchen, the smell of stew wafted past my nostrils and my stomach clenched.

Their home was warm and welcoming and cozy.

And safe.

I crumpled between Jonas and L, both of them crying out as they moved to catch me.

"For haven's sake," L complained.

They picked me up and helped me into a seat at the table. I slumped back in it, thankful to be off my feet.

"L, there's water boiling over the fire. Bring it." L's mother scooted into a chair opposite me and smiled softly. "Ye be Rogan, that right?"

"Yes, ma'am," I replied politely.

Her grin widened. "Ma'am. Ye be hearin' that, L? Perhaps ye can be learnin' some manners."

L grunted.

"I be Sarah Moss. Ye met L—Elizabeth, but she be preferrin' L—and my husband Jonas. And that one there"—she nodded warmly at the little boy—"is Jonas Jr. We just be callin' him Jr."

"I'm pleased to meet all of you," I wheezed. "You have no idea." Tears I couldn't control spilled over.

"Aw, lass," Sarah tutted. She turned to L, who had placed the hot water before her. I watched through blurry eyes as Sarah rolled up a cloth and dipped it into the water. "L, why don't ye and yer papa make us up some bowls o' stew, eh?"

L and Jonas did so without complaint.

I, on the other hand, waited warily as Sarah leaned over with the wet cloth and dabbed at the blood on my face. I winced as she touched my bruises. My nose must have been swollen as well because it hurt horribly.

I was so glad there was no mirror in the room.

For a while, all Sarah did was wash away the blood from my cuts. She drew a deep breath and put the cloth aside. Then she reached for me with her bare hands. At the touch of her soft fingertips on my face, my eyes widened at the tingling rush of energy that shot through my nose. My eyes teared as the swelling disappeared, as my cheeks returned to normal, as the cut on my lip sealed. I said not a word as she turned those healing hands to all my wounds, even my feet.

Sarah looked exhausted by the time she settled back in her chair. L and Jonas had ladled out the stew and were already busy eating.

"You're a Dravilec," I whispered in amazement.

She nodded. I shook my head, glancing between Sarah and L. A Dravilec and a Glava in the same family. L caught my look and seemed to understand. She smirked.

"How is that possible?" I asked.

Jonas replied, "I have Glava in my family history. Sarah, Dravilec."

That really wasn't what I meant. What I had meant was that,

for a world whose mages were apparently dying out, I'd encountered many of them. Haydyn's evocation wasn't the only thing in Phaedra changing.

More mages were being born.

I chewed my lip as I wondered what this meant.

Of course, the Moss family didn't know I'd encountered many more like them, so my puzzlement was bemusing for them. I shrugged it off. This wasn't the time.

At Sarah's insistence, I ate the stew, but slowly, because my stomach still fragile. But as I ate the stew and warm bread, and sipped the apple juice Sarah pushed toward me, my body began to shut down in a sudden lassitude now that I felt safe.

"No, no, Lady Rogan." Sarah shook me, and I was surprised that it didn't hurt. Of course. She had healed me. I smiled dopily at her. I could have kissed her for that. "First, we need to get you washed up."

Again I was too tired to argue. Sarah shooed the rest of the Mosses from the room and set about undressing me. I let her wash me as my own mother had done years before, too exhausted to be embarrassed. She was gentle, even rinsing my hair out and braiding it into a coil on my head.

At last she dressed me in one of her own clean, soft, cotton nightgowns, and led me to a room at the back of the house. It was small with two single beds and a chest of drawers opposite them. Floral curtains were pulled across the window. In the bed closest to the door lay Jr., already fast asleep. In the other bed was L. She sat on the edge of it in cotton long johns. It didn't surprise me she didn't wear a nightgown to bed.

"She all right?" L whispered.

"She will be," Sarah replied. "She just needs sleep." She turned to me. "Ye can share L's bed. She don't mind."

At that moment, I didn't care if she did or not. I crawled into the bed and slipped under the covers.

L craned around to look at me. "Make yerself at home." She grunted and then slid in, too, pulling the covers around us. She reached over and tugged the other side of the quilt so that I was completely covered. Then she turned to Sarah and whispered, “Night, Ma.”

“Night, L. Proud o’ ye, lass.”

“Thanks, Ma.”

I must have fallen asleep as soon as my head hit L’s pillow because I didn’t remember a thing after that.

CHAPTER 26

The next morning I awoke snuggled up next to L.

She gave a huff of laughter because I'd trapped her in my embrace and she couldn't get out without waking me up. I blushed beetroot, but she merely waved away my apology.

Apparently everyone else was already up for breakfast. It was midmorning, L told me. They'd let us rest longer. I was grateful. I already felt so much better than I'd ever thought I'd feel again. L gave me clothes—we were of a similar height. I pulled on the soft trousers and shirt, eyeing the stockings and the too-big boots with dread because I knew my feet would soon be wrecked again.

As we dressed for the day, L mentioned I'd woken her up thrashing through what she surmised was a nightmare. I couldn't remember it and I apologized profusely. Again.

Again, she seemed truly unbothered by the disruption I'd caused.

"I only mentioned it because ..." She seemed embarrassed and I raised an eyebrow. "Well, because ye might be wantin' to talk about what happened to ye. Ye can talk to me." She shrugged as she turned from me.

I smiled, sad but grateful. "Thank you, L. I don't ..." I bristled at the way my body still clenched in fear at the thought of the mountain man. "I can't just yet, but thank you."

L shrugged again and headed into the main room.

BREAKFAST WAS DELICIOUS.

Eggs, toast, goat cheese. More of Sarah's delicious apple juice. The Mosses were kind and considerate of not only me but each other, and I enjoyed their teasing banter at the breakfast table. Their home was happy and warm. It was so nice to see that again after what I'd encountered up here in the Alvernian Mountains. It soothed my jangled nerves.

L told me she knew about Haydyn and the sleeping disease. None of them looked particularly worried by that, and I realized it was because it didn't really affect them way up here where the evocation didn't reach. But as L went on, I gathered they realized the importance of the evocation for the rest of our world. Although my own opinion on the evocation had changed with this journey, I was still determined to save Haydyn's life.

The Mosses saw this. They knew there was no stopping me.

And I could see in L's eyes that she knew for me it was personal—that I felt about Haydyn the way she felt about Jr.

"So, the Pool of Phaedra." L shook her head. By now I knew she was nineteen, Haydyn's age, but she spoke to me like I was twenty years her junior. "Quite a quest. Ye've certainly made a muddle o' it so far, hasn't ye."

"L, be polite," Jonas scolded.

"Just sayin'."

"I'm doing my best. I won't stop until I get that plant, even if I have to face a million mountain men to get it."

I watched L's eyes glimmer with a hint of respect.

"Well, I be gettin' an idea," Sarah piped up. "Our L is as tough as they come, knows these here mountains better than anyone. If ye follow yer magic to the Pool, L will be keepin' ye safe and right."

"Although I don't appreciate bein' offered up as a guide without my say-so, I do see the wisdom in the suggestion," L agreed. "I'll do it."

I rather liked the idea of having a savvy, crossbow-toting mountain girl with me but I didn't want to endanger anyone else. "I appreciate the offer, but you don't have to help me. You've already done so much."

L scowled. "I don't offer help unless I be wantin' to. I'm comin'. Isn't no 'yes thank ye, no thank ye' about it. I leave yer lily-white ass to saunter through these here mountains, and Phaedra will be doomed—ye eaten alive by the Aran, and Phaedra fallin' to nothin' without that princezna o' yers."

Minutes before, I'd thought having her along might be a wonderful idea. Now I grimaced. With L's obnoxious, superior attitude, I might as I well have brought Wolfe along.

Then I remembered the mountain man.

I eyed L's crossbow leaning against the wall near the fire.

I pasted on a strained smile. "Thank you. I appreciate it."

❧

WE LEFT SOON AFTER, BOTH OF US OUTFITTED IN WARM jackets, each with a pack of supplies.

L carried her crossbow, and I carried one of Jonas's hunting knives. I'd lost my pack and dagger at the stream when the mountain man had taken me.

We took off at a brisk pace, and I marveled at how rejuvenated I was, as if I had never undergone such horror at the mountain man's hands.

The boots didn't begin to rub as quickly as my previous pair, but when I did eventually feel a niggle of discomfort, I ignored it.

Our march upward was silent until we broke for a late lunch.

Sweat soaked my back already. As we sat to eat the biscuits and bread Sarah provided, L decided she was bored with the silence.

"Ye don't talk much for a fancy person with fancy learnin'."

I shrugged.

I thought that would be the end of it, but as we walked again, L encouraged me to tell her about my "fancy" society life. Anything I said or explained was answered with phrases such as, "Well, that just sounds stupid" and "What would ye be wantin' to do that for?"

Surprisingly, I enjoyed L's chatter. Her speech may have been of the mountain people but her rough slaughter of our language belied a keen mind and sharp wit. I couldn't help but agree with her assessments when I told her about the scandalous things society members got up to.

L was pragmatic and straightforward, much as I'd always thought I was. She knew the mountains well, traipsing through them without a care, physically stronger than I. I puffed a little to keep up. She wondered aloud how I'd survived this far without her, especially after I squatted to relieve myself and she saved me just in time from squatting on poisonous leaves.

After that, L pointed out the different species of plants in the forest, what each of them was called and what their properties were. I was amazed by how knowledgeable she was on the subject, and she told me her grandfather had taught her before he died a few years ago.

WHEN WE STOPPED FOR THE NIGHT, MY MAGIC VIBRATING through me stronger than ever, L didn't build us a fire.

When I asked why, shivering in my jacket, she told me it would attract the mountain dogs. My heart had thundered as I remembered warnings from Brint about the dogs. I was glad L said we should huddle together for heat.

We fell asleep with our arms tight around one another.

"WHO'S WOLFE?" L ASKED AS I TRIPPED OVER A TREE ROOT I hadn't seen.

I picked myself up, dusting the soil off my hands. It was early morning, we'd already eaten, and we'd been walking for half an hour.

I glanced sharply at L.

She smirked, her young, fresh face bright with amusement. "Ye said his name in yer sleep last night. And the night before."

Whatever she saw on my face made her laugh. "Ah, I be seein'. I just got a wee picture o' ye kissin' a fine-looking specimen o' a man. Wee bit soft perhaps, but mighty fine."

I felt the heat of indignation. "Wolfe is anything but soft," I snapped.

L grinned mischievously. "He yer man, then? Yer betrothed?"

Like a thirteen-year-old, I blushed, shaking my head. "It's complicated."

I was rewarded with a scowl. "I can be keepin' up."

With a weary sigh, I went on to tell L about my family, about what Syracen had done to them. That Wolfe was Syracen's son. How all these years I'd thought Wolfe had been after revenge. How I had recently discovered what Syracen had done to Wolfe. That Wolfe had feelings for me. That I had feelings for Wolfe but I knew that acting on them was a betrayal of my family.

I talked myself hoarse, surprised by how much I'd come to trust this girl in so little time. L listened patiently, her eyes betraying her interest and her sympathy.

Still, when I finished, she scratched her cheek and said gruffly, "Well, I isn't no expert on these here things, but from what ye be tellin' me, sounds to me as if ye be gettin' things a wee bit backward."

"Backward?" I puffed out a breath, glaring at her back. L turned and caught the look. She chuckled at my expression as we dug our feet into the hill, the incline growing steeper.

"Well, yer parents tried to protect ye, told ye to run. They died for ye."

"Yes," I replied through clenched teeth, hissing the *s*.

"Well, that be sayin' to me that they was good folks. They just wanted ye to be free and happy."

I frowned, wondering at the direction of her point, and if she was ever going to make it. "Yes?"

"If this Wolfe man—ha ha, wolfman." She chortled and then noticed my belligerent expression. "Never mind. If this Wolfe makes ye feel free, makes ye happy, isn't that all that be matterin' to yer parents?"

"But his father killed my parents. Being with his son would be a betrayal of their memory."

"That don't be makin' no kind o' sense. Ye brought yer parents murderer to justice, Rogan, and ye saved Wolfe and his mother from a life o' misery at that evil-doer's hands. And this Wolfe person, he sounds like he be an upright kind o' fella. And don't he be some kind o' nobility?"

I wiped the sweat off my forehead, my fingers trembling. "A vikomt."

L grunted. "Lass, ye be gettin' yerself a rich man. That's every parent's dream," she joked.

When I didn't respond, she threw me a wicked smile that transformed her from ordinary to pretty. "Ye joined giblets with yer Wolfe, then?"

I frowned, searching my brain for a translation.

L laughed at my confusion. "Has he bedded ye, Rogan?"

I grimaced at her forthright question, my cheeks flushing hotly. "No," I bit out.

L sobered quite abruptly. "Ye a maiden, then?"

"Yes. Aren't you?"

"O' course."

I nodded, having expected as much.

"Think on this then, Rogan ..." She stopped to freeze me in her guileless stare. "What if I had no' got to ye? Is that how ye would have wanted it? Raped and abused by a stranger in these here mountains, instead of it bein' right and true with the man ye love?"

I was instantly chilled at the thought.

Then panicky, hot flutters melted the ice she'd created inside me with her directness.

"If there be one thing these here mountains learn us, Rogan, it be life is often harsh ... and always temporary. Don't run from love because ye lost so much o' it as a child. Instead ... love while ye can."

Gulping back the emotion clogging my throat, I somehow managed to respond, "Is that what you intend to do, L?"

She threw me another quick grin before turning back up the mountain. "As soon as I be finding love like Ma and Papa's."

As I followed her, I found myself drowning in L's practicality. I had been since the moment I met her, and now her pragmatism was starting to make sense. And with Wolfe, I didn't want it to make sense.

"My plan wasn't to marry—*ever*."

"My plan for this week was to show Jr. how to be layin' a trap without takin' his hands off. Instead I'm stuck up in these here mountains with the dumbest smart person I ever be meetin'."

"You know, L, I'm feeling overwhelmed by your kindness and charm."

"I try to leash the potency of the charm but it's too exhaustin'." L grinned crookedly over her shoulder.

I shook my head and burst into reluctant laughter.

❧

By the third day, we had made it up through the Alvernian Mountains with little mishap.

We'd heard a few howls in the distance that had given us pause, but so far, we hadn't come across the mountain dogs.

My magic told me we were close. Very close.

It was midafternoon, and the mountain had already begun to plateau under our feet. L drew to a stop as a new scent drifted by on the wind—lilacs and damp moss.

"I guess we be here." L smiled at me. At my confused look, she pointed. I walked around her, my feet throbbing. Light sparkled through the trees in front of me, and I grinned in relief.

"We're here."

Together we took off at a run and burst out of the trees into the bright light. Before us the grass at our feet slid down toward a glistening lake, enclosed on all sides by higher ground. A small waterfall cascaded from one of the mountains, descending into the lake, causing puffs of foam to rise in the water. Fresh lilacs and orchids bloomed around the lake's edge, interspersed with dewy plants and buttercups. I stared in amazement. It was the most enchanting place I'd ever seen.

"Wow." L nudged my shoulder. "Impressive."

I nodded, smiling in awe. "The Pool of Phaedra."

I was finally here. My lips trembled and tears prickled behind my eyes.

"Yer no' be gettin' all watery, are ye?" L teased.

I gave her a little push, and she laughed. I didn't know what I would have done without her. Impulsively, and so unlike me, I threw my arms around her and pulled her into a hug. At first she tensed with surprise ... and then tentatively, she returned my embrace. When I eventually released her, she gave me a mock look of bemusement. I grinned and then walked away, following the tug of my magic.

It took me behind a large rock by the edge of the lake. There grew a blue plant, the color of the lake itself, vivid and alien, the sweet smell of molasses drifting out of it.

"The Somna plant?" L asked from behind me.

I nodded, reaching for it.

"No' much left."

No, there wasn't. "I'm taking it all," I whispered, reaching for my pack. "We have alchemists back in Silvera who might be able to plant this to grow more crops. Mayhap they can withdraw its properties and discover other uses for it."

She glanced around warily. "Alchemists. Properties. Who cares, Rogan, just be gettin' the damn thing and put it in yer pack."

I frowned as I pulled the plants out by the roots and wrapped them in cloth. "What's wrong?" I asked as I carefully stashed them in my pack.

L exhaled shakily. "Well, I don't be wantin' to alarm ye but I be sensin' we might be hittin' a spot o' trouble on the way back down."

My heart thumped, visions of the mountain man making me dizzy. "Trouble? What kind of trouble?"

She shook her head, her eyes narrowed in frustration. "I don't be knowin' yet. Sometimes my gift, as Ma calls it, has a warped sense o' humor."

WITH ONE LAST LONGING LOOK AT THE POOL OF PHAEDRA, L and I hurried back into the woods.

I trusted that L had been paying attention to the route we'd taken but that didn't mean I hadn't been paying attention either. L led us back the way we'd come without faltering.

We were both tense and anxious as we moved swiftly through the Arans. All I wanted now that I had the plant was to get back to Silvera and Haydyn as quickly as possible.

When the woods creaked and cracked around us, we would pause, warily cocking our heads, our eyes wide as we stared through the trees, searching for signs of danger. There would be nothing. We'd look at each other, surmise we were safe to carry on, and we'd head off again, our departure faster downhill that it had been going up.

Dusk passed into dark and still we strode through the woods, desperate to get back to L's home. For now, L searched the woods, looking for the perfect place to bed down for the night.

When more time passed, my feet aching and stomach growling, and still L hadn't stopped, it was almost on the tip of my tongue to beg L to just choose somewhere already, when the hair on the back of my neck rose.

A low growl sounded from my left and I drew to an abrupt halt. L heard it, too, and spun around. Her eyes followed the sound.

"Mountain dog," she whispered. Slowly, silently, she took her crossbow and brought it up, aiming it somewhere to my left. "I thought we might be comin' upon one o' these dung-bred lowlifes."

Frightened but needing to see for myself, I turned my head. My eyes widened at the sight of the large dog mere yards from me. Its body was skinny but muscular, its coat rough with bald patches here and there. Its muzzle was pulled back over its sharp teeth, saliva dripping from his rotting gums.

Its eyes were feral.

"We've got to be takin' this mutt down and then be goin'. Its pack can't be too far behind."

Just as the dog moved to attack, L shot the arrow. It plunged with perfect aim into the dog's flesh. It whined and collapsed mid jump. I exhaled in relief and turned to thank L, only to yell out as another dog lunged out of the woods at her.

It took L down, clamping its jaws into her shoulder as she struggled beneath it, attempting to reach for her crossbow, which had fallen from her hands.

I acted without thought.

With the hunting knife in hand, I leapt on the dog, plunging the blade deep and up into its belly. It snapped out at me, missing me by an inch, before it whined and slumped unconscious on top of L. I grabbed her biceps and pulled her out from under it. The dog's blood stained her trousers.

Her own stained her jacket where the dog had ripped it open and tore into the muscles of her shoulder. The bite was deep.

She swayed a little, and I reached to catch her. In her usual gruffness, L batted me away.

"We need to go."

When she took off at a run, I followed, anxiety gripping me. L was running on adrenaline. When that dissipated, I needed to get her home to Sarah as soon as possible.

Finally, L drew to a stop, the pallor of her skin worrying. I pulled out the cloth the Somna plant was wrapped in and put the plant back into the pack. With a briskness I knew L would appreciate, I removed her jacket and shirt, using the cloth to tie a tourniquet over the awkward wound. It would stem the flow of blood, but that was about it.

Hastily, I put her shirt back on as she lolled in my arms. Next her jacket. I forced a couple of sugary biscuits into her mouth, followed by water. And then I wrapped my arms around her, watching as I attempted to keep her from slipping into unconsciousness.

CHAPTER 27

I'd never been so thankful in my life to see a house.

With L growing weaker by the hour, we weren't as quick as I would have liked in returning her to the Mosses'. I was glad I'd paid attention to the route we'd taken, for L was disoriented. In those hours spent looking after her, keeping her conscious, I was more like myself again. This person, this young woman in control, was me. And with my old determination, I pushed both L and I to our limits, not stopping for food or rest until I had her back to Sarah. I wasn't letting anything happen to the girl who had saved my life twice without ever asking for anything in return.

As if she'd sensed us, the door to the shack flew open, and Sarah rushed to meet us as I dragged L up the garden path.

"What happened?" Sarah's eyes blazed with anxiety.

"Mountain dog," I bit out, relief making me weak. Thankfully Sarah took hold of L and carried her the rest of the way into the house.

When I stepped over the threshold, I took in Jr. staring wide-eyed at his mother as she laid L on the table.

"Jr., heat some water," Sarah threw over her shoulder as she ripped L's clothes away. She hissed at the sight of the wound and

I flinched seeing how putrid it had grown with infection. Sarah stroked her daughter's face tenderly. L barely registered the touch. "L, my love, ye got yerself a fever. I'm goin' to be sortin' that out, all right, honey?"

I just stood there, gazing on uselessly. This was all my fault. I should never have taken L with me. Sarah caught the guilt and concern on my face and smiled reassuringly.

"Now, don't ye be lookin' like that, Rogan. Things happen up in these here mountains. L's goin' to be all right."

Jr. struggled with the pot of hot water so I hurried to take it from him before he splashed and burned himself. Sarah took it from me and set about cleaning L's wound. She stirred a little at her mother's touch. And then, as she had done with me, Sarah put her fingertips on the wound and released her energy into L. I watched in amazement as the wound began to close, the color returning to L's face with surprising swiftness. L's eyelashes fluttered and she groaned, looking at Sarah's happy but now weary expression.

"Ma." Her head rolled and she saw me standing over Sarah's shoulder. She smiled. "Knew ye wasn't completely useless." She turned to Sarah now. "Here, Ma, Rogan saved my life."

"Well, don't that be somethin'." We all turned at the sound of Jonas's voice. He stood in the doorway to the house, his eyes bright on his daughter, a dead rabbit slung over his shoulder. He winked at me and then stepped farther into the house. A shadow moved behind him, and my heart faltered. There was a man with him, taller, broader. As he stepped inside beside Jonas, his familiar eyes bored were inscrutable and probing.

"Wolfe!" Jr. shouted happily and flew past me to hop at Wolfe's feet. "This be my sister, L, Wolfe." He pointed at L lying on the table. I glanced at L as she pulled herself into a sitting position. Her eyes flicked between Wolfe and me before she bestowed me a knowing smirk.

I exhaled and turned to Wolfe.

I couldn't believe the fool had come after me. Where was the damn Guard?

When our gazes locked, despite the inscrutability of those pale eyes, a delicious relief—like coming home after months of miserable absence—swept over me.

❧

IT WAS STRANGE SITTING AROUND THE MOSSES' KITCHEN TABLE with Wolfe.

I knew I'd only known the family a few short days, but I had a bond with L that made me feel closer to all of them, and it was strange to share them with Wolfe. We hadn't spoken yet about my running off on him, but he wasn't unpleasant to me.

However, I knew that was more for the Mosses' sake than mine.

We'd been eating for five minutes and having already exhausted the story of mine and L's rescue of one another from the mountain dogs, Jonas and Wolfe discussed hunting techniques while Jr. desperately tried to get in on the conversation. The young boy was obviously enamored with Wolfe.

As he did with everyone, Wolfe had enchanted the Moss family.

He took up a lot of room at their table. I forgot how large he was. The warm military jacket he'd been wearing when he appeared with Jonas was hanging up on the Mosses' coat pegs, the fur around the cuffs and collar proclaiming Wolfe's wealth. His shirt and waistcoat were finely made, as were his boots and trousers. The white-gold hilt of his sword gleamed propped against the wall.

He was from an entirely different world than the Mosses.

He was from my world.

And as much as I was grateful to the Mosses, their home had not felt like home until Wolfe sat within its walls.

Just being near him made me feel safe.

I thought of L's words of wisdom in the woods and longed to reach out and brush his hair off his face, stroke his arm, anything to feel the heat and life of him under my fingertips. But he refused to look at me. I watched him talk animatedly with Jonas. From what I'd gathered, Wolfe was very familiar with the Mosses.

The question was, how?

L stared at me. Her eyes demanded me to question Wolfe about it, but I was frightened any conversation might spark an argument between us.

She kicked me under the table and I muffled a cry of pain. I glared at her and exhaled, turning to Wolfe.

"So, Captain, when did you arrive?"

The sound of my voice made Wolfe tense, and he glanced sharply at me. "Apparently a few hours after you and Miss Moss left for the Pool. Sarah and Jonas convinced me you were in safe hands and that it would better if I stayed with them to await your return." That last word he emphasized with an edge, his eyes suddenly dark with pure, undiluted fury.

My heart lurched.

I had expected him to be mad, but this ... he looked ready to explode. "Jonas told me how he and L found you. *Where* they found you. With *whom*. In what *state*."

The breath whooshed out of my body. I hadn't ever wanted Wolfe to know about the mountain man. I looked away and scraped at my plate. "I see."

"Rogan ..."

"Later, Wol—Captain."

Just as I had not wanted to, Wolfe and I created a chilled atmosphere. I shifted uncomfortably.

"So, Captain Wolfe," L piped up, "how be ye findin' Rogan?"

Yes, I thought, glancing over at him. How had he found me at the Mosses'?

Wolfe shrugged. "I'm a Glava as well, Miss Moss. I have a heightened sense of intuition."

L threw me a look. I had told her about Wolfe being Glava but had not mentioned this ability. I shrugged back at her. I hadn't *known* about that ability. I sighed and refused to look at him. Wolfe was powerful. Extremely powerful. He could move things with his mind, call upon the elements, and he had some psychic talent as well. I had never heard of the like. Perhaps that's why he hadn't trusted me enough to tell me.

I chanced a glower at him but Wolfe caught it. His expression was so clear, it was almost as if I could read his mind: "Don't be mad at me for not trusting you. You who didn't trust me and got yourself almost raped in the Alvernian Mountains."

I grimaced and turned from him.

L threw me a sympathetic smirk.

CHAPTER 28

The sun bit into the morning chill, and I breathed in the crispness of a summer morning in the Alvernian Mountains, feeling far more exuberant than I had in weeks.

I had the plant, I was no longer alone, and I was heading back to Silvera to save Haydyn.

Sarah, Jonas, and Jr. stood on the porch of their home while L helped me with my pack. I could feel Wolfe waiting impatiently behind me at the end of the garden path, having already thanked the Mosses for their hospitality and made his goodbyes. Jr. was not amused by Wolfe's sudden departure and blamed me for it. He refused to say goodbye to me.

"Right," L said briskly, handing over the hunting knife.

I shook my head. "I can't take anything more from you." I was already wearing her clothes and carrying their food. They had so little and yet they gave so generously.

L gave me one of her characteristic scowls. "Ye be refusin' to let me escort ye down the mountain, so ye be takin' the damn knife."

I hid my smile. Last night, L had made quite a stink when I told her she was staying with her family, that I would be all right now that I had Wolfe with me. She'd given Wolfe, in his fine clothing, with his nice hair and skin, a dubious look. Wolfe had good naturedly let her pick at his "obvious uselessness" as she called it. I experienced an ache in my chest as L had gone on and on, pretending to be put out. She was worried about me.

I took the knife and held her gaze. "You and your family must come to Silvera to see me, L. I'll arrange it." I looked past her to Sarah and Jonas. They smiled at the idea, so I took that to mean yes.

"Ye isn't meaning that." L sniffed, kicking dirt on the path, uncharacteristically self-conscious. "Ye'll go back to yer fancy world and forget all about me and mine."

"L." I grinned, grabbing her arms. "L, you're just about the most unforgettable person I've ever met. And if you don't come to see me in Silvera, then I'm going to crawl all the way back up this mountain to you."

She reddened a little but looked pleased. "Well, no need to be gettin' all melodramatic on me," she drawled, waving me off.

I laughed, feeling that pang again. I felt as if I'd known her forever, and I was sorry to leave her and her family up here in these forsaken hills. I'd be back for them, though. I was going to make sure they never had to worry about anything again.

Ignoring L's gruffness, I tugged her into a hug and was surprised by how tight she held me. After a moment, she patted me on the back and pulled away, our eyes bright.

"Ye be careful," she warned, and then peered around me to Wolfe. She threw him her famous scowl. "Ye be watchin' o'er this one, Captain Wolfe."

"I promise, Miss Moss."

"Miss Moss," L muttered under her breath and then threw me a look. "Ye ever heard the likes." Still muttering under her breath like an old woman, L turned on her heel to join her family on the porch. Wolfe and I waved one last time and then I walked away with him in a mixture of reluctance and anticipation.

. . .

We'd been walking an hour and still Wolfe hadn't said a word.

The tension between us was thick and uncomfortable; even my gums ached with it. I concentrated on watching where I was going, thankful to Sarah who had healed my new blisters again. I'd probably have a few by the time we got off the mountain, but maybe not so many. My feet were already feeling harder and stronger.

That morning, as I'd pulled on L's trousers and shirt, I realized how much weight I'd lost since I'd left Silvera. My calves and thighs had slimmed with muscle; my stomach was flatter from eating sparingly and walking the hills. Still, despite our similar heights, L was wiry and I was curvy; she wore her trousers tight, and on me, they were indecent. I'd forgotten all about propriety up in the mountains without anyone from home to see me. But now that Wolfe was around, I was painfully aware of how revealing these clothes were. I'd put my borrowed coat on over the top of the trousers and shirt before Wolfe had seen them. I wouldn't be removing it.

The silence continued between us, Wolfe keeping a careful distance, enough for me to know he wasn't speaking to me, but not enough so he couldn't keep an eye on me. I kept waiting for his explosion of indignation and anger, and when it didn't come, I was strangely peeved.

The tension only grew thicker as the afternoon wore on and we found ourselves at the outskirts of Shadow Hill. Before I could warn Wolfe, he turned to me with a finger to his lips, hushing me. He knew about Shadow Hill. Either the Mosses had warned him, or he may have already met Brint in Hill o' Hope and Brint had warned him.

We moved around the outskirts of the town with stealth, the voices in the distance making my heart pound. I grew unbearably warm under my coat. It was with a sigh of relief when we made it past the Hill without incident and carried on at a quicker pace down the mountain. Again, we were making good time.

An hour or so later, I heard the trickle of the stream in the distance and something about the wood seemed familiar. I shivered. We were close to where I'd been taken by the mountain man. Without explaining, I picked up my feet, almost running to get away from the spot, my skin crawling, my neck prickling. I felt as if his shadow were watching me, taunting me. I trembled in revulsion and began to run. The sounds of Wolfe's running footsteps grew louder and closer, but I couldn't stop.

Abruptly, I was forced to a halt, Wolfe's hand catching my arm and dragging me around to face him. His features were fierce with anger, the golden striations in his blue eyes prominent with passion. "What the hell were you thinking?" he yelled, not caring if his voice carried now that we were miles from Shadow Hill.

I struggled to get out of his grip. "I just felt like running."

"Not that, Rogan." His jaw clenched. He looked close to violence. I struggled harder to get away from him, but he only pulled me closer. "I'm talking about you running off from Arrana, alone, without an escort—about lying to me and making a fool of me—of nearly getting yourself raped and killed!"

Like always, his overbearing attitude caused my knee-jerk reaction—to dispute him. "Nearly. *Nearly*, all right. I managed well enough without you, Wolfe."

"Well enough? Jonas told me how he found you, Rogan, and he spared me no details!"

"Will you stop yelling? Are you trying to get us into bother?" I hissed, glancing around to make sure we were still alone.

"Stop trying to wriggle your way out of discussing it."

Using all my strength, I tugged out of Wolfe's grasp, my cheeks hot with frustration and anger. "Did you ever stop to consider I might not be ready to discuss it?"

Wolfe's expression changed instantly. Concern softened his features. "Rogan ..."

I shook my head.

"Fine. But what about my first question? You ran away, Rogan. From me. You knew I would come after you and as far as you knew, I had no way of knowing which way you went. I could have gotten lost up here."

Guilt gnawed at me and I shook my head in denial. "No. I didn't … I thought if you did chance into the mountains, you would bring an escort. Chaeron. Or a few of the men. I didn't think you would be foolish enough to come all the way into the mountains after me alone."

"You're lying," he hissed. "You knew I'd come after you, Rogan, you had to have known that."

I clenched my jaw trying to stop the tears that choked me. Hanging my head, I didn't say anything in return. Was he right? Had I known Wolfe loved me enough to do that? I knew what kind of man he was. Because of my fear of being alone with him, a fear of my own damn feelings, had I selfishly put him in danger? I didn't know. I had no response. There was nothing I could say.

All this time I'd fretted that his parentage meant perhaps he didn't deserve me. But really … I didn't deserve him.

"I don't know what I was thinking. I just knew I had to get this plant. For Haydyn."

"And still she lies," he whispered bitterly.

We didn't speak after that.

THE JOURNEY DOWNHILL CUT THE TIME IN HALF.

By late night, Wolfe and I broke out of the trees and into Hill o' Hope.

I chanced a glance at Wolfe. "You came through here too?"

He nodded, not looking my way. "I stayed with a man called Brint Lokam. He told me he'd sheltered a young woman who was looking for the Pool of Phaedra."

My mouth fell open. "He knew I was a girl?"

Wolfe flicked me a patronizing look. I harrumphed. I'd so thought my disguise had worked. Had all of Hill o' Hope known I was a girl? My cheeks flamed with embarrassment.

We crossed through the quiet hill, noise, cheer, and light spilling out of Hope Tavern. Wolfe didn't stop. He headed toward the Lokams' shack. I shook my head in wonder at the thought of Brint. He'd been such a gentleman. No wonder he'd seemed so concerned about letting me go into the mountains alone. He knew I was a girl!

The door to the shack opened before we even reached it and the tall figure of Brint appeared. He squinted in the dark, holding up a lantern, and then grinned when he recognized us. "Well, hullo there."

I waved and followed Wolfe up to the door.

"Brint." Wolfe held out his hand to shake. "Could we perhaps trespass upon your hospitality one more evening, Mr. Lokam?"

Brint took Wolfe's hand, shaking it heartily as he grinned. "No needin' to be askin'." He shook us off gruffly and grinned wider as I passed. Brint must have seen the look on my face because he said, "Ye wasn't thinkin' ol' Brint was bein' fooled by the boy's outfit o' yers? Not even wee Tera. She likes a bonny maid does our Tera."

Wolfe raised an eyebrow as I blushed, but I refused to tell him about the night at Hope Tavern. Not that I was sure he'd appreciate me speaking to him anyway.

Anna was happy to offer us food and ale, and they put down blankets by the fire for us to sleep on. Wolfe was so mad at me, he slept at the kitchen table.

❧

I DIDN'T THINK I HAD EVER BEEN HAPPIER TO BE ON FLAT ground in my life.

I celebrated my last step off the Alvernian Mountains by

rushing into the arms of Lieutenant Chaeron, who, unlike Wolfe, was happy to see me. I ignored Wolfe's grunt as he strode past us. Chaeron squeezed me hard and I pulled back. Half the Guard filled the narrow trade road leading away from the mountains. They all pretended to be indifferent to my clothing and the fact that I was informally hugging Chaeron, treating him as a friend. But he *was* a friend. And I was thankful to see him again.

"Another hour and be damned Wolfe's orders, I was coming up to get you both. I am delighted to see you are well, Miss Rogan." Chaeron smiled wearily at me. I wondered if he'd slept much since my running away.

"You too, Chaeron. I got the plant!" I whispered excitedly.

He smiled in relief and then lifted his gaze to Wolfe, who was taking off the winter coat and replacing it with his emerald jacket. We both watched as he mounted his horse.

"He's not speaking to me," I said forlornly.

"You frightened him, Miss Rogan. Give him time."

I nodded, but I didn't think even time would fix the situation between me and Wolfe. Chaeron had no idea what I'd gone through up on that mountain. For that to have happened to me surely made Wolfe sick. He was a man who felt it his calling in life to protect others. And I hadn't let him protect me. I hadn't trusted him.

With another woeful look at the man who had so surprisingly complicated my life, I turned and mounted the horse Chaeron had waiting for me.

"Don't you wish to remove that coat, Miss Rogan?" Chaeron inquired as he pulled up beside me.

"Don't you dare." Wolfe was suddenly in front of us, his eyes blazing. "It's indecent what you're wearing, Rogan. You will not take that off in front of my men."

"Indecent?" Chaeron's brow furrowed.

"You saw?" I blushed, half-aghast, half-annoyed at his overbearing command.

"At the Mosses'." He nodded. "Before you put the jacket on."

A strange look entered his eyes, and I could have sworn a flush rose on the crest of his cheeks. He shifted on his horse and then glared at me. "Keep it on." And then he headed off, leading the way for me and Chaeron to move through the men (who all nodded their relieved greetings at me) so we were in front of the entourage.

"Indecent?" Chaeron asked again.

I shrugged, tempted to take the damn coat off to remind Wolfe I wasn't one of his men to be ordered around! "I'm wearing trousers. They leave little to the imagination."

"Ah." Chaeron shifted his attention to Wolfe who began to gallop ahead of us. His mouth broke into a wide, knowing grin. "I think you'll be fine, Miss Rogan. You and Wolfe both."

IT WAS COLD AND BLACK AS TAR OUTSIDE BY THE TIME WE entered Arrana and were allowed entrance into the vojvoda's home.

I still had the coat on. Not because Wolfe had ordered it but because my own sense of modesty did. After a day of blazing heat in the valley, my clothes were sticking to me. I needed a bath. Badly.

As soon as we were inside the mansion, Chaeron took care of everything. I was led to the room I had been given before, and I watched impatiently as the servants filled a tin tub with hot water, leaving rose-scented soap for me. After the last maid had laid out one of my dresses, I politely asked them to leave and removed L's now-dirty clothing.

Sinking into the tub was like sinking into my own piece of haven. I breathed a sigh of relief, not really able to comprehend that I had succeeded in retrieving the plant, that I was off those forsaken mountains. I felt as if I'd spent months up there.

And just like that, I began to cry.

My chest ached with the harsh sobbing, my throat closing and opening as I struggled to draw breath. Tears scored my cheeks as they rolled down quick as rainfall. I hugged my body, trying to blot out the memory of the mountain man, assuring myself that he'd never get near me again.

"My lady?" a voice asked, followed by a tapping on the door.

I swiped at my tears. "I'm fine," I called out, my voice quavering. "I'm all right."

"Are ye sure, my lady?"

"Yes. Thank you."

I waited for the sounds of fading footsteps and then reached for the soap, scrubbing the bar over my body and lathering it into my hair. I couldn't think about the bad things that had happened to me in Alvernia. I had to think of the good. Like Brint. And L. Especially L. Had I really only known her a matter of days?

I smiled through my tears, thinking of gruff L Moss who had saved my life and burrowed her way into my much-guarded heart. Haydyn would love her. I couldn't wait for them to meet. I couldn't wait to repay the Mosses for all of their kindness.

Once I had calmed myself, I changed into my dress. The fabric felt strange swishing about my ankles. Encumbering. I kicked out with my legs. I actually missed trousers. Sighing, I braided my hair and frowned at the way the dress lifted from my waist. My clothes no longer fit well.

Vojvoda Andrei Rada and his son the markiz awaited me with Wolfe in the moody, masculine dining room.

"There she is," Vojvoda Andrei called out, approaching me with a fatherly smile. He took my hands, and I found it difficult to smile politely back at him. "Lady Rogan, what a scare you gave us, taking off to tour Alvernia alone."

I grimaced at our lie. I grimaced at the way the vojvoda looked down on me condescendingly, in his gated home and isolated city. Where was he for the people of the mountains?

All my anger and frustration over everything that had happened seethed to the surface. If I'd known this was going to be my reaction at seeing him again, I would never have come down for dinner.

"Well." He shrugged, seeming nonplussed by my silence. "I'm very glad the good captain caught up with you to keep you safe. How did you find my rough lands?"

I thought of L and her forthright honesty. Of the Mosses' kindness and sincerity. Of Brint Lokam and the people of Hill o' Hope's generosity.

"Like everywhere else in Phaedra, Your Grace. Populated with good people and bad people ... and poorly governed." I straightened my shoulders, jutting my chin defiantly. "If you'll excuse me."

And leaving all three of the men with their mouths hanging open, I spun on my heel and left them to it.

CHAPTER 29

The days ahead were filled with a mixture of anticipation and a sickening coldness.

I barely ate a thing as we galloped through Daeronia. We stopped to collect the two soldiers in the mining village. The villagers now greeted us with hospitality, offering us bread and shelter. But we didn't stay long. If our pace had been grueling before, now it was frantic.

I knew the Guard were curious, that they all suspected something more was afoot, especially since my escape into the mountains. They wondered what on earth had possessed me to go up there. But I didn't want to panic anyone, especially when we were so close to saving Haydyn. I'd rather they think I'd gone light in the mind than know the truth.

The times I did sleep, I twisted and turned with nightmares. I dreamed of arriving in Silvera only to find we were too late and Haydyn was gone. I dreamed the mountain man was still alive and chased me into the empty palace and as much as I fought and fought, I could not seem to save myself from his deranged lust.

And I dreamed of Wolfe.

Always he stood on the edge of the Silver Cliffs, his eyes

pleading with me. I'd make a move toward him and feel a tug on my hand. I'd turn to find Haydyn, shaking her head at me, my parents and little brother behind her, disapproval on their faces. When I looked back at Wolfe, he'd glare at me, hatred filling his eyes. And then he'd fall right over the cliffs into the crashing water.

I didn't need to be a scholar to interpret the dream.

WE REACHED CAERA IN RECORD TIME, NOT STOPPING LONG enough for incidents to occur.

I was exhausted by the time Vojvodkyna Winter welcomed us into her home. Taking in my bedraggled state, she was even kind to me. As she ushered me to the guest suite herself, ordering a bath and food tray, I forgot to be jealous of her. I even came to the conclusion that, as before, I may have judged her too harshly.

THE NEXT MORNING AS THE MAIDS GIGGLED IN THE HALLWAY, all my good feelings toward Winter died.

It was easy in a household as large as Winter's for the gossip to reach my ears. Wolfe had been seen leaving Winter's bedroom early that morning.

I stumbled when I heard the gossip, pain hitting me in the chest with the force of a sledgehammer. I turned, no longer hungry for breakfast, or able to stand the sight of Wolfe and Winter together. I could barely draw breath; my whole body ached with the grief. With the betrayal.

But he wasn't mine, so it wasn't a betrayal.

Sniffling back silly tears that were best not wasted on him, I drew on my traveling cloak and clutched the pack with the Somna plant inside.

It was time to leave.

❦

CHAERON AND THE OTHERS WERE VISIBLY CONFUSED.

Before Caera, Wolfe had been the one not talking to *me*. Now every time he came near me, I was so cold in attitude, it was a wonder ice didn't crystalize in the surrounding air. Wolfe seemed just as perturbed by this and grew even more indignant. I imagined the lieutenant and the Guard were just as exhausted with us as they were of the journey.

WE CROSSED INTO RAPHIZYA, STOPPING IN RYL TO STAY WITH Matai's cousins again.

This time I met Mr. Zanst, who welcomed us into his home just as warmly as his wife had. From his dark good looks to his charming stoicism, he reminded me much of Matai ... and I longed for home. Mrs. Zanst was so worried for me, I felt terrible for deceiving her, for having been foolish enough to be kidnapped by the Iavii in Ryl. She asked me if I had been treated badly, and I assured her I had escaped unscathed.

After a wonderfully civilized and pleasantly refreshing evening with the Zansts (perhaps because Wolfe stayed away), the Guard and I set off for Peza. It rained the entire journey. I wasn't sure if it was because my body had hardened with its recent experiences, but I escaped the head cold that swept through the Guard. Mayhap because of their position distant from the Guard, Wolfe and Lieutenant Chaeron escaped it too. Still, I was glad to reach Grof Krill Rada's home. I'd never heard men complain so much in my life, and all over a little cold.

Grof Krill came bounding out of his mansion with Strider, the wolfhound, at his side. Strider seemed to remember me and my generosity at the dinner table and licked my hand when I reached out to pet him. Grof Krill grinned at me so happily, I was taken aback. We hadn't exactly left on the best terms.

"My lord." I bobbed a curtsy.

"You are a vision, Lady Rogan." There was no flirtatiousness in his tone. He seemed genuinely *delighted* to see me.

Bemused, I replied, "Thank you, my lord."

"Come. I want you to meet someone."

As I took his arm and followed him inside, a suspicion grew.

No. It couldn't be. Could it?

As the door was swept open by the butler, my heart pounded. I prayed my suspicion was correct.

As soon as we stepped inside, I saw her. I broke out into a choked laugh. "Ariana?"

The pretty young woman came forward in a hurry, her gray eyes brimming with happiness. "Is this her, Krill?"

"This is she." He spun me around, gripping me by my upper arms. "How can I ever repay you for writing that letter, Lady Rogan?"

Ariana joined us, pulling me into a hug, joyful tears filling her eyes as she told me all about receiving the letter; how she couldn't believe the Handmaiden of Phaedra had written to her; how she so wanted to believe me about Krill's love for her; how she'd left her life behind and took a chance on what I had confided.

I chuckled as she barely drew breath.

Grof Krill and Ariana married three days after her arrival in Peza. She was now Grofka Ariana.

Exhausted and incredibly elated that I'd done one thing right on this quest of mine, tears welled in my eyes.

"Lady Rogan, are you all right?" Grof Krill asked anxiously, seeing my eyes shine.

"I'm fine," I whispered hoarsely. "I'm just delighted for you and ... so very tired."

"Oh." Ariana looked aghast. "Here we've been monopolizing your time when you must be so weary from your journey. How ill-mannered of us."

"No, no," I rushed to assure her. "I am so pleased to meet

you, Ariana, and I am so happy I had a hand in bringing you and Grof Krill together. It's just been such a long trip."

I struggled to hold back the frustrating tears.

With a perception that bothered me, Grof Krill straightened his spine in alert. "Nothing untoward has happened to you, Lady Rogan?"

"No, no. Please ... I just need to rest."

"Krill, stop pestering the poor girl," Ariana admonished gently. She took my arm. "Come, I shall show you to your room."

Ariana left me in the suite I'd stayed in my last visit and sent for a supper tray to be brought to me. With one last grateful hug, she departed the room, and I flopped down on the bed. I was glad the grof had gotten his happily ever after. At least someone had.

The food arrived, and delicious though it was, I barely tasted it as I shoveled it down. I kept seeing Winter at the door to her mansion, waving her handkerchief at Wolfe with that knowing, intimate look in her eyes.

I slid back on the bed and rested my head against a fluffy, gold-brocade pillow, willing the nightmares away tonight. I'd give anything for a restful, dreamless sleep.

My eyes were just closing when I heard the handle on the door turn. Someone was entering without knocking. I bolted upright at the impudence, the blood whooshing in my ears when the intruder revealed himself.

Wolfe.

He closed the door behind him and turned the lock.

I glared at him as he leaned against the door, his expression inscrutable.

"Grof Krill and Grofka Ariana are so sickeningly happy, I had to get away from them."

I was surprised by his even tone. There was no ice in his eyes.

"Get out," I snapped, feeling the hurt roll over me again in crashing waves.

Wolfe's expression hardened. "No." He shook his head and

pushed away from the door, striding toward me. "I'm fed up with fighting with you. It's exhausting. I keep waiting for you to come to your senses ... but I realized something today."

I continued glowering. "What was that?"

He stopped inches from me so I had to crane my neck to meet his eyes. "You never just come to your senses, Rogan. You have to have them shaken into you." He reached out to touch my cheek and I jerked away, ignoring his wounded look as he dropped his hand. "I love you, Rogan."

All the pain and anger I felt brimmed over in my eyes. "Then why did you bed Winter when we were in Caera?"

Wolfe looked stunned.

Then he slowly lowered himself onto the bed beside me and attempted to reach for my hands.

I shook my head at him.

He sighed. "Rogan, I never bedded Winter. I never touched her. I shared a room with Chaeron that night. You can ask him. You know he won't lie to you."

Confusion plus his proximity made my skin flush hot. "What?"

"I was nowhere near her. The last time we were in Caera, I told Winter there would never be anything between us again because ... because I love you. I'm in love with *you*."

I trembled, hope desperately clambering its way back into my heart. I tried to shake it out but it clung on. "The servants were gossiping about you. They said you were seen leaving her bedroom in the morning."

Wolfe huffed in exasperation. "Winter likes to use her servants for her little games. She wants me back, Rogan. She's trying to build a wall between us."

"You refused to converse with me, even look at me. There was already a wall."

He reached for me, his fingers whispering down my cheek. Then his hand slid beneath my hair to cup my nape. I shivered at his gentle touch. "I was terrified, Rogan. Every time I think about what could have happened ... what did happen ... I—"

"Wolfe, don't," I urged, shushing him. I reached for his other hand and threaded my fingers through his. His skin was warm and rough against mine.

"I don't want a wall between us ever again," Wolfe whispered.

I looked up to find his eyes on my face. I saw his fear. Fear of rejection. And I hated that I was the cause of it.

Slowly, my breath hitching, I leaned across the space between us and pressed my lips to his. Wolfe sat tense, unmoving as I kissed him, as if he was afraid to touch me.

I retreated.

There was desire in his eyes but also wariness, uncertainty, and concern. It took me a moment to understand what had put all of that there. "He didn't hurt me, Wolfe. He didn't ... rape me."

Wolfe swallowed, his eyes glistening. "Promise?"

"Promise."

Tentatively, he lifted our clasped hands off the bed and kissed my knuckles.

"Are you going to seduce me, Wolfe, or am I going to have to seduce you?"

Wolfe's eyes darkened as his lips curved into that wicked smile. "I'm happy with either scenario."

Made bold by his declaration of love, I pressed my lips to his throat. He groaned, tilting his head back a little as I kissed my way up to his jaw. He needed to shave. His stubble tickled my lips, and something about the feel of it scratching my skin made me burn hotter.

With a growl of impatience, Wolfe's lips crashed down over mine.

His kiss was deep, hungry, coaxing; his tongue gently teased mine. As I melted into it, he laid me back on the bed. My thighs naturally parted and he fell between my legs, covering my body with his. I pulled at his shirt until I could slip my hands beneath it, forcing the fabric up so I could explore his hard stomach. The ridges of muscle me tremble with want. He was hard to my soft, and the evidence of his utter masculinity pleased me. A ripple of hot sensation moved deep and low in my belly.

Wolfe broke the kiss, but only so he could remove his shirt. He threw it behind him and I let my eyes wander down his torso.

Goose bumps awoke all over me.

He was so beautiful.

"I don't think anyone has ever called me that before," he murmured, amused. And I realized I'd spoken out loud.

I grinned, nervous but excited for what was to come. "Should I undress?" I whispered.

His eyes flashed with hunger. "Let me help."

I sat up and turned so he could unbutton my gown, my pulse racing at the feel of his fingertips brushing my silk chemise.

"Lie back."

I did as he asked and gazed up at him in wonder as he pulled on the sleeves of the dress and then tugged the fabric down over my breasts. His eyes darkened as the thin chemise was revealed. My nipples were visible through the fabric. I flushed hotly, wondering if I pleased him as much as he pleased me.

The way his eyes turned molten suggested so.

"Rogan ..." He practically growled with impatience as he slid down the bed, pulling the dress with him until I lay there in nothing but transparent silk.

I took hold of the chemise and raised it up as I lifted one leg out toward him, toe pointed. "Stockings next."

Wolfe's chest rose and fell in shallow breaths as he climbed back onto the bed on his knees. My eyes dropped to follow his movements, and I saw his arousal straining against his trousers.

I experienced another tug deep in my womb and let out a mewl of need.

"I'm trying to be gentle and patient," he said, his voice hoarse as he reached for my outstretched leg. "But if you keep making noises like that, I might lose my mind."

I bit my lip, rather enjoying the power I seemed to wield over him.

As if he read my thoughts, Wolfe shook his head, but he wore a teasing smile. A smile that darkened as he coasted his fingers up my calf, tickling the back of my knee, before coming to a stop on my thigh where the stocking ended.

Sensation shot along my skin in luscious tingles from his point of contact. The higher his fingertips tickled my thighs, the more it felt as if he were touching me between my legs.

I tingled there, too, and felt the wet of arousal.

"Wolfe," I begged, wanting him to touch me there more than I wanted anything in this world.

"Patience." He stroked my inner thigh, his jaw clenching.

And then he curled his fingers into my stocking and slowly guided it off my leg.

It was torturous waiting for him to do the same with the other.

When he was done, he wrapped his hands around my calves and then glided his hands up my legs as he kneeled between them. Our eyes held, my breath caught in my throat, as he moved up the back of my thighs until he reached my underwear.

"Your skin is like silk," he whispered, hovering over me like some pagan god, the shadows of the room flickering across his muscled arms and torso.

I wanted to touch him, but he was too far away.

"Come to me." I reached out.

Wolfe gave me a teasing smile. "Not yet. I want to kiss you." His fingers curled around the edge of my underwear.

I gasped as he tugged on them but lifted my hips to help him remove them. "To kiss me"—my breath hitched as cool air caressed me between the legs—"you have to come closer, where my mouth is."

He grinned. "Ah, but that's not where I want to kiss you."

A memory assailed me. I'd once accidentally walked in on one of our guests with a housemaid. She'd been sprawled across a desk in a palace study, skirts above her waist, with the nobleman's face between her legs.

"Oh." Suddenly, I understood.

I experienced another deep pull there.

Seeing I understood, Wolfe tossed aside my underwear and demanded, "Take off the chemise."

I sat up to do so with urgency, very much impatient to experience this kiss. Lying back on the bed, naked as the day I was born, I waited, chest heaving.

Wolfe could only stare. His expression darkened as he took in every inch of me.

"Wolfe?"

He shook his head, as if dazed, and then his eyes came back to mine. His voice was thick with emotion. "There cannot be anything, anyone, or anyplace in this land, in any land, that matches your beauty, within and without."

Tears pricked my eyes.

I'd never thought of myself as such, but he made me feel like the most beautiful being in the world in that moment.

"I don't deserve this gift." His hands coasted up my thighs, and a fierceness flashed across his face. "But I'm a selfish bastard, and I'm going to take it."

I wanted to disagree, to tell him that he deserved everything he wanted, but suddenly his head was between my thighs and—

"Wolfe!" I gasped in amazement at the feel of the first lick. I lifted my hips, widening my legs, wanting more. So much more! I groaned with sheer pleasure as he kissed and nuzzled and licked and sucked until I was writhing with coiling tension.

Then there was pressure as he pushed two fingers inside of me. He moved them in and out, causing the tension to climb to a breaking point. My heart raced so hard. My skin was hot and damp with sweat. I couldn't take much more of this!

And then my whole body stiffened, and it was like a tidal

wave of ecstasy rolling through me as my inner muscles rippled around Wolfe's fingers. I cried out, unable to stifle the sound of my release.

Wolfe covered me, swallowing my gasps in his deep, voracious kisses that made me feel light-headed on top of my climax. When he pulled back, his muscles seemed to strain with need, and then I felt him scorching and throbbing at my core. I whimpered as renewed need flooded me. "Are you ready? It will probably hurt the first time."

"I know." I wound my arms around his shoulders and stroked my fingers across his smooth, hot skin. His muscles were hard beneath my touch. "But I want you."

Wolfe kissed me again, slower, gentler, brushing his mouth across mine, and then he nudged his arousal against me. I braced for his entrance but instead, his lips left my mouth to caress my jaw and then my throat and chest ... He kissed every inch of me, sucking on my nipples until they were hard and tender and my thighs were climbing his hips. As he lavished attention on my breasts, he undulated between my legs, his arousal kissing me, teasing me, until I was desperate for more.

"Wolfe," I moaned, my nails biting into his back, "I can't ..." I needed him inside me. I needed us to become one.

"I can't wait any longer," he said harshly, and I nodded.

"Yes, yes, come inside me."

His hands depressed the mattress on either side of my head, his chest lifting up off my body. He nudged my knee with his and I opened my legs wider at his silent request.

I looked up into his eyes.

He stared back at me, his cheeks flushed, his expression bright with desire and love. My pulse raced faster, impossibly so. I slid my hand around his nape, my fingers curling in his thick, soft hair, and I gently pulled him toward me.

Our lips brushed, causing my mouth to tingle, but as I traced my tongue along the edge of his upper lip, Wolfe sank into the kiss. I sucked on his tongue and Wolfe stiffened with shock before his groan vibrated down my throat seconds.

He thrust into me.

I cried out, the sound swallowed in his deep kiss. A flare of pain rippled up from my lower back to sprinkle shivers across my shoulders, and Wolfe broke the kiss, holding himself above me, still, tense.

"Rogan," he panted, "are you all right?"

As the pain dissipated, I felt only pressure, fullness. "I think you should move."

"Stop?" A bead of sweat slid down Wolfe's temple as he strained above me for control.

"No." I assured him, my fingers biting into his shoulders. "But there is more to this ... isn't there?"

He gave a huff of strangled laughter. "Yes," he said. "Let me show you how much more."

Wolfe withdrew until he was almost gone and then pushed back in. I still ached but as he withdrew again, and glided back in, pleasure began to stir beneath the pinch. And then Wolfe reached between our bodies and his thumb found the bundle of nerves he'd licked and sucked earlier, and my pleasure grew tenfold. The next time Wolfe withdrew, I muffled a cry of surprise at the delicious sensation that moved through me, and I arched my hips trying to pull him back.

"Haven, Rogan. Your body is haven," Wolfe growled, and his thrusts picked up speed.

I slid my hands down his back and clutched at his buttocks, pulling him into me, and his eyes widened marginally.

"Rogan," he grunted. "I'll lose control."

"Yes," I gasped, pushing into the fast pumping of his strong hips. "Yes, Wolfe. Please. Lose—ah!" I tensed and then as before, it shattered, but this time the feel of my muscles rippling around him was even more exquisite. My lower body shuddered against his drives and then Wolfe suddenly froze above me. He threw back his head and yelled his pleasure as his hips juddered against mine. He throbbed inside me, pulsing and pulsing as he found his release.

"Fuck," he panted, collapsing over me, one elbow braced to keep from crushing me. He nuzzled my neck as his other hand caressed my body, my breasts, my waist, my hips. He ground into me as if he didn't want to lose our connection.

Lifting his head from my throat, our eyes locked.

I felt known. I felt known and loved down to my very soul.

CHAPTER 30

I never knew I could feel this close and connected to anyone.

We lay together after our lovemaking, his arm around me, my head on his chest. His heart thumped under my ear, not quite steady.

Despite my willingness to abandon myself to Wolfe's loving, reality crept in quickly. My plan had never been to marry. If I were honest with myself, it was because I was afraid to care about too many people. The more people you loved, the more chances you had to lose one of them.

I didn't want to love someone as much as I loved Wolfe and have to deal with the pain of losing him. Or worse, have children live with the daily fear of losing them too.

I'd wanted desire, passion, but not love.

Yet I loved Wolfe.

I could no longer use his parentage as an excuse to keep him at bay. L, in all her pragmatism, had knocked that wall down so I couldn't hide behind it anymore. But I had other reasons not to be with Wolfe. I did! This bond with him would mean abandoning Haydyn to become a wife.

Not only did Haydyn need me but, as much as I loved Wolfe,

I couldn't imagine giving up my freedom to become a society wife. Haydyn and I had years of work ahead of us to reform Phaedra, work that would not be seen as appropriate for the wife of a vikomt. Work that only the Handmaiden of Phaedra would be allowed to do.

It wasn't just a choice between Wolfe and Haydyn.

It was bigger than that.

It was a choice between Wolfe and the person I wanted to be.

What he and I had was wonderful now, but in a year's time, I knew myself well enough to know I'd come to resent the cage of marriage.

Perhaps I could have Wolfe for a little while. Without marriage. An affair. We could be happy with that ... I tried to convince myself.

For now, as we lay entangled, I didn't voice any of my concerns, knowing those words would break this beautiful spell we were under.

Goose bumps spreading up my arm in the wake of his fingertips stroking my skin. "This is nice," I whispered.

"Mmm," Wolfe murmured and pressed a kiss to my temple.

I snuggled deeper against him.

"Thank you for coming after me into the mountains, Wolfe. I should have said that before."

"You're welcome."

"So ... you have psychic abilities now?"

He chuckled. "How long have you been waiting to pester me with questions about that?"

"Since the night at the Mosses'."

"I didn't say anything about it because I don't want people to fear me."

"Because you're this astonishingly inconceivable, all-powerful mage?"

"Yes."

I snickered and shook my head. "No one would be afraid of you, Wolfe. You're too kind to people for them to fear you."

"I can be fearsome if I want to be."

I hid my smile. "I know."

"I can be plenty fearsome."

"Oh, I know."

"I can—"

Afraid he'd want to prove how fearsome he could be, I cut him off. "You know, I've discovered something interesting on this quest of ours."

Wolfe grunted at having been interrupted. "What's that?"

I drew away from him to lean up on my elbow. I stared down into his handsome face. "Mage, Wolfe. Quite a few of them."

Wolfe frowned. "Well, there have been some ..."

I shook my head impatiently. "For a world in which the mages are apparently dying out, I find it strange to have come across over a handful of them since leaving Silvera. I mean, it seems like too much of a coincidence."

"Meaning?"

"That mages are out there." I gestured beyond the walls of the bedroom. "Lots of them. I'd bet Haydyn's Somna plant on that."

"Perhaps you're right. If so, then ..."

I sighed. "It has to be taken into consideration with everything else."

"Everything else?"

Lying back down in his arms, I went on to tell Wolfe about all I had discovered, what I thought of the people of Phaedra and the way we governed.

"What's the use in the evocation if we don't support it with good government? There are places in Phaedra—Alvernia, for one—where good people are lumped in with the bad, and nothing is done to help them."

"You know my feelings on the subject. I agree that people are people, no matter their situation or location, have both light and dark within them. And there are certain people I intend to see punished for their crimes, such as Markiz Solom and those damn Iavii. But the bad people will stop being bad when the evocation strengthens again. When Haydyn is well."

I growled in frustration. "Not in Alvernia. Haydyn's evocation begins to wane, and people like L and her family are the ones who suffer, having to live side by side with uncivilized, foul people who need laws and consequences." Butterflies flapped wildly in my stomach as I drew on my courage to voice my real concern. "What if the evocation is wrong, Wolfe? Do you really think it gives us peace and freedom? Or is it just the pretense of it?

"We're so afraid of that shadows you spoke of, of the fire of people's passions flaming out of control, that we've relied on a magic that will die out if Haydyn's heir is not born with the evocation. Shouldn't we stop relying on it? Learn to govern without it? Shouldn't we trust in the light? That the fire within us can live without burning the world to the ground? We're suppressing human nature, and I'm not sure that it is our right to do so."

His chest rose and fell beneath my ear with deep exhalation. "Rogan ... what you're suggesting could have far-reaching consequences. I'm not saying that you aren't right ... but these questions can really only be posed to one person."

"Haydyn."

"Yes." Wolfe kissed me lightly on the lips and slid out of bed.

Despite the turmoil raging inside me, I took great enjoyment watching him dress. I bit my lip. Intimacy between lovers was all Haydyn promised it would be. "Where are you going?"

Wolfe grinned as he buttoned his shirt and then he leaned over to kiss me. Deeply. I moaned at the taste and wrapped my arms around Wolfe, trying to pull him back down. If he left the room, I was afraid we'd never have this again. The thought panicked me.

Laughing against my mouth, Wolfe pulled away, his eyes

telling me it was with great reluctance. "I have to leave before someone finds me here."

I released him.

We couldn't be caught together. That was something I'd have to think about if we did begin an affair. We'd have to be careful not to get caught.

I nodded, wrapping my arms around my drawn-up knees so I wouldn't touch him again.

"You are so beautiful," he told me hoarsely.

I smiled. "So are you."

Within and without.

Wolfe threw me a boyish smile as he picked up his jacket and strode to the door. Just as he was about to depart, he turned to me.

"We'll work it out all, Rogan," he promised, his expression tender. "After Haydyn is well and good, we'll get married, and then we can take all the time we need convincing Haydyn of what's right."

Wolfe was gone before I could respond. I groaned and flopped back on my pillow. Damn it. I'd have to tell him.

I was not looking forward to that.

Not one little bit.

CHAPTER 31

Ariana was quite possibly the sweetest person I had ever met, even more so than Haydyn, which was quite a feat. In contrast to L, it was almost shocking to sit and converse with Ariana—one so gruff and straightforward, the other so gentle and affable. Despite the impact L and the Mosses had made on my life, I found it soothing to sit at a beautiful breakfast table, with refined people, and eat sumptuous food.

I almost snorted, thinking of all the times I'd argued with Wolfe for calling me Lady Rogan instead of Miss. He'd be happy to know in the end, he was right. I'd been raised a lady since I was a girl, and that had made more of a mark than I'd realized. It was time to accept who I was.

The Handmaiden of Phaedra.

We ate companionably, just Ariana and I, as Grof Krill had business to attend to. He still hadn't returned by the time I was ready to leave. I asked Ariana to thank him for his hospitality and to inform him that I looked forward to seeing them both at the annual Autumn Ball Haydyn held at the palace.

"I cannot wait to meet again, Lady Rogan." Ariana hugged me. "It's been such a pleasure. I do wish you could stay longer."

I thought of the pack being tied to Midnight as we spoke.

The pack with the Somna plant. Haydyn was waiting. We were so close now. I smiled. "We will see each other soon."

Catching sight of Wolfe out of the corner of my eye as he mounted his horse, I flushed. Tingles cascaded down my spine and my heart raced like a galloping horse. I needed to tell him. Mind you, I narrowed my eyes in thought, it wasn't as if he'd actually *asked* me to marry him. He'd just *told* me.

With another farewell to Ariana, I lifted my skirts and strode over to Wolfe. I touched his leg, and he glanced down, his mouth widening into the warmest smile he'd ever bestowed on me. I was struck dumb for a moment.

"Lady Rogan?"

For once I didn't argue with the title. "Wolfe," I responded in a low voice, glancing around to make sure no one was close enough to overhear. I raised an indignant eyebrow. "Marriage?"

He exhaled heavily, sensing my tone. Wolfe dismounted and towered over me, standing far closer than propriety allowed. "We made love, Rogan," he hissed in my ear. "I took your virginity. We *have* to marry."

Have to marry?

I flinched. "No." I crossed my arms over my chest and glared. All the reasons I had for not marrying him disappearing. All I cared about in that moment was that he hadn't asked me, and he bloody well was acting like marrying me was a duty, not a desire!

Wolfe drew a hand through his hair, looking exasperated. "Rogan, don't do this." He glanced around, catching Chaeron's eye, who quickly looked away, whistling under his breath as if he hadn't been trying to eavesdrop. "We'll discuss this later."

I harrumphed. "There's nothing to discuss. I'm not marrying you."

And like the society girl I tried to tell myself I was nothing like, I flounced away in a dramatic air of petulance and mounted Midnight without looking at Wolfe again.

Despite my fury, I kept picturing that smile he'd given me

when I'd approached him on his horse. That smile made me want to throw all my reasons against marriage out the window.

I was such a befuddled mess.

Without Haydyn, I had no one to confide in, and it seemed I was incapable of processing my emotions, sorting out the truths from the excuses. I smiled wearily at the lieutenant as we set off through Raphizya.

Once we administered the cure to Haydyn, I could think about my feelings for Wolfe. Talk them over with her. Decide what the best course of action would be.

I just needed time.

WOLFE WAS NOT A MIND READER. HE DIDN'T KNOW MY reason for rejecting him; he just knew I had.

He clipped orders at me like I was one of his men and snapped at me when I dared to wander away from the Guard when we took our lunch break. I was exhausted by the tension between us, and my chest ached every time I saw that damnable hurt in the back of his eyes.

When we crossed the border into Sabithia and began traveling through Lumberland, pain squeezed my temples from all the overthinking. Despite my resolve to put aside my worries over Wolfe until we returned to Silvera, all the questions kept whirling around in my head. Moreover, I was anxious to return to Haydyn.

My head was throbbing by the time we came upon the village of Woodmill again. Wolfe sidled his horse next to Midnight.

"Lieutenant Chaeron, perhaps you can speak with Mr. Dena regarding accommodation for Lady Rogan."

Chaeron grinned at Wolfe's pointed dismissal and trotted off ahead of the Guard, dismounting as Jac Dena came out of his factory to greet him.

"Rogan," Wolfe said so softly, so gently, I had to turn to him.

Expecting to see pain and panic in his eyes, I was surprised to see angry determination. I knew that look. It was the look he wore when he wanted something and refused to back down until he got it.

"What?" I asked warily.

"Not marrying me ... that means some time in the future, you'll marry someone else. *I* will marry someone else."

Jealousy scored a vicious talon across my heart. I lowered my eyes. "I have no intention of marrying anyone, Wolfe. That's what I was trying to explain earlier."

"But I'll marry, Rogan. I must. For the title. And I want a family. Could you stand to watch me marry someone else?" His voice deepened. "Because I will."

I thought how painful it had been when I'd suspected he'd bedded Winter. If he married, I'd have to go through that pain every single day. I glared up at him now, my cheeks flushed with rage. "Why are you doing this? It's cruel."

Wolfe searched my face for a long moment and then he nodded. "It's only cruel if you feel for me how I feel for you."

I glanced away. This wasn't the time or the place to explain why I couldn't marry him.

Snapping his stallion's reins, Wolfe took off to meet up with Chaeron and Dena, leaving me on Midnight. If I didn't marry him, mayhap he'd marry Winter.

I struggled to draw breath.

But my fear of losing Wolfe couldn't distract me from the truth.

Marrying him might mean losing myself.

And I'd just finally found her.

ALTHOUGH THE DENAS' SONS WERE ON THEIR BEST BEHAVIOR, dinner was awful. I pushed my food around my plate, not able to eat under the heavy emotional weight I carried. It didn't help that Wolfe hadn't taken his eyes off me the entire meal. The Denas had been surprised and honored to have Wolfe sit at their table, but I would have given anything for Chaeron's easy company. I was grateful when dinner was over and enough time had passed for it to be polite to retire to my room.

This time I slept in the extra bedroom by myself. Or tried to sleep. I sat huddled on the bed, my brain refusing to succumb to sleep as I went over and over Wolfe's warning.

What would Haydyn say? I worried my lip.

I shook my head, snorting out loud. Haydyn was a romantic. I knew exactly what she'd say. She'd tell me to throw off all my concerns.

On the one hand, there was the pain I'd experience when I inevitably began to resent my life as a bored society wife. Never mind the fact that I was still terrified that by marrying him, I'd only grow to love him more deeply and then inevitably lose him in some way.

On the other hand, there was the pain I'd experience watching Wolfe live his life with another woman. To see him with the children she'd bear.

Or, back to the first hand: I could just tell Wolfe that marrying him would be dependent upon him agreeing that I remain at Haydyn's side to help her govern. He would not like it. I didn't know any nobleman who would not be affronted by the idea of a wife who worked. A wife was supposed to look after the household and rear the children. I would, of course, try to be a good mother, but the household would have to be maintained by either Wolfe's mother or the housekeeper.

Wolfe would never agree to it.

You could ask him.

And have him reject my proposal? Reject me?

Surely it would hurt less to be the one who did the rejecting from the outset?

I growled in frustration. "This is it, Rogan. You've managed to overcome the fact that he's the son of the man who killed your family, but you cannot overcome your own fears?"

I was a coward.

How could I be a coward after all I'd gone through?

Yes, there had been moments during this entire rescue mission that I'd fumbled and hated myself for. But I retrieved the plant! I escaped ruthless gypsies, dirty rookery thugs, and a perverted mountain man, and saved L's life to boot! I'd even brought two star-crossed lovers together. I had faced a great deal in my life. How could I not find the courage to do the simplest thing of all ...

To love Wolfe.

To trust him.

I loved Wolfe.

I *loved* Wolfe ...

It be as simple as that, I heard L's smirking, know-it-all voice in my head.

At the sound of the door handle rattling, I froze. When it rattled again, I slid one leg out of bed, thinking of the hunting knife I still carried in my pack. Just as my foot touched the cold wooden floor, the door opened and shut quickly. A familiar shadowed figure leaned against it.

"Wolfe?" I whispered, half-relieved, half-stunned.

The floorboards creaked as he tiptoed over to the bed. Then he slid in next to me without even asking permission!

"*Wolfe.*" I tried to act outraged but my body hummed with anticipation.

His eyes sparkled in the light from the moon outside the window, and he grinned at me, playfully yanking me under him. My cry of surprise was swallowed by his mouth.

Trust him.

In the morning I would tell him my worries and chance his rejection. Otherwise I'd regret it for the rest of my life.

I smiled against his lips and kissed him back. When he took a breath, I caressed his face with my fingertips. There was a little drop of eternal fear inside me that would always worry that one day he might disappear. I had to accept that and stop letting it govern my life.

Pushing thoughts of it away, I flashed Wolfe a saucy smile. "What made you think I'd be amenable to you sneaking into my room?"

Wolfe grinned wickedly. "I hoped perhaps I'd finally gotten through to you. And ... I don't know." He frowned. "Something told me you wanted me here."

My lips parted in shocked realization. "Your magic? Can you read my mind now?"

He laughed against my cheek and whispered seductively in my ear. "No. Intuition again." He nibbled my earlobe and I shivered. "I gather my intuition assumed correctly? You want me here?"

I gasped as sensation rippled through my belly. Fierce need flooded me. "What do you think?" I replied, pushing him onto his back to straddle him. "I'm not throwing you out, am I?"

WOLFE LOOKED GUILTY AS HE LEANED OVER ME AFTER OUR lovemaking. I reached out to smooth his furrowed brow. "What?"

He exhaled slowly. "You might be carrying my child, Rogan. You *have* to marry me now."

The truth was, I wanted a life with him, even at the risk of losing everything we would build together. I could doubt myself and the choices I had made in this life, but deep down, I had always prided myself on the fact that I wasn't a weak-willed person.

I wasn't a coward.

Not yesterday. Not today. And definitely not tomorrow.

But I did need to start having more faith in people. "I need to speak with you first."

Wolfe nodded solemnly and sat down on the bed beside me.

Our eyes locked, and I prayed he would prove himself the man I believed him to be. Or at least hoped he could be. "If we were to marry, you must not be under any illusions that I would be a typical society wife, Wolfe. I have a duty to Haydyn and to Phaedra, and it is an essential part of who I am. If we marry, I would not spend my days running our household. I would be at the palace, at Haydyn's side, helping her govern."

He studied me with heated intensity. "And what about children?"

Hope bloomed. He had not outright rejected my plans. "I would want children with you. And I would try to be a good mother. But I would still wish to work at the palace as an advisor to the kralovna, if Haydyn wished for me to do so."

Wolfe nodded thoughtfully. "It would be unusual and not well looked upon for a vikomtesa to have duties outside of what society deems appropriate."

I exhaled heavily. "I know."

He smirked. "It's a good thing, then, that I couldn't give a damn what society deems appropriate."

"Really?" I whispered, unsure I'd heard him right.

He clasped my face in his hands. "I love you, Rogan. I love how protective of Haydyn you are, and I admire how much Phaedra means to you despite everything it's taken from you. I could not ask you to give up who you are when it is the very reason I want you."

Tears brimmed in my eyes. "You promise?"

"I promise, my darling. I promise. I will do whatever it takes to make you happy." His eyes glowed with the fire of his passion. "Now say you will marry me, Lady Rogan, and put me out of this infernal misery."

I laughed softly, clutching at his shirt to bring him closer. "Yes."

"You'll marry me?"

"Yes."

His answering kiss was so deep and hungry, when he broke it, I panted for breath. He rested his hand over my chest so my heart thumped against his palm. "Am I in here then, Rogan?"

I realized that I hadn't reciprocated those three little words.

I nodded and covered his hand with mine. "I love you."

At my quietly spoken declaration, Wolfe's eyes closed, relief softening his features, his whole face growing younger before my very eyes.

I suddenly remembered he was only twenty-five years old.

A tension I hadn't even known was there visibly melted out of his body. Wolfe opened his eyes again. "I love you too. I have ever since you punched Niall Tromskin in the nose for pushing Valena in the courtyard and making her cry."

My jaw dropped at the revelation. "I was but fourteen!"

"I know." He swept his thumb across my cheek, his expression, his touch making me feel cherished. "I have loved you for a very long time."

CHAPTER 32

With our love declared and our engagement decided, we galloped toward Silvera with renewed determination. I think Chaeron suspected something had happened between me and Wolfe. To be fair, I think the entire Guard suspected, considering we kept sharing intimate smiles.

Now all I wanted was for Haydyn to be well. If I saved her, somehow managed to banish my nightmares of the mountain man, and convinced her to withdraw the evocation and reform Phaedra, then everything would be almost perfect.

I was glad when Wolfe spent the nights with me. He was furious about my nightmares—or the cause of the nightmares—and I'd worried it would only remind him that I hadn't trusted him before. But Wolfe didn't throw my foolishness in my face. Instead he soothed me back to sleep and held me tight in his arms. The nightmares didn't go away. I wasn't sure they would for a while, but at least when I woke up, I wasn't alone.

Wolfe snuck into my room at Mag's Inn in Sabith Town, and as he tiptoed toward the bed, his eyes were so filled with mischief and happiness, he looked more boy than man. I wondered, then, if we'd ever grow weary of another. I also wondered about his other women but was too afraid to bring up the subject for fear it would only hurt me. And it seemed pointless, anyhow, now that I knew he loved me.

"You know," Wolfe mused as he pressed kisses across my stomach, "I think I'm starting to miss you arguing with me."

I huffed. "That can be easily remedied, Captain."

I felt him grin against my skin. "Mmm. I imagine it could." He looked up abruptly, frowning. "One thing I keep wondering about ..."

"Mmm?"

"You've stopped objecting to being called Lady Rogan."

I nodded, stroking my fingers through his hair as he crawled up my body. He braced himself above me. "Perhaps I've come to the conclusion that you are right. I am a lady. I've been raised a lady, despite circumstances of birth."

"Finally, you see the wisdom in agreeing with me," he teased.

"Just because you came to this realization before I did—"

"That's not why I insisted on calling you Lady Rogan."

I frowned. "Why, then?"

Instead of answering, he kissed me—a deep, sexual, voracious kiss that had me undulating beneath him, ready for more. "I insisted on it"—he breathed raggedly—"because one day, I knew you were going to be my wife and I wanted you accustomed to being called Lady Rogan."

"You're lying," I panted. "How could you possibly know that, especially considering our past?"

"I didn't have to know." Those aquamarine eyes blazed down at me, all masculine arrogance and determination. "I always get what I want, Rogan. Always."

"And what about what *I* want?"

Wolfe pressed a soft, tender kiss to my lips, the arrogance giving way to deep sincerity. "I'll always give you what you want, Rogan. Always."

WE ARRIVED IN SILVERA WITH A FIERCE BURST OF RENEWED energy. I galloped by Wolfe's side, Chaeron and the men at our backs, as we tore through the city, through the marketplace and out past the palace to the cliffs. We ignored the cries of surprise and shock as we forced people from our paths. The Silverans watched with troubled countenance as we raced by them. While Chaeron drew the Guard to a halt in the palace courtyard, Wolfe and I continued on.

We made haste beyond the palace, out onto the rough trail that led us to the cliff side. Our horses kept their footing and made the half-hour journey to the Land's End cottage in twenty minutes. Both our horses' coats were thick with sweat, our own clothes plastered to our skin by the time we arrived.

I dismounted so fast, I nearly fell, and I ignored Wolfe's yell of concerned admonishment as I thrust open the door to the cottage. Rowan, who stood in the hallway, startled, almost dropping the tray of sandwiches in her hands.

"Lady Rogan!" she gasped, her eyes alight with relief. "You've returned."

"Where is she?" I demanded. There was no time for pleasantries.

"Upstairs." Rowan jerked the tray toward the narrow stairwell. "Valena is with—"

"Rogan!" Raj appeared in the doorway to the sitting room just as Wolfe entered the cottage. The healer hurried toward me. "You have it?"

I held up the pack. "I have it."

My heart pounded hard as we hurried up the stairwell to the large bedroom Haydyn loved. It was the view. She loved a view. The wide window captured the Silver Sea like a frame around a master painting created by nature.

I hugged Valena when she threw herself at me, and my eyes drank in the sight of Haydyn.

I felt a raw, choking burn in my throat at how pale and slight she appeared lying on the bed, her moon-colored hair spread across the pillow. "Oh, haven," I whispered. "She looks—"

"You're in time, Lady Rogan," Raj reassured me, removing the blue plant from the pack. He breathed a sigh of relief and then turned to us all. "I hate to ask it of you, but I need time alone with the princezna to do this. I'll require Valena's help, of course."

I didn't want to leave. That old stubbornness of mine wrapped around my legs, gluing them to the floor. Wolfe, however, slid his arm around my shoulders to draw me away, and it was only then I saw Matai standing by the door. He gestured for me to follow him out of the room.

"Matai," I mumbled as Wolfe guided me downstairs in a daze. I was exhausted. It felt as if my body might just float up into the air and drift away on the wind.

Before it could, Matai enveloped me in a tight hug. "Thank you, Rogan," he whispered in my ear, hoarsely, grief and worry and heartache soaking every word. "Thank you so much."

I gave him a watery smile and let Wolfe draw me back into his arms. I rested my head on his shoulder as we waited.

"We're betrothed," Wolfe told Matai.

"What?" Matai choked. "Dear haven, has the world gone topsy-turvy?"

"Actually, yes," I replied, turning my head on Wolfe's chest to meet Matai's gaze. "You should see it out there, Lord Matai. What a mess."

"We'll fix it," Wolfe insisted, rubbing his hand up and down my back.

"I hope so."

Matai lowered himself into a chair. He looked weary. "Tell me all that happened."

I PUT IT DOWN TO HAYDYN'S LOVE FOR THE DRAMATIC THAT instead of Raj coming down to tell us she was cured, a tousled blond head peeped around the door frame of the sitting room, followed by a stunning face blooming with color.

"Haydyn!" I screeched like a little girl, pulling from Wolfe's embrace to rush to my best friend. She squealed and crossed the room to meet me halfway. As we shook in each other's arms, crying somewhat hysterically, no one would have guessed that the princezna of Phaedra had only hours before been moments from death.

I pulled away, barely able to see her through my tears. "Look at you! Should you be out of bed?"

"Not really," Raj opined from the doorway, his eyebrows drawn together in consternation.

Haydyn shrugged. "I don't care. My body aches all over but I feel so awake! I've been sleeping forever, Rogan. Don't make me go back to bed."

I laughed and pulled her tight, afraid to let go of her. "Don't ever do anything like that to me again."

She huffed against my shoulder. "It's not like I could help it. Oh, Rogan." She retreated, her eyes brimming with love. "How can I ever thank you for what you did for me? Raj explained everything. How you went all the way to Alvernia, into the mountains, for the cure! Rogan—"

"You would have done it for me."

"In a heartbeat."

"Well, it took a little longer than that, but—"

"Can I perhaps ...?" Matai appeared at our side, his eyes fixed on Haydyn as if he couldn't believe she was real.

Reluctantly, I stepped away to let the two lovers embrace.

I raised an eyebrow at Wolfe when they kissed in front of Raj. Raj, for one, didn't look surprised.

"Ah ... happily ever after," Valena sighed dreamily from the doorway.

CHAPTER 33

If I could have wished for anything in this life, then I would have wished for Valena's words that day to be true.

But unfortunately, life just doesn't always work out that way.

HAYDYN AND I HAD MUCH TO CATCH UP ON ONCE WE returned to the palace.

The sight of Haydyn put paid to all the rumors and gossip of her illness that had spread across Sabithia and even into the neighboring provinces. Calm swam through the provinces like the tide flowing in at night. With the evocation stronger than ever, word reached the palace that Markiz Solom Rada had begun working on ridding Vasterya of the rookery as well as his little army he'd been building.

It was too late, however.

The Guard had been sent out to arrest the markiz. He would be tried before the court of the Rada for treason. Jarvis was furious and left little doubt in my mind that the markiz would be dismissed from the Rada and imprisoned.

Moreover, upon my discovery of the mages, Jarvis was interested in conducting some kind of census to discover just how many mages were being born every year. The thought of magic truly returning to our world swept Silvera with excitement.

I received a letter from Kir confirming the rumors in Vasterya and the worry in Pharya over the markiz's arrest. He promised to keep me informed while the Rada dealt with the markiz. As we wrote back and forth, I was glad for his friendship again. He was unsurprised to learn of my betrothal to Wolfe, having discerned Wolfe's feelings for me during our time in the rookery.

I grimaced at that. I really had been a blind fool.

Jarek *was* surprised to learn of my betrothal to Wolfe. He was a little skeptical even, but nonetheless happy for me, proving I was right when I suspected I was nothing but a mere flirtation to him.

The Iavii, now that they were caught in the trap of the evocation, agreed to settle in a few acres of land on the northern border of Javinia. As for Tiger, Bird, Vrik, and a few others, they were imprisoned in the palace jail for murder, theft, and kidnapping. No one questioned it, now that the Dyzvati reigned supreme again.

Haydyn was so busy at first with meetings with the Rada that I couldn't seem to get her to sit long enough for me to explain my concerns. Finally, exasperated upon hearing she had a meeting with a dignitary from Alvernia, I urged Haydyn to postpone it and talk with me. There was much she needed to know, including the fact that Markiz Andrei was not a good match for her.

Seeing how troubled I was, Haydyn agreed and we headed to her suite. My palms were damp and my heart raced with all I had to tell her.

"I haven't spent nearly enough time with you, Rogan, and after all you've done—"

"Haydyn, don't—"

"We haven't even had time to discuss your betrothal to

Captain Stovia. Wolfe, Rogan! You've barely given me any answers to how that really came about. And none of that fluff about realizing how you felt about one another." She grinned, her eyes bright. "I want the luscious details."

So I told her. But not just about Wolfe. I told her everything that had happened to me. She already knew some of it. About the Iavii and the rookery. But this time, I didn't leave out any details. I told her about Alvernia. About the good people of Hill o' Hope. About the mountain man. About L and the Moss family.

When I drew quiet, Haydyn promptly burst into tears.

I reached for her hand but she drew away. "Don't. How can you even touch me after all you've been through because of me? That man, Rogan ... what he did to you ..." She shook her head, her eyes so full of anguish.

"Haydyn," I said sternly. "I didn't tell you to make you feel guilty. Nothing happened to me that couldn't be dealt with. But I came to question things ... important things ... about Phaedra. About the way we govern. About the evocation. I need you."

She still looked pale and uneasy. "For what? What about the way we govern? What about the evocation?"

"Didn't you hear what I told you? There are issues in your provinces, Haydyn. Issues the evocation cannot fix, and I'm not sure it should. What right do we have to suppress human nature? That is not freedom. It is the opposite of freedom."

Haydyn flinched like I'd hit her. "The evocation makes sure peace reigns in Phaedra."

Frustration burned in my throat. "But what if something happened again to the evocation? We'd be left with a world that isn't properly governed because we're so afraid of our true natures. Perhaps we should accept who we are as a people and be true to ourselves. Govern without the evocation."

Haydyn stood up now. "I heard all this the first time around, Rogan. I understood. Believe me. The provinces have been left in the hands of the Rada who have relied upon the evocation for everything. Laws need to be instituted to protect people like that kind family you met in the mountains. And they will be. It will just take time." She drew a breath. "In fact ... I've decided to move the palace to Vasterya. I was just discussing it with Jarvis and Ava."

"What?" I asked, shocked.

"The province is central. From there, my power will be absolute. It will even reach Alvernia. What happened to you need never happen to anyone again. But as I say, this will all take time. Patience, Rogan." She smiled.

For a moment, I was taken aback by how determined and self-possessed Haydyn was. Then again, I had witnessed a change in her these last few weeks. She was taking charge with remarkable aplomb. The sleeping disease had changed her as much as I.

Still ... I needed her to *understand*. "Perhaps once you've set up proper government, you might think about easing Phaedra out of the evocation?"

Haydyn guffawed. "Are you jesting, Rogan?"

I frowned. "No."

"Why would I take away the evocation? It's my purpose in life."

"Your purpose in life is to reign over your people and take care of them. Make decisions that will better their lives. Not control them."

Horror slackened her features. "Control them?"

I sighed. I was doing this all wrong. "Not control them. That's not what I meant. I meant ..." I searched the room, looking for the words. They landed on Haydyn's bed, where I'd kissed her forehead weeks before, promising I'd wake her up. "We're all asleep under the evocation. We're not free to be truly ourselves. You more than anyone must understand the imprisonment of sleep, Haydyn. We're not prepared for what will happen when we wake up. We never will be unless we stop relying on the evocation. We have to stop being afraid."

Something happened to her as she stood before me. I saw her shoulders stiffen, her spine lengthen, her chin jut. Her eyes were still kind, still loving, but there was obstinance in them. "In sleep we don't get the choice between dreams and nightmares. With my evocation, Phaedra sleeps peacefully. Without it ... it could be a waking nightmare. And why should we worry about there being no evocation? That's not going to happen. I won't let it. You won't."

"I wouldn't want anything to happen to you ever. And you're right: I will do anything to make sure nothing ever happens to you again. But surely we should prepare for the worst when we're talking about securing the future of our land."

"I am securing the future of our land. I will marry. I will have children. I will teach those children to use the evocation. After everything you've gone through, how can you tell me the evocation isn't worth it?"

I could feel myself losing my grip on this discussion, so I said the one thing I thought may penetrate. "It's dangerous to rely on this, Haydyn. You can't guarantee your children will be born with the evocation."

Haydyn paled. "The Dyzvati reign has not been broken in all these centuries. I doubt it's going to end with me. But since you insist on being a pessimist, I'll remind you that the contingency plan, as you suggest, is to enforce the evocation with proper legislation and closer involvement in each of the provinces."

I gave her a bittersweet smile. "I'm not going to convince you otherwise?"

My best friend shook her head and then laughed softly at my expression, her eyes pleading with me to understand. "You wanted me to wake up, Rogan, and take control of my lands. Well, this is what I see now that I'm awake."

I sighed heavily. Haydyn was right, of course. All these years, all I had ever wanted was for her to be the kralovna I knew she could be. I had just never realized that when she did, we'd see things differently. Governing Phaedra, making decisions for our people, had never been my journey. My journey had been saving the person who was destined for that ... and in saving her, I found myself. I wanted to make a difference, and I could only do that through Haydyn.

I wasn't ready to give up on what I believed in. It would take time, but maybe one day I would convince her that freedom to be who they were, good or bad, was what our people really deserved.

I thought of Wolfe and how I knew he'd support me in my decision to stay on to advise Haydyn, even if we did not see the same future for Phaedra just now.

Thinking of Wolfe made me think of Matai.

"And Matai?" I asked, almost dreading her reply.

Pain and sadness painted a bright sheen in her eyes. "An alliance with Alvernia would be advantageous for everyone. It's difficult enough sticking my nose in the Rada's business, but as the wife of the son of the Rada of Alvernia, it would be within my rights to do what I could for the land and its people. I could bring so much to your friend L and her family's life. But ... if I marry Matai, a man of lower rank, then people will see it as a weakness. They'll know I married for love. They might think me frail and too sensitive to rule. I cannot afford to be seen as weak."

I flushed with anger, not only on Matai's behalf but because I was terrified Haydyn would make the wrong choice and spend her life miserable because of it. I knew what it was to love now, and I didn't want her throwing that away. "I told you," I argued, "you have all the power. They're not going to object to anything you do."

Haydyn sat down, leaning over to take my hand in hers, her eyes begging me to understand. "I need time to think on it. I'm still holding the ball. I'll make my decision then."

I remembered Wolfe's warning when I refused to marry him. "Matai won't wait forever, Haydyn."

She pulled back from me again, hurt in her beautiful and

kind gaze. "You were the one who told me to make my own decisions. Now you're angry because you don't agree with them!"

I closed my eyes, my shoulders slumping in exasperation. Again ... she was right. I glanced up at her through my lashes and nodded. "You are correct." I tried to shrug off my misgivings. Haydyn wasn't a little girl anymore. I had to let her make her own choices and believe she could cope with the consequences when they came. "I am glad you're making your own decisions. Our opinions may differ but ... all that matters"—I took her hand again—"is that I have faith in you. I went to the ends of the world because of that faith. I'm not going to give up on it now."

She grinned back at me, relief thrumming visibly through her.

"Now, if we cannot agree about the evocation, have faith enough in me to believe when I say that Markiz Andrei and his son are not good men. They are not suited to rule at your side."

Her eyes widened at the fierceness in my voice and she slowly nodded. "I believe you. I'll find another way to gain influence in Alvernia."

Relief filled me but I still worried for our future. For Haydyn's future. For her happiness and for the wisdom of her decisions. I had seen the truth of Phaedra because I'd journeyed through it.

Perhaps it was time to stop coddling Haydyn and push her out into the world. "Mayhap," I pondered, "it might not be such a bad thing if you were to see Phaedra for yourself."

"What do you mean?"

"Visit the provinces. All of them."

She considered this. "I suppose I could do a coronation tour once I'm kralovna."

I smirked. "I was thinking something a little more daring."

Haydyn raised an eyebrow. "Daring how?"

"You. In disguise. Traveling the provinces with a guide. A very capable, albeit a little rough around the edges, guide." I pictured L leading Haydyn through the provinces and although I experienced more than a pinch of fear for Haydyn's safety, I needed her to make an informed decision about the evocation. She couldn't do that without seeing the world for herself, without everyone sugarcoating it for the princezna, soon to be kralovna.

The spark of adventure lit in Haydyn's eyes. "You mean, sneak about Phaedra, pretending to be a commoner?"

I nodded. "For research. L Moss could be your guide."

A slow smile pushed at the corners of Haydyn's mouth. "You would really aid me in running away from the palace?"

"If it allows you to have the knowledge you need to make the decision you think is best for our world, then yes."

Her eyes narrowed. "It might not change my mind about the evocation, Rogan. In fact, I'm certain it won't."

I shrugged. "If it doesn't, then I'll support whatever decision you make. But how can you rule Phaedra unless you *truly* know it?"

She raised a delicate eyebrow. "You believe I can do this?"

"I believe you can do anything."

Haydyn beamed. "Then I think we better send for a messenger. Miss Moss is required at the palace."

EPILOGUE

Although Haydyn's happily ever after was uncertain, I knew I was as close to mine as I would ever be as I sat beside Wolfe on the cliffs outside the Land's End cottage. After weeks of traveling, I wanted nothing more than a bit of haven out here on the cliffs, away from everyone else. The quiet was wonderful. Back at the palace, Haydyn was arranging my wedding to Wolfe while juggling our clandestine plans for her journey through Phaedra.

Now and then, I'd feel more than a stab of worry that I was putting our future kralovna in unnecessary danger, but I had to believe this was the right thing for everyone.

As for my wedding to Wolfe, it was to take place the first day of the autumn season, and Haydyn was turning it into a lavish affair that made my head spin and my ears bleed.

Wolfe had finally come to my rescue and absconded with me to the cliffs.

I sighed contentedly, snuggling into his side, loving the drizzle of sea spray that caught on the wind and kissed my cheeks. I knew I would have to deal with all the trappings that came with being a vikomtesa—the large wedding, getting to know the dowager vikomtesa. Wolfe's mother was a bird of a woman who twittered at me nervously.

She was gentle and kind, and I could see how easy it must have been for Syracen to hurt and abuse her. We were a different breed of woman, but for Wolfe's sake, I would try to be a good daughter to her, even if that meant discussing dress fittings, menus, and sheet music. I'd have plenty of time in which to get to know her better, as Wolfe had agreed to move into the new palace in Vasterya so I could work with Haydyn, but only under the condition that we didn't leave his mother behind in Silvera. Of course, this would all be after Haydyn returned from her research trip.

One bright spot in my busy social schedule was L. The two messengers I'd sent into the Alvernian Mountains (two of the Guard well equipped to deal with the harsh hills) had returned two days ago from their visit with the Moss family with a message from L.

They had agreed to come to the wedding and more importantly, L had agreed to act as Haydyn's guide.

I couldn't believe it. I'd thought it would take blackmail to get L off that mountain of hers. I couldn't wait for Haydyn to meet her. I wouldn't push L to meet anyone else in society if she didn't want to. I knew what their reaction to her rough speech and unladylike ways would be, and she was too good a person to be subjected to that. But, deep down, I secretly hoped that after traveling with Haydyn, L may come to like my world. Mayhap even think of making a new life in Vasterya with me and Wolfe and Haydyn.

I smiled inwardly. It was a bit of a fairy tale, I knew. But I could hope.

And if L and her family did decide to return to the Alvernian Mountains, then I'd make sure they were sent supplies every month, and perhaps have a larger home constructed for them. Wolfe had already told me to rein in my plans for the Mosses in case I overwhelmed them. But I wanted to overwhelm them. With kindness. Appreciation.

They'd saved my life.

And I'd owe L once more when she brought Haydyn home safely to me after their trip.

"When does the princezna plan to move us to Vasterya?" Wolfe asked quietly, stroking my back.

I shivered at his touch, still amazed that he had this effect on me. "As soon as the rookery is depleted. And she has architects overhauling one of the mansions in Pharya for her arrival. She'll no doubt live in the fanciest mansion we've ever seen until palace construction is completed."

"She seems strong," Wolfe assured me, as if he heard the concern in my heart, in my words. "In control. She appears to know what she's about."

"She is," I agreed. "She really wants to make a difference after everything I told her."

Wolfe made a huffing noise. "Still annoyed she didn't take your advice?"

I slapped at him half-heartedly. And then after a minute, I shook my head, leaning back on my palms, my fingers digging into the rich grass below us. I smiled into Wolfe's eyes, feeling lighter, lighter than I'd felt since lazy summer days by a brook in Vasterya. "No. I have to confess something ... but in doing so, you have to promise you won't get in our way."

He raised an eyebrow. "I promise."

"I mean it."

Wolfe looked affronted. "If a gentleman offers you a promise, do not insult him by suggesting he won't honor it."

"Okay, I apologize." I studied him intently and once more put my faith in him. "After the wedding, Haydyn is going away. She's going to travel around the provinces in disguise with L Moss as a bodyguard."

It took a full five minutes to convince Wolfe not to strangle me and Haydyn. And he cursed a great deal the entire time. "You promised!"

"I know. But this is reckless, Rogan! Anything could happen to her."

"How can she possibly make a decision about the evocation if she doesn't have all the facts?"

The muscle in his jaw flexed with his anger as he glared out at the sea. "I can't allow it."

"You promised." My heart crashed against my ribs.

Wolfe glowered at me but I could see the conflict in his eyes. "Rogan, my duty in life is to protect Haydyn. This would be the opposite of protecting her."

"But you know I'm right."

He cursed under his breath again. "I know you're right," he growled. "But I still can't allow it."

"Wolfe—"

"Not as it stands." He held up a hand to quiet me. "Matai and a number of the Guard will accompany them. Chaeron, perhaps."

"But that defeats the purpose. People will question who she is if she has an entourage."

"Then Matai and L will travel with Haydyn. Chaeron and a few of the guard will follow in disguise so they can be there if anything happens. That is the only compromise I'm willing to make."

I scrunched up my nose in annoyance but mostly because it was a good plan and I should have thought of it myself. I'd just been so worried about anyone learning of it and telling the Rada.

"I love you."

I softened, melting against him. "I love you too."

"Then you agree to this new plan."

"It is a good plan."

He exhaled heavily, reaching up to brush the hair off my face. "I'm glad. You set out to wake up the princezna ... and that's exactly what you will do, Rogan."

I smiled, bussing into his touch. I reminded myself that this surreal feeling of contentment was real.

Months ago I would never have imagined loving Wolfe, how, in doing so, I was finally putting the past behind me, finally learning that by accepting my future, I wasn't turning my back on my family's memory.

Moreover, I'd changed.

I'd grown up.

Never would I have imagined becoming friends with Alvernian mountain people or thought I'd have the strength to accept what could and couldn't be changed.

Or that I would finally come to terms with who I was.

"Better yet ..."

Wolfe brushed his lips across mine. "What, my love?"

I smiled. Happy. "I woke up too."

WAR OF HEARTS

Read more from S. Young

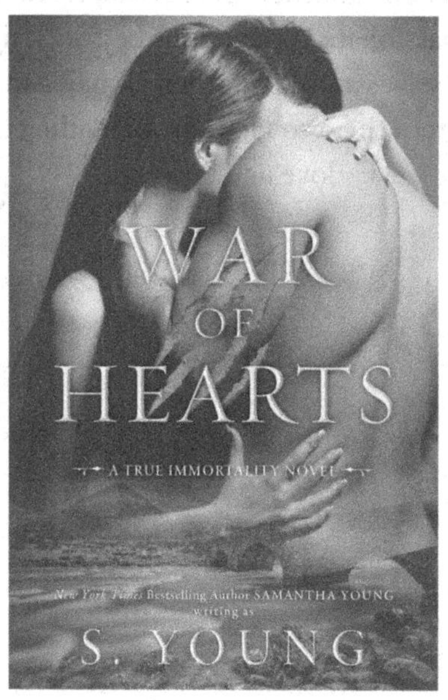

Thea Quinn has no idea what she is. All she knows is that her abilities have been a plague upon her life since she was a child.

After years of suffering at the hands of a megalomaniac, Thea escaped and has been on the run ever since.

The leadership and protection of his pack are of the utmost importance to Conall MacLennan, Alpha and Chief of Clan MacLennan, the last werewolf pack in Scotland. Which is why watching his sister slowly die of a lycanthropic disease is emotional torture. When Conall is approached by a businessman who offers a cure for his sister in exchange for the use of Conall's rare tracking ability, Conall forges an unbreakable contract with him. He has to find and retrieve the key to the cure: dangerous murderer, Thea Quinn.

Thea's attempts to evade the ruthless werewolf are not only thwarted by the Alpha, but by outside dangers. With no choice but to rely on one another for survival, truths are revealed, intensifying a passionate connection they both fight to resist. At war with themselves and each other, Conall and Thea's journey to Scotland forces them to face a heartrending choice between love and betrayal.

ABOUT THE AUTHOR

S. Young is the pen name for Samantha Young, a *New York Times*, *USA Today* and *Wall Street Journal* bestselling author from Stirlingshire, Scotland. She's been nominated for the Goodreads Choice Award for Best Author and Best Romance for her international bestseller *On Dublin Street*. *On Dublin Street* was Samantha's first adult contemporary romance series and has sold in thirty countries. *True Immortality* is Samantha's first adult paranormal series written under the name S. Young.

Visit Samantha Young online at
www.authorsamanthayoung.com
BookBub
Instagram @AuthorSamanthaYoung
Facebook @AuthorSamanthaYoung
Facebook Reader Group
Goodreads

CPSIA information can be obtained
at www.ICGtesting.com
Printed in the USA
LVHW092136301122
734382LV00035B/2149

9 781838 301705